A MOMENT OF TRUTH . . .
AND SWEET DESIRE

"Say my name," he commanded. "I want to hear it from your lips. I want to drink it from your mouth." He reached up and drew her head down as if he meant to kiss her. "Say it, sweet Emma."

Emma felt bewitched; she had lost control. Anything at all might happen between them, and she might allow it. "Alexander," she whispered.

"No." He shook his head. "Sikander. Say my real name."

When she hesitated, he drew back to study her face. "Does my Indian name disgust you? Do *I* disgust you?"

The hurt in his tone tore at her heart. He had openly admitted he was part Indian; now, he was asking if she could accept it. He was an outcast from two different cultures. She ought not to trust him, to want him. Yet how could she refuse to say his name, when she did want him so very much?

"Sikander. . . . My dear Sikander. You could never disgust me."

He pulled her down and kissed her—a tender, burning kiss that flooded her heart with bittersweet yearning . . .

WILDWOOD

Katharine Kincaid

Zebra Books
Kensington Publishing Corp.

http://www.xebrabooks.com

ZEBRA BOOKS are published by

Kensington Publishing Corp.
850 Third Avenue
New York, NY 10022

First Printing: November, 1996
10 9 8 7 6 5 4 3 2 1

Printed in the United States of America

In Loving Memory of
Ruth A. Wakelin

January 15, 1918—January 27, 1995

My mother and my friend,
may you rest in peace.

Prologue

"And to my obstinate, rebellious daughter, Emma, I leave the sum of one shilling. I urge her to spend it wisely—more wisely than she has thus far spent her wretched, misguided life."

Emma sat stunned and silent as the will of her deceased father, Sir Henry Whitefield, was read by his solicitor, Mr. Cross. As expected, her younger brother, Oliver, had inherited the entire estate, including Whitefield Hall and the London town house. Her father had doted upon his only son. In stark contrast, Sir Henry had seemed not to like Emma even when she was a child and more biddable—but for her to be cut off without a small annuity or the ownership of her favorite mare came as a great shock. Until just this moment, Emma had not realized precisely how much her father must have hated her.

She struggled to swallow the huge lump in her throat. Across the polished mahogany table in the library of Whitefield Hall, Oliver glared at her triumphantly. The very image of their late sire, Oliver was prematurely bald, heavy-jowled, and as somber as an avenging angel in his elegantly cut clothing. He had a way of curling his upper lip that set Emma's teeth on edge. Just so had her father always curled *his* upper lip when he took Emma to task for some infraction of proper behavior.

"Well, Emma. It appears the pigeons have all come home to roost, haven't they? You wouldn't be in this unfortunate position had you accepted one of the several marriage proposals Father arranged for you, now would you?"

Withholding a response until Mr. Cross gathered up his papers and excused himself, Emma suppressed a shudder at the memory of the objectionable men her father had chosen for her. All had had valuable connections in trade or society, but one had been a hopeless drunkard, another old enough to be her grandfather, and a third not only shorter than she by a good fourteen inches but burdened by a surly disposition. Not one had been interested in her personally—not that she expected them to be, of course.

Tall, slender as a blade of grass, and unfashionably outspoken, she had always been considered plain and spinsterish, bearing only a faint resemblance to her beautiful mother who had died when she was only seventeen. Now, at twenty-seven, she was "on the shelf," a place that until now she hadn't much minded because marriage didn't appeal to her. Having witnessed the stormy relationship of her glowering father and the petite, bubbly Lady Jane Anne, Emma had long ago decided to forego the dubious pleasures of the marriage bed. Instead, she found satisfaction in other pursuits— becoming a highly accomplished horsewoman and sketching modest scenes of horses and the hunt in pen and ink. She also had her "causes." They took up a great deal of her time and had earned Sir Henry's incessant disapproval. He simply could not understand why she found it necessary to champion overworked peasants or children forced to perform the labor of adults.

Sir Henry was always accusing her of stepping on toes, causing tongues to wag, and embarrassing the family name. Well, he had finally gotten his revenge, and his son and heir was plainly delighted.

"I will give you one year to make a suitable marriage. If you haven't done so by then, I will cast you out as you should have been cast out years ago—with naught but a shilling in your palm and the garments on your back."

Emma did not hesitate to wield her only weapon: what her father had called her "rapier tongue." "But what will society think of you then, dear brother? Father never cast me out for fear of the scandal, and you are less of a man than he was."

"Shrew! You shall pay dearly for comments like that, sister of mine. You have just reduced your grace period to three months instead of a year. And don't think you can ride Morgana anymore, either. She is mine now, so stay away from her."

Emma's spirited black mare delighted in dumping any rider whose attention foolishly wandered, and Emma's heart shattered at the prospect of losing the beautiful, fiery creature. "You will not be able to handle her," she warned.

"I shall handle her. Just as I am handling you. The trick is to give no quarter and show no mercy. If she does not behave, she will find herself on the way to the knacker."

Oh, Morgana! Emma wept inwardly. *What will become of us?*

"Why do you hate me so, Oliver? When we were children, you were sometimes my ally in childish rebellions. We . . . shared things. But then something happened to turn you against me."

"I grew up, and embraced my heritage and its attendant duties—something you never did. You never have understood what it means to be a Whitefield. Like Father, I find it tiresome to constantly have to defend the family reputation."

"I fail to see where I have besmirched it," Emma began.

"That's precisely the point. You never *have* seen how extraordinarily outrageous your behavior is. Women of our class simply do not go 'round making speeches on street corners and distributing inflammatory literature. You've championed nearly every cause Father fought against: making employers responsible for accidents to their workers, insisting upon all children going to school—even those of the lower classes, permitting wives to keep property from their husbands . . . and your latest folly, giving the vote to agricultural laborers. Why, next you'll be fighting for the rights of females to have a say in running the country."

"The third Reform Act is long overdue. It's a matter of simple fairness. As for females running the country, they could do as good a job as you yourself, Oliver—maybe better."

"And I suppose you also support Home Rule for the Irish!" Oliver's jowls quivered indignantly.

"You suppose correctly. I never have been able to understand why the British aristocracy believe themselves superior to—"

"Bah!" Oliver pushed back his chair and stood. "I don't care to listen to any more of your radical opinions. Find yourself a husband, Emma. I intend to take a wife soon, someone young and malleable, and I'll not have you contaminating her mind with your dangerous notions."

"And if I do not, you will truly cast me out? You would actually do that to your own sister?"

Oliver's pale blue eyes were as cold and unforgiving as marble. "I'll tell everyone you've gone off to visit relations in Scotland."

"We have no relations in Scotland."

"You, my dear Emma, are the only one who knows that. And I hardly need worry that you'll go running to some mutual friend to tell them what I have done. We no longer have any mutual friends; you have turned them all against you."

"You presume much, Oliver. I do have friends."

"Do you, Emma? If so, I am glad for you. I encourage you to flee to them. That way I shall not be tempted to feel guilty about putting you out."

He would not feel guilty at all, Emma realized. He had

truly become his father's son, except that he was younger and more ruthless than Sir Henry had ever dreamed of being.

"Three months, Emma. That is all you have."

He left Emma sitting alone in the library, pondering her fate. She *did* have friends, but few of her own class. Her friends were the people she had helped with her time, money, and tireless efforts to fight injustices. None of them were rich. None could help her. The one person in society to whom she could always turn was her dearest friend, Rosamund, or Rosie as Emma had always called her. Unfortunately, three years ago, Rosie had married and moved to India with her new husband, an official in the Indian Civil Service.

Sighing, Emma rose and headed for her mother's chambers, the only place in the drafty old hall where she had ever known warmth, love, laughter, and acceptance. Ten years had passed, but Emma still missed her mother terribly. Without the loyalty and friendship of the servants, she could not have borne living in the same abode as her father and brother.

Entering her mother's sitting room, she found a fire already lit in the small cheery chamber with its worn blue carpet and heavy gold draperies. Someone—the doddering old butler perhaps?—had guessed that she'd be searching for solace in the patchouli-scented room that still contained her mother's beloved vases, art objects, and wall tapestries.

Emma sank down on a chair drawn close to the fire's warmth. She hadn't wept since her mother's death. Tears were a waste of time and effort; only the weak indulged in them, and Emma fancied herself strong and resourceful—only she did not feel strong at this particular moment. She felt terribly alone and abandoned, her prospects for the future as dismal as any of the poor unfortunates she had tried to help over the years.

She could always search for employment among those acquainted with her family's pedigree. However, she had her pride, and it would be humiliating to beg the very same people who shared her father's and brother's view of her political activities to now hire her to help run their households or raise their children. They might refuse. Even Rosie had once begged her to cease making a spectacle of herself, or Rosie's parents were going to forbid Rosie to associate with her.

Yet what else could she have done? Her causes had all been worthy ones, and Emma was proud of herself for having had the courage of her convictions.

As she stared unseeing into the fire, someone cleared his throat. Mr. Weston, the old butler, stood off to one side, his feeble, shaky hands encircling an ornately carved small chest which he now held out to her. "Forgive me for intruding, Miss Emma, but the time has come for you to have this."

From the highly decorated style of the cask, Emma surmised that it had come from India, though she could not recall ever having seen it before. Her mother's rooms contained many items from that faraway country, for her father had once served as viceroy in the state of Madhya Pradesh in Central India. Sir Henry had always claimed that he hated every moment of his tenure there and could not wait to return to England, but Lady Jane Anne had spoken of India with fondness and nostalgia, regaling Emma with tales of what a wondrous, fascinating place it was with its jungles, tigers, elephants, heat, and torrential rains. Emma had just missed being born there and, as a child, had often fantasized how different her life might have been had her parents remained in India during her childhood.

"What is it, Mr. Weston?"

The old butler reverently extended the wooden box with its fine filigree of entwined leaves and flowers. "A gift, Miss Emma. A gift from your dear Mama. She entrusted it to my care many years ago and instructed me to give it to you only in the event of your father's death and her own. It was her last request, which she made to me as she lay dying from the mysterious malady which finally claimed her life."

"Why . . . thank you!" As she reached for the cask, Emma's hands shook as badly as Mr. Weston's. A gift from her dying mother! Why had her mother insisted that it be kept from her for so long?

Bowing, the old butler retreated from the room as unobtrusively as he had entered it. Several moments passed before Emma could muster enough courage to open the box. The gold clasp was simple in design, and she had no trouble releasing it. Balancing the cask on her knees, she lifted the hinged lid. Red satin lined the inside of the cask, and on it lay a coil of lustrous pearls, all perfectly matched. Next to the pearls was a gold-embroidered silk pouch tied with a cord.

Emma's heart was thundering. The pearls must have cost a fortune. She opened the pouch, and a single large ruby slid into the palm of her hand. The gem's blood-red depths nearly blinded her with its pure brilliance.

Emma was sure she had never before seen these lovely pieces. Upon her mother's death, her father had confiscated all of Lady Jane Anne's jewels. "Why bother adorning a peahen with the feathers of a peacock?" he had said, referring to Emma. "Nothing will help her anyway, short of locking her up and excising her tongue."

Had her father known about these treasures? Perhaps they had belonged to her mother *before* her marriage, and her father had merely forgotten them . . . yet they had the look of India, and Lady Jane Anne had only visited India with Emma's father.

Emma suddenly noticed several folded sheets of foolscap in the bottom of the cask. Quickly, she set down the jewels and unfolded the papers, immediately recognizing her mother's tiny, slanted handwriting on the top sheet.

"My darling Emma," leapt out from the sweet-smelling page. Tears welled in Emma's eyes and spilled unheeded down her cheeks, as Lady Jane Anne revealed the true reason for Emma's father's hostility—his deep suspicion that Emma was not really his daughter.

"And indeed, he was not . . . Emma dearest, your true

father was a dashing, brilliant, kind, sensitive man I met in India during the first difficult months of my adjustment to life in a foreign country. A great naturalist, horseman, and huntsman, your true father was an officer in the British Army . . ."

So that explains why I love horses and hunting, Emma thought giddily, while my father and brother never did take to it, and neither did my mother.

"I make no apologies for my behavior, dearest daughter, for I did not set out to betray Sir Henry, and it was at least partially his fault that I came to love your father."

Lady Jane Anne then explained that during one of Sir Henry's journeys through the huge state of Madhya Pradesh, she had become ill and was left to recuperate in a *dak* bungalow—while Sir Henry, in a fit of pique over the inconvenience her illness was causing him, continued with his plans to hunt tiger in the Mahadeo Hills. While they were separated, the Indian mutiny of 1857 had broken out, causing havoc all over the country and preventing Sir Henry's return to collect Lady Jane Anne. Major Ian Castleton had rescued her . . . *Her real father's name was Major Ian Castleton! . . .* from certain death at the hands of the rebellious natives and sheltered her in a small plantation in the jungle, until such time as she could be reunited with Sir Henry. There, their love had blossomed until they could no longer resist their mutual attraction.

"My love for your father was the high point of my entire life, Emma. Sadly, not long thereafter, Major Castleton died fighting in one of the many skirmishes that took place as a consequence of the mutiny, and I was left with naught but bittersweet memories and the gifts he had given me: the pearls, the ruby, and the deed to his plantation, Wildwood, a beautiful, isolated place where he had hoped to advance his fortunes by harvesting the surrounding jungle of teak, Indian ebony, rosewood, sal, and hardwickia."

Emma reread that section of the letter, then scanned the

deed itself, the last yellowed page of the papers contained in the cask. *Wildwood. What a beautiful name!* It conjured images of dense, thick trees where parrots screeched and panthers crouched on hidden branches overhead.

"Finding myself pregnant, I had no choice but to return to my lawful husband and try to rebuild a life with him. I never told him about my indiscretion nor showed him the jewels or deed, but he knew that I had changed and suspected the cause of it. He never forgave me, Emma, and his anger inevitably fell upon you."

The last paragraph of her mother's letter read: *"These precious jewels and the plantation, Wildwood, where I knew my greatest happiness, are all I have to give you, my darling. I pray you will never have need of them, but if you do, I have instructed Weston to give you this cask. With loving felicitations, Your mother, Lady Jane Anne Whitefield."*

On the back of the deed to Wildwood, Emma discovered a roughly sketched map. It showed Wildwood in the state of Madhya Pradesh, south of Delhi and west of Calcutta, in the vicinity of Bhopal near the Narmada River. Rosie's husband was stationed in Calcutta!

Emma fingered the perfect pearls; the sale of one or two of them ought to be enough to. . . . Rising from the chair, she crossed to her mother's writing table and searched the drawers for a sheet of patchouli-scented paper. *"Dear Rosie: Good news! I am coming to India to take possession of my very own plantation, Wildwood. By the time you receive this, I shall already be en route, so pray do not attempt to persuade me to abandon the notion. I shall come directly to you, so that you may advise me as to how I might best get on in India . . ."*

Emma paused, thinking of Oliver. How pleased he would be to get rid of her! And how glad she would be to leave England and seek a new life in a fascinating foreign land. In India, she would be free. She could live her own life in her own way. No one except Rosie would know her. She could start over, begin anew, make a whole new life for herself.

"Thank you, Mama. Oh, thank you!" she whispered fervently, and then—finding the paper and writing materials—pulled out the chair, sat down, and began her letter.

One

Calcutta, 1885

"Why, Emma, I was right! Those pearls do wonders to dress up that gown. At the ball tonight, Mr. Griffin will find you irresistible, and before the year is out, you'll marry and be comfortably settled right here in Calcutta in a house within walking distance of my own."

Clapping her hands in excitement, Rosie spun around the airy, high-ceilinged room, but Emma peered doubtfully into the cheval glass. Her mother's pearls did seem to relieve the starkness of her best black bengaline silk gown, which was caught up by a huge silly bow at the bustle in the back, but Emma wondered if anyone would notice that three pearls were now missing from the strand draped across her slender bosom.

Surely, they would notice that her skin looked sallow, suggesting a liver ailment, and her fashionable coiffure with its absurd curls and ringlets piled precariously on top of her head made her resemble some silly chit just out of the nursery. Rosie had insisted she abandon the neat, unpretentious hairstyle she usually wore, but nothing could help the fact that her hair was brown—plain, uninteresting brown—and it framed a face without a hint of prettiness.

"I rather doubt Mr. Griffin will be impressed," she muttered under her breath, but Rosie nonetheless heard her.

"Of course he will be impressed! You must not think disparaging thoughts, Emma. You are most attractive when you make the least effort. You have good skin, bones, teeth, and hair, and your greenish-colored eyes are quite striking, definitely your most becoming feature. In any case, Mr. Griffin is a serious-minded gentleman who will admire you for your mind, if not your beauty."

"No doubt he's desperate, what with marriageable Englishwomen being scarce as hen's teeth in this part of the world. That should increase my appeal a hundredfold." Emma turned from the mirror in disgust. "None of this would be necessary if you would just let me go my own way. Sooner or later, I'll find someone willing to take me to Wildwood."

"Perish the thought, Emma! Must we discuss this again? There is absolutely no way you can travel to Central India in search of your jungle plantation. 'Tis a journey of over a thousand miles just to Delhi, then you must travel south to Gwalior, and finally to Bhopal . . . and after that, who even knows how much farther? Why, it's completely uncivilized in that part of India, a jungle wilderness, and as you already know by now, India is nothing like England. You cannot possibly travel alone all that distance, nor could you trust Indian servants to protect you, nor . . ."

Rosie rattled on for several moments, causing Emma to wonder how a woman gowned in palest pink and white, a woman with great, innocent blue eyes, fair white skin, and golden blond hair could sound like such a crier of gloom and doom. Yet from the moment Emma had arrived in Calcutta after her long voyage by steamship, Rosie had been regaling her with all the reasons why she must remain in Calcutta, "among her own kind," and not dare venture into the *mofussil*, which was anywhere outside of the major cities of India.

But the people Emma had thus far met were not her kind at all. They were just like the people she had fled in England. She had been expecting India to be totally different, but it wasn't. Not really. The entire time she had been here—six weeks now—she had associated solely with the English, lived in an English manner, and pursued typically English diversions. Her sightseeing had been limited to the Maiden, a huge open park surrounding Fort William, St. Paul's Cathedral, the *Raj Bhavan,* or Government House, St. John's Church, and the Racecourse, where the Calcutta Polo Club occupied the central oval. Even her shopping had been confined to the Army and Navy Store, Hall and Anderson's, and Whiteway and Laidlaw's, all popular emporiums for the British.

Interesting as all these were, especially the polo club, Emma had yet to set foot inside an Indian temple or mosque, an Indian home, or the bustling, colorful, smelly, supposedly dangerous Bow Bazaar. And the only Indians she had met were household servants who came and went as silently as shadows. Every Englishman in India seemed dedicated to the preservation of a slice of his homeland in this foreign country, and their wives were even worse. Rosie herself went to extreme lengths to run her spacious, thick-walled house with its wide veranda and tall white pillars exactly as if she were still living in Shropshire. The only differences were the *punkahs* or ceiling fans in nearly every room, and the little brown *punkah-wallahs* or fan boys who operated them. . . . And oh, yes, when going outside, everyone donned a *topi* or solar helmet to protect him or herself from the sun.

And now Rosie had concocted a match-making scheme to ensure that Emma never would have a chance to explore the real India—the one that beckoned to her with tantalizing glimpses of exotic sights, sounds, and smells—or find the plantation she had inherited. The man on whom Rosie had set her sights was named Percival Griffin, a high-ranking official in the ICS, the Indian Civil Service, where Rosie's husband was also an officer. Mr. Griffin had excellent prospects of one day becoming the British Land Administrator of Central India, and both Rosie and her husband thought him a capital fellow and a fine choice to marry Emma.

But Emma could summon little enthusiasm for the plan. She hadn't come to India to find a husband, but to gain her independence and a means of supporting herself—and to have adventures before she became too old to enjoy them. Nor was she impressed by Mr. Griffin's impeccable credentials. Virtually every man she had met in India was an official of some sort. At dinner parties, hostesses made a great fuss to ensure that everyone went into dinner and was properly seated at the table according to rank and importance.

Emma had had to bite her tongue to keep from remarking upon the absurdity of all this posturing. Yet she was determined not to embarrass Rosie . . . and that was why she was primping in front of a mirror to impress a man she had no desire to meet in the first place.

"Now, you do promise to behave yourself, don't you, Emma, and to give Mr. Griffin a sporting chance?" Rosie had gone from a recitation of the perils of travel into another diatribe on why Emma should marry and settle in Calcutta.

"This is your golden opportunity, dear friend. Here you need not compete with young misses twitching their bustles at every gentleman they meet. An unmarried English female is a great rarity in India, and every unattached Englishman at the ball tonight will be eager to make your acquaintance. You'll find none as suitable as Mr. Griffin. Save several dances for him, won't you Emma? The two of you were made for each other."

"Rosie," Emma caught her friend's hand. "Please don't be too disappointed if I don't like your Mr. Griffith—"

"Griffin . . ."

"I will try—honestly, I will. But I cannot guarantee that he will appeal to me nor that I will appeal to him."

"Well, if you meet someone who appeals to you more, you don't need *my* permission to pursue the relationship."

Rosie shook her blond curls. "Only do have a care not to associate with the *wrong* gentlemen, dear Emma."

"The *wrong* gentlemen?" Emma released her friend's hand and smoothed down the folds of her black silk gown. She could not imagine that *any* of the men she might meet tonight would be as interested in her as Rosie claimed, much less that she would have to watch out for scoundrels among them.

"There are a few black sheep who sometimes dare to show their faces at our affairs; they are not considered to have the best reputations or to be one of us."

"One of . . . us?" Emma stiffened. Back home in England, Rosie had shown no inclination toward snobbery. That was the main reason she and Rosie were friends—because they could laugh together over the foolish conventions of society. They still did so privately, though not with the same frequency or enthusiasm they once had, what with Rosie striving so hard to aid her husband in his career. . . . Had Rosie changed so much since her marriage? Emma had noticed many distressing alterations, but had hoped that at heart, Rosie still shared the same basic philosophy of life.

"I am referring to men such as . . . as Alexander Kingston, for example. If *he* should appear, stay away from him, Emma, for I have heard the most shocking tales. Handsome though he is—and he *is* deliciously handsome—he's apparently a devil."

"What sort of shocking tales?" Emma was immediately ready to leap to the man's defense, simply because others had condemned him.

" 'Tis said he doesn't observe the unwritten rules of British society here in India. Not that I fault him for that, exactly. You know I am no snob, at heart."

I used to know that, Rosie. Now I am not so certain. "What sort of rules?"

"Well, he has been involved in many scandals—escapades involving other men's wives. And he also consorts too closely with Indians. He socializes with them, meets them in their homes, takes part in their festivities . . ."

"Why is that so terrible? Socializing with Indians, I mean—not becoming involved with other men's wives."

"Because it isn't done here, Emma. The two societies never mix. The members of the Raj have a distinct identity; indeed, it would be awkward and difficult to mix with the Indians and still rule them . . . and that's why we're here—to rule them, or so William keeps reminding me."

"I see." Emma grappled with a deep dismay and disappointment. Rosie had indeed changed since her marriage. What her friend had just described seemed like the trouble with the Irish all over again, except that India was far larger and more complex.

Well, *she* certainly had no intention of trying to rule the Indians. But neither would she abuse her friend's hospitality by repeating the mistakes of her past; so she forbore to question what right the English had to rule anybody outside their own borders.

Rosie pursed her pink lips in disapproval. "Alexander Kingston has a good English name, but he may be Eurasian or part-Indian, what is known as *"kutcha butcha,"* as the Indians call a half-baked loaf of bread. Actually, no one knows much about him. If he has a wife and children, no one has ever seen them. Nor has anyone visited his home."

"Perhaps he's like me—a social misfit."

"You are *not* a social misfit, Emma. You have only been misunderstood all your life, and since your mother died, subjected to relentless criticism. All that is finished. Tonight marks the beginning of a dazzling new future. So avoid Mr. Kingston, be nice to Mr. Griffin, and let us hope something develops. . . . Are you ready? I believe we should go downstairs now. William is probably wondering what's taking us so long, and the horses must be stamping in their harnesses."

"You run along. I . . . I have something to do first."

"What more could you possibly do? As I've told you, you look lovely."

"I wish to tidy my belongings. They are in shocking disarray."

"The servants can do that. You must accustom yourself to Indian servants, Emma. They do everything according to caste. If you perform the duties of the servant in charge of this room, you will only anger him and my major-domo. Don't bother with such trifles."

Emma stubbornly stood her ground. "Go ahead and tell William I'm coming. I promise I will be there soon."

Shaking her head, Rosie gathered up her skirts. "If you insist. I recognize that unyielding tone when I hear it. I'll expect you downstairs in a few moments then."

As Rosie departed, Emma headed toward the large black trunk containing her things. Opening it, she removed the deed to Wildwood. Everywhere she went, she took it with her in the hope she would encounter someone who would look at the roughly drawn map and say, "Yes, I know precisely where Wildwood is, and I'd be happy to take you there."

It hadn't happened yet, and Rosie was annoyed that Emma kept trying. But someday, it *might* happen—hopefully before Emma had to sell all her pearls and the ruby, too, or worse yet, was forced to marry the next desperate man she met. She prayed she would never have to sell the ruby and dreaded parting with more of her pearls—unless it was to make improvements to her plantation. She couldn't live forever on Rosie's generosity. William was very nice, but Emma sensed there were limits to his hospitality. He was not at the top of ICS officialdom, and his income was modest. Yet Emma had noticed that Rosie spent money freely, needing a great many gowns to attend the almost daily social events and also entertaining in a lavish fashion, citing Emma as her excuse.

These functions bored Emma, and she dreaded becoming a source of conflict between Rosie and her husband. Worse yet, she was beginning to feel stifled. The more she saw of British society in Calcutta, the less she liked it. Marriage to Mr. Percival Griffin wasn't the answer. It would be too much like sealing herself into the tomb of stuffy British propriety.

Slipping the deed to Wildwood into her reticule, Emma again studied herself in the cheval glass. Perspiration filmed her forehead and upper lip, and it wasn't even the hot season yet. She wiped a finger along her brow; the British didn't dress properly for such a warm climate. They dressed as they did at home for this time of year.

"I must get out of Calcutta and find the real India," Emma whispered to the tall, frowning woman in the mirror. "And when I do, when I finally get to Wildwood, I shall never wear a bustle, long sleeves, or petticoats ever again."

Alex took a moment to critically examine himself in the filigreed gold mirror set atop a gold stand in one corner of his bedchamber. Sakharam had done his usual excellent job of selecting appropriate English clothing for tonight's formal occasion, but dress alone could not disguise Alex's exotic foreign appearance; he did not look English.

His Western height, muscular build, and blue eyes notwithstanding, he looked pure Indian, his features unmistakably stamped with his Mughal heritage—except he wasn't pure Mughal, either.

"Kutcha butcha," he hissed, turning away in disgust.

Crossing to a small teak table supported by an exquisitely carved elephant with ivory tusks and diamond eyes, he snatched up his gloves, nearly knocking over the table in his haste. Quickly, he grabbed and steadied it. The table was a gift from his aunt; centuries old, it had been handed down through the ruling families of the Mughal dynasty and symbolized all that India once was and would never be again. . . . Alex kept it with him when he traveled. It reminded him of who he was, at least in part, the part that he most cherished but could not publicly embrace.

Tugging on his gloves, he hated the very feel of them upon his fingers. He didn't want to attend this evening's function—didn't want to be in Calcutta. It was a waste of time. His appearance at the ball tonight would win him no more friends among the British, but for Michael's and Victoria's sake, he must keep trying. He dare not quit, or his children would pay the price.

The British Raj wasn't going to disappear overnight—and unless his young son and daughter learned to look, think, and act British, they might easily lose all he had fought for so long and hard to achieve. Alex could not afford to bury himself—and them—in the jungle forever. Without his British contacts and their money, trade connections, and good will, his entire empire would soon collapse, leaving nothing to hand down to his son. Nor would little Victoria be able to marry among the Raj, and she certainly could not marry the cream of Indian society—not with her tainted blood.

Resigned to making the best of a long, tedious evening, Alex picked up a gold-knobbed walking stick and turned to leave—only to be confronted by Sakharam who had padded silently into the chamber.

"Shall I wait up for you, Sahib?" The white-coated, white-turbaned servant salaamed, his soft cultured tones belying his attitude of humility. Such a falsely obsequious manner greatly annoyed Alex, who had grown up feeling the weight of Sakharam's brown thumb on his shoulder, holding him back, censuring him, always attempting to modify his rash behavior. Sakharam was closer to him than his own father.

"Stop calling me Sahib. When we're alone, I prefer you call me by my usual name—Sikander."

"Better I should call you by the English version: Alexander." Sakharam's unruffled dignity was his most notable feature. Whether he was facing fire, flood, snarling tiger, or rebellious youth, he never raised his voice in anger or altered his smooth, untroubled expression.

As a boy, Alex had ceaselessly tested Sakharam's patience, but the only display of emotion he had ever provoked was a slight flaring of Sakharam's chiseled nostrils and a darkening of his already dark eyes.

"I prefer Sikander," Alex argued for the sake of arguing.

"Perhaps you do, but that is inappropriate. You plan to introduce an English *ayah* to your household, so we must all accustom ourselves to calling you Sahib, for that is what Indian servants always call their English masters."

"You can call me that when she comes—and only in her presence. She won't be an *ayah,* either; she'll be a nanny."

"A *nanny?*" Sakharam's brows rose. "Is that not the same word used to designate a female goat?"

"Don't ask me to explain; I can't. But that's what we will call her—a nanny. And she'll be responsible for turning Michael and Victoria into proper young English children."

Sakharam's eyes unmistakably darkened. "They are already proper and well-mannered. I myself have seen to their upbringing, just as I saw to yours."

"In Indian fashion, not English. English rules of etiquette are different from ours, and I won't have my children making the same mistakes I've made along the way. You did the best you could, Sakharam. I don't hold you responsible for my failure to behave in the prescribed manner."

"That is good, because my teachings were not at fault. Too often you have allowed the base side of your nature to lead you astray, Sikander. And tonight will probably hold many temptations. No strong spirits, I beseech you. And no dalliances with pretty women, married or otherwise."

"I'll be careful." Alex tucked his walking stick beneath one arm. "You need not lecture me, old friend. I know what I've already lost and still stand to lose. Let's hope the evening will prove fruitful in repairing what's been broken—and that someone at the ball tonight knows of a suitable nanny whose services I can procure for the children."

"I pray she will be old and ugly, or you will have no peace at Paradise View when you take her home with us. The women of the *zenana* will conspire against her, and the gossips here in Calcutta will further shred your tattered reputation."

"Enough, Sakharam. Do you never tire of giving advice? If my carriage is ready, I am going now. Don't wait up; I doubt I'll make it back before dawn. Just make sure all is ready for us to depart as soon as I have located the right woman. Once I've found her, I don't wish to tarry, or she might change her mind about accompanying us all the way to Paradise View."

"All will be ready, Sahib." Sakharam executed another elaborate salaam, much to Alex's annoyance. When he rose, he was smiling, pleased to have nettled Alex, even in so small a matter. Nettling Alex was one of Sakharam's main pleasures in life; other than that, the tall, inscrutable Indian lived solely to make himself indispensable.

"Sikander, damn it." Alex strode toward the front door of the small, modest house he kept in Calcutta for those times when a visit to the city was unavoidable, and he dared not stay with his Indian friends.

His carriage was waiting outside in the street, and he paused a moment to inspect the horses before he climbed into it. The matched chestnuts were not as fine as the horses at Paradise View, but they were well fed and groomed. He must thank Sakharam for that, too. Sakharam knew how particular he was about his horses. Some might say he esteemed them more than his friends or family—an absurd notion. But where he was concerned, there would always be gossip and criticism; a *kutcha butcha* could truly please no one. Indians and British alike rejected, scorned, and regarded him with deep suspicion. That was why Alex was fighting so hard to win acceptance for his children. His children would have it easier than he had; he would see to it or die trying.

Percival Griffin was a wholesome-looking gentleman of medium height with sandy-colored hair, beard, and mustache. He wore very proper evening clothes and spoke so politely that Emma could not discover his opinion on much of anything. He was, in a word—colorless.

He was also attentive, regularly inquiring after her comfort. Was she too warm? No? Then was she chilled? Would she care for a drink of the quite excellent rum punch? What about the tiny iced cakes? He was such a *nice* man; why couldn't she feel any attraction to him? Especially since he seemed quite taken with her.

"My dear Miss Whitefield," he gushed as they sat together on a settee watching couples whirling across the floor of the large room, which had been cleared of everything except the huge *punkah* fan moving slowly overhead and an assortment of enormous ferns and tropical plants.

"My dear lady, you can't know how delighted I am to meet someone of your obvious intelligence and refinement here in Calcutta."

"Do you mean to say that the women in Calcutta are all stupid and ill-bred?" Emma forced a smile. "I hardly believe that can be the case, Mr. Griffin."

"Oh, it's not!" he denied, flustered. "It's just that . . . well . . . the women sent out from home are usually so young and untried. So . . . immature."

"Ah, yes, the Fishing Fleet. I have heard of it. It's comprised of young ladies who for one reason or another failed to ensnare husbands at home and hope to find them here, where the competition is not quite so fierce."

"The Fishing Fleet, yes . . . a terrible way to describe a shipload of eager young women, but rather apt, I'm afraid."

"I did not come to India to go fishing, Mr. Griffin. I have

no wish to marry and am well past the age where marriage is any great concern to me."

"How can that be? You're a vibrant woman, and marriage is the normal object of all women, a state to be devoutly desired. Have you no wish for children?"

"Children I could tolerate, perhaps even enjoy. But a husband? I don't know, Mr. Griffin. I am accustomed to my privacy. Unlike many women, I do not abhor solitude. It would be difficult for me to learn to share my life with another."

His hand covered hers where it rested on the red brocade between them. "Not if you married a man who understood you, Miss Whitefield, and was willing to give you plenty of breathing space. In my present position, I travel a good deal, and if I should be so fortunate as to one day become Land Administrator for Central India, I should be traveling even more. The last thing I need is a woman who fears being alone and would cling to me like the proverbial ivy vine."

Emma gently extracted her fingers from his. "I should like to try the rum punch, after all, Mr. Griffin. This conversation is becoming too personal. Please remember we only met this evening."

Percival Griffin's ears turned a bright crimson red. They were prominent ears, too, Emma noticed, the sort that suggested he might sail away in a good strong gust of wind. "Forgive me for being forward, Miss Whitefield. I assure you I have only the best intentions. Your friends have told me all about you, you see. They made you sound so . . . so perfect for a man like me. Then, when I finally met you, I . . . well, my enthusiasm and eagerness quite ran away with me."

"No apologies are necessary, Mr. Griffin. Don't distress yourself. I, too, have been bombarded with excellent reports. Rosie has praised you to the heavens. However, I think we should tread carefully and not rush into marriage, merely

because our mutual friends have decided we suit one another
so well."

"Then you are not angry?" Tobacco stains and some evidence of tooth decay were revealed in Mr. Griffin's grin.

"Of course not. I'm only thirsty. I really would like some
of that rum punch."

Mr. Griffin jumped up. "I'll get you some straight away.
Don't go anywhere. Promise me you'll stay right here."

"I assure you I will." Emma had no wish to lose one of
the few places in the room to sit down.

Grinning from ear to ear, Percival dashed toward the line
of gentlemen waiting to fetch refreshment. Looking for
Rosie, Emma searched the crowd of whirling couples. She
finally spotted her dancing with William and smiling happily
into his eyes. . . . Oh, to be so much in love! To be so happy.
Emma was glad for her friend. The only thing marring
Rosie's joy in her marriage was that she had not yet conceived a child. Twice since Emma had arrived, Rosie had
burst into tears while speaking of it.

But at least she has love, Emma thought, and a man who
adores her. She is not alone.

Emma gave herself a stern mental shake. Only a few moments ago she had been telling Mr. Griffin how much she
cherished privacy and solitude. Had that all been a lie?
Slowly, she scanned the room, searching for some man—any
man—who might appeal to her more than Mr. Griffin, a man
with whom she *might* actually want to spend the rest of her
life . . . and then she saw him: A tall, exotic-looking gentleman standing alone in an alcove and watching the dancers
much as she was doing.

He was very dark, dark as an Indian, with hair so black
it was almost blue-black. And he was dressed all in black,
except for the snowy-white shirt that contrasted sharply with
his skin and hair. Emma shamelessly admired his physique.
He was very nearly the tallest man in the room, and his
shoulders were wide, his waist narrow, his stomach perfectly

flat. Lithe, graceful, and as fit as a jungle cat, he reminded her of some sleek, black panther avidly stalking its prey.

His eyes roved the room. They looked right at her and moved on. . . . Good Lord! He had *blue* eyes. Even from a distance, she could tell they were blue—an incredibly brilliant blue, the exact shade of the Indian ocean beneath the hot noon sun.

Emma suddenly realized she was holding her breath. The man wasn't *that* handsome, and he did not seem at all kind or pleasant. His features were rather sharp; some might say cruel, or at least, disturbingly arrogant. His nose was too long, his lips too full and blatantly sensuous, his gaze too challenging. She instinctively distrusted him. He radiated danger, though *she* had nothing to fear.

She wasn't the sort of woman *his* sort of man ever noticed. He might be younger than she. She narrowed her eyes, studying him, and decided that no, he couldn't be younger. Fine lines bracketed his eyes and mouth, as if he spent time in the sun without a *topi*. How reckless!

Two women suddenly strolled in front of her, their heads together, blocking her view. "Can you believe it? Alexander Kingston has arrived. Do you see him? He's right over there, looking every inch as if he thinks he belongs here."

"What nerve! To show his face in decent society."

"I can't think he was invited. Our poor hostess will have the vapors. What do you suppose he's doing here?"

"Well, he can't spend *all* his time hunting tigers in the *mofussil*, now can he? Perhaps he's come to sample civilization for a change. Where he lives is nothing but jungle, so I've heard. I've also heard he's rich as a maharajah."

"Paradise View, his plantation is called, isn't it? It's somewhere in Central India near the Narmada River. South of Delhi, I think."

Emma almost fell off the settee straining to hear what they were saying. Wildwood was in Central India, near the Narmada River!

"Is it exposure to the sun that makes him so . . . brown?"

"So you've heard the rumors, too. No, it isn't exposure to the sun. It's impure blood. Half-caste or not, you can't find fault with his blue eyes. Or with the rest of him. Look at those wide shoulders and narrow hips! He should have been named Lucifer; he's got the look of a fallen archangel—and the reputation of one, too. I wonder what he's doing here."

"Shall we go and ask?"

"Maude! You wouldn't dare."

"No, I wouldn't, more's the pity. Any woman who speaks to him is risking her good name. We'll have to ignore him, I suppose. But what a shame. He's the most wickedly handsome devil I've seen in all India. No wonder women cannot resist him. If I were a tiny bit younger . . ."

"Come along, Maude. It's time we find our husbands."

The two women moved off, and Emma was annoyed to discover that Alexander Kingston—if that was the name of the man she, too, had found so dangerously attractive—had disappeared. She rose to her feet. She would just have to find him again. And ask him about his plantation. And show him her map. Maybe he had heard of Wildwood! . . . Rosie wouldn't like it if she engaged Alexander Kingston in conversation, but the opportunity to meet someone who might know the location of Wildwood was too good to let pass.

Emma caught a glimpse of broad shoulders and shining black hair passing through the foyer behind the dancers and she hurried toward the man. "Mr. Kingston? Mr. Kingston! Do give me a moment of your time, will you, sir?"

Two

At the sound of his name, Alex spun around to see who was calling him. The voice was appealingly feminine, soft and throaty, with the kind of velvet texture he associated with the bedchamber. But the woman he saw determinedly pursuing him through the crowd resembled the sort of bird often seen swooping down on small prey in the jungle.

She was gowned in stark black, his least favorite color on a woman, and her pale features looked pinched and strained. Her mouth was set in a grim line, and the only alluring thing about her were her eyes. They were greenish in color and held a glint of something akin to passion.

Too plain. That part of his brain that unwittingly assessed every woman he met dismissed her as unworthy of his attention—until she came up to him. Then he noticed that she had beautifully sculpted cheekbones, an aristocratic nose, and delicately fashioned lips that might be intriguing were they not so colorless. The severity of her gown, absurd arrangement of her hair, and lack of enhancing cosmetics had doomed her to unfavorable comparisons with hawks or crows. Given the right garments—get rid of that awful bustle!—add some color to her fine features, and let down her hair, and the woman herself might match the seductive promise of her voice.

He wondered what she wanted with him; surely, it wasn't his body! He cast a critical glance down her fragile form.

Too thin. He liked his women slender, but not straight as a spear. Again, the gown was probably at fault. It managed to conceal any curves she might possibly possess.

"Mr. Kingston?" She halted breathlessly in front of him, and his senses leapt at the sensual quality in her voice. He could suddenly imagine her moaning Sikander in his ear and sliding down the front of his naked body to tongue his nipples, then take one between her even white teeth and nip him sharply. The image was startling and ridiculous—considering that it involved this thin, sallow woman in her ugly black gown.

"Yes, what is it?"

"I . . . My name is Emma Whitefield," she burst out.

Whitefield. He didn't know any Whitefields. And he had never before met this woman with the seductive voice and falcon-like demeanor. Yes, that's what she resembled: a peregrine falcon. From the way she was looking at him, as if he were a serpent, he knew she was a virgin who had probably never tongued a man's nipples in her life—or had her own nipples tongued, either. He doubted she knew she had nipples.

"And?" he prompted.

She blinked her green eyes. Without doubt, her eyes were the best thing about her. Her eyes and her voice. The rest was completely forgettable. "I . . . I wish to speak with you."

"Here and now?" He glanced away long enough to notice that others were avidly watching; Miss Emma Whitefield seemed oblivious. Her glance met his with unwavering intensity.

"Yes, I thought . . . that is, I wish to question you concerning . . ." The quiver in her voice betrayed her uncertainty. So she very well knew she should not be speaking to him. She had been warned.

"Over here, Miss Whitefield." He pulled her behind a huge potted plant in a nearby alcove. It wasn't private enough to cause a scandal, but out of view of most of the guests.

"Now, what is it you want?"

"I . . . I . . ." She fumbled in her reticule, extracted a piece of paper, and thrust it under his nose. "I own a plantation named Wildwood that is located somewhere in Central India. You see? Here is a map, sketched on the back of my deed to the property. I understand you also own a plantation in the same general vicinity. Have you ever heard of Wildwood?"

It was dim behind the maidenhair fern; large green fronds blocked the light spilling from the nearest wall sconces. But Alex didn't need much light to recognize the general boundaries of the land she was pointing out. He also recognized the name—Wildwood. And he knew exactly where it was located.

His heartbeat wildly accelerated, but he kept his tone cool and calm. "Where did you get this map and deed, Miss Whitefield?"

"It's rather a long story. In brief, my mother died some years ago and left me the property—Wildwood—which I've only recently come to India to claim. Tell me. Do you know it?"

She lifted the paper, and he pretended to study it. Wildwood was located at the very center, the very heart of Paradise View. What had once been Wildwood lands constituted a large portion of his total holdings—the most important portion, where he had built his home, stable, personal polo field, and numerous outbuildings. An extremely valuable hardwood forest from which he was currently harvesting trees had once belonged to Wildwood. The eight hundred acres of land Miss Whitefield was claiming were hers were in reality *his,* but due to a recent fire in the Calcutta land office, he possessed no legal proof of it.

"There's obviously some mistake," he began.

Emma Whitefield pressed closer, and he caught a whiff of some musky, elusive scent completely at odds with her drab appearance. "A mistake? What sort of mistake? I can't be certain the map is accurate, but I know the plantation itself exists. How could there be a deed for it, if it didn't?"

He waved the paper aside. "I don't know, but I'm well acquainted with the area in question. My own plantation, Paradise View—some three thousand acres of jungle and hardwood forest—is located in the exact same region, and I myself have never heard of Wildwood."

"You've never heard of it?" She looked crestfallen.

He shook his head, the lie coming more easily as he thought of all the trouble it would be to have to prove the validity of his own deed over hers—particularly since he lacked that precise document.

"Miss Whitefield, let me try to explain. During the tempestuous period following the Mutiny of 1857, land throughout India frequently changed hands and was bitterly fought over until the East India Company and the British government regained control and settled the disputes by redefining certain states and kingdoms. The great holdings of the old *rajahs* were divided and subdivided, often on the basis of who had remained loyal to the crown during the uprising. Have you looked at the date on this deed?"

Miss Whitefield peered at the date in question. "It's dated 1855, two years before the Mutiny, and three years before I was born."

That meant she was twenty-seven, no longer a young woman, but still several years younger than he. "Then that's probably why I haven't heard of Wildwood," Alex lied smoothly. "Because it no longer exists. Following the Mutiny, nearly all of the land in that region reverted to the old Begum of Bhopal, who disposed of it as she saw fit."

And I bought as much of it as I could afford and persuade her to part with before she died, including your Wildwood.

He had never told anyone, but he had obtained it at a fraction of its market value on the understanding that the *Nawab*, the son of the old Begum, would receive fifteen percent of all profits made on the hardwoods. If any claims on the lands were to surface at a later date, they would be dealt with on a case by case basis. He had even signed an agreement stating that if a valid claim *did* surface, he would surrender the disputed area and reimburse the rightful owner for the loss of property resulting from the harvesting of the trees. From the very start, the venture had been risky, but the possibility of making a fortune had outweighed the risks—and he *had* made a fortune, one he was not about to share with Miss Emma Whitefield, whether her belated claim proved valid or not.

She had one hell of a nerve, appearing out of nowhere at this late date with a mysterious deed that might or might not be valid. He had known of several similar cases, where men had fought over lands dispersed following the Mutiny, but these cases had occurred long ago—within several years of the Mutiny itself, not twenty-odd years later. Why, he had owned Wildwood lands for well over a decade!

"I am truly sorry, Miss Whitefield, but there is no such place as Wildwood anywhere in that entire area. The map itself is in error, as were many maps of India drawn during that period. Some parts of the country are still not thoroughly explored. Did no one tell you this before you came to this country seeking such a doubtful inheritance?"

"N—no," she stammered, her green eyes shimmering dangerously. "I just assumed the map and deed were valid. No one ever explained what you just did—but who is this Begum? Couldn't I go to her and *show* her this document? Perhaps she would recall—"

"I doubt it. The present *Nawabzada,* the son of the *Nawab* who succeeded the Begum, is barely out of boyhood. I know him well. He's still a child, hardly privy to his father's or grandmother's dealings. His father died quite suddenly, a young man himself, and it will be months, if not years, before the boy sorts out all his responsibilities."

"How sad!" Miss Whitefield frowned. "But surely there

must be someplace where old deeds were recorded. I cannot believe I have the only copy of this one."

"The land office here in Calcutta." Alex was glad to be able to tell her a bit of truth, at least. "Unfortunately, a recent fire destroyed many original papers, so that old boundary lines, land descriptions, and agreements were lost. The fire has created a terrible mess, for myself personally, as well as for many others. That's one reason why I'm here in Calcutta—to file new papers showing my own holdings, so there can be no mistaking them."

"I had no idea it would be so complicated. Do you think if I went to the land office and—"

"No, it wouldn't help," Alex hastened to discourage her. "As I said, the date is too old. Without consulting the archives, now destroyed, the officials in the land office could make nothing of it. Even for current holdings, they are thinking of sending out designates to tour properties and give the final seal of approval on boundary lines. Were you already in possession of the land, you might stand a chance, but since you aren't sure of the exact location . . ."

"You mean I would have to be able to identify it beyond doubt just to support my claim, wouldn't I?"

He was glad she finally understood. Now maybe she would crawl under a rock somewhere and leave him in peace. "It would seem so. Excuse me, Miss Whitefield, but I see an acquaintance I must waylay before he disappears entirely. Besides, I believe you have already done irreparable harm to your reputation by spending so much time talking to me."

"Please, Mr. Kingston, wait a moment." Miss Whitefield touched his sleeve with a small, slender hand. Her fingers were extraordinarily long and graceful, he noticed, and a slight tremor ran through him at her hesitant touch.

"Miss Whitefield?" He gazed pointedly down at her hand. A flush crept up her cheeks as she removed it. Did she abhor touching him—a man with inexplicably brown skin, one considered unacceptable in polite society, both Indian and British? Staring directly into her eyes, he noted her confusion and embarrassment, and he suddenly wanted to lash out at her, to punish her for being everything he wasn't—white, prim, proper, and pure-bred.

"Have a care, Miss Whitefield," he hissed. "You wouldn't want to contaminate yourself any more than you have already. I'm sure the gossips are tearing you apart for daring to seek me out this evening."

The color in her cheeks deepened to a ruddy hue that quite transformed her face, giving her a vibrancy that truly astonished him. He felt as if he had poked a kitten and discovered a tigress hiding in its skin. "I don't care a fig for what others say of me, and I wonder that you should care, either. Do you relish your somewhat tarnished reputation, Mr. Kingston? It certainly causes the ladies to speculate and sigh over you, as I'm sure you've noticed."

He was taken aback by her vehemence and the clarity of her observation. "I don't relish anything. I merely noted that you have tarried overlong in my questionable company. What more do you wish from me?"

"Are you returning to Paradise View in the very near future?" she demanded, quite undaunted.

"As soon as possible. I still have business to attend to here in Calcutta, and then I am returning."

"What sort of business?"

Was there no end to her brashness and curiosity?

"Not that it's any of your concern, but I'm looking for a nanny to educate my two children," he blurted without thinking.

Her remarkable green eyes widened. "And what ages are your children, Mr. Kingston?"

"I can't imagine why you should be interested, but my son is five, nearly six now, and my daughter just turned four."

"You've kept your wife busy—except in recent years."

Her forthrightness stunned him. No other *memsahib* in all of India would be so quick to let fly with her feelings and opinions—or make references to what a man did with his wife in the bedchamber.

"The children's mother died in childbirth four years ago." He watched in satisfaction as the color drained from her face. The set-down might have been more enjoyable had she not gripped his sleeve again, her green eyes stricken.

"Forgive me, Mr. Kingston. I'm so sorry. You cannot imagine the trouble my errant tongue has caused me in the past. One day, I vow, I shall be forced to tear it out altogether."

He could barely suppress a smile. "On the contrary, Miss Whitefield, I very well *can* imagine what troubles your tongue has gotten you into. Perhaps you merely need to learn new uses for that particular organ."

Shock flared in her eyes, though he was sure she couldn't have the same thought in mind that he had for the use of her tongue. She made a visible effort to gather her dignity about her like a protective cloak. "About the nanny you wish to hire, Mr. Kingston. You need look no further. Despite your unsavory reputation, I am offering my services."

"*You?*" The idea appalled him. "Impossible, Miss Whitefield. I would not consider it."

"And why not?" She efficiently refolded her deed and stuffed it back into the black beaded reticule hanging from her wrist. "You need someone to educate your children, a task for which I am marvelously well-qualified. And I need someone to take me to Central India, where in my free time I can search for Wildwood, make the acquaintance of the young *Nawabzada,* and hopefully, discover what has happened to my inheri—"

"Absolutely not! You aren't of the servant class, Miss Whitefield. Not at all the sort of woman I'm looking for. If you doubt it, ask anyone here, and they will gladly tell you how inappropriate it would be for you to accompany me more than a thousand miles into the *mofussil.*"

"How were you planning to protect the reputation of the *servant* woman you expected to hire? Or doesn't *her* repu-

tation count? Are you saying I'm not of the proper *caste,*
Mr. Kingston? Or is it that you merely don't like *my* character? Come now, I demand an answer to these questions."

*Blast this interfering female and her damnable deed which
could cause him so much potential harm!* At the very least,
she would inconvenience him intolerably.

"Miss Whitefield, I have already secured the services of
an *ayah* to protect the reputation of the nanny I intend to
hire. However, you are a gentlewoman, not a servant, and
the rules are different for you. In your own way, you British
are every bit as caste conscious as—"

"We British?" she inquired insolently.

He damned himself for that revealing slip of the tongue;
he might as well have come right out and admitted what he
was.

"You—we, have it your own way, Miss Whitefield. In any
case, I have practically promised the position to another female who comes highly recommended by a friend of mine."

"And what is her name, sir? Perhaps I have met her."

Having only just heard of her the other day, Alex had
meant to learn more about the lady this evening. All he could
remember was that she had previously been employed in a
family with whom he did business, but now the children had
returned to England for the remainder of their education, and
she was desperately seeking another position before the family cast her out on the streets.

"Abigail. Abigail Lundy." The name sounded right. "And
she is—was—a valued member of Sir Samuel Braithwaite's
household. I have an interview scheduled with her for tomorrow afternoon."

"I have met the Braithwaites, though I haven't met Miss
Lundy. With her credentials, she will have many offers. I
doubt you can secure her. Therefore, you ought to take me,
Mr. Kingston. I am presently unattached, living on the good
graces of friends, and eager to escape Calcutta and see some
of India. If I have no fear for my reputation, why should

you? Your *ayah* will afford me all the protection and female companionship I could desire."

"No, Miss Whitefield. I refuse to consider it. It has been ... interesting, making your acquaintance." He bowed low from the waist. "I must take my leave now. Good evening."

Before she could protest, Alex slipped from behind the potted plant and made his escape. He immediately sought out several gentlemen, so that Miss Emma Whitefield could not approach him again. In case Abigail Lundy refused to accept the position he meant to offer her, he queried everyone he met as to whether or not they could recommend a reliable Englishwoman who might be interested in a position in his employ. There were none available—at least, not to him.

True, British servants were hard to find, but *maharajahs* and other upper-class Indian families seemed able to get them, particularly nannies. Many an Indian prince and princess grew up under the influence of a beloved British *ayah,* who remained with the family long after the children had grown. Unlike so many of the British, the Indians did not abandon their faithful servants once their services were no longer needed. They treated them like family and cared for them until death—pampering and honoring them in their old age.

If Alex were *pure* Indian, he knew he'd have no trouble hiring a nanny. Englishwomen would be banging on his door looking for employment. Whether he found one or not, the one thing he wouldn't do was hire Miss Emma Whitefield and take her home with him to Paradise View. He had no use for someone who might dispute his claim to his holdings—especially now, when a land inspection might possibly face him in the near future. He didn't want any of his enemies—or his young friend, the *Nawabzada* of Bhopal—to hear even a breath of controversy surrounding his claims. Miss Whitefield's deed more than likely could *not* be proven, but its mere existence threatened his security and peace of mind ... as did Miss Whitefield herself. She was a bustle-full of trouble; he could smell it. And he hoped he never saw her again.

* * *

After her disappointing encounter with Alexander King-ston, Emma drifted back into the main ballroom, where a distraught Percival Griffin pounced upon her.

"Emma!—Miss Whitefield. I have been looking all over for you. I brought your rum punch." He thrust a glass in her direction, and amber liquid sloshed over its side and splat-tered down the front of her gown. "Oh, no! How clumsy of me. I must get a cloth and repair the damage to—"

"No, no . . . Don't distress yourself, Mr. Griffin." Emma took his arm. "Forget the rum punch. We have more impor-tant things to discuss."

"We do?" Mr. Griffin blinked, and an expression of hope-fulness flooded his face. "We do?" he repeated joyously.

Ignoring the haughty, disapproving glances directed her way, Emma again steered Mr. Griffin toward the still empty red brocade settee in the corner. "You must tell me every-thing you know about the land office here in Calcutta. Since you aspire to one day become the land administrator for all of Central India, you must know a great deal."

An air of quiet pride and self-satisfaction stole across his features. "I have just returned from Bombay, where I was assured that the position will soon be mine, Miss Whitefield. The current administrator is retiring—returning to Eng-land—and I am due for a promotion. I am not yet privy to all the inner workings of that esteemed office, but I have quite a flair for organization, and everyone agrees that the land office is in grave need of reorganization."

Emma concealed a yawn. "Fascinating. You must tell me more. I have heard there was a fire there recently."

"Oh, yes. . . . Frightful thing. Destroyed all sorts of valu-able papers. Left an unbelievable tangle to sort out." Mr. Griffin sat down beside Emma on the settee. "William told me you came to India to find some property your dear mother left to you. I fear you must abandon the notion, Miss Whitefield. That part of India is wild and most dangerous. Moreover, it will be impossible for you to establish a claim on any property dating back ten or more years. Land in India has changed hands many times since then."

"You are the second person to tell me that this evening. However, I am not about to give up, Mr. Griffin. Surely, when you undertake your new position, you will be able to help me."

"Well, of course, my dear, I'll certainly try."

Emma reached for the remaining glass of rum punch he still held in one hand. "Marvelous." She lifted the glass to her lips and drained it in a single long, thirsty swallow, while Mr. Griffin watched in apparently boundless amazement. "Now, Mr. Griffin, I have one other favor to ask of you."

"Anything, dear Emma. Anything at all."

"Do you happen to know where the Braithwaites live in Calcutta? I have been there before but I don't know if I can find it again, especially on foot."

"But you mustn't attempt *walking*, my dear. You must take a palanquin or better yet a carriage. Ladies of your station can't be too careful, you know."

"So I have been told." Emma didn't explain why she wanted to visit the Braithwaites, but she did accept Percival's offer to send his own carriage for her the following morning. That way, she wouldn't have to explain to Rosie where she was going. Percival himself was going to be busy all morning, so she'd have ample time to seek out Miss Abigail Lundy and discourage her from accepting employment with the disreputable Mr. Alexander Kingston. Mr. Kingston did not as yet know it—because he did not know *her*—but he wasn't leaving Calcutta without her.

"What were you thinking, Emma?" Rosie roundly scolded her later that evening after the ball. "To skulk behind a potted fern with that scandalous man and beg him to hire you to care for his children! Why, you must be daft! You—the daughter of Sir Henry, a baronet and the former Viceroy of India—a mere nanny! And for the offspring of Alexander Kingston, of all people."

"His offspring don't deserve to be tarred with the same brush he is. They are only children, not some horrific monsters." Once again standing in front of her mirror, Emma quietly pulled the pins from her hair. "I'm sorry you disapprove, Rosie, but I'm determined to get to Central India one way or another."

Rosie paced the floor in her agitation. "I suppose I can't talk you out of pursuing this course of folly. I know you well enough to realize that once your mind is made up, you will do what you like, regardless of what anyone says to you."

Emma shook the ringlets from her hair, then reached for the brush on the ornate bedstand. "I don't wish to cause you pain or embarrassment, Rosie. Trust me to be discreet."

Rosie came to a halt. "Discreet! When have you ever been discreet, Emma? Doesn't it matter to you that *my* reputation will surely suffer along with yours? If you do succeed in persuading Mr. Kingston to hire you, everyone in Calcutta will soon hear of it. There will be terrible gossip and speculation—and 'tis *I* who will have to deal with it."

"He may not hire me," Emma said reasonably. "The position may well go to someone else."

"No one else will be interested." Rosie narrowed her eyes at Emma. "Besides, if I know you, Emma Whitefield, you will make certain no one else gets it. . . . What about poor Mr. Griffin? Have you thought about what *he* might think?"

"Mr. Griffin is sending his carriage for me at nine tomorrow morning. Rather, I should say *this* morning." Emma failed to mention that Percival would not be in it. Nor did she say where she was going. "I haven't totally discounted any role Mr. Griffin might play in my future."

"He'll have nothing further to do with you if you create a scandal, Emma. For once in your life, can you not behave conventionally? This is a chance for you to set aside the mistakes of your past and start anew. You must let me guide you—for your own sake as well as mine. British society here in India is even more narrow and circumscribed than it was at home. You simply cannot afford to—"

"Ah, but that is the problem, isn't it?" Lowering her hairbrush, Emma turned to face her distraught friend. "Rosie, please forgive me if I hurt you by what I'm about to say. I cherish our friendship and am most grateful for all you have done for me. But, Rosie dear, I am suffocating here in Calcutta! I must get out of this stuffy society and search all India, if necessary, until I locate what I came here to find."

"But darling, Wildwood is beyond your reach!"

"I don't mean just Wildwood. It's more than Wildwood. It's . . . it's . . . oh, I don't know how to explain, Rosie. It's . . . who I am, perhaps. It's my identity, my very being. Wildwood is why I came, that's true, but now I see that my entire life is sorely lacking. I don't fit anywhere, and each day I am growing older. Life is passing me by, and I still don't know where I belong."

Pausing in her impassioned speech, Emma crossed to the tall open window admitting the soft, floral-scented night air. "Somewhere out there is the real India, Rosie. And there, too, is my future. I can feel it." She inhaled the breeze carrying the exotic scents of India and gazed upon the waning stars; it was only an hour or two until dawn.

Then she turned back to Rosie who was watching her with great dismay. "I must find Wildwood. Maybe then I will know who I am and where I belong. . . . Who knows? Perhaps I will decide it is here in Calcutta with Mr. Griffin. Or England will draw me home again. I only know I have this great emptiness and uncertainty inside me. I've had it all my life. I've never felt I belonged anywhere. Somehow, I must set things right for myself. Dear Rosie, can you understand?"

Tears glimmered in Rosie's eyes as she crossed the room

to embrace Emma. "Oh, Emma! I do have an idea of what you mean. The first time I met William, I knew I had found the other half of myself. We were fated to be together—to meet, marry, and spend the rest of our lives together. Did you have any such feeling when you met Percival?"

She drew back to study Emma's face, and Emma could only shake her head ruefully. "I'm afraid not. Maybe I'm the sort for whom such things must grow over a period of time."

Amazingly, Emma thought of Alexander Kingston. She *had* felt a flare of instantaneous attraction to *him*. But the very idea gave her chills. She wanted nothing personal between herself and that dark, disturbing man; she only wanted to use him to get to Central India and find Wildwood . . . and he would certainly never be attracted to *her*. Given his good looks, he could have his pick of nearly any young woman in India—except for the very proper or married ones, and even they might be tempted. . . . Oh, she must be careful not to allow that brief tempest of feeling to become a full-fledged storm! After she visited Abigail Lundy, she would again confront Alexander Kingston—only this time, she would force herself to remain cool, calm, and completely in control.

Bidding Rosie goodnight, Emma sought her bed with its wooden cage of mosquito netting. The legs of the bed were stuck in saucers of water to deter climbing insects, but the flying ones flapped against the netting, reminding Emma that India truly was a foreign country and different from any place she had ever lived or visited. . . . Maybe she wouldn't fit here, either. Then again, maybe she would. If she had enough courage and determination, anything was possible.

Three

Emma had no difficulty persuading Abigail Lundy that she ought not to accept the position being offered by Alexander Kingston. The plump, elderly, foulard-clad woman had two other offers to consider, neither quite as lucrative, but both with respectable English families—one in Delhi and one in Calcutta itself.

"My Lady," she said to Emma over tea in the Braithwaites' sunny, overgrown garden, "Thank you for coming to warn me about the perils of traveling to Central India with Mr. Kingston, but on the advice of my current employer, I had already decided to decline his offer."

"Oh? And why is that?" Emma sipped cautiously at her tea, an excellent gunpowder-green, then set the cup on the three-legged teapoy between them. Both Sir Samuel and his wife were out this morning, so it hadn't been necessary to offer an explanation for why she wished to visit with their soon-to-be departing nanny. She had intended to say that she understood that Abigail had already been hired by Mr. Kingston, and that if Miss Lundy were foolish enough to actually undertake this ill-advised journey, she wished to ask her to make inquiries about Wildwood on her travels through India.

Emma was relieved not to have to make awkward excuses for her visit. She had been able to come right to the point with Abigail, who seemed an imminently sensible woman making the best of a sad and precarious situation.

Blue eyes caught in a web of wrinkles, graying hair piled into a tidy mass atop her round head, Abigail exuded wholesome British propriety. She looked like the perfect nanny as she leaned forward to pour more tea into Emma's still full cup.

"Even before you mentioned the gossip concerning Mr. Kingston, Sir Samuel advised me it would be imprudent to enter a household about which so little is known, Miss Whitefield. I had therefore decided to accept an offer that will allow me to remain here in Calcutta, where I have a small circle of friends whose acquaintance I should hate to sacrifice at this late date in my life."

"A wise decision. When will you tell Mr. Kingston?"

"Why, this very afternoon. We have an appointment for an interview at three o'clock."

"Here? Or does he have offices somewhere in Calcutta?"

"Oh, he won't come here! I can't say he'd be welcome, since he's not on intimate terms with Sir Samuel, if you know what I mean. They have business dealings, but socially. . . . Well, I've agreed to go to his office, though it's located in a rather unsavory part of town. Sir Samuel has said I might use the barouche, however, so I trust I'll be quite safe."

"Why don't I save you the bother, Miss Lundy? Tell me where his offices are located; I'll take care of it for you."

"*You,* my Lady? Oh, I couldn't. It wouldn't be at all proper for a gentlewoman to be seen in that part of town."

"But I wasn't thinking of going myself," Emma fibbed. "I will simply send a messenger to make your excuses and explain that you've accepted a position elsewhere. It's the least I can do, considering that I came here expressly to discourage you from taking Mr. Kingston's offer."

"You would actually do that for me, my Lady?" Abigail looked ready to burst into tears. "I am quite amazed that you have assumed such responsibility for a stranger's well-being. This is a most difficult time for me, you see, and I do so appreciate your kindness. I had thought to grow old in Sir Samuel's employ, but . . ." She stopped, dabbed at her eyes with a handkerchief, and smiled bravely. "Well, things do not always work out as one expects, do they? I still have a few good years left before I have to worry about what I shall do when I become infirm. Long before then, I hope to make a permanent place for myself with a new employer."

At your age, you shouldn't have to worry about such things, Emma silently sympathized. Unfortunately, she herself was no more secure than Abigail Lundy. All that stood between her and destitution was a handful of gems . . . and Wildwood. Which was why she was willing to do anything to obtain her inheritance. Already, she had told several lies; who knew what else might be required before she was finished?

She much preferred tackling problems head-on, but that approach had done little for her in the past, except make enemies. Emma dug into her reticule, extracted a few precious sovereigns, and pressed them into Abigail's plump hand. "I wish you every success, Miss Lundy. If there is anything else I can do for you, please do not hesitate to call on me. You know where I am currently staying."

Miss Lundy nodded through a wash of tears. "Oh, Miss Whitefield, I don't know how to thank you! Really, this is quite unnecessary."

"Has Sir Samuel provided any severance for you?"

Miss Lundy miserably shook her head.

"I thought not. People of my station do not always consider the problems of others; it's a peculiar sort of blindness they have."

"Nor do they sit down and take tea with their inferiors," Miss Lundy added. "You are one in a million, my lady."

"Nonsense, Miss Lundy. I am merely a fellow traveler on the hard, rocky road of life . . . and now, I must continue my journey. I can see myself to the door; you need not get up."

But Miss Lundy did accompany Emma to the door and again profusely thanked her. This greatly embarrassed Emma who did not think she really deserved it, especially since the next step in her plan was to appear in Miss Lundy's place at her three o'clock appointment with Alexander Kingston.

The carriage ride to Mr. Kingston's office was fascinating, as it offered Emma a chance to view parts of the city she had never before visited. What she saw amazed her. Calcutta not only catered to the British, but also to the Chinese, Muslims, Parsis, Hindus, and other national, ethnic, and religious groups.

There were so many architectural styles she could not identify them all, nor did she recognize the different races of people crowding the busy thoroughfares of the bustling, over-crowded city. Emma passed through an area where virtually all the faces were Oriental, then went down a street where Muslim tailors competed with Chinese shoemakers and a succession of sweet and tea shops.

She saw temples, mosques, Christian churches, and synagogues. There were tall white buildings with marble steps and brass signs, structures that resembled old medieval castles, and sandstone edifices boasting mosaics, colored glass and stone, and Mughal, baroque, neoclassical, and other styles. Seeing these forbidden places was both exhilarating and overwhelming. Emma was heartily glad she hadn't tried to walk the distance from the mansion area behind Chowringhee, where the European community resided, to the small side-street somewhere near the Hooghly river where Alexander Kingston kept his office in a tall, narrow, faded, pastel-colored building that stank of rotting garbage and other unpleasant things.

Emma could not have found her way back to Rosie's house if her life depended upon it, which it probably did. But she had frequented worse areas in London in pursuit of worthy causes, so she was not about to have the vapors now, when her own cause demanded a stalwart heart.

After instructing the dubious carriage driver to wait for her in the crowded street, she entered the building. The inside was far more pleasant than the outside. Gleaming wood and brass, high white ceilings adorned with *punkah* fans, and an eerie hush greeted her. Almost immediately, a white-turbaned figure intercepted her, bowed with mock servility, and offered his assistance in flawless English.

"I am here to see Mr. Kingston."

Emma lifted her chin in an imperious manner that never failed to intimidate uppity servants back home in England, but this man looked anything but intimidated. Tall and slender in his pristine white garments, he possessed a dignity and formality matched only by the most proper English butler. Intelligence shown in his black eyes, and the merest hint of scorn curled his upper lip. "Whom shall I announce wishes to see him?"

"The Honorable Miss Emma Whitefield." Emma used her formal title, which she rarely employed with anyone else.

"He is expecting you, *Memsahib?*"

"No, he is expecting Miss Abigail Lundy, but I have come in her place. You may tell him that."

"Very well, *Memsahib*. Wait here while I convey your message."

The servant disappeared behind a set of carved wooden doors, and Emma amused herself studying the contents of a beautiful case containing swords and other curios. In one corner stood a small statue of a female with naked breasts and long black hair. Leaning closer to get a better look, Emma discovered that the statue had red palms, a red mark in the center of her forehead, and was sticking out her tongue, also painted a bright blood-red. Perfect down to the tiniest detail, miniature gold chains, bracelets, and a necklace of tiny human skulls, garlanded the unusual figure.

"You are interested in the Goddess Kali?"

Emma jumped and whirled around, embarrassed to be caught staring at a replica of a half-naked female sticking out her tongue in an obscene manner. "Is that who she is— the Goddess Kali? I've never heard of her."

"No doubt because she's an Indian goddess." Dressed impeccably in somber gray with a crimson vest, Mr. Kingston looked even more handsome and dangerous than Emma remembered. "If you are interested in learning more about her, you should visit the Kali Temple here in Calcutta. It was built in 1809, but the site was devoted to her worship long before that. Human sacrifices are known to have taken place there, though today, usually only goats and the occasional buffalo are offered in her honor."

"Usually?" Emma echoed breathlessly.

"As far as I know. There's always gossip, but whenever I've been there, all I've ever seen offered was goat milk mixed with water from the Ganga."

Alexander Kingston's eyes were the precise color of a peacock's feathers. Emma had thought they were turquoise or ocean-blue, but they were even bluer than that, and framed by long black lashes that gave them a hooded, mysterious look. . . . Why had he gone to an Indian temple in the first place? Was it merely to see the sights—or to worship? Was he telling her all this in a deliberate effort to shock her into fleeing? If so, he would find she was not so easy to rout.

"Perhaps I shall visit there sometime. If I am lucky, I'll be able to witness the offering of human flesh—*yours* preferably."

Alexander Kingston smiled, his teeth a brilliant flash of whiteness in his dark face. "You aren't the first person to express a desire to witness my demise. Why are you here, Miss Whitefield? Where's Miss Lundy?"

Emma glanced about the outer room, expecting—hoping—to state her case in a more private place. They were quite alone, and Mr. Kingston did not seem about to invite her into his inner office, so she launched into her explanation. "Miss Lundy isn't coming. She bade me inform you that she has already accepted a position elsewhere. I'm afraid you will find no one else to hire, Mr. Kingston. Therefore, you should bow gracefully to the inevitable and accept *my* services."

After a moment of studying her with unnerving intensity, Mr. Kingston gave a shout of laughter that quite startled her.

"What is so funny?"

"You, Miss Whitefield. I have underestimated you. *You* are the reason Miss Lundy isn't coming, aren't you? And I don't doubt for a moment you will find a way to discourage any other applicants I might unearth. What did you do—tell her I eat little children and old nannies for breakfast?"

Emma smarted beneath his too-knowing scrutiny. "No, I merely told her the truth: No self-respecting Englishwoman would dare risk her good name by accompanying a rogue like you into the *mofussil.*"

"But *you* would take that risk, wouldn't you? Don't I frighten you, Miss Whitefield?" Moving closer, he forced Emma to back up a step—until her hips brushed the curio cabinet.

She stared into his blue eyes. They were as mesmerizing as a serpent's. In the pit of her belly, something quivered and quaked, and she was suddenly acutely conscious of his height. He was taller than she by a full head. And his shoulders were wider than most men's. His hair was black as a crow's wing—and his scent! It was a peculiarly masculine odor hinting of leather and . . . and . . . sandalwood?

"You don't frighten me in the least, Mr. Kingston," she lied, with her pulse pounding and the blood rushing to her head. "So you might as well stop trying to bully me and let us get on with the business at hand. I insist upon the customary wages afforded to nannies and governesses here in India, payable in English coin on the first of each month. As for working conditions, I demand my own living quarters, which need not be lavish, but must at least contain minimum comforts, such as storage for my clothing and my extensive collection of books. I shall require Saturdays and every other Sunday off, and before we depart Calcutta, I insist upon meeting the *ayah* you have engaged, so that I can determine how well we will get on together. If she is not to my liking, nor I to hers, I will engage my own traveling companion, though you, of course, will pay her wages."

Watching her with an amused expression, Mr. Kingston backed off somewhat, though it wasn't as far as she would have liked. "You are really quite something, Miss Whitefield. Nothing deters you. Not even knowing that I have no intention of taking you home with me to Paradise View."

"One way or another, I intend to change your mind."

"But what will all your friends say? You risk ostracism from your own kind by insisting upon this course of action."

"In all India I have but one true friend, Mr. Kingston. I can only hope she will understand why I am doing this and not sever our friendship because of it."

"If you persist, your friendship will surely be doomed."

"Then it will be doomed anyway, because if you refuse to allow me to accompany you, I will make such a pest of myself bothering the officials here at the land office in Calcutta—and whomever else I might meet that could possibly be able to help me—that she will be mortified by my unladylike behavior. Really, it would be much easier all around if you just let me go with you. My friend is the only one in Calcutta who needs to know where I've gone and what I'm doing there. Everyone else can be told some innocuous tale I can concoct on a moment's notice."

Mr. Kingston regarded her silently, as if seriously weighing the matter. Emma wasn't sure what she had said to cause him to do so, but she decided to risk a bit more in hopes of settling the issue. "Mr. Kingston, am I correct in assuming that you wish your children to be raised with . . . shall we say . . . a strong British influence?"

A flush consumed his dark cheekbones. "What are you implying, Miss Whitefield?"

Ignoring the flash of anger in his blue eyes, she plunged recklessly onward. "Do your children take after *you*, Mr. Kingston—or do they favor their mother?"

"They take after both of us," he snapped. "And their mother

was dark, even as I am. Nonetheless, they are beautiful children. Unfortunately, the world as we know it today is run by fair-skinned, blond-haired Englishmen—so yes, I want a strong British influence upon them. I want them to look, speak, and act British. To be totally at home with British values and customs. That's why I need an English nanny—to exert this influence before they grow too old to reject it."

Emma felt a sudden stab of empathy for Alexander Kingston. Only his love for his children could induce such a proud man to seek that which he obviously scorned. "Why do you not bring them here to Calcutta—so they can rub shoulders with other British children? Buried in the jungle, they must have little association with anyone English."

"How I choose to raise my children—and where—is my concern, not yours. If I wanted them raised here in Calcutta, obviously I would have brought them here. However, they would be subjected to the same cruel gossip I have suffered. No, I would never expose them to that. But one day, when I send them to England to complete their educations, they must be able to fit in there. They must know the language and customs. That is where *you*—or rather, a nanny—comes in."

"Me, Mr. Kingston. Do let it be me, for I can think of no one better qualified to teach the subtleties of English manners to your children. I have lived with those subtleties all of my life. As the daughter of a baronet, I know far better than Miss Lundy what one must do to blend with the ruling class."

"Do you *blend*, Miss Whitefield? You strike me as something of a rebel, and I don't want my children to rebel against the ruling class, but to be absorbed into it."

"I know *how* to fit in, Mr. Kingston. I can teach your children all the silly, meaningless little games one must know to get on with the gentry. Isn't that what you want?"

"Yes. Yes, it is." He paused a moment, studying her, then said brusquely, "So if you want it, the job is yours. Be at the train station at four o'clock tomorrow afternoon, Miss Whitefield. We will leave Calcutta then."

"Tomorrow afternoon! But . . . but what about my other demands?"

"I accede to your demands. You may meet Tulsi then, too, and determine if the two of you are compatible."

"Tulsi?"

"The *ayah* who will supposedly protect your virtue."

"What do you mean—*supposedly?*"

He grinned—a wicked grin that sent a ripple of alarm down Emma's spine.

"Miss Whitefield, the presence of ten *ayahs* will not protect your reputation if the British community here in Calcutta gets word of this. You won't be able to show your face on an English veranda in all of India. If someone hasn't already explained that by now, they should."

"I've already told you: I don't care what people think."

"That's because you haven't had them think the worst of you."

Yes, I have, Emma silently retorted. She didn't say it aloud for fear of changing his mind about her suitability to teach his children correct behavior.

"I'll be at the train station at four o'clock. Thank you, Mr. Kingston. Now, I must go. I have much to do before then."

She turned to leave at the exact same moment as the tall slender Indian servant appeared at the door. Had he been standing nearby, out of sight and eavesdropping?

"I bid you good day, *Memsahib*." Again he bowed with an attitude of doing so only because it pleased him, not because he thought she was in any way superior.

"Good day," she said and sped for the waiting carriage.

"Sikander, what have you done?"

"What I came here to do; I've hired a nanny." In no mood to debate his decision, Alex headed toward his inner office.

Not about to be ignored, Sakharam followed. "Sikander, why that one? She will be trouble. Anyone can see it."

"I don't wish to discuss the matter. It's settled." Alex sat down at his polished wood desk and began rifling through some correspondence. If he was indeed leaving Calcutta tomorrow afternoon, there was a great deal he must do also. "We leave tomorrow afternoon. See to it."

Sakharam planted himself obstinately in front of Alex's desk. "You are making a mistake, Sikander. Do not take that particular Englishwoman with us."

Alex plowed his fingers through his hair in irritation. "I have to, damn it! If I leave her here in Calcutta, Emma Whitefield will spend every waking moment at the land office trying to convince them she owns *my* land!"

"*Your* land? Do you mean Paradise View?"

Alex sighed and told his friend the whole story. "Her deed can't be valid, of course, but she still represents a great threat to me, Sakharam."

"Can you not settle a modest sum upon her, *Sahib*, and remove the threat? She does not know the value of the land, having never seen it. Simply tell her you wish to purchase the property—which you can claim is all worthless jungle— and you are willing to make a fair offer on it."

"I don't want her to know that I know of the property in question! First of all, she doesn't strike me as a reasonable sort who'd be willing to sell her inheritance for any price. And second, I haven't the necessary funds to buy her out, at the moment. All my cash is tied up in the cost of feeding and clothing my sometimes worthless servants and in the expense of harvesting the wood on that land. Moreover, the *Nawabzada*, who claims to be my friend, is now demanding twenty-five percent share of the profits on every tree I harvest—or else he is threatening to raise questions with the authorities over the authenticity of my deeds, the originals of which were destroyed in that fire in the land office."

"Ah, I perceive the problem."

"It is worse even than that," Alex glumly informed him. "There have always been those who resent my success, Sakharam—both among the British and my own countrymen. If they knew I was vulnerable in any way, they would seek to destroy me—and what better way than by relieving me of the best portion of my holdings? I know some who would pay three or four times what I could afford to offer Miss Whitefield to gain possession of her questionable deed."

"Your cousin, Hyder Khan."

"Yes, him especially, but also my half-brothers. They have always lusted after what I've been able to gain by dint of hard work and scheming."

"The worthless dogs! They who work not should eat not. They loll about on their silken couches just dreaming of ways to thwart you for daring to share their royal blood."

Sakharam was referring to the fact that Alex's mother, dead from fever some fifteen or more years now, had been a high caste Brahmin connected to the family of the Maharajah of Gwalior in the state of Madhya Pradesh.

"If your father still lived, he would help you now," Sakharam said. "He would do it; I know he would—discreetly, of course."

"I doubt it. He may have been a high-ranking official of the British East India Company, but it isn't the same India now as it was thirty years ago, when he held power."

"Yes, I know. How well I remember . . ." Sakharam sighed. "In those days, no one found anything shameful in an alliance such as your parents enjoyed. Not until the women of the Raj began arriving by the boatload did it become unacceptable for men like your father to consort with women like your mother. It grieved your father sorely to have to set you both aside, Sikander. I wish you would remember that."

"But he still did it, didn't he? And though my mother's family willingly took her back, they never could accept *me*, could they?" The old hurt and bitterness rose up chokingly in Alex; his mother had been reabsorbed into her family much as if she'd never left it—she had even married and borne other children before she died! But he himself had been ostracized . . . always on the outside looking in, taunted mercilessly by his cousins.

"Not all of your mother's family hates you, Sikander," Sakharam gently reminded him.

"No," Alex conceded. "There is Santamani . . ."

Santamani was his aunt, Hyder Khan's mother, who had given him many precious gifts, like the elephant table, over the years. Alex had had a serious falling out with her over her son's behavior some years ago, but before that, she had helped further his career by discreetly exerting her considerable influence in the family. Alex deeply regretted the loss of her friendship; he owed much to her, but even her intercessions on his behalf had not been able to soothe the sting of rejection he still felt, first from his father, then from his mother's family.

Family was supposed to help and support family, but other than Santamani and one or two others, no one on either side had been willing to claim him openly. He was a shame and an embarrassment to everyone. Had his father not at one time saved Sakharam's life—and committed Alex to Sakharam's care—Sakharam himself might not have stood by Alex all these years. Alex had been eight years old when his father abandoned him; it made no difference that there had been tears in the man's eyes when he bade Alex goodbye; Alex had never forgiven him . . . and he hadn't shed a tear at the news of his death some years later.

"So we are taking this English *memsahib* home with us in order to keep her from frequenting the land office here in Calcutta; is that what we are doing?"

Alex nodded, his thoughts returning to the present. "Yes, and perhaps on our long journey to Paradise View, we can arrange for her to lose her precious deed, so that nowhere on paper is there anything to support the validity of what she claims—that her mother once owned a piece of property called Wildwood and willed it to her. Without the deed, it will make no difference if she does go to the *Nawabzada*, the land office, or Hyder Khan. The paper is worthless, but I would still feel much better if it were destroyed."

"Leave that to me, Sikander. I will take care of it." Sakharam salaamed deeply.

"No *Sahib* today? I've decided I might enjoy receiving a bit more respect from you, Sakharam. Perhaps you do need practice saying it. And you could bow a little lower, too."

Sakharam rose, his dark eyes glowing. "Do you wish for me to lick your boots while I am down there, *Sahib?*"

"Why not? Might do you good to learn true humility."

"Beware I do not bite your big toe while I am doing it," Sakharam warned, his eyes flashing.

Alex laughed, his good humor restored. "Go and prepare for our departure, my friend. And don't forget to purchase an extra railway ticket for our new nanny."

Four

After another argument and a tearful departure from Rosie, Emma set out for the railway station in a hired buggy and soon found herself standing on the train platform surrounded by several trunks and wooden boxes filled with all her worldly possessions.

Anxious and worried, she craned her neck looking for Alexander Kingston. She didn't see him, but she did notice many other interesting things. The station was a commodious building with elegant touches of brass and marble, but there were too many human beings crammed into it. Whole families of Indians squatted in the station or on the platform. Waiting for the arrival or departure of trains, they had brought their bedding, cookpots, and servants and were going about the details of daily living with complete disregard for their surroundings.

Dogs, chickens, and even a stray cow wandered about searching for scraps of food. Hawkers with trays on their heads were busy selling green coconuts, mangoes, lemonade, soda water, and jugs of spicy-smelling, milky-looking tea. The station itself had rows of stalls where one could buy oranges, bananas, figs, hot curry or spicy snacks, all manner of sweets, and cool sherbet.

Walking through the building, Emma had been accosted by vendors bearing huge wooden trays with arrangements of glass bangles or clay toys painted with brightly colored birds and flowers . . . and she had been forced to turn away beggars who plucked at her skirts and wanted to show her their oozing sores and crippled limbs.

There was no way she could help them all, and she had been repeatedly warned that to help even one would mean that the rest would pester her unceasingly and even follow her to her destination in an effort to persuade her to widen her sphere of generosity. Beggars did seem to be everywhere in Calcutta, and Emma had already observed that once she refused to hand over any coins, bent old crones sometimes straightened and walked away with a youthful swagger, and limps were miraculously cured. Still, it went against her grain to turn a blind eye on human misery. She felt guilty and uncomfortable in her serviceable clothing and sturdy shoes, while others went about barefoot and clad only in rags.

"Where are you, Mr. Kingston?" she fumed under her breath. "You had better not have left without me."

A shrill whistle signaled the arrival of a train, and a moment later, belching smoke and making a terrible commotion, it clacked into view around a bend in the track. Emma clutched her reticule more tightly to her bosom and prayed that this wasn't the train she and her new employer were supposed to be boarding. She had no way of finding out for certain.

Over Rosie's protests that such efforts were unnecessary, Emma had been diligently studying Hindustani ever since her arrival in India, but she still didn't know enough to converse intelligibly with complete strangers. Several Europeans shared the platform with her, but Emma didn't want to approach them for fear they might begin asking questions she herself was loath to answer. She had convinced Rosie to circulate the story that she had gone off to visit old family friends in Darjeeling and had even persuaded her to tell Percival Griffin she was looking forward to spending more time with him upon her return. There was no sense destroying all her chances for the future; if things didn't work out as she hoped in Central India, she might welcome the idea of returning to Calcutta and marrying Percival—assuming he still wanted her. It wouldn't do to meet someone in the station who knew Rosie and William and might dispute her story at a later date.

The train ground to a screeching halt in front of Emma, and passengers began to pour out of the railway carriages. Emma immediately noticed that Indian men and women traveled separately—men in one carriage, women in another. Europeans occupied their own compartments. . . . How would she and Alexander Kingston travel? Would they share accommodations?

A group of Indian women in brilliantly colored *saris* stepped off the train, and Emma gaped, for they were the first upper-class females she had seen up close. Their mysterious garments floated about them, the colors gloriously clashing in impossible shades of brightest pink, blue, yellow, orange, and scarlet trimmed with borders of gold, silver, and bronze. Another carriage disgorged women wearing short satin skirts of pale cherry and emerald green, quantities of gold lace, handsome ornaments, and flowers in their glossy black hair. They were completely unlike the women in the *saris* and didn't seem to be speaking the same language. Emma stared at them in mingled wonder and curiosity.

"Parsee," said a male voice behind her, and Emma whirled to discover that once again, Alexander Kingston had managed to sneak up on her. "Those women you are gawking at are Parsee."

Just then a flock of birds settled upon the platform and began cackling and fighting over crumbs dropped by passersby.

"Are you acquainted with those birds?" Mr. Kingston's tone was pleasant and conversational. "They're called the Seven Sisters because they always fly in flocks of seven."

Emma was only slightly distracted by his easy patter. "At

the moment, I'm not interested in birds. Where have you been? Is that our train that just pulled in?"

"Yes, but don't worry. We've plenty of time. It won't leave without us." He motioned to several partially clad men wearing the voluminous lengths of cloth Indians often adopted in place of trousers. Emma thought they were called *dhotis*. Behind Mr. Kingston, she spotted the tall, haughty servant she had first seen in Mr. Kingston's offices.

With a nod of his head, Mr. Kingston indicated Emma's baggage, and the men in *dhotis* scrambled to grab hold of her things. "Tell them to have a care, please," she implored. "I shouldn't want those boxes broken and to have my garments scattered about for all the world to see."

"Oh, especially your *unmentionables*." Mr. Kingston gave her a mocking smile. "That would be a terrible tragedy."

He said something to the men, and they immediately began to exercise more caution as they disappeared inside the train with Emma's belongings.

Relieved, Emma studied Mr. Kingston from beneath her lashes. Today, he wore a dark blue traveling suit with a thin elegant stripe. It fit him like a kidskin glove. His vest was a deep burgundy color and fashionably adorned with a gold watch chain. Both his dress and manner were pure English, but to Emma, Alexander Kingston in no way resembled the other Englishmen sharing the platform. He was too dark. Too vivid. Too outrageously handsome. And entirely too self-possessed.

Her throat closed with sudden dread. What was she doing preparing to accompany this exotic stranger into the interior of an unknown land?

Taking her arm, he smoothly inquired: "Having second thoughts, Miss Whitefield? It's not too late to change your mind, you know."

"Once I've decided upon a course of action, I rarely, if ever, change my mind, Mr. Kingston."

Eager to escape his all-knowing gaze, Emma watched another group of women veiled entirely from head to foot. Not even their eyes were visible. And all about them, pushing and shoving, were men of every shape, size, skin color, and manner of dress—some swathed in yards of white muslin, some in skirts or *dhotis*, others with skull caps or colored turbans . . . and then she saw a half-naked creature clad only in a loin cloth. His wildly rolling eyes, long tangled locks, and stick-thin body in which every bone was visible, struck unreasoning terror in her heart. . . . She didn't mean to gasp, but she couldn't help it.

Alexander Kingston turned to see where she was looking. "Don't be afraid." His grip on her arm tightened. "It's only a *sadhu*, a holy man. He means you no harm."

She jerked away. "I'm *not* afraid—not enough to go running back to the security of my British friends. Shall we board the train, Mr. Kingston, or do you intend to stand all day on this platform pointing out people and objects of interest?"

His grin infuriated her. "Good thing you're a brave woman, Miss Whitefield. You will need a hearty dose of courage on this journey; once we leave Calcutta, you'll be entering a world completely foreign to you."

"I relish the thought. After all, Wildwood is a part of that world, and I know somehow I shall find it."

His grin disappeared. "In that you will be disappointed. If you are embarking on this long journey only to find your inheritance, you will be sadly disillusioned."

"I am also coming to teach your children—and to see India. So you may resume your informative lecture as soon as we are settled on the train. At that time, I shall welcome your comments and observations, I'm sure."

"Let's be about it then."

They boarded the train, where an Indian porter directed them to a single large compartment containing four leather benches and a large block of ice. Emma presumed the ice was to keep it cool, though the hot season hadn't yet descended.

When she opened a small door, she discovered a thunderbox in one corner and a shower that drained away through a hole in the floor. Embarrassed, she hurriedly closed the door and instead examined the train windows, which were quite complicated—consisting of a layer of glass, a blind to keep out the dust and the sun, and a netting to deter insects.

"This is most satisfactory, Sakharam," Mr. Kingston remarked to his servant. "Weren't you able to secure a separate compartment for Miss Whitefield?"

"No, *Sahib*," the servant replied without a hint of regret. "She will have to stay in here with you—or else she can join the *pattah-wallahs* in the only other carriage available."

Emma suppressed a shudder at the thought of traveling with all those half-naked men crammed into one tiny area. Mr. Kingston's lips curved slightly upwards. "We'll have to share then. If she can bear such close proximity, I can."

Emma gingerly seated herself on one of the benches and peered through the window coverings. Mr. Kingston sat down opposite her. After several awkward moments of relative silence, the whistle blew, the train gave a lurch, and the entire compartment began to sway, shake, and rumble.

"What? No disinfectant?" Mr. Kingston drawled, stretching his long legs out in front of him, unbuttoning his coat and vest, and making himself shamelessly comfortable.

"No disinfectant?" His meaning eluded her.

"Most *memsahibs* would already have out their disinfectants and be swabbing down the benches by now with a bit of lace. Don't you fear contamination, Miss Whitefield?"

"Should I?"

"Disease is ever-present in this country, if not in England," he said reasonably.

"Just how well do you know England?"

"I attended school there for some years." He sounded evasive. "But I pined the whole time for India. I was born here and consider it home."

Emma debated whether or not to question him in greater

detail. She was intensely curious but did not wish to offend him, especially since he had already demonstrated a sensitivity to gossip. She decided to forestall her questions until she knew him better.

"Home for me was Shropshire. But I don't miss it at all. Indeed, I'm very glad to be here in India, setting out for Paradise View. I've no wish to be anywhere else."

"How fortunate for you." He leaned his head back against the wall of the compartment and promptly closed his eyes, inviting no further conversation.

The train went slowly at first, but then it finally picked up speed, and the noise was deafening. Emma leaned her own head back against the wall and let her body absorb the motion and vibration. She strove without much success to match Mr. Kingston's apparent relaxation. She was hungry, but didn't know when or how they would eat. She grew sleepy, but couldn't imagine where she might lie down—or sleep.

Mr. Kingston dozed, his disturbing blue eyes mercifully closed. He breathed deeply, his mouth fully closed—a feat she envied. She might have succumbed to her own weariness, but feared having her jaw drop open, thereby making a spectacle of herself and earning more of Mr. Kingston's scornful amusement. She finally moved closer to the nearest window, raised the netting and shade, and watched the lush green countryside glide past. She had envisioned India as being hot, dry, and dusty, but at this time of year, the state of Bengal sported a lush verdancy—the same she had witnessed on her boat trip up the Hooghly upon her arrival.

Coconut, banana, and date palm trees grew abundantly. In the distance were rice fields. The banks of the Hooghly had been studded with mansions, but the housing in this area was far more modest—more typical of the *dak* bungalows she had heard so much about. Buildings were square, made of mud-brick with thick walls to keep out the heat, and had thatched or tiled roofs. The more prosperous-looking ones had verandas.

Emma amused herself speculating about the occupants of the houses and what their lives were like as the train slowly chugged away from Calcutta and all that was faintly familiar.

When evening came, Sakharam entered the compartment, set up a small table between Emma and Mr. Kingston, and returned a few moments later bearing two china plates, each tied up in a spotless white napkin. With a flourish, he set them down, produced silverware, and removed the napkins from the plates. A complete hot meal consisting of a savory-smelling vegetable curry served over steaming rice, chutney, fresh fruit, and some sort of compote awaited her.

She was further amazed when Sakharam served wine in crystal goblets. "I don't indulge in spirits," she demurred when he offered her one.

Mr. Kingston arched a brow sardonically. The light from a swaying paraffin lamp cast shadows on his face and gave it a saturnine look. "You don't have a peg now and then?"

A peg was a whiskey with soda, which came in thick green bottles. It was a popular drink for both men and women at British Clubs in India, as was gin with Indian tonic, called a gimlet. The peg was so named because each was a peg in one's coffin. Even Rosie drank them, but Emma had thus far resisted.

She shook her head. "On very special occasions, I might have a glass of rum or milk punch."

"So sorry, but I don't believe Sakharam can furnish that, can you, Sakharam?"

Something shifted in Sakharam's dark eyes. "No, *Sahib*. Forgive me for being remiss in my duties."

"I really think you should try the wine, Miss Whitefield, or else you are bound to go thirsty. Fresh water will be scarce during our journey, and where it is available, it cannot be trusted. I shouldn't want you to fall ill. Thus, we must drink wine or other mild spirits, except of course, when we resort to tea, which will mainly be served at *chota hazri*—excuse me, breakfast—tiffin at noon, and tea-time."

Emma made an instant decision to be accommodating. "All right then, I shall try the wine."

To her great surprise, the golden liquid slid down beautifully with the delicate curry, the finest she had yet tasted in India. She decided she liked wine with dinner, though she had always mistrusted it because of the great quantities of claret and burgundy her father and brother had consumed at meals, which had made them red-faced and temperamental. In future, she resolved to drink the light-colored vintages and avoid the red at dinner parties.

By meal's end, Emma was suffused by a rosy haze and desperately trying to remain upright, as befitted a lady. Sakharam suddenly appeared with an armload of bedding and calmly began making up the two remaining benches. It was then she realized that she and Mr. Kingston would be sleeping together—or as nearly together as a male and female could be without actually sharing a bed. They would be lying no farther apart than if they *were* sharing the same bed.

Belatedly, Emma remembered that she was supposed to have a female companion. "Where is the *ayah* you promised would be accompanying us?"

"Sakharam, where is Tulsi?" Mr. Kingston calmly inquired as if he himself had only just thought of her.

"In a carriage with other females, *Sahib*."

"I shall go and join her." Emma rose unsteadily. "It isn't proper for me to spend the night alone in this compartment with you."

"It isn't proper for a *memsahib* to travel in the company of Indian women," Mr. Kingston disputed. "Europeans don't share railway carriages with Indians."

"Then what shall we do? This . . ." she indicated the

makeshift beds, ". . . is impossible, Mr. Kingston, as I am sure you know."

"We'll have her join us. It may be a bit crowded, but it's the only solution. Sorry I didn't think of it sooner."

"She ought to have eaten with us," Emma fumed. "I never should have spent so many hours isolated in here with you."

"Nonsense. You've been perfectly safe—and who is there to pass judgment? No one on this train knows either of us."

"*I* know I have been alone with you. So do you, Mr. Kingston. We must observe the proprieties. They exist for a reason."

"What reason, Miss Whitefield? Do you fear ravishment? Is that it? I assure you I have no intention of ravishing you."

His tone implied she wasn't worthy of ravishment. Emma had a sudden mental image of Alexander Kingston's elegant brown hands on her white body. She shivered uncontrollably, and her reaction did not go unnoticed.

"Don't be ridiculous, madam," he snarled. "I've never had to force myself upon women in the past, and I doubt I shall have to do so in the future. Nor am I attracted to women who are unattracted to me. Your repugnance arouses a similar response, I assure you."

Emma's cheeks burned with mortification. It didn't help that Sakharam was standing in front of the closed door to the compartment, absorbing every word. In the midst of her excruciating embarrassment, Emma was aware that she did *not* feel repelled by the person of Alexander Kingston. The thought of him putting his hands on her body made her blood leap with a sudden wild, inexplicable yearning. She had never experienced anything like it, and it terrified her to the depths of her prim, proper soul.

"Please send for Tulsi," she managed in a shaky voice. "And from now on, she must remain here with us—or else one of us must vacate this compartment and leave it to the other."

Mr. Kingston's gaze was plainly challenging. "The rumors

you have heard are all true, Miss Kingston. I am not gentleman enough to bed down in a compartment full of unwashed *pattah-wallahs* merely to set your mind at ease concerning my intentions. If my word is not good enough to allay your fears, 'tis you who must find another place to sleep—and that will be difficult, I think, as the train is already over-crowded."

Emma refused to be intimidated. "Tulsi's presence will give me all the security I need."

"Sakharam, fetch Tulsi, and make up another bed please. We wouldn't want our new nanny to fear for her virtue. Would it offend you too much if I removed my jacket, madam?"

His scathing tone made Emma long for his gentle mockery. "You may remove your jacket, sir. And I shall remove my *topi*. That way we will both be comfortable."

"I sincerely hope you don't snore," he said rudely. "For I am not a heavy sleeper."

Emma hoped she didn't also. That would be too, too mortifying. She sat back down on the bench while Sakharam went to fetch Tulsi, and Mr. Kingston disappeared inside the washroom. Tulsi turned out to be a tiny, plump woman wrapped in a mustard-colored *sari*. Her ebony-black hair, parted in the middle and pulled back to form a large mass at the back of her neck, was streaked with gray. She wore a caste mark in the very center of her forehead and spoke not a word of English.

"How am I to communicate with her?" Emma had somehow expected the *ayah* to know at least a few words of English; most servants did.

"Tell me what you wish to say, *Memsahib*. I will translate for you," Sakharam volunteered in his haughty manner.

"Oh, just tell her I am pleased to make her acquaintance!"

Tulsi bowed and smiled and chattered incomprehensibly. Then she lay down on one of the benches which Sakharam had made up into a bed. Within seconds, she fell asleep . . . and snored loudly the whole night through.

Five

Nothing could have tasted better to Emma the next morning than the hot tea Sakharam served, along with thick wedges of fresh mango, a light, sweet rice dish, boiled eggs, syrupy pastries, and some bland, satisfying things called *chapattis*.

She couldn't help remarking on how delicious everything tasted and how surprised she was that such fine food was available on a train. From all the horror stories she had heard, she had been expecting severe deprivation, not better fare than she had eaten at Rosie's.

"Sakharam will be pleased," Mr. Kingston said with a distant politeness. "That in turn will please the assistant cook who carries his little stove with him wherever he goes and takes great pride in what he does. They chose this morning's offerings with an eye toward your enjoyment; at least, they did not wish to disgust you or make you ill."

"Well, I have appreciated their offerings immensely." Emma wondered which of the barefoot, untidy servants was the assistant cook. Somehow she had not expected Mr. Kingston to travel with one cook, much less two, and she realized then how privileged she was—to have her meals served on fine china, to drink wine from crystal goblets, and not to have to worry about how or where the meals were prepared, or what happened to the dirty dishes. With grave dignity, Sakharam and his retinue of servants took care of everything.

After breakfast, Emma attempted to make conversation with Tulsi, but Tulsi only smiled and nodded at everything Emma tried to say, and she soon gave up in disgust. At last, Tulsi said something, which Sakharam obligingly translated.

"Your *ayah* wishes to know if you would object to her joining a friend traveling in another carriage. She promises to return before nightfall."

The request surprised Emma, but she did want to deny it merely because she felt uncomfortable being alone with Mr. Kingston. Still smarting after last night's set-to, Mr. Kingston had said hardly a word to her all morning. Sakharam had brought him several newspapers, purchased during one the train's frequent short stops, and he had been engrossed in them ever since.

"No, no—I have no objections. I am sure she would rather spend her time with someone proficient in her own language."

"You should forbid her," Sakharam scolded with a disapproving frown. "Her duty is to keep you company, not visit with friends who happen to be aboard this same train."

"I don't mind—really, I don't. I will just sit here and look out the window. Perhaps Mr. Kingston might consent to share his newspapers with me."

Mr. Kingston glanced up from his reading. "Only one of these is written in English. But if you are bored, you are welcome to look it over."

He tossed a newspaper in her direction, which she caught before it fell to the floor. "Thank you."

After Tulsi left the compartment—having expressed her gratitude in an incomprehensible outpouring—Emma perused the *Civil and Military Gazette*, which was published in Lahore, not Calcutta. Unfamiliar with the names of people or places listed in it, she found little of interest. She wished Mr. Kingston would talk to her, but having made such an issue of being alone with him, she didn't know how to initiate a conversation. She hadn't meant to offend him, but he ought to have understood that she couldn't possibly spend the night alone with him in the compartment.

He looked up suddenly to catch her staring. "What is wrong now, Miss Whitefield?"

"Nothing's wrong, Mr. Kingston. I was just wishing you would put down your paper and talk to me. I thought you were going to tell me all about India."

He seemed about to refuse outright. It certainly wasn't customary for an employer to accede to an employee's demands. Nor did the master stoop to entertain his servant. However, they both knew that their relationship was hardly ordinary; she was going to be his children's nanny, but they were social equals. If anything, her status exceeded his, though he would never admit it.

With a small sigh, he set aside his newspaper and sat up straighter. "What do you wish to know, Miss Whitefield?"

Hoping to set things right between them, she gave him her sunniest smile. "Oh, everything! Perhaps you could begin with . . . with . . ." She cast about for an innocuous topic. "Food!" she burst out, inspired. "You could tell me more about the foods of India. Other than the two I've had on this train, my meals have been typically English, and much of what I have eaten has come from tins. My friend, Rosie, was quite proud to have served me tinned asparagus and salmon, when I was quite longing for something fresh. Alas, the only fresh fish I have tasted thus far is boiled pomfret. There must be more than that available."

Mr. Kingston gave a short laugh, his blue eyes lighting with amusement. "Indeed, there is, Miss Whitefield, and I would be happy to tell you about all that India offers, including the many varieties of fish. But you must tell me something first: isn't it considered vulgar to discuss food and appetite? Such behavior is more typical of the lower classes, something ladies of quality avoid at all costs."

Emma realized she had sailed into dangerous waters. "It is considered impolite to compliment the hostess on her table, for it implies she did the cooking herself, which everyone knows she didn't. But away from the table, there's nothing wrong with discussing food."

"So that is the distinction. I'm glad you explained it, as I've always wondered and broken the rule on any number of occasions. Fortunately," he gave her a sharp look, "my children will never make such an error. You, as their nanny, will make certain they do not."

"I shall do my best." Emma thought of all the hundreds of social errors a man like Alexander Kingston could make. Had he not had a proper English nanny? She managed to restrain herself from asking, lest he retreat once more into infuriating silence.

"About the food, if you please, Mr. Kingston."

"Ah, yes, the food. Shall I tell you how the Indian views food—or will you be satisfied with a mere recitation of items one can find in a typical bazaar?"

"As I said, I wish to learn everything."

"Everything. I was afraid of that." He rubbed his chin contemplatively. If she could tell anything about character from his chin, Emma judged Mr. Kingston to be extremely stubborn. He also radiated strength, and she suspected he had opinions on nearly everything—strong opinions.

"Well, let me see. . . . To the Indian, food is a serious business, a gift of the gods. As such, it is treated with respect and subject to innumerable prescriptions . . . or so I have heard."

"What sort of prescriptions?"

"The time of year, the climate, the locale where it is eaten—even the age of the food itself—governs each meal's ingredients. A meal ought to include six *rasas* or flavors; no meal can be considered perfect—or even satisfactory—if it does not contain something sweet, salty, astringent, sour, bitter, and pungent."

"My goodness!" Emma tried to remember if the two meals she had taken with him thus far had contained such flavors.

"How droll. Is there some logical reason behind this dictate?"

"Of course. Each is believed to have a particular physical benefit, when consumed in proper ratio to the others. I can't vouch for any of this personally, but my Indian friends claim that food influences behavior as well as health. The further one strays from what is considered proper, the more health problems one is likely to encounter."

"How fascinating! Though it's not so very different from what we believe, except that we also include the manner and sequence of eating certain foods to be of immense importance. A dinner usually begins with soup, then progresses to fish, and on to a cutlet, a roast fowl, then perhaps some game . . . but do continue. What are some of the most important foods peculiar to India?"

Mr. Kingston leaned back and extended his long, muscular legs. "I had best begin with spices, which are used throughout all of India not only to flavor food but to stimulate the appetite. Again, the time of year matters. Heating condiments are employed primarily in winter . . ."

Emma listened in rapt attention, as he identified the most common spices, discussed the importance of milk products in Indian cooking, and the use of *ghee* and *dahi* as the basis of many dishes. *Dals,* or split lentils, were common to all India, but featured in distinctly regional dishes, as were various other vegetables and grains. So extensive was his knowledge and enthusiasm for the subject that Emma began to learn geography and cultural customs, along with culinary facts.

Her mouth watered as he described in great detail some of the luscious dishes for which various parts of the country were known. She wondered aloud why Rosie and her circle of friends had never mentioned these delicacies, nor indeed seemed aware of them.

"Because the British think that British cuisine, as well as British politics, government, customs, and religion, set the standard for how the rest of the known world should live, worship, and eat. They cannot imagine that anyone anywhere can conceive of doing anything better than they can."

"You sound bitter, Mr. Kingston. I take it you yourself do not ascribe to that particular view?"

He gazed at her in that hooded fashion she was beginning to greatly dislike. "Considering my British ancestors, I ought to, Miss Whitefield, but since I regard India as my home, I entertain grave doubts that Great Britain has the answers to every question. What works in England does not necessarily work here. Moreover, India is so complex that what works in one part of the country cannot possibly work anywhere else. Even so simple a thing as rice will be cooked one way in the South, another in the North—yet rice dishes in the Punjab can be as nourishing and delectable as rice dishes in Madras or Bengal. One must learn to appreciate variety."

Yes, one must, Emma thought. *In people as well as food.*

Yet she knew that most of Rosie's friends would be horrified by the thought that she was sharing a railway carriage with Alexander Kingston, earnestly discussing a vulgar topic like food, and going off into the *mofussil* to be a nanny to his children. The British did not celebrate variety; they regarded it with great suspicion and not a little contempt.

She was heartily glad she had escaped Calcutta. Eventually, despite her best efforts to control her behavior, she would have done or said something unforgivable and thoroughly embarrassed Rosie. It was therefore ironic that she should have to prove to Alexander Kingston that he and she were like-minded in so many things. Of course, she didn't have to prove anything at all to him—but she suddenly wanted to convince him that *she* was not typical of her narrow-minded countrymen. She was ready and willing to experience all India without condemning it; but how was she to tell him that?

"Please assure Sakharam that he must feel free to offer me anything he would normally serve you," she finally said.

"I have a more adventuresome palate than most English-women and would relish tasting every one of the Indian delicacies you have just described."

Mr. Kingston's brows rose, and his blue eyes glinted with interest. "I shall certainly tell him, but you might then be surprised at what he serves us."

"If you can eat it, so can I."

"I'll remind you of that when the situation warrants."

Emma had the strong feeling they were not speaking only of food. An awkwardness descended, until she thought of more questions to ask about regional differences in condiments and seasonings, and the conversation veered away from the personal. The day passed quickly, and she slept that night in eager expectation of a stop the train was scheduled to make on the following morning. Mr. Kingston had promised they might debark for several hours and take in the sights, and Emma couldn't wait to stretch her legs and see a bit of the country through which they were passing.

The next day, she got her first good look at a town or hamlet in the *mofussil*. She had expected it to be depressingly primitive, barely more than a handful of natives, rude huts, and wandering animals. To her surprise and delight, the village contained an assortment of charming temples, churches, mosques, and even an old palace from the days of the fabulously wealthy maharajahs. From the train window, she could easily pick out French, Portuguese, and other foreign influences, evidence of all those who had attempted to colonize India before her arrival. There were also swarms of natives, a stinking bazaar, and beggars who descended upon her in a horde the moment she set foot off the train.

"Maama! Mamaaa!" They cried as if she was their long-lost mother.

Emma shrank against Mr. Kingston's side. "Why are they calling me that?"

"Because it's the only English word they know. Wait here a moment. I will deal with them." Mr. Kingston motioned to Sakharam, extracted a hefty pouch of coins from the inside pocket of his elegant, dark blue jacket, and gave it to his head servant. "Take care of the neediest ones, Sakharam. If there's any left after that, give it to the widows and children. Send only the fakers away empty-handed."

He was completely matter-of-fact about his generosity, as if he did this every day of the week. Sakharam nodded, apparently accustomed to doling out large sums of money to beggars. The beggars immediately flanked Sakharam, freeing Emma and Mr. Kingston to continue on their way unmolested.

While Emma pondered her companion's surprising compassion for the less fortunate—a compassion her compatriots in Calcutta did not share—Mr. Kingston hailed a passing pony cart and convinced the reluctant driver to step down and allow them the use of his rig for a sight-seeing tour through the small town. The vehicle allowed for little space between the two of them, but Emma forgot to worry about their close proximity. Mr. Kingston was an expert driver, and she was soon gawking at all the temples. There was a flat-roofed Bengali structure dedicated to Krishna, several smaller ones devoted to Kali, another with many tiny exquisite towers, and unexpectedly, a Shiite mosque.

All were decorated with innumerable carvings that seemed to waver and jump in the hot glare of sunlight. Emma began to suffer a headache. She had worn her *topi*, but still, the weather seemed to be growing warmer each day as the hot season approached. The land continued to display a lush verdancy, with the usual tropical vegetation she had seen in Calcutta, but a change was in the air. For the first time, Emma sensed the utter remorselessness of the sun; she had no trouble imagining what it must be like when everything lay baking and shriveling in the heat.

Longing for coolness and shade, she made a daring request. "Could we stop and visit one of the temples? I should love to look more closely at some of the carvings and paintings on the walls."

"You would?" Mr. Kingston sounded skeptical. "All right, I'd be pleased to accommodate you."

He drove the pony into the shaded courtyard of the very next temple which stood on its own square of cobblestones and was itself shaped in a small, precise square with arched towers at each corner. Emma took her time alighting from the cart. If the temple proved as interesting as it looked, she resolved to spend at least an hour discovering its treasures.

The building appeared deserted. After waiting for Mr. Kingston to secure the pony to a convenient ring affixed to a pillar in the courtyard, Emma eagerly entered its shadowed portals. "To what sect or religion do the worshippers who come to this temple belong?"

"I don't know—yet." Mr. Kingston took her arm to guide her through the semi-darkness. "I'm sure we'll discover the answer to that question soon enough."

Emma paused to peer at the wall depictions, many of them glinting with gold. "You go ahead. I'd like to take my time and examine these at leisure."

Mr. Kingston nodded, released her arm, and strolled toward the center of the building while Emma leaned closer to study the brilliantly colored miniature paintings adorning the inside walls. After a moment, she drew back in shock. The paintings depicted partially and fully nude figures—of both men and women—engaged in all sorts of sexual activities, half of which she hadn't known existed until just this moment. Why, in one scene, half-naked women were dancing around a male figure standing on a pedestal, his male organ obscenely distended as the women paid homage to him—or to *it*.

Inhaling deeply of the incense-scented air, Emma fought for breath. Her heart thudded in her ears as she wondered what sort of place this really was. Once again, she bent to look at the paintings. No, she was not mistaken, male and female figures were engaged in what could only be called an orgy of procreation and wanton revelry.

Simultaneously fascinated and repelled, Emma hiked up her skirts and went looking for Mr. Kingston. In her haste, she stumbled into a huge inner chamber, at the center of which stood a statue. In front of it, several heavily veiled women had gathered. Darting for the safety of a pillar, Emma cowered behind it until she got up enough courage to discover what the women were doing. What she saw made her gasp, but she immediately muffled the sound by clapping a hand over her own mouth.

Smoking lamps and braziers on either side of the statue clearly illuminated the bizarre scene. The statue itself was a . . . a stone carving of the male sex organ! Hugely distorted in size and sticking almost straight out. Directly below it was a large basin of water where white blossoms floated . . . and the women—good heavens, the depraved women!—were pouring water over the sculpture, stroking it, and crooning to it, as if it was their lord and master.

Emma stood rooted to the spot. She had heard that Indian religions were strange and primitive—but this! This surpassed all boundaries of human decency. As she watched, shocked to her very soul, one of the women leaned forward, discreetly lifted her veil, and *kissed* the grotesque appendage!

"Have you seen enough, Miss Whitefield?"

Emma stiffened. *"Quite* enough, thank you."

With as much dignity as she could muster, she turned on her heel and swept past Mr. Kingston, heading in the direction of what she hoped was the entrance. Once outside, she leapt into the pony cart and sat waiting for Mr. Kingston to appear and climb up beside her. When he did so, she clasped her shaking hands together, gripping them so tightly that her knuckles turned white. "You might have warned me. A gentleman would have done so."

"I have never claimed to be a gentleman." Mr. Kingston

calmly took up the reins and clucked to the pony. "Moreover, I didn't know it was a temple dedicated to the worship of Shiva, as the seed of life. Shiva is worshipped in many aspects, as the Great Yoga meditating on Mount Kailasa, as the Lord of Dance, creating and destroying, as—"

"They were worshipping his . . . his . . ."

"*Lingam?* I believe *lingam* is the word for which you are searching. Yes, they were worshipping his *lingam* and paying homage to it as the source of life and fertility. To the Indian, there is nothing obscene in the creation of life, Miss Whitefield. Rather, it is the European mind that makes something dirty and ugly out of something so inherently beautiful. The European derides sex, sniggers about it, and tries to pretend it does not exist. In stark contrast, the Indian celebrates it, rejoices in it, and accords it the status of being a proper pursuit for a man during a particular period of his life."

"And what period might that be?" Emma snapped, quite unmollified.

"The period of *kama.*" Mr. Kingston slanted an amused glance at Emma's still flaming face. "Do you really want to know about this, Miss Whitefield? It isn't a fit topic for a lady of good breeding, even one who dares to talk about food."

Struggling to regain her equilibrium, Emma watched a pack of *pariah* dogs fighting over some garbage. "I really want to know," she answered at last. "Do explain it to me."

Mr. Kingston turned a corner and drove the pony down a street of crowded market stalls, then headed out of town toward the verdant countryside, where rice paddies glimmered in the distance. "The ultimate goal of the traditional Hindu is the attainment of *moksha*, which can be explained as a kind of liberation from the cycle of existence. Until *moksha* is obtained, a human being is subject to rebirth each time he dies. Each time he is reborn, the conditions of his life are determined by his *karma*, or the cumulative result of the deeds he performed in his previous lives."

"Interesting . . ." Emma wasn't at all sure she was following him.

"Aside from the attainment of *moksha*, three other goals are recognized as worthy ones: *kama*, which encompasses pleasure, including the pleasures of the flesh; *artha*, which pertains to prosperity and fame; and *dharma*, the highest of these lesser goals, which relates to truth and righteousness."

"And how is one to achieve all these things?"

"By striving toward them as one passes through the four stages of life: learner, when one must learn to exercise self-control and abstain from excess; householder, when *kama* and *artha* are valid pursuits; detachment, when one turns away from worldly concerns; and finally, renunciation, when one begins to lead a wholly spiritual life, preparing for *moksha*."

"And how does the average Indian keep all this straight?" Emma was beginning to be intrigued, though she did wonder what all this had to do with the worship of *lingams*.

"Through the caste system." Mr. Kingston flicked his whip over the pony's back. The bony little animal obligingly broke into a brisk trot, carrying them away from the town sights and smells, and into the green countryside.

"Whether one is born a *Brahmin*, the highest caste of priests and teachers, or a *Shudra*, the lowest of unskilled workers, is partly determined by one's *karma*. If a man is fortunate enough to have a skilled *guru* and diligently practices *yoga*, he can hope to proceed from physical control through mental control, and eventually be able to recognize himself as pure spirit, a condition the Buddhists call *Nirvana*."

"I see," Emma murmured, not sure she did. "It all sounds so complicated."

"To the outsider, yes. To the Indian, it makes perfect sense. Outsiders rarely take the trouble to try and understand, which is why they are able to casually dismiss an entire system of beliefs that is older than anything in Western history. Primitive, they call it. Disgusting. Obscene."

"Worshipping someone's *lingam*, even a god's, *is* primitive and obscene."

"Why?" Mr. Kingston's blue eyes skewered her. "What we saw struck me as entirely innocent and childlike."

"Innocent and childlike! One woman actually *kissed* it!" Emma sputtered indignantly.

"Don't be so quick to condemn what you haven't tried, Miss Whitefield. In some situations, that act can be full of reverence and truly beautiful. It connotes great love and respect—even cherishment."

"Cherishment! I'm not certain there is such a word," Emma was truly scandalized.

"If there isn't, there should be. . . . And the same can be said when a man chooses to kiss a woman's *yoni*. By the way, I have heard that some sects revere the *yoni*, rather than the *lingam*, as the cradle of all life."

"If *yoni* means what I think it does, 'tis well they should. In any case, I cannot believe we are having this conversation."

"You wish to end it? It is too risque for you? But we have only been discussing religion and certain gestures of love and affection. What can be offensive about that?"

"Oh, you are impossible! By any standard I have ever known, this is an improper and incredible exchange."

"*British* standards, you mean, of course."

"Of course. What other standards could there be, given that I am British? I can't help what I am, Mr. Kingston. And you have pushed me too far."

"But you hinted you might be different from most Englishwomen, Miss Whitefield. And I didn't plan for you to see what you did today. It just happened. Such incidents are part of the fascination of India. Here, you will always be confronted by the unexpected, the mysterious, the not immediately explainable. If you are not prepared to deal with it, you should board the next train going back to Calcutta. Like most Englishwomen, you should cling to your own kind and attempt to construct your own little slice of England right here in India."

This so nearly paralleled Emma's own thoughts as to what Rosie and her friends had done that she could scarcely continue the argument. He was right; if she was ever to know and appreciate this vast country, she must be prepared to accept the occasional shock along the way—the challenge to every moral precept in which she *did* believe. Just because she didn't understand something and had never seen anything like it, didn't mean it was wrong . . . did it?

"Where are we going now?" she demanded as a lovely fowl spread its wings and rose out of the foliage beside the road, nearly spooking the pony.

"Out into the country, where the fresh air will help clear your head."

She nearly objected that her head did not need clearing, but realized he was right again. Never had she felt so muddled or unsettled, and he wasn't helping any. Alexander Kingston was as perplexing as everything else in this strange country. Was he a devil, as everyone claimed, or an angel in disguise? His treatment of the beggars had left her confused, and his defense of all things Indian struck her as laudable, not contemptible.

She settled back in her seat and tried to concentrate on the gold-washed charms of the countryside, but her head spun with questions only time could answer, including the most important one: Would she be open-minded enough to recognize the answers when they came?

Six

In the days following the incident in the temple, the train stopped at other small towns and villages. During layovers, Emma and Mr. Kingston went exploring, though they found no more temples dedicated to Shiva, as the seed of life. At every stop, Mr. Kingston took care of the inevitable beggars, making certain Sakharam aided those most in need before any others. In one instance, he directed Sakharam to give the entire sack of coins to an old woman clad in rags and smelling so bad that Emma feared she'd become ill if she had to spend more than a few moments in the poor soul's presence.

"Why did you single her out?" Emma asked him afterward, wondering what had set the old woman apart from the rest, some of whom were pitiful-looking children.

"Didn't you notice? She was blind, and her hands were covered with open lesions. She has leprosy or some other hideous disease."

The old woman had been honoring the tradition of *purdah*—which meant she never showed her face in public. The woman's odor had so appalled Emma that she hadn't noticed her hands or her tell-tale walking stick. "You are far more observant—and generous—than I," she said quietly, ashamed of the repugnance that kept her from noting such important details. She had always congratulated herself on her willingness to champion the poor, but now she was learning she didn't even *see* the poor, much less go out of her way to champion them.

"Don't paint me as some sort of hero, Miss Whitefield. I give from my excess, not from my want, and I do so only to those who cannot survive without help. That is only simple human decency, what sets us apart from animals. You mustn't deduce that I'm soft of heart, for I assure you I'm as greedy and grasping as the next man."

"I did not say you were a saint; however, you do seem less of a charlatan than people paint you."

"If you mean people in Calcutta—*British* people—you are probably right. They know very little of me."

"You don't permit them to get to know you."

"If they did get to know me, they still wouldn't like me. If anything, they'd like me less."

Emma could scarcely refute the statement, for he always steered their conversations away from the personal. She had learned nothing more about his children, private life, or Paradise View than she had known when the journey started. But she was learning a great deal about India. Mr. Kingston turned every sight-seeing excursion into a history lesson or a verbal treatise on culture. When there was no architecture of any great interest, they explored the native bazaars, where one could purchase every spice from coriander to ginger. She tasted such delicacies as crisp, golden *jelabis*, dripping with syrup, and *papads*, roasted or fried pastries made of rolled and dried lentil or rice dough, a popular treat in India.

She discovered that Mr. Kingston had a sense of humor, astonishing in one normally so aloof and serious. He could burst out laughing at a moment's notice—as when a monkey suddenly dropped down from the twisted limbs of a banyan tree, landed on his shoulder, and proceeded to steal a bit of *barfi,* or milk cake, he was about to eat. Anyone else might have been horrified, fearful of contracting a disease or fleas from the hairy, wizened creature, but Mr. Kingston found such humor in the incident that Emma herself laughed until her eyes watered.

She laughed often in his company, expressed her opinions forthrightly, and took true delight in Mr. Kingston's ready wit, endless supply of knowledge, and sparkling conversation. Even when she didn't agree with him, he made her think and question. As the train inched its way deeper and deeper into the heart of India, they spent hours debating various topics without interruption. Tulsi was usually off visiting friends in another compartment, and Sakharam retreated to wherever it was he went when he wasn't dancing attendance on Mr. Kingston.

Sometimes the poverty of the small towns and villages depressed Emma. They saw many funerals, often for babies and small children, and the animals—dogs, cows, goats, and horses—were usually little more than ragged hides stretched across flea-bitten skeletons. The contrast between rich and poor could not be ignored. People were either one or the other; not much existed between the two extremes.

Once they visited a small palace of the dynasty period, and Emma was awed by the precious artwork decorating every inch of the magnificent structure. Exhibiting a strong Mughal influence, it was built entirely of marble and precious woods and surrounded by gardens and fountains. Set like a jewel in the midst of a garbage dump, the palace exemplified the vast differences that separated the upper classes from the lower in Indian history and society.

"I had no idea people lived in such luxury," Emma said as she peered at a solid gold stool that had once supported a royal bottom.

"This doesn't compare to the palaces and tombs I have seen elsewhere. One day you must visit the Taj Mahal in Uttar Pradesh. I presume you have heard of it?"

"What visitor to India hasn't? 'Tis said to be very beautiful."

"It is exquisite. You must see it to believe it."

"Forgive me, but I do not recall why it was built."

"It is the mausoleum of Empress Mumtaz Mahal, the beloved spouse of Shah Jahan who died in 1631. The shah and his wife rest in a domed, two-storied, octagonal building with four tall minarets at the corners, all built of brick and encased in marble."

"He must have loved her very much to have constructed such a monument for her." Emma chanced to look at Mr. Kingston and discovered him gazing off into the distance. His blue eyes held a dreamy, nostalgic expression, his mouth was relaxed, and for once, she saw none of the bitter cynic.

" 'Tis said their love lasted into eternity—if one believes in such nonsense." Sarcasm edged his tone, belying her brief glimpse of his romantic side. "Do you believe it is possible to love someone so much that your love endures until the end of time, Miss Whitefield?"

"I . . . I've never experienced such a thing myself," she admitted.

"Nor have I. . . . Oh, I cared for the mother of my children, and I grieved when she died, but I can't say I was moved to build a marble monument in her honor. Perhaps I am incapable of emotions on so grand a scale."

"Perhaps I am, too; I can't imagine what it's like."

Emma gazed into Mr. Kingston's brilliant blue eyes a moment longer than was comfortable. Then, they both looked away. But in that moment, something changed for Emma. She found herself foolishly wishing that this train journey might continue forever—and during it, she could somehow probe the depths of Mr. Kingston's soul and find true communion with him, perhaps even a love to last throughout eternity.

Shortly thereafter, the train trip abruptly ended. It was early morning, and Emma had just taken the first sip of her tea. The rest of the meal lay before her on a small ivory-inlaid table supported by a carved wooden elephant with fake diamond eyes and tusks of imitation ivory. Emma was certain that the ivory and gems couldn't be real, because no man in his right mind would subject such treasures to everyday use and the perils of traveling, not even Mr. Kingston.

Setting down her cup, she remarked: "I wish I had a reliable map on which to mark our progress. It's disconcerting to think I have no idea exactly where we . . ."

Suddenly there was a grinding noise, and the table slid against Emma's knees and overturned, dumping hot tea and rice down the front of her skirt. An ivory tusk gored her thigh, and she was thrown backward against the wall of the compartment. Everything happened so quickly there was no time to grab hold of anything to steady herself. Emma had the terrifying experience of being tossed about like a wood chip in a wind storm. Glass shattered, and metal crunched. Emma's bones crunched, too. Her cheek struck a cold hard surface, sparks danced before her eyes, and the next thing she knew, she was lying crumpled on her side, her hair covering her face, and every muscle in her body protesting the harsh treatment it had just endured.

She could not get her breath. "H-help . . . me," she gasped, choking on a whiff of oily black smoke.

Inhaling required extreme concentration and effort; Emma suspected that her ribs were either cracked or broken. She tasted blood in her mouth, and her ears rang with metallic grinding noises and distant screaming. Then Mr. Kingston was dragging her to her feet, or trying to do so. Half of her body was caught under something.

"Get up!" he shouted over the din. "I smell smoke. We've got to get out of here."

Emma could already hear the crackling of flames. She reached down to push herself off the floor—except it wasn't the floor; it was the smashed window. Shards of glass pierced her palm, and blood spurted everywhere. Her only sensation was the painful constriction in her chest. She sagged against the wall, except it wasn't the wall; it was the floor.

The carriage was lying on its side, and the wall with the

door was now the ceiling. Mr. Kingston pulled open the door, which departed its hinges altogether. Tossing it aside, he indicated they would have to climb up through the hole overhead. "Come along. It's the only way out."

"Sikander! Sikander!" Sakharam's anxious face, covered with soot, appeared in the opening. "Are you all right?"

Sikander? Emma questioned. Her dazed mind grappled with the terrifying possibility that she could not climb out of the doorway. None of her limbs seemed to be working properly. When she tried to stand, her knees buckled, and her left ankle refused to cooperate. Somehow, she remained upright, clinging to Mr. Kingston's arm.

"Sakharam will help you. Reach up. Take his hand," Mr. Kingston urgently advised.

Sakharam immediately withdrew the slender brown appendage. "Sikander, I cannot. The *memsahib* is untouchable."

"Damn it, Sakharam, do it! I don't care if she's untouchable or not; we've got to get out of here before the entire train goes up in flames, and we're all roasted alive."

"You should not be touching her, either. You will lose caste," Sakharam lectured above the chaos.

Children were wailing, women shrieking, men groaning. . . . The metallic grinding noises had stopped, but the sounds of human misery and burgeoning hysteria had grown louder, and the smoke was thicker, too. Emma reached a trembling, bleeding hand up to Sakharam. He was still peering doubtfully down at them through the opening. He saw her outstretched fingers and shook his head.

"Forgive me, *Memsahib*. I will fetch a man from a lower caste to attend you. There are several sweepers among the *Sahib*'s servants. One of them will help."

"Sakharam!" Mr. Kingston loosed a string of curses that surpassed anything Emma had heard down on the docks in England. Then he wrapped his hands around Emma's waist, picked her up, and shoved her through the aperture in the ceiling.

Skinny brown legs passed within inches of her nose as she scrambled out of the opening. As soon as she was free, she tried to assist Mr. Kingston, but she had neither strength nor dexterity. Fortunately, he had enough for both of them and was soon on his hands and knees beside her. She rose to her full height, but again, her ankle gave way. Pain jolted up her leg. She had to grit her teeth to keep from crying out.

All around them in the narrow corridor, people were pushing and shoving. If not for Mr. Kingston catching her around the waist, she would have fallen. "Easy," he soothed. "This way."

Emma wondered how he could see through the smoke and confusion. Dirt and dust made her cough. Flames leapt up behind them, eating through the wood underfoot. The floorboards were hot as cinders. Mr. Kingston stopped and said, "We'll have to climb out right here and then jump off the carriage. It's our only chance."

Someone shrieked inside the carriage below them. Swept with panic, Emma clutched at Mr. Kingston's sleeve. "People are trapped down there!"

His grip on her arm remained strong and firm. "Once you are safe, I will go and help them."

Someone began banging, and Mr. Kingston bent down and jerked open the door to the carriage below. Then he opened the door overhead. Mercifully, the windows in the carriage above them had already been broken, and the occupants had escaped.

"In you go . . ." He lifted Emma through the doorway, then helped her wiggle out of the window. "Can you make it from there by yourself? Jump down from the carriage and get as far away from the train as you can."

Doubts assailed Emma. She wanted him to stay with her, but more screaming from inside the train stilled her protests.

The crackle of flames was louder now, the smoke thick as a veil. "I can do it. You must help those still inside."

He nodded and disappeared into the bowels of the train. Emma shakily got to her feet. Ignoring the excruciating pain in her ankle, she hobbled to the edge of the railway carriage. It was a long way down to the embankment. But the ground looked sandy, and lush vegetation grew nearby. Knowing she had no choice, Emma lifted her skirt and jumped as far as she could. On impact, a blinding pain shot up both legs and through her wrists. Crumpling into a ball, Emma rolled. When she stopped rolling, she found herself wedged against rock. Blackness descended. With a sigh of disappointment at her own weakness, she succumbed to it.

When she awoke, she was lying on her back some distance away from the burning train wreck. Four small men in loincloths and turbans were jabbering away as they ministered to her. She caught the words, "*Memsahib* and *Ma-baap*," another Indian form of address for Europeans that had something to do with the terms mother and father. The latter implied she was an important personage, a caregiver, though the last thing she could have done right now was care for anyone.

Groaning against the pain, she sought to sit up, which brought a storm of protest. One of the men scurried off and returned a few moments later with Sakharam. "Do not move, *Memsahib*," the servant ordered, looking only slightly less immaculate than usual. "The *sahib* will be along shortly."

"Is he all right? Where is he?" Glancing about, Emma noticed that the little elephant table—smoke-blackened and with one leg broken—lay on the ground nearby. Someone—Sakharam?—must have risked his life saving it.

"The *sahib* is helping the victims of this most unfortunate accident," Sakharam informed her.

"But you—his servant—do not help. God forbid you should dirty your hands." Emma could hardly restrain her ire. She recalled how he had referred to her as "untouchable" and refused to pull her from the burning railway carriage. Yet this same man had probably gone back to rescue a table.

"I *am* helping, *Memsahib*. I am directing my inferiors in assisting with the injured and recovering important belongings. . . . Would you have me lose caste? Once lost, 'tis not so easily regained—and besides, there are plenty of others who can do what needs to be done."

"I will never understand your foolish caste system! You should be ashamed to look me in the eye."

" 'Twas I who saw to it you were pulled to safety, removed from the area near the burning wreckage," Sakharam stonily informed her. "You owe me your life, *Memsahib*."

Emma brushed at her rumpled, soiled clothing with a bloody hand. "If I owe anyone my life, it's Mr. Kingston. He's the one risking his life to save others while you stand here debating social customs."

She struggled to rise on an ankle now swollen to twice its normal size. The pain made her dizzy. She also felt as if she were trying to breathe through a broken bellows.

"More fool he." Sakharam made no move to help her as she stood swaying and gasping. "But then he has never gracefully accepted his limitations."

"Thank God for British obstinacy, or we'd all be dead!"

For all her ranting and raving, Emma realized she would have to stay where she was until Mr. Kingston arrived and decided what should be done next. She suddenly spotted him over near the train giving orders to a group of Indian survivors. He was soot-stained and disheveled, only his erect posture clearly identifying him as someone in authority—someone in control. Admiration surged through Emma; for the second time that morning, her heart raced, and she could hardly draw breath. . . . He had saved her life and undoubtedly saved others, too. It made no difference what caste they were or what language they spoke. His only concern had been to get as many as possible out of the burning train, which for some mysterious reason had derailed and turned over.

"I don't care what anyone says of him," she murmured under her breath. "I will never forget this day, and I will tell everyone I meet what a hero he truly is."

"He will appreciate that, I am sure." Sakharam bowed to her in his imperious fashion. "Please excuse me now. I have much to do. Tiffin will be served at noon, as usual."

"Tiffin!"

Sakharam was not in the least intimidated by her tone of voice. "The *memsahib* has been injured, and the *sahib* has strenuously exerted himself rescuing people from the train wreck. You will both need to take tiffin at the usual hour, and 'tis my duty to see that you get it."

He left Emma staring after him and wondering if she would ever understand the Indian mentality, which Sakharam seemed to exemplify in all its infuriating complexity and casual disregard for human life.

As it happened, tiffin wasn't served until four o'clock, and then it consisted of a single greenish banana and some dried biscuits procured from heaven only knew where. Emma was too ill to eat, but Mr. Kingston insisted she must.

"You're looking pale as a bowl of *dahi,* milk curds, Miss Whitefield. Modest though it is, the food will give you strength."

Nausea, not bravery, made Emma refuse. "There must be many in worse shape than I am. Give it to them, please."

"The survivors are being well cared for, or as well as can be expected given the distance to the nearest town. We came out of this rather well—only sixteen dead and twenty-eight injured. Considering the damage to the train, I would have thought those counts to be much higher."

Sixteen dead did not sound "rather well," to Emma, but she hid her dismay and took a biscuit to mollify him. She was lying in the shade of a thorny tree on a rug Sakharam had located in the wreckage, and Tulsi sat beside her, gently fanning her with a palm leaf to keep away the whining insects. Emma counted herself among the fortunate, for the majority of the injured passengers were forced to lie in the sun on the sandy ground. Apparently, no one wished to go into the shady jungle for fear of snakes, stinging ants, or other dangers.

"Has anyone discovered the cause of the derailment?" she asked between bites of the hard-as-nails biscuit.

Mr. Kingston wiped soot from his forehead with a no-longer-white shirt sleeve and shook his head in a weary gesture. "No, but I suspect it was caused by the usual reasons: poor maintenance, or animals uprooting a portion of the track. That occasionally happens when a herd of the larger ones moves through a remote area."

"Elephants, do you mean?" Emma had seen only one or two tame elephants since her arrival in India and no wild ones whatsoever.

He nodded. "Possibly. Anything can happen this near a jungle. Help should be arriving soon, however. I sent *pattah-wallahs* in every direction."

"I still cannot believe no one in our party was hurt."

"Except you."

"Oh, I daresay I shall recover quickly. I checked my . . . my lower limbs, and nothing appears to be broken—only badly sprained, I believe."

"You've no other injuries?" Mr. Kingston narrowed his eyes, as if he thought she might be hiding something.

"Well, my . . . my mid-section is sore and bruised, but . . ."

"We must have someone examine you. There were several European women on the train, and one of them might have experience in these matters. I've located a couple of bullock carts and drivers to take the lot of you to the nearest plantation or *dak* bungalow. As soon as I find out where that is,

I'll be back to load you into it. I just hope it will be before nightfall."

"I hope so, too." Emma eyed the jungle with misgivings. She had heard stories about the perils of night travel in the jungle. Despite her thirst for adventure, she did not feel up to any more adventure at the moment. Whenever she moved—or breathed—the pain was sharp as a lance.

Mr. Kingston left her and returned to sorting out the wounded and bringing order to the chaos. Only a portion of the train had been totally destroyed by fire, but the rest was severely battered. It was a miracle more people hadn't been killed or injured. Had the train been going any faster, the damage would surely have been much worse.

Resting her head against the base of the tree, Emma dozed. She awoke to the sound of a female voice inquiring whether or not she was awake. "Are you quite all right, my dear? We had heard you were hurt, not seriously, apparently, but you've suffered some minor injuries?"

Emma opened her eyes to discover three women bending over her . . . three women dressed in proper English garb, their stylish gowns bearing evidence of the misfortune they had just endured. She sat up. "I . . . I'm sure I'll be fine by tomorrow."

"Stay where you are, my dear. I am Mrs. Honoria Gatewood, wife of Major Reginald Gatewood." The eldest of the trio knelt down beside her. "This is Mrs. Alice Groat. Her husband is a sanitary commissioner in Lucknow, and Mrs. Vere Stephens, who is married to the Government Solicitor in Delhi."

Emma struggled to remember her manners. Mrs. Gatewood had revealed the social status of each of the three women, along with their names, but in her muddled state, she could not recall if a government solicitor took precedence over a sanitary commissioner or not. Only one thing was certain; a major's wife was definitely at the top of the pecking order.

"I am the Honorable Miss Emma Whitefield." Emma greeted each of the ladies in turn, beginning with Mrs. Gatewood, then Mrs. Stephens, and lastly, Mrs. Groat. Tired as she was, she hoped she wasn't making a mistake. Not even a train wreck could excuse a serious breach of etiquette, especially with these ladies. She could tell by looking at them.

The introductions completed, the ladies explained how they had come to be traveling on the train. All three were journeying to join their husbands in Lucknow or Delhi. They had met en route and joined forces, rarely showing their faces outside the safety of their shared compartment, which was why Emma had been unaware of their presence. Two of the ladies had only boarded the train recently, they told her, while little Mrs. Stephens, the youngest and prettiest, had gotten on just outside Calcutta.

"And you, my dear . . ." Mrs. Gatewood looked down her rather long nose at Emma. "What were you doing on the train? Have you family here in India?"

The light was fading from a sky streaked with purple, pink, and orange, and Emma had to squint to see her clearly. "No, I don't—at least not now." She debated how much of her situation to reveal and finally decided that she stood to lose nothing by being honest. This was a chance meeting; after she parted from these women, she'd never see any of them again.

"I am traveling to Central India to find a plantation left to me by my mother who lived here during the Mutiny of '57. I didn't wish to travel so far alone or to expend all my funds along the way, so I accepted the position of nanny to the children of Mr. Alexander Kingston."

"Mr. Kingston . . ." Mrs. Gatewood pounced upon the information. "Is he the gentleman who has taken charge—the one who sent us over here to meet you?"

"Yes, he is. However, I am not traveling alone with him. I have an *ayah*." Emma indicated Tulsi with a nod. The plump little woman smiled and continued waving her palm frond as if it were a *punkah* fan. The mosquitoes were out in earnest now; the slight breeze didn't keep them entirely away, but did seem to distract them.

Mrs. Gatewood pursed her lips and glanced meaningfully at her two companions. "And have you known Mr. Kingston for very long, my dear?"

"No, not long. I haven't been long in India. But I'm most impressed with Mr. Kingston. His behavior during this tragedy has been wonderful, don't you agree?"

"Oh, yes, yes, quite." Mrs. Gatewood sniffed the air as if suddenly detecting a noxious odor. "We shall find ourselves much indebted to him before this nightmare is over. Ah, here he comes now . . . quite full of himself, I might add."

All three women gazed at him with falsely polite expressions. In the waning light, Emma could read their suspicions in the slight curling of their lips and the cool disdain in their eyes. They barely knew him, yet they had taken one look at his dark skin and begun to speculate about his breeding, a fact which angered her immensely.

"Ladies, my retainers tell me there are two *dak* bungalows not far from here. As soon as we load you and your belongings into the bullock carts coming up now, we can set off for the nearest one. By nightfall, you'll be safely under a roof."

"We cannot thank you enough, Mr. Kingston," Mrs. Gatewood gushed. "I do hope you were able to locate our trunks and other baggage. I should hate to lose anything or leave it lying about for thieves."

"I've done the best I could. Miss Whitefield is the only one whose belongings are still missing. They may have been destroyed in the fire."

"Poor, poor girl!" one of the women sympathized, but the news barely fazed Emma. When others had lost their lives, she saw no reason to complain about belongings.

"I can manage without them. I keep my most important possessions on my person anyway. Other than the deed to my plantation and a few other things, I don't own much of value."

"Is that so?" Mrs. Gatewood made a clucking sound. "It grieves me to hear you have fallen upon hard times, my dear. From the way you introduced yourself, I took it you were the daughter of some important person."

Emma perversely decided not to reveal the identity of her stepfather. She simply nodded, leaving Mrs. Gatewood to wonder and speculate.

"It's a good thing you didn't pack the deed to Wildwood in one of your trunks." Mr. Kingston offered Emma his hand to help her rise. In the twilight, his eyes were an intense, shadowed blue that revealed nothing of his thoughts.

"Yes, isn't it?" she whispered, too low for the others to hear. "I shouldn't want to lose that deed, valid or not. I carry it with me always. In Calcutta, I made a special pouch to keep it in; now, I'm glad I had the foresight to do that."

Emma managed to get to her feet, but once there, she swayed unsteadily—daunted by the prospect of having to walk as far as the bullock cart. Without a word, Mr. Kingston swept her up into his arms and carried her—as if she were an infant—over to the conveyance. He deposited her carefully on the rough wooden seat, then assisted each of the other ladies in climbing into the cart.

They were crowded, but no one suggested they divide themselves between the two carts. There was no room in any case. The second was filled entirely with the baggage of the three ladies. Deprived of a seat in his own cart, the driver ran alongside, screaming, shouting, and cracking his long whip over the heads of the huge lumbering beasts.

"Dear me," Mrs. Groat murmured. "I imagine we are lucky to have this, but it's still an uncomfortable way to travel, isn't it? I do hope the bats will not bother us as we pass through the jungle."

"I hope we get to the bungalow before it gets much

darker," moaned little Mrs. Stephens. "The jungle is always so frightening."

"The bungalow had better have room for all of us. If it doesn't, we three shall stick together—won't we?—while you, Miss Whitefield, must avail yourself of the remaining shelter," Mrs. Gatewood suggested in a tone that brooked no argument. "Considering your injuries, I'm sure you'll be more comfortable without all of us crowding in upon you."

"As you wish." Emma was glad to be excluded from their select circle. All they had done so far was complain; they hadn't even offered to help her or to look at her injuries.

The women gave up trying to talk over the creaking, squeaking, groaning sound of the cart. But as they entered the black depths of the jungle, all sorts of strange night noises could be heard. "About Mr. Kingston," Mrs. Gatewood said. "This may be the only opportunity I shall have to speak to you privately concerning him, Miss Whitefield."

"Privately?" Emma wondered how the woman could consider it private when her two companions and the driver were all listening—though the driver probably didn't speak English.

"Alice and Vere shan't mind what I have to say. I am sure they would only agree with me."

"Why should you have anything to say, Mrs. Gatewood? You have only just met the man, and so far, he has done nothing but help rescue you from a difficult situation."

"You did say you haven't been long in India, didn't you, Miss Whitefield?"

By now, it was too dark to see the woman, but Emma could hear her well enough, and she did not like what she was hearing—or about to hear. "Yes, I said that."

"Then you should be more willing to accept advice from someone who has lived in the country for nine years. Mr. Kingston appears to be Anglo-Indian, as we British call ourselves after we have lived for a while in India. But I can't help wondering if he is not more Indian than Anglo."

"You mean *kutcha butcha*."

"Yes, dear, that's it exactly. I see you know what the term means."

"Yes, I know, but how do you know if he is or isn't? I haven't noticed him wearing a sign on his forehead."

"Oh, the signs are all there, my dear, if one knows what to look for."

"And what exactly does one look for?" Emma longed to turn around and punch the nose of the woman who sat perched behind her. "Perhaps his dark skin is due to going about in the sun too much without his *topi*."

"No, my dear. I sincerely doubt it. Why, if you want to know the truth about him, you have only to examine his fingernails. The little half-moon at the base of each nail is always darker in a person of mixed blood. As are his gums. The next time he smiles, study them. You will probably note a bluish caste that's quite unmistakable."

"I have seen his smile. His teeth are exceptionally white."

"We are not discussing his teeth, but his gums. Study his gums, my dear. They will tell the story of his breeding better than any other indicator you might use."

"I'm not interested in his breeding, but in the sort of person he is."

"Breeding determines character, my dear. Never forget it. Especially in India, where one must beware of all associations which could possibly affect one's social standing and indeed one's very life. If he is partly Indian, you will never be able to trust him, no more than you can trust a mongrel dog not to turn on you and bite you, when you least expect it. With a purebred, at least, you know what sort of behavior is most common to the breed."

"This conversation is utterly distasteful," Emma flatly declared. "I refuse to engage in it. You can't compare people to animals; even if you could, just because a dog is a mongrel doesn't mean it's worthless."

"Now, don't take offense, dear. I am only trying to help.

You say you are going to serve as nanny to his children. But what—really—do you know about this man?"

"All I need to know, thank you."

"Well, I hope you are right, my dear."

A silence fell on the group after that. Emma could sense the withdrawal of each of the women in the cart. She knew she'd not be sharing a bungalow with them. If they did not refuse, *she* would. Their bigotry and prejudice infuriated her. Did they honestly expect her to go up to Mr. Kingston and demand that he open his mouth like a horse up for auction, so she could inspect his teeth—his gums, rather? She despised them for their snobbishness! But as she jolted along in the ox cart, an insistent little voice nagged at her unmercifully: *What indeed do I know about Alexander Kingston?*

Not as much as she wanted to know, though his breeding and background was the least of it.

Seven

By the time Alex reached the first bungalow, it was blacker than the inside of a funeral urn. He cursed under his breath when a servant informed him that Miss Whitefield had gone on to the next one, which meant that he himself, not to mention all his bearers and *pattah-wallahs*, would lack a roof over their heads that night.

He wondered why she had chosen not to join the other three ladies at the thick-walled house. It was small and sparsely furnished, but large enough to accommodate all of the women without too much trouble. Hadn't anyone realized that if they split up, it would be considered improper for him, much less his retinue, to share a shelter with only one woman, or even more than one? He was amazed that Miss Whitefield herself hadn't thought of it—as conscious as she was of observing the proprieties.

What made it doubly inconvenient was that he had located her baggage and brought along a small, sturdy cloth bag containing her everyday necessities. It was the bag she always took with her into the washroom on the train. She would be glad to have those items tonight, he suspected. Tomorrow, she could examine the rest, whereupon she would discover that one trunk was partially charred and another quite flattened.

He had known the state of her things all along; they were the first he had found after the accident. But he had decided that now was as good a time as any for her to "lose" her belongings. The wreck made a perfect excuse—only he should have known she would keep the deed on her person, along with whatever other valuables she had brought with her.

As he continued through the darkness with Sakharam and several bearers carrying extra bedding and food supplies, Alex wished he need not worry about the deed. He felt guilty about his efforts to deprive Miss Whitefield of her belongings. It was a terrible thing to do to a woman on a long journey in a foreign country. She didn't deserve to be treated that way—but then he didn't deserve to have the damn deed hanging over his head like some freshly sharpened sword.

He had to protect himself. Another opportunity to gain possession of the document would come along before they reached Paradise View. Now that he knew she carried it in a small pouch on her person, he had to figure out a way to get it. Since Miss Whitefield wasn't the type to allow him to undress her, this would require some inventiveness on his part. Perhaps he could enlist Tulsi's help. The sooner he took care of the matter, the better. Then he could relax and try to make the journey as pleasant as possible for Miss Whitefield, by way of making up for her loss.

Damn, but he liked the woman! He had enjoyed her company thus far on the trip. Though absurdly prim and proper, her greatest fault, she did not complain unceasingly as other women of the Raj so often did. Rather, she endeared herself by displaying an almost insatiable curiosity about India— except for certain topics, such as *lingam* worship.

He enjoyed challenging her, baiting her, educating her, and arguing with her. She stimulated him intellectually, as women almost never did. Hindu women did not, not even his young wife, the girl who had borne his children. The women of India were far too sheltered and uneducated to verbally spar with a man. They had been raised to defer to men, not contradict them—except for Santamani, who as a young girl had defied custom and learned to read and write. Indian women had extremely narrow outlooks. They were far more concerned with the doings of the *zenana*, than the world.

As for Englishwomen, until Miss Whitefield, Alex had considered the lot of them to be a bunch of whining, snobbish bitches, too shallow of mind and character to be of interest anywhere but in bed. Even there, he soon tired of them.

It was a pity Miss Whitefield had not been born a man; with her attributes, she would have gone far in the Raj. Friendship might have been possible between them. Her adventuresome nature, sense of humor, and superior intellect were wasted on a mere female, especially one so . . . plain. Not that she was entirely unattractive. There were moments when her face lit with interest or laughter that made her unexpectedly appealing—but she simply wasn't the sort of woman a man dreamed of taking to bed with him. Not unless he wanted to talk all night.

Alex grinned to himself as he tried to picture Miss Whitefield in the throes of passion. She would never permit herself to indulge in pure sensation. He could better imagine her suddenly sitting up in bed and demanding to know how camels or elephants performed the act. Did they make noise while they did it? Was the female submissive? Exactly how did she indicate a readiness to mate? Those were the kind of questions Miss Whitefield would be likely to ask.

He nearly burst out laughing picturing it. After a day sorting through bodies and separating the dead from the living, Alex needed a good laugh. It had been a soul-wrenching experience. Now he was so exhausted it was all he could do to put one foot ahead of the other and follow Sakharam through the jungle. Fortunately, his bearers were conscientious about beating the thick vegetation on each side of the path with their long sticks, because he couldn't summon the energy to care if a tiger was lurking in the foliage. He wondered if he could convince Miss Whitefield to let him sleep inside the bungalow after all. Maybe he could sleep there without her knowledge. If he left before first light, she'd never know.

By tomorrow, Sakharam would have located tents, and he'd be quite comfortable in his own private quarters, but tonight. . . . Oh, what he would give for a pallet inside a safe quiet building, so he wouldn't be kept awake by chattering servants or have to keep an eye open all night watching for predators! It hardly seemed fair that after all his efforts to make certain everyone on the train—Indians and Europeans alike—had found shelter in the nearest towns, villages, or plantations, he himself would be reduced to sleeping in the open.

When they finally arrived at the second bungalow, Alex decided to risk it. The structure was typical of the sort of shelter available to Europeans at stations across most of India: a solid, square building consisting of thick, mud-brick walls with small high windows encased in shutters, and a tile roof. Unless this one was somehow unique, it had a beaten mud floor covered with grass or bamboo matting, several rooms opening directly into each other, *punkah* fans, and a cloth stretched across the beams of the ceiling to keep snakes, lizards, rats, and insects from dropping down upon the inhabitants.

This one had a large veranda screened by vines. Lamplight spilled through the partially open front door, and Alex hoped that Tulsi, not Miss Whitefield, was the one still up. The *ayah* would be easy to handle; he would simply command her to go to bed, and when she had done so, he could enter the bungalow and take over the front room.

Sakharam nodded toward another dimly lit structure—a three-sided hut—not far away, where several *pattah-wallahs* had already gathered. "Sikander, there is a stable. Shall I make up your bed there? A *sahib* must have his own quarters, so I shall tell the others to sleep elsewhere."

"No, this close to the jungle, they need shelter, too. The

stable is the next best thing to tents. Just be sure to keep a small fire burning through the night."

"But Sikander, where will you sleep? With the *memsahibs* occupying both of the *dak* bungalows, there is nothing else available."

"Don't worry about me, Sakharam. I will be fine."

In the light of the torch he carried, Sakharam's dark face looked forbidding and unhappy. "But Sikander . . ."

"I said don't worry . . . and don't question. Whatever I do, I don't intend to disturb any of the *memsahibs*."

"If you say so."

"I do say so. Goodnight, Sakharam. Sleep well. Tomorrow is sure to be another long, trying day."

Alex left his servant staring after him in frustrated disapproval. Quietly, he made his way up three small steps to the veranda of the bungalow. Setting down Miss Whitefield's cloth bag, he eased open the front door and stuck his head inside. Like a hundred other rooms in *dak* bungalows across the face of India, this one held an odd assortment of Indian, Kashmir, and Burmese tables, stools, and screens—plus a few long-dead maidenhair ferns and a *punkah* fan made of polished wood, rather than cloth.

Beneath it, seated on a stool and finger-brushing her long loose hair by the light of a coconut oil lamp, sat Miss Whitefield. Alex inhaled sharply. For Miss Whitefield, this was a scandalously relaxed pose. The front of her gown was partially unfastened, revealing a modest but very feminine cleavage, her sleeves were pushed up to flaunt slender white arms, and she had removed her shoes and stockings and tucked her toes under her skirts like a carefree young girl.

Best of all was her free-flowing hair, spilling to her waist and glistening like the smoothest satin in the dim warm light. Glints of gold, auburn, and chestnut shone in the silky brown mass. Were the glowing strands as soft as they looked? Alex had always known that having her hair down could make a profound difference in a woman, but in Miss Whitefield, the effect was stunning. Suddenly, she epitomized all the things he did not usually associate with her: she was feminine, mysterious, ethereal, beguiling . . . and most of all, vulnerable.

Swallowing hard, Alex couldn't help staring at the amazing transformation. He must have made some sound, for Miss Whitefield suddenly glanced up and saw him standing there. Immediately, she straightened on the little stool, tucked her bare feet further beneath her, and blushed furiously, as if he had caught her naked.

"I'm sorry I disturbed you." He picked up her bag, entered the room, and nudged the door shut behind him. "Where's that worthless Tulsi?"

"Sleeping in one of the other rooms. The train wreck left her exhausted." Miss Whitefield rose to her feet, wincing as she did so. Quickly, she rearranged her features into a polite, expressionless mask. "Shall I fetch her?"

"No, no. . . . You are the one I came to see. How are you feeling? Do you need anything? I brought your bag . . ." He set the bag on the floor near her bare feet. "I can probably find some fruit if you're hungry. Tell me how you're faring."

"I'm managing well, thank you, though I admit I'm happy to see my portmanteau. Still, when others have lost so much . . . well, you mustn't concern yourself over me."

"But I am concerned, Miss Whitefield." She seemed smaller without her shoes—small and fragile—making him feel tall and clumsy beside her. "You are my responsibility. Did one of the other women have a look at your injuries?"

"No, I . . . there wasn't time really. And Tulsi can look at me in the morning, if you think it's necessary."

"No one's checked to see if you broke any bones or cracked your ribs?"

"Cracked my . . . ?" She couldn't seem to say the word in front of him. Discussing one's body parts with a man was simply not done by women of her class. Biting her lower lip, she glanced away self-consciously. "Everyone is too tired to bother, Mr. Kingston. I have some swelling and soreness. Nothing serious. By morning I'll be my old self again."

"I will be the judge of how serious your injuries are. Sit down, Miss Whitefield. It's obvious you can hardly move without pain."

She remained standing ramrod straight. "Perhaps I *will* have Tulsi examine me in the morning. You must go now, Mr. Kingston. It isn't proper for you to be here."

"It isn't proper for you to suffer in silence. Now, sit down. I wouldn't trust Tulsi to know how to help you. She has no experience as a healer. She isn't qualified to do much of anything—except snore at night. Snoring is what she does best."

A tiny smile played about the corners of her mouth—a very tender, soft-looking mouth. Placing his hands on her shoulders, he gently pushed her down on the stool. Again, she grimaced. She really was in pain, he thought—but too stubborn to admit it.

"Where do you hurt, Miss Whitefield? Don't be shy. I'm not leaving here until I find out, so you might as well make it easy on both of us and tell me."

"H-here, I suppose." Timidly, she thrust out one foot.

"You suppose?" Shaking his head, he dropped to one knee in front of her. "Your ankle, I gather."

She withdrew her foot before he could lay a hand on it.

"Stop being a feather-wit," he chided. "Give me your foot."

"But it's not proper for you to see my lower . . . limbs."

"Tulsi's sleeping, and no one else knows I'm here. What harm will be done if I merely look at it?"

She sighed. "All right, look then."

Her tone implied he had better not touch, but he seized her foot just as she stuck it out. "Mr. Kingston!"

He ignored her and carefully examined the foot while she sat cringing on the stool. Her toes were small, pink, and utterly feminine, the nails neatly trimmed but still longer than a man's might be, and her skin was as soft as a flower petal. Unfortunately, her ankle had a huge, unnatural bulge, and the flesh there was greatly discolored. "Why have you discarded your stockings? Wouldn't your ankle be more comfortable if you still wore them to provide support?"

"Probably. But they . . . constrict me, so I took them off to relieve that particular discomfort."

"No wonder it hurts. Your ankle is all black and blue." He gently rotated it. "However, no bones appear to be broken."

"I believe I already told you that," she retorted with some asperity.

"You should lie down and raise your foot on a pillow. It cannot be good for it to bear your weight."

"I've been sitting or lying down all day. I just wish there was something I could rub on it to alleviate the swelling and soreness."

"Sakharam might know of something—some poultice perhaps. But he can't go looking for the right plants until daylight."

"Sakharam will do nothing for me. He called me an untouchable."

Her eyes were sparkling with anger, the green in them heightened. She really did have beautiful eyes, long-lashed and expressive. "You mustn't hold his beliefs against him, Miss Whitefield. Caste is extremely important to an Indian. It governs his entire life."

"Sakharam said *you* would lose caste if you touched me."

Alex well knew the importance of his response to that comment. "Sakharam has been with me so long that he tends to think I've come to share his beliefs. He has often tried to convert me to Hinduism. In his not-so-humble opinion, I would be perfect if I just adopted his religion and all of his customs. He's managed to convince himself I must be a Brahmin, except I do not always behave as a Brahmin should."

"No, sometimes you behave like an Englishman." Miss Whitefield actually smiled then, and he smiled with her, pleased they could share a joke that would be incomprehensible to anyone else.

"Your ankle should mend nicely, with or without any further attention. We shall see about a poultice for it first thing in the morning. Now, where else do you hurt?"

Her hand went to her side, but she still refused to say the word "ribs." "I appreciate your concern, but there's nothing you can do about my discomfort in this particular area, Mr. Kingston. You certainly cannot examine me here."

"Here in this room, do you mean?" he teased. "Or here on your body?"

"You *know* what I mean."

"I do know, Miss Whitefield, and I intend to examine you anyway. If you've broken a rib, I will have to bind it, and nothing you say or do will deter me. Be sensible. Shall we awaken Tulsi or send for one of the other Englishwomen to keep you company while I do what must be done?"

"No!" The response came more quickly and vehemently than he had expected. "This is embarrassing enough without having witnesses. If you are so set on it, just do it and be done with it."

Holding herself absolutely rigid, she clenched her jaw and fastened her gaze on the wall opposite him. Alex almost laughed out loud at her expression. She looked like a woman about to be executed by an elephant. He had never personally witnessed the phenomenon, but his aunt had once vividly described the cruel punishment sometimes decreed by the old maharajahs in the not too distant past. The victim was forced to the ground and held there while an elephant stomped on his head. Miss Whitefield had the grim expression of someone awaiting that particularly unpleasant demise.

Alex tried to be gentle as he lightly ran his fingers over her ribs. She gasped when he probed a particularly sensitive spot—just beneath her left breast—where a small, firm protrusion indicated something amiss.

"Miss Whitefield, I'm sorry, but I think you might have a broken rib. It hurts right here, doesn't it?"

Tears sprang to her eyes, but she merely nodded and bit her lower lip as he continued examining her entire ribcage through her clothing. He took great care to avoid her breasts but it was next to impossible not to brush them occasionally. She actually did have breasts, he was pleased to discover, and they were quite adequate in form and size. Indeed, he found himself wishing he could examine them, too, at his leisure. Miss Whitefield winced when his fingers located another sensitive spot, but nothing seemed to hurt as much as the first spot. She could scarcely bear for him to touch her there. "I think if I bind your mid-section, you will feel more comfortable. But you'll have to remove your garments first, at least from the waist up."

"Can't I do this myself?" Pleading green eyes met his. "Or can't Tulsi do it?"

"Not without supervision. Nor can you possibly do it yourself. Better me than some inept servant, Miss Whitefield. First, I need to find some strips of cloth."

"I can provide those," she said wearily. "If you will just turn your back for a moment."

He thought about telling her how silly her modesty was in view of the fact that he had already witnessed any number of females in various states of undress, but he didn't know if the information would ease her mind or terrify her further. Standing, he turned around to face the door.

A moment later, he heard several long ripping sounds, and then she calmly inquired, "How many strips of cloth will you need? Must I demolish an entire article of useful clothing?"

"A half-dozen should be plenty. Would you like my shirt? I'd be more than happy to donate it to the cause."

"Don't you dare remove anything! It's bad enough that circumstances force me to disrobe in front of you. If you start disrobing, too, we'll be violating every known standard of decency."

Grinning at her tone of voice, he rocked back on his heels. "You're making too much of this. The act of disrobing is only titillating when two people have intimacy in mind. An infant is hardly titillated when its mother bares her breast so it can nurse. Similarly a mother isn't titillated when she disrobes her child so she can bathe it."

"There are no infants or mothers here, Mr. Kingston. Rather, we are man and woman, male and female, and this is embarrassing in the extreme. . . . You may turn around now. Do hurry and finish this."

He turned, intent on doing just that, but the sight of her arrested him. She had stripped to the waist and was sitting on the stool hiding herself from his gaze with her long hair and discarded upper garments. Her bare shoulders gleamed in the lamplight, and she looked so feminine and vulnerable that desire flashed through him like a bolt of fire, rendering him temporarily speechless.

Her cheeks were crimson, her eyes a smokey green, and she was panting with nervousness. "The cloth strips you need are there," she nodded toward the floor near her bag.

He couldn't speak for the lump in his throat and could only hope she didn't notice any other swellings on his anatomy. Who would have guessed that Miss Emma Whitefield could be so provocative? He had certainly never suspected it. The way she dressed and wore her hair, the colors she chose, all conspired to conceal her femininity, to make her seem drab, dull, and uninteresting. . . . Yet as he studied the graceful arch of her throat, her delicate bone structure, and tender pale skin, he wished he could seduce her right then and there. Her shy innocence stirred something deep within him, making him feel simultaneously protective and predatory. She was no match for him in experience or sexual expertise, but he didn't doubt he could awaken her passions and melt the icy reserve she fought so hard to maintain. Oh, how he would love to try!

He longed to take her in his arms and make her melt against him in boneless surrender. Aside from the challenge she represented, Alex knew he would relish teaching her to employ her mouth and hands in ways that would absolutely horrify her maidenly heart—and pleasure him endlessly. In return, he would relish pleasuring her, making her sigh, whimper, and cry out with the force of her feelings. Suddenly, he *could* imagine Miss Emma Whitefield convulsing beneath him in total ecstasy, moaning "Sikander!" and clawing his back.

Thinking of it made his blood boil.

"Do cease looking at me like that!"

He uttered a short, sharp laugh. "Like what? I am only deciding how best to wrap your ribs, Miss Whitefield. What else did you think I was thinking?"

"You . . . have a most wicked gleam in your eye, so there's no use denying that your thoughts are not gentlemanly."

"On the contrary. My thoughts are *most* gentlemanly—depending, of course, on what you consider worthy thoughts for a gentleman to be thinking. We may have a difference of opinion on that topic."

"I'm sure we do. And if you do not begin this unpleasant business immediately, I shall clothe myself at once and refuse to allow you to touch me."

Picking up the first strip, Alex advanced upon her. "You wound me, Miss Whitefield. All I was thinking of was how to make this business *much* more pleasant for you. Alas, since you suspect me of knavery, I shall cease considering your comfort and simply do the job as quickly as possible."

"Thank you," she murmured as he knelt behind her and passed the first length of cloth around her waist.

With quick, efficient movements he bound her ribs snugly, tucking the ends of the cloth strips in place beneath the final wrap of the cloth. When he had finished, she released an almost inaudible sigh. "Oh, that does feel much better. Where did you learn to bind a person's . . . ribs . . . with just the right amount of pressure?"

He smiled. So he *had* made progress tonight. She had actually said the word "ribs."

"In the army. I served for several years in the army in my youth." He did not elaborate—did not explain that after numerous citations for bravery and service above and beyond the call of duty, he had never been able to rise very high, had not, in fact, qualified for the elite British cavalry, despite being a crack shot and an accomplished rider with a string of fine horses. His British schooling had been excellent, but even attendance at the best schools had not eliminated the suspicion that he had mixed blood and was not, therefore, worthy of the honor of being appointed to the cavalry.

"You served in the British Army?" She turned her head and leaned back slightly to gaze up into his eyes with great interest. Too late he realized he had broken his own rule to reveal nothing of his past to her. In answer, he cupped the curve of her cheek in one hand, and to satisfy his own sudden impulse as much as to distract her, he lowered his head and brushed her mouth with his lips.

The brief contact made her gasp, and the little sound was his undoing. Repositioning himself more comfortably, he gathered her into his arms and kissed her thoroughly. Her lips were as delectable and sweet as an Indian pastry. She felt incredibly soft and womanly against him, arousing his carnal instincts and making him yearn for contact of a deeper, more intimate kind. But after a moment's brief surrender, she began struggling against him and managed to free her mouth.

"Mr. Kingston! What do you think you're doing?"

Her hair swirled about them as she tried to extricate herself from his arms without dropping the garments concealing her breasts. In the face of her rising panic, he reluctantly released her. "There, there, Miss Whitefield. Calm yourself. I was only consoling you for the pain you've suffered."

"A kiss to make me feel better?" White-faced and trembling, she shrank away from him.

Her sarcasm surprised him. It was a tool in *his* arsenal, yet he didn't know why he should be so amazed that she might use it. He himself resorted to it whenever he felt threatened; why shouldn't she?

"I was trying to make you feel better, yes. However, I also kissed you because . . . because you looked so kissable."

"I am the last woman in the world that men have ever considered kissable. Pray do not belittle me, Mr. Kingston. I am not at my best tonight and cannot deal with your . . . your scorn."

The glint of tears in her eyes amazed him, and he suddenly wanted to pummel whatever man—or men—had convinced her that she was undesirable. Tonight had taught him that she could be *most* desirable; he was in great discomfort because of it. But he knew if he pushed her too far, she would flee like a wounded fawn into the forest.

Unable to stop himself, he reached out and fingered a strand of her soft, silky hair. "I am not belittling you. You seemed imminently kissable to me just now, Miss Whitefield. I apologize if I frightened you by acting upon a wayward impulse."

"This is most . . ." she hesitated.

"Improper?" he supplied with a grin. "It is, but perfectly understandable. We have both experienced a shock today— due to the train wreck. If you do not need comfort and consolation, *I* do. I am glad we are still alive, and I kissed you to celebrate our good fortune."

She would not meet his eyes. "I think you had better go now. You have finished your task, and it has grown late."

"Ah, but I have a favor to ask of you," Alex belatedly remembered. "My men are sleeping out in the stable. If I join them, they will think they must relinquish the shelter, which means they will be forced to sleep in the open. And as you know, we are surrounded by jungle."

"What are you proposing?" A small frown marred the

smooth, unblemished skin of her forehead. She tilted her head slightly, revealing a sweep of white throat, and it was all he could do not to nuzzle it.

"I propose that I sleep here in your front room—while you sleep in one of the other rooms, perhaps even join Tulsi," he quickly added when he saw she was about to object.

"But that is . . . improper," she whispered sheepishly, half-smiling as she said it. "Goodness, I do use that word all the time, don't I?"

"Isn't it a shame so many reasonable things are considered improper? . . . Would you risk having one of my bearers eaten by a tiger or trampled by a wild elephant simply to preserve the proprieties?"

She released a small sigh. "No, but I know of some women who would."

He knew who she meant. "The very proper *memsahibs* in the other bungalow?"

She nodded. "That's why I am here, and they are there; they don't approve of where I'm going and . . . with whom."

Alex steeled himself against the old familiar twisting of his gut and the sudden swell of bitterness and rejection. "Ah, I see. . . . However, they did not succeed in changing your mind, did they?"

"No, they did not. But that doesn't mean I do not have my own standards to uphold, Mr. Kingston. I may be "on the shelf" as they say, but I am not about to . . . to do anything foolish simply because . . . because . . ."

"Of course, you are not. Nor would I seek to take advantage of the situation, Miss Whitefield." He rose to his feet and towered over her. "Do not worry about me. I will find somewhere else to sleep tonight."

She rose also. "No, I didn't mean . . . that is, I don't want you to go. You certainly must stay—here in the front room, while I sleep in another chamber."

"Are you certain?" He studied her closely—the delicate high cheekbones, the beautiful eyes . . . the regal nose, the open, earnest expression. He had been so wrong when he had first dismissed her as plain, ordinary, and unattractive! Her face had a striking, unforgettable quality about it; she simply could not be compared with other women, using conventional ideas of loveliness. Her beauty was uniquely her own—and he wished he could convince her of it.

"I'm certain," she answered breathlessly.

"I'll leave before first light. But you must realize it will probably be days—perhaps even a week—before repairs can be made to the train, and we can continue on our journey."

He didn't mention the possibility of Sakharam obtaining tents tomorrow. Sakharam could find anything anywhere; it was a particularly useful and laudable trait, but Alex intended to tell him not to look too hard this time.

"You must sleep here for as long as necessary," Miss Whitefield insisted. "Providing you leave before first light . . . and . . . and you don't try to kiss me again."

"Was it that distasteful?" he couldn't resist asking, as a blush climbed up her cheeks.

"A true lady would never answer that question."

That's when it occurred to him. Of all the British women he had met both here in India and in England, Miss Emma Whitefield just might be a "true lady." Until now, the only true ladies he had ever known were his mother and Santamani. He regarded all other women either with indifference, disrespect, or downright contempt. They didn't measure up to his standards—and that included his dead wife and his present mistress.

"Goodnight, Mr. Kingston." Leaving him standing there, Miss Whitefield quietly departed the room, taking with her all the warmth and brightness.

Eight

Emma could scarcely sleep that night—and it wasn't just because Mr. Kingston was sleeping in the outer room. After all, she had been sleeping in the same train compartment with him at night, within full sight and sound, for almost two weeks now. In the bungalow, the actual distance between them was greater, but the proximity must be considered more dangerous, since they were in a house.

However, it wasn't any of this that bothered her; it was the fact that he had kissed her. He had pressed those warm, firm, arrogant, beautifully chiseled lips to hers, and kissed her as if he actually enjoyed the act . . . but how could he? Mr. Kingston must have kissed many beautiful women in his lifetime—while she had kissed, or rather *been* kissed, by only a very few men.

And they hadn't kissed her on the mouth. Nor had they opened their mouths when they did it. And they hadn't done it as if they were promising to do much more if they had the chance. The few—very few—kisses she had experienced had been pitifully poor, dry-lipped things that had embarrassed, even repulsed her. . . . Not that she had enjoyed being kissed by Mr. Kingston. She hadn't. Not one little bit. His kiss hadn't moved her at all. The earth hadn't trembled. The sky hadn't opened and showered diamonds. Her heart hadn't jumped out of her chest; it had only fluttered a tiny bit faster.

But—and this was the important thing—she did have to

admit that his kiss had had possibilities. For the first time in
her life, she had sensed that a kiss was capable of doing all
those things. If he had kissed her longer . . . or kissed her
more than once, or . . . or done anything else, she might possibly—there was the remote chance—that she could swoon
at his feet! And *that* would be too embarrassing to contemplate, almost as embarrassing as having to remove half of her
clothing and endure his touch while he bound her ribs.

That, too, had had possibilities as an erotic act. Yet she
was reasonably certain that if it had been Percival Griffin or
any other man performing the chore, she would have felt
perfectly comfortable. Well, maybe not comfortable, but certainly not as bothered by it. She had always been a sensible
female, flouting convention, yes, but only when the occasion
warranted it. . . . So why now was she behaving like some
silly young chit knowing nothing of men or life?

It simply wouldn't do to allow her imagination to run wild
and conjure all sorts of ridiculous notions. Mr. Kingston had
succumbed to an impulse, nothing more. She ought to have
slapped his face when he did it. Instead, she had taken an
absurdly long time to register an objection and hadn't been
outraged nearly enough. If the kiss hadn't been bad enough,
she had then consented to allow him to sleep in the bungalow!

And assured him that for however long it took for the train
to get underway again, he might share her quarters. What
had possessed her to *do* such a thing! If the ladies in the
other bungalow ever found out about it, they would spread
the story to every European they met. Word might somehow
get back to Calcutta, to Rosie and Percival Griffin.

Emma heartily regretted having admitted to the three
women that Mr. Kingston had hired her. She wished she had
told them nothing of her plans or destination, and had concealed even her name from them or given them a false name.
Their reaction to Mr. Kingston, after all he had done for
them, proved that no matter how far she traveled into the

heart of India, she was never going to escape staid British attitudes. They would follow her wherever she went. How could she have forgotten—even for a moment—that she could not afford to alienate her own countrymen, especially knowing that she might one day have to make a life among them?

She had left England with the idea that she could never return; there was nothing more there for her. If she could not find Wildwood and claim it for her own, there would be nothing for her in India, either. She must not make enemies every time she turned around. Not like she had done at home.

For her own sake, as well as Rosie's, she must be discreet, and she had not been discreet with Mrs. Gatewood, Mrs. Groat, and Mrs. Stephens. Now she was throwing caution to the wind by allowing Mr. Kingston to share her bungalow.

So she got little sleep that night, and her worries multiplied a hundredfold when Mr. Kingston sought her out late the next morning and informed her that it might be *several* weeks—or even months—before the train and the track would be repaired enough to continue the journey.

She was sitting on the veranda enjoying the shade and the view of the surrounding jungle when he delivered the bad news. "I have just spoken to Mrs. Gatewood. She and the other ladies have decided to hire a bullock cart and driver and go on to Delhi by way of the Grand Trunk Road. I'll be making arrangements for their departure this afternoon. They hope to be underway within a few days. Considering that the hot season will soon be upon us, they've made a wise decision. If we are laid up long waiting for repairs to the train, we ourselves are likely to have a miserable journey and may not arrive at Paradise View before the coming of the monsoon. And as you may have heard, the rains make travel almost impossible."

"But what can we do? Perhaps we, too, should consider continuing by way of the road." Emma gently fanned herself with a palmetto fan she had found in the bungalow. To her, it felt as if the hot season had already arrived. Her clothes were sticking to her back, and it wasn't noon yet.

"There aren't enough bullock carts available for everyone who wants one. Also, the road is the long way to get where we're going. No, I'm considering traveling up the Ganges by boat to the home of a friend who can provide all we need to set out cross-country for Paradise View."

"Cross-country! Oh, I should love to see the land far from the main traveled roads."

"It would be far from the main traveled roads all right." Mr. Kingston smiled. He was scandalously informal this morning, not yet having donned jacket, vest, or *topi*. He wore only skin-tight breeches, tall black Hessian boots, and a white shirt with a high collar and gold-embroidered sleeves. His attire—the shirt especially—was shamefully Indian in cut and style, not at all what a proper English gentleman would wear, but on him, it looked marvelous, the perfect foil for his dark coloring. All he lacked was a snowy white turban, and he'd be as grand as a maharajah. Emma was deriving great pleasure just from looking at him.

"The isolation is what worries me, Miss Whitefield. Were I alone, I should definitely go cross-country, enjoying good hunting and the rugged, wild scenery. But with you along— and Tulsi—I hesitate. The area through which we will be traveling is tiger and wild elephant country—hardly a fit setting for women. You will have to ride horseback the entire distance, except for the first leg of the journey, which, as I said, will be by boat."

"But I am an excellent horsewoman, Mr. Kingston. And you mustn't worry that my injuries will hold me back. By the end of the boat trip, I should be sufficiently healed to spend long hours in the saddle. . . . Oh, please let's do as you have suggested."

"Whoa, Miss Whitefield. Your enthusiasm is galloping away with you. Don't forget Tulsi. Can *she* survive mountains, rivers, and jungles on horseback? And what about the supplies

I am taking to Paradise View? I must make arrangements for their safe transport. We will have to travel lightly and live off the land. Much of our time will be spent in *shikar*."

"*Shikar*?"

"Hunting. We'll need to hunt for our food, and hunting is a dangerous sport. Often it involves riding deep into untrod wilderness, following game, and jumping whatever obstacles might block our path . . ."

"I know something of firearms," Emma sniffed. "In England, hunting was my favorite sport. I practically lived on horseback, and my mare could jump anything. You are underestimating me again, Mr. Kingston."

"The last thing I would do is underestimate you again, Miss Whitefield. . . . Let me investigate the possibilities. First, I must speak to Tulsi and see about our supplies. But are you sure you can withstand the rigors of such a journey? Most *memsahibs* would violently object to being deprived of the luxuries available on the railways and main roads of India. There may not always be a *dak* bungalow available."

"I should think *you* might mind the deprivations before I do, Mr. Kingston. Weren't you the one complaining about sleeping in the open this near the jungle last night?"

Flashing his brilliant smile, he saluted her. "Your hit, Miss Whitefield. 'Twas indeed I who sought shelter and comfort last evening. But I am no fool. I will not undertake such a journey without a few basic comforts. There will be separate tents, one for you, one for me, and another for the servants. And we will still dine on white linen and enjoy an occasional bottle of fine wine. If I do not insist upon these amenities, Sakharam will. He will lose caste if his master does not behave in a manner befitting his station."

"He will lose—amazing! I could live in India for a lifetime and never fully understand this puzzling culture."

"Don't be too hard on yourself. One must be born here to understand the culture—and even then, it is sometimes incomprehensible. But just imagine for a moment how difficult it would be for an Indian to take up residence in England."

"Try the shoe on the other foot, you mean. Yes, I can see that our customs might be equally difficult to explain—or defend." Had Mr. Kingston committed grave social errors in his youth, of the sort she had so often committed? If so, it was one more link between them, one more thing they had in common. More and more, Emma found herself perceiving such similarities—they both felt an empathy for the poor, they enjoyed exploring. They were both rebels who didn't fit in safe little niches. . . . But no, she must not make more of these discoveries than actually existed—and all because he had kissed her. *The kiss meant nothing.*

"I will let you know what I decide." Mr. Kingston bowed slightly. "Rest today, Miss Whitefield. If we do set out for the Ganges, I wish to leave as soon as possible, perhaps as early as tomorrow. I've done all I can for the other passengers on the train. Now I think it's time to make haste toward Paradise View."

"Whatever you think best, Mr. Kingston. Today, I intend to do nothing more than watch the passing scenery from the shade of this pleasant veranda."

"If you need anything, ask Sakharam." He turned to leave, then paused. "Is Tulsi inside? I might as well talk to her here and now as later."

"You're too late. She left immediately after breakfast— excuse me, *chota hazri*—to go find her friends and see how they are faring."

"You gave your permission?"

Emma nodded. "She asked Sakharam to ask me, and I said yes. Shouldn't I have?"

"She's neglecting her duty to you, Miss Whitefield. Sakharam's right; the woman is completely useless. I don't know why I hired her."

"You were doing what's considered proper."

He grinned. "So I was. And you see what that's gotten me? Naught but irritation and annoyance."

"Perhaps she will prefer to remain with her friends, rather than continuing cross-country with us."

His glance was as sharp as a sword. "And if she does, will you still come away with me?"

He made it sound like an intimate assignation. It wasn't, of course, but Emma knew she was making a momentous decision. If she said yes, she would be breaking *all* the rules. There would be no turning back. Without an *ayah* to claim as companion and chaperon, she risked having her reputation irretrievably ruined. Any Europeans they met would assume she was the wrong sort of woman. Had she not had an *ayah* for this part of the journey, Mrs. Gatewood and the other two ladies might have refused to acknowledge her, train wreck or not.

"If Tulsi does *not* accompany us, we will take care to avoid other travelers, particularly members of the ICS." Mr. Kingston was still closely watching her. "And when we reach Paradise View, I will find another *ayah* for you."

"Talk to Tulsi first, and see what she says. If she refuses to accompany us . . . well, I shall think about it."

"You may take all afternoon to consider the matter. But don't let what happened last night have a negative bearing upon your decision. I apologize once more for succumbing to . . . a wayward impulse. You needn't worry it will happen again. And as I said, we'll avoid anyone who could possibly carry tales to your friends in Calcutta. I'm well acquainted with the less than tender mercies of grapevine gossip, and if I can help it, I won't expose you to that sort of viciousness. Though it could be said you've brought it on yourself by insisting on becoming a governess to my children."

"I have, haven't I?" Emma lowered her lashes against his all-too-potent gaze. "Considering how I hounded you for the position, you shouldn't concern yourself with my reputation."

"It's difficult enough for a man to survive when the sharks are circling, let alone a woman," Mr. Kingston softly admonished. "But never say I didn't warn you, Miss Whitefield. I believe I did."

"Yes, you did, so I'll never say that. Whatever happens will be my fault."

Emma realized she was speaking as if Tulsi's absence was a foregone conclusion and she had already agreed to go without her. "Talk to Tulsi. Perhaps she will surprise us."

Tulsi flatly refused to embark on what she saw as a dangerous, uncomfortable journey. Her friends assured her that many British families in Delhi were looking for servants, and so she wished to stay with them. Mr. Kingston explained the situation to Emma over dinner, which consisted of a wonderful *pilau* of rice, vegetables, and nuts, and some light-as-air curry puffs that almost made Emma forgive Sakharam for calling her an "untouchable."

Pouring a second goblet of wine for her, Mr. Kingston leaned across the table set up on the veranda. "So have you decided, Miss Whitefield? Will you come with me cross-country? Or would you prefer waiting here until the train is repaired and then continuing the journey by yourself?"

"By myself? You said nothing about going by myself. How would I find Paradise View? How would I manage? I don't yet know the language, much less the countryside."

Emma was deeply upset by the notion, but Mr. Kingston merely sat back in his large cane chair and regarded her solemnly over the rim of his wine cup. "I've thought it over carefully and decided that you could travel to Delhi with the other three British ladies. In Delhi, they would surely help you locate transportation to Gwalior. I will give you the name of an Indian family in Gwalior—friends of mine—with whom you can stay until I can send someone to get you or come myself. The plan makes more sense than having you accompany me, riding all that distance, encountering all sorts of possible hazards. You've never been through a hot season in India, Miss Whitefield. In the jungle, it's not only hot but humid, and the humidity saps your strength. Sometimes, you are stricken with fever. I'd feel much better if I knew you were in a civilized place, and—"

"Are you seizing this opportunity to be rid of me, Mr. Kingston?" Rising to her feet, Emma didn't flinch from the pain in her ribs and ankle. "I can endure anything you can. I absolutely refuse to be fobbed off onto Mrs. Gatewood and her two stuffy friends. I am coming with you to Paradise View, and I'll hear no more about it. Why, I could be stuck in Delhi or Gwalior forever. You might never send for me. I might lose this chance to look for Wildwood and never find another. I won't stand for it; do you hear? I simply won't stand for it."

She stopped in mid-diatribe when she realized that Mr. Kingston was leaning back in his chair in wry amusement. As soon as she fell silent, the laughter rolled out of him— warm, masculine, and rife with pleasure. "Ah, Miss White-field, you do not disappoint. I knew you would say that."

She suddenly realized he had been teasing her—or testing her, ensuring that she refrain from agonizing over the matter, which she certainly would have done had she had more time to think about it. "You knew I'd come, with or without Tulsi."

"I expected you would. I hoped so. But no, I didn't know for certain until just this minute. You might have been all bluster and no substance. Most people are. Now I know you truly are a kindred spirit—a rebel at heart. We are much alike, you and I. Once we set our goals, nothing on earth can deter us. Especially not the opinions of others. It's amazing, isn't it, that fate has thrown us together?"

They stared at each other in sudden, awkward awareness. Emma's heart beat so violently she was sure he could see it thumping—except he wasn't looking at her chest. He was gazing into her eyes, as if he could see to the very depths of her soul . . . and she was so shaken by the intensity of the moment, the sheer wonder of it, that her knees quivered. Slowly, in a dream or a daze, she made her way back to her own cane chair and sank down upon it. "How soon will we leave?"

Her voice sounded throaty and far away, not at all like her usual self. It could have been a stranger speaking.

"Tomorrow after *chota hazri*. If the poor old horse I've found can make it to the Ganges, you and I will ride in a rickety old victoria. Sakharam will follow in a bullock cart. Only a few bearers will accompany us. The rest must remain here with the baggage we cannot take with us. Have you had a chance to go through your belongings yet?"

Emma shook her head. Several bearers had brought her things before dinner, but she had not yet had the opportunity.

"Do so this evening. Pack only your portmanteau and perhaps one other bag for the journey—something easily borne by a horse or, better yet, by a man."

"I shall not require much. Should I simply plan on wearing my riding habit?" Emma was already making a list in her mind: two calico nightgowns, two—no maybe three—muslin bodices, four pairs of lisle thread stockings, three petticoats, a single tea gown, an evening gown in case she had to dress for dinner somewhere along the way. . . .

"Wear whatever is cool, light but sturdy, and most important of all, comfortable. On no account should you pack a bustle. And no corsets, either. Where we're going, you won't need one."

Conscious of maintaining the dignity of the Raj, Emma protested. "But if we should be entertained anywhere, even by Indians . . ."

"I've already told you. We'll avoid all company for whom it would be necessary to wear a bustle or a corset. I'll go through your bags and toss by the wayside anything that resembles either."

Emma blushed. Gentlemen *never* spoke of bustles and corsets.

"When we get to Paradise View, I will send for a *durzi*, who can make up anything you desire," he told her.

"A *durzi* is a tailor," she murmured to cover her embarrassment. "I have heard of them."

"Good. Then you know they can quickly reproduce any item of apparel down to the tiniest detail."

Emma nodded. She did not mention that Rosie had once had a gown reproduced, and the *durzi* had copied everything perfectly, even the makeshift patches in the skirt and the bit of mismatched ribbon Rosie had used because she could not find a matching one. Fortunately, the gown had been one she wore only when she arranged flowers or oversaw the gardening.

Mr. Kingston stood. "Can you be ready to depart by morning?"

"Morning will be fine." No matter how much her injuries still hurt, Emma was determined to be ready—or die trying.

"Excellent. Then I will see you in the morning."

"Until tomorrow, Mr. Kingston."

Not wanting her wine to go to waste, and also to dull the throbbing in her side, Emma lifted her still-full cup to her lips. Neither of them mentioned that he would be sleeping in her front room again, and that Tulsi might not be there to provide the security of her presence. Emma had not seen the woman all day. From now on, she would be spending each and every night alone in Mr. Kingston's company. Except for Sakharam and the bearers, there would be no one else—no female companionship, in particular.

"Mr. Kingston, wait!" she called as he descended the steps of the veranda. "How long will the boat trip take?"

At the bottom, he turned and gazed up at her—and he was so heartrendingly beautiful in the rosy twilight that her throat convulsed with some swift sharp emotion she feared examining too closely.

"Traveling from Calcutta to Delhi by boat normally requires a month. But we will be aboard only a week or two, I should think, until we get to Allahabad. Were I certain we could find horses and supplies at Mirzapur, we would go only that far on the river, but I doubt it's possible. Besides, my friend in Allahabad has everything we'll need, most importantly good horses. I know, because I myself bred the horses and sold them to him. He won't mind if we borrow them."

"*You* bred the horses? Then I shall be most anxious to see them. The polo horses in Calcutta—and the race horses—were most impressive."

"Wait until you see mine. You won't find better in all of India."

He loves horses, she thought. *And so do I.* It was one more thing they had in common.

"I can hardly wait. In a week or two, I'll be ready to ride."

"You'd better be." He lifted his hand in farewell. "Good evening, Miss Whitefield."

"Good evening, Mr. Kingston."

After he had gone, Emma perched on the edge of her chair to finish her wine before she started packing. As night fell, the jungle noises seemed to grow louder; there were sudden loud shrieks, low muffled growls, and the incessant whirring, chirping, and rustling of insects and other night-roaming creatures. Each night when the sun went down, Emma had to fight off a wave of uneasiness. Slapping at a huge mosquito, she contemplated her impending great adventure. Would she be capable of facing all the challenges she might encounter? The heat, the bugs, the harsh terrain, the foreign language, the isolation, the lack of female companionship, the strange foods and customs, the absence of privacy, the unknown dangers . . . all of these she could probably handle without too much trouble. But could she handle her own growing feelings—her unexpected and ungovernable responses—to Alexander Kingston?

He was a riddle whose meaning she was trying to discover. Each day she received more clues, more insight into his character. But the essence of the man still eluded her . . . and while she was pondering it, she was becoming more and more enamored of him. More aware of him with every fiber of her being. Did he feel the same? She couldn't be certain, but she thought he did. The way he looked at her, with that piercing, intent expression . . . the way he had laughed at her today, as if he found her truly delightful . . . and of course, the way he had kissed her, all contributed to her belief that he felt *something*. He was not indifferent.

Yet she feared to put too much stock in these superficial impressions. She had been disappointed too many times in the past to let vanity mislead her now. She hadn't grown any younger or prettier in recent weeks. And she was far too sensible to entrust her heart to someone she still barely knew. Perhaps this cross-country journey would provide all the answers to the questions that continued to plague her . . . and perhaps she would not gain those answers until she actually arrived at Paradise View.

Until she met Mr. Kingston's children, saw his home, witnessed how he lived so far from civilization, she wouldn't truly know the man. Until then, she couldn't form a final opinion—or risk getting hurt by caring too much. Whatever she felt for him must be ignored. She had to remain focused on the purpose of this trip, which was to search for Wildwood, a fact she had nearly forgotten since she'd left Calcutta.

She patted the square cloth pouch that contained her deed, the remaining pearls, and the ruby. It was tied by a silken cord around her waist so that it hung down at her side, concealed in the voluminous folds of her skirt. She ought to stitch up something more sturdy and waterproof to protect her valuables, particularly her deed. A piece cut from her mackintosh ought to work nicely. She hated to ruin the garment made of rubberized cotton, which according to *Real Life in India*, a guidebook for newcomers to the country, was an indispensable item with which to face the monsoons, but surely, protecting her deed was every bit as important as staying dry during the wet season.

If she was careful, she could cut away enough of the fabric to make a waterproof pouch without entirely destroying the mackintosh. She still had her ulster, the new long overcoat from Ireland, to protect her from dampness, and she mentally added the item to the list of garments to be packed.

"Emma, Emma," she chided herself. "Why are you sitting here drinking wine and wool-gathering when you have so much to do yet tonight? Get moving, girl, and be quick about it."

Jumping up, she hurried into the bungalow in search of her mackintosh and a pair of scissors.

Nine

The victoria Mr. Kingston had found was an old, dilapidated model with worn seats, just big enough for two people. It had reasonably good springs, but the drive to the river was a nightmare due to the constant jolting of Emma's healing ribs. The sun's heat poured down on their heads as they left the jungle and headed across a stretch of flat land bisected by rice paddies shimmering in the green-gold light.

Emma wore her heavy *topi*, a Meerut version covered with pelican skin and a few feathers that Rosie had assured her was quite dashing. Emma thought it gave her a demented air, and beneath it, she sweltered, frequently having to dab away the perspiration with a lace-edged handkerchief. It was now early March, and the hot season wasn't fully upon them yet. When it descended, it would remain until June and the arrival of the monsoon. Emma told herself that the heat was nothing, yet by noon, her sturdy brown riding habit was limp and damp, and she was in true agony from the bump-bump-bumping of the victoria.

She closed her eyes against the glare of the sun, but could still feel the steam rising from the earth. Her brains were sizzling, and she struggled to keep from slumping against Mr. Kingston who had his hands full discouraging the poor nag pulling the victoria from stopping in the middle of the track to snatch at the passing greenery. The sight of the horse's graying nose and muzzle, skeletal frame, and long-suffering expression had initially stirred her sympathies, but now, she could spare no pity for the beast's misery when her own was so great. She just wished he would go faster and get to the river before the flesh on her bones melted.

"Feeling poorly, Miss Whitefield?"

Jerking upright, Emma forced her parched lips into a smile. "Not at all, Mr. Kingston. It's rather a pleasant day for a drive through the countryside, don't you agree?"

"To me it is, but you seem pale and tired. Are you in pain?" Mr. Kingston clucked to the horse and snapped the whip over its bony hips, which he had been doing almost non-stop since their departure that morning.

"No, I'm perfectly wonderful. Never better, I assure you."

"Glad to hear it, because I'd like to skip tiffin and keep going until we reach the river—unless you have some objection."

Emma had been praying they would stop soon, but she gritted her teeth and urged him to keep driving. "Don't worry about me. I'm not in the least hungry."

She wasn't lying; the mere thought of food made her queasy. If she ate, she would probably lose the contents of her stomach.

"Oh, I wasn't worried," Mr. Kingston drawled. "It's not hot enough to be uncomfortable, and this track is in better shape than I thought it would be."

Emma barely managed to conceal a groan. They went a little farther, and suddenly the horse skidded to a stop and began snorting and prancing like a colt in springtime.

"What is it?" Emma craned her neck to see over the animal's bobbing head. "Something has startled the poor creature."

"Easy, old boy. Whoa . . ." Mr. Kingston spoke soothingly to the horse as the animal backed up against its breeching strap and tossed its head, trying to see the track ahead. The horse's blinders severely limited its vision, and Emma could not decide if this was a blessing or a liability.

"Take the lines." Mr. Kingston thrust them at her. "I'm getting out."

She barely had time to grab them before the horse started rearing. Mr. Kingston jumped down from the victoria, his movements as smooth and liquid as a panther's. Stalking to the horse's head, he grabbed its bridle and swiftly brought it under control, then stroked its nose and spoke calmly to it. Emma still did not know—and could not see—what had frightened it. Heart thumping, she sat very still until Mr. Kingston returned, calmly resumed his place beside her, and reclaimed the lines from her trembling hands.

"What was it?"

"Just a snake. A large python. Nothing to cause concern."

"A snake," Emma's hand flew to her breast. She knew that India was full of snakes and other loathsome creatures. Rosie had warned her to always examine her shoes before putting them on in the morning, lest a scorpion or something equally dangerous be lurking inside one. But this was the first time she had come so close to a snake—and a python yet!

"You aren't afraid of snakes, are you, Miss Whitefield? With a skittish horse, the last thing I need is a skittish woman." Mr. Kingston clucked to the horse, who had calmed down considerably, and the jolting began anew.

"Didn't I tell you? I am enchanted by them! Do let me get down to make the acquaintance of this one. With your permission, I'll pat him on the head and wish him a good afternoon."

Mr. Kingston's laughter was startling. "Never fear, Miss Whitefield. I'll provide you with a mongoose when we get to Paradise View. You can make a pet of it, and it will keep the snakes away. However, you really only need to be careful of them when you bathe. They sometimes come in through the drain in the bathing chamber. It's rather disconcerting to be sitting in a tin tub, enjoying a good soak, and suddenly discover a large cobra flaring its hood and hissing at you."

"I imagine it is." Emma suppressed a shiver—an amazing reaction considering the heat.

"Kraits are more dangerous. They're much smaller and more difficult to see. Beware of kraits, Miss Whitefield. Shake out your clothing before you put it on, and never reach into an enclosure without looking first. When we get to Paradise View, you may wish to sprinkle carbolic powder throughout your quarters, as a deterrent. Some people swear by it."

"And what will deter tigers, leopards, and bears, Mr. Kingston? No doubt I shall encounter them, too."

"No doubt. For those, you keep a rifle close at hand."

"Do *you* have a rifle? Could you have shot that python?"

"I had only to call Sakharam, and he would have brought my gun. But why should I have shot the python? He meant us no harm. If a creature—human or animal—threatens me or mine, I destroy it without a qualm, but so long as it leaves me alone, I leave it alone."

"A person, too? You kill people who threaten you?" Emma found his casual reference to murder most disturbing. She didn't mind if he shot pythons, but the idea that he might shoot humans gave her pause.

He slanted her a dark glance, his eyes suddenly hooded and unreadable. "Man or woman, Miss Whitefield. It makes no difference. I fight for what is mine, and I use all the weapons at my command. Luckily, murder has never been necessary, but if I had to, I would resort to it."

Something in his tone personalized the challenge—as if she herself had said or done something to threaten him. Emma could think of nothing extraordinary about her behavior; the conversation had been about snakes, but now it was about . . . something else entirely, something far more important, only she couldn't say what.

She only knew that she had been warned, and as charming as Mr. Kingston could be, he was also dangerous. She wouldn't want him for an enemy. He could be ruthless and vindictive; it was a side of him she had not yet seen, but now knew existed. They continued in silence and by evening, reached the wide, placid Ganges, one of India's most sacred rivers. A stone pier marked the landing place, or *ghat* as Mr. Kingston called it, and tied up to the *ghat* was a long, low barge with a huge striped awning stretched over the deck.

Mr. Kingston held up an oil lantern so Emma could see where she was going as he took her hand and helped her board. "This will be home for a while, Miss Whitefield. You'll find it comfortable, a perfect place to rest and heal in preparation for the more rigorous part of our journey."

Emma was so miserable she could have knelt and kissed the floorboards of the old, gently swaying boat. Hurricane lanterns illuminated several natives hunkered down in front of a small cookstove, amidst a welter of deck chairs, trunks, coils of rope, and crates, including one containing chickens. Though crowded, the deck seemed a cheery place, and one section of it was partitioned off by a well-patched sail. As Emma noted the boat's two masts and the benches where rowers could sit when the wind failed, her stomach rumbled with hunger pangs brought on by the smell of cooking food.

"Are we going to sail up the Ganges?" she asked, as Mr. Kingston led her to a rattan chair with a sloping back, raised footrest, and armrests, one of which had a hole in it to hold a tumbler. The chair was behind the partition, which offered a measure of privacy to her and whomever joined her in the second identical chair.

"No. This is an old sailing boat, but it's been converted to steam. Our progress will still be slow, for we'll be traveling upstream all the way."

"I see." Emma sank down gratefully into the chair, which boasted a plump tasseled pillow. Perhaps she was meant to sleep here, and sleep she would, if the mosquitoes didn't keep her awake.

A moment after she sat down, one of the squatting men immediately rose, pushed past the partition, and offered her a green coconut. No sooner had she reached out to accept the offering when Sakharam descended upon her and snatched the coconut from her outstretched hands—without touching her, of course. He said something in a furious tone to the little man in the soiled *dhoti*, and the man scurried away, looking most chagrined.

"Why did you do that?" Emma was longing for the cool nectar of the denied refreshment. She was about to demand that he give it back, when Sakharam unceremoniously tossed the coconut into the river.

"If the *memsahib* desires a green coconut, it will be my pleasure to obtain one for her," he intoned in his haughty manner. "And I myself will serve it."

"Well, serve me something." Irritated by his high-handedness, Emma didn't care how pettish she sounded. "I am thirsty and famished. How soon shall we eat?"

"In a very short time, *Memsahib*. I beg your indulgence. 'Tis only that one cannot trust men of his caste to choose one's food. He overstepped his place. 'Tis my duty and mine alone to see to your needs."

"Then see to them." Emma stubbornly squared her shoulders against the lift of Mr. Kingston's dark brows, indicating his disapproval of her confrontation with Sakharam. When the white-turbaned servant had bowed to her and hurried off to do his duty, she glared at him. "I'm sorry, but there are times I can't abide your head servant's attitude. I did not consider it an insult to be offered that coconut; I don't know why Sakharam should be so offended by the gesture."

"I have told you before that Sakharam has his own notions of what is proper. Please remember that we are in India, not England, so his notions take precedence over yours." Mr. Kingston sat down in the seat beside her and stretched his long legs out in front of him. "Don't be rude to him, Miss Whitefield. He is more to me than a mere servant, just as you are more than a mere nanny."

Emma wasn't sure what he meant by that remark and

hoped he would see fit to explain. As he had earlier that day, he looked unfriendly, even forbidding. "I have given you far greater latitude than I would have given Miss Lundy, had she accepted the position. Surely, you've noticed. But I will not allow you to behave churlishly to Sakharam or any of my other servants."

Emma silently pondered his rebuke. Twice now in one day she had glimpsed the darker side of Alexander Kingston. What was making him so testy? He wasn't the one with a broken rib or injured ankle. Still, she was suddenly ashamed of herself. She didn't normally snap at servants—either here or in England. They were human beings, with feelings to be considered. She just wished Sakharam were not so certain of his innate superiority over everyone else.

"Forgive me. I apologize for my behavior. It was indeed rude, and I shall not make a habit of it."

Mr. Kingston rested his head on his own pillow and closed his eyes. "I'm pleased to hear it. Forgive me for mentioning the matter. I don't usually remind people of their inferior positions, if I can avoid it."

Emma's heart softened. What was there about this man that made it so easy to flare up at him—and so easy to forgive? He was an intriguing mixture of kindness, sensitivity, and strength. Underneath it ran a dark vein of . . . ruthlessness. Wildness. Barely restrained passion, and she was forced to admit, violence. He had such elegant manners, yet Emma suspected he was about as tame as a tiger. She lay back in her chair to wait for dinner, but her thoughts centered on Mr. Kingston. Would she ever truly understand the man?

Miss Whitefield fell asleep almost immediately after she had eaten, but Alex stayed awake a long time, gazing up at the stars and savoring a tumbler of brandy he desired only on rare occasions such as this one. Sakharam had rigged up nettings so neither of them would be attacked by mosquitoes or bothered by the huge, silvery-winged moths swooping about the lanterns. The boat would remain moored at the *ghat* until morning, for night travel on the river was dangerous due to submerged obstacles, shallow water, crocodiles, or other watercraft traveling without lights. Day travel was much safer, and Alex was glad for the night quiet, broken only by distant jungle sounds that were soothing and familiar.

Tonight, he could hear jackals howling, their discordant melody as calming as the lapping of the river against the hull. Miss Whitefield would probably abhor the jackals' music, but he was not put off by it. . . . He just wished it would do a better job of distracting him from his troubled thoughts.

This boat trip would be an excellent opportunity to make certain Miss Whitefield got a thorough dunking in the river. If she was well and truly soaked, the deed to Wildwood would be destroyed. The ink on it would run, making the print illegible. Then he could relax for the rest of the journey.

As he had told her, he could not abide threats to his empire. He met them head on, fought like a demon, and never regretted doing whatever was necessary to survive . . . so why did he feel guilty about the prospect of dunking Miss Whitefield in the river? He didn't intend to let her drown; he only wanted to destroy that deed! And now was the perfect time. He had been thinking about it, planning it all day. And all he had accomplished was to lose his temper nearly every time Miss Whitefield looked at him.

One particular expression annoyed him tremendously. Her eyes would suddenly get dewy, her lips curve into the barest of smiles, and she would give him the most . . . liquid . . . innocent . . . trusting . . . look. It made him want to slap her silly and say, *What's wrong with you? Don't you know I only hired you because I feared the damage you might do if I left you in Calcutta? I intend to rob you of your inheritance. If I have my way, you'll never find your precious Wildwood, you'll lose all proof that it ever belonged to you, and as soon as I can be safely rid of you, I will.*

That would be the prudent course: get rid of her as soon as he had destroyed the deed. Why keep her with him and take her to Paradise View so she could snoop about trying to find Wildwood, even though she'd lost the deed? Why had he gone as far as he had to befriend her? Why in hell had he kissed her?

He didn't like what she was doing to him—seducing him with her personality, character, and dewy-eyed looks—actually making him desire her! She was a prickly old maid, for God's sake. The first time he had seen her she had reminded him of a crow. Was he *that* desperate?

Alex took a hearty swallow of brandy. He was spending too much time in her company; that was the problem. When it came to women, he was weak. He could bed a woman he completely scorned—and enjoy it. Here was a woman he genuinely liked, so of course, he wanted to bed her. Even if it wasn't in his own best interests.

He *must* resist his feelings for once, carnal and otherwise, and cold-bloodedly adhere to his plans. Much as he detested the idea, he must arrange for his proper little nanny to fall overboard, at which time he would save her from drowning. After he saved her, she would be so grateful to him she'd probably welcome him into her bed with open arms!

Not on the boat, where there was no real privacy—but later, when they had tents. He would pay her a visit one night, after everyone had gone to sleep. Her ribs would be healed by then, and once she was thoroughly healed, softened, ripened, and prepared, he would teach her what lovemaking, pleasure, passion, hunger, and need were all about.

Damn, but he hadn't wanted a woman this much for a long, long time! The memory of her soft, delicate skin and sweet, tender flesh haunted him, as did the thought of her hair. He longed to bury his face in that mantle of silk and inhale her scent, which teased him unmercifully every time he got close to her. He had started out wanting Miss Whitefield's deed, but now he wanted her body, too. Indeed, the only thing about her he *didn't* want was her affection.

Having her fall in love with him would seriously complicate things, making it difficult to eventually abandon her. When a woman fell in love with him, he always felt responsible, even if he didn't love her. Lahri was a good example. She understood that he would never marry her, that she would never have a more exalted position in his *zenana* than that of mistress, that he would use her body for his own pleasure without surrendering his heart, and that when he was finished with her, he would never take her to his bed again. She understood all this, because he had explained it to her—and still, she loved him. Or so she claimed.

In return, he felt responsible for her and would never simply cast her out. She would always be welcome to live in his *zenana*, or if she preferred, he would find her another protector when their relationship ended. He had explained all this to her, too, and he might very well have to make good on his promise when he got back to Paradise View.

For reasons he couldn't begin to fathom, Lahri had ceased to captivate him. When he pictured her in his mind, his body did not react. He tried imagining her naked, her long black hair spilling down her back, her kohl-lined eyes warm and eager, her slender body anointed with oils and scent, her breasts rouged as she sometimes did in an effort to excite him . . . and he felt nothing. Lahri knew every trick to prolong a man's pleasure from dusk until dawn, but here he was—pining for a dried-up spinster who didn't know the first thing about pleasing or seducing a man!

Tossing down the rest of his brandy, Alex shook his head at his own folly. He was a fool to want Miss Whitefield more than he wanted Lahri, especially since Miss Whitefield was the sort of woman to demand emotional and legal commitments, while Lahri demanded nothing. If he did manage to seduce Miss Whitefield and keep her with him, he could just imagine what would happen when they reached Paradise View.

She would take one good look at Lahri and his *zenana* and conclude that all six of the women he sheltered there existed to answer his summons to the Love Pavilion whenever he called for them. She'd never believe that Lahri was his only mistress, and the rest simply lived there because they had nowhere else to go. Whether he seduced Miss Whitefield or not on this trip, she would not approve of the life he led at Paradise View; he had known that back in Calcutta. In Calcutta, he hadn't cared if she approved or not. Working for him had been *her* idea, not his. He certainly hadn't been planning on seducing her.

So what was he going to do about all this? *First, destroy the deed.* Destroy the deed, and then worry about the rest of it, he decided. Carefully replacing his tumbler in the hole in the armrest of his chair, Alex stole one last look at the woman in the chair next to his. Dim yellow light shone through the partition, and starlight glowed overhead, brushing her fine features with enough illumination so that he could easily distinguish them. She wasn't beautiful by conventional standards, but she was . . . compelling. Tonight, more than ever. At sunset, she had removed her ugly *topi*, and her hair was now an untidy mass cushioning her head against the pillow and framing her face in soft-looking wisps. Alex longed to brush them back from her elegant cheekbones and run his finger along that petal-soft skin. In repose, she looked so young and innocent, almost childlike, and he wondered what sort of child she had been.

Probably difficult. Most certainly precocious. Undeniably intelligent and filled with enthusiasm for life. Much like his own children, particularly Victoria who loved nothing better than freedom from restriction and having her own way. Alex readily admitted that he doted on his little daughter—spoiled her outrageously—and loved her as he had never loved any female. Miss Whitefield had probably been the mirror-image of Victoria, a child most people would consider far too forward and inquisitive.

Victoria would never fit into Indian society—not with her volatile nature. Whether or not she could fit into British society remained to be seen. That was why he had decided to hire a nanny. Victoria was dark and exotic-looking, but in the right gowns, with the right education and comportment, and backed by lots of her father's money, she stood a good chance . . . and Alex intended to see that she got it.

Miss Whitefield might be the perfect nanny for Victoria— a stunning example of what a British lady could and should be: a blade of fine steel sheathed in silk, except that Miss Whitefield eschewed silk in favor of coarse, plain fabrics that did nothing to enhance her femininity. Not that it needed enhancing.

Alex wished he dared raise the mosquito netting, gather the contrary Miss Whitefield into his arms, and make love to her with all the mastery his years of experience had given him . . . All in good time, he cautioned himself. *First the deed, and later, the seduction.* When they got the tents, he promised himself. Only then would he mount his campaign to make a woman of the very virginal Miss Emma Whitefield . . . and only after that would he decide what to do with her.

Emma awoke to the sensation of movement. The boat was moving! Her nose and ears confirmed the fact. She could hear a rhythmic chug-chugging and smell an acrid, burning odor. The voices of the boatmen made a low murmuring sound, almost like the river itself as it gently rocked the boat in an incredibly relaxing motion. She hadn't slept this well since her arrival in India.

She opened her eyes to discover a dazzling blue sky overhead. Someone—probably Sakharam—had removed the cage of netting and turned back the awning. She was lying in a patch of shade created by the partition, and Mr. Kingston's chair was empty, so she was alone behind the barrier. Stretching luxuriously, she sat up and examined her surroundings.

Beside her was a small table set with china and silverware. Beneath the chair was her portmanteau and a pink and white china pot with a lid. As usual, Sakharam had thought of everything. It really was churlish of her to dislike him so much when he waited on her so well, anticipating her every need. Other *memsahibs* may have grown to expect perfect service from the Indians, but to Emma, it was still a novelty. On the one hand, she couldn't help but enjoy it. On the other, she wished Sakharam were *less* attentive.

She had no wish to grow helpless and pampered, dependent on others for basic necessities. At home in England, she had often dismissed her servants early in the day and looked after herself. They had always had enough to do waiting on her father and brother.

Rising, Emma prepared for the day. Sakharam must have heard her, for after a decent interval of time, he clapped his hands outside the partition to announce his presence and then asked if she was ready for a cup of tea. Emma pushed back the barrier and smiled at the sober-faced Indian in his spotless white attire.

"Indeed, I am, Sakharam. Thank you for all you have done—and continue to do—for me. I am most grateful."

Sakharam's expression remained inscrutable. "I do my best, *Memsahib*, though my best may not always please you."

"Oh, but it does please me! I apologize for yesterday. Fatigue and discomfort made me bad-tempered."

"Think nothing of it, *Memsahib*."

Sakharam snapped his fingers, and an ugly little man clad in a loincloth and dirty turban scuttled like a crab toward the china pot Emma had used, picked it up, and proceeded to dump the contents over the side of the boat. He was, she deduced, the sweeper—a man of the lowest possible caste whose duties consisted of emptying chamber pots, removing dead animals, and performing other loathsome chores. Sakharam's attitude toward him was that of a god condescending to tolerate a mere mortal, and Emma was irritated anew. But she kept smiling—determined not to treat Sakharam as he treated those beneath him.

"Good morning, Miss Whitefield." Mr. Kingston suddenly materialized at Sakharam's side. "You look well-rested. In contrast to yesterday, your color is good—your cheeks are actually rosy—and that white thing . . ." With a wave of his hand, he indicated the ruffled, high-necked blouse she was wearing over a sensible dark blue skirt, ". . . is most becoming. White suits you better than the dark colors you favor, though I'd still enjoy seeing you in brighter, more cheerful attire."

Emma didn't know what to say. He *had* complimented her, hadn't he? "I slept unusually well, Mr. Kingston. River travel must agree with me."

"Good. Let's enjoy the scenery while we eat, shall we?"

He offered her his arm to lead her back to the deck chair, which Sakharam was already raising to an upright position. Mr. Kingston wore the same boots and breeches as yesterday, but had changed to a clean shirt and had not yet donned his *topi*. So she did not don hers. His boots were polished to a high gloss that must have taken Sakharam half the night to achieve, and his buff-colored breeches were spotless. Sakharam truly was a marvel.

They ate an excellent breakfast of mutton chops, kidneys on toast, and the little curry puffs Emma had grown to love. She was surprised by how British it was and could only surmise that Sakharam wished to impress the boatmen with the importance of their position—and his, as head servant.

The scenes along the banks of the Ganges soon enchanted her, and the day passed swiftly. At this point, the riverbanks were lined with a tall, coarse grass, ten or twelve feet high, with a feathery head of downy white seed. It was called *moonge* or *jeplasse*, Mr. Kingston told her, and in places the grass grew so thick it resembled a heavy fall of snow.

The heat had not yet destroyed the flowers, and hedges of blossoms in purple, red, and white signaled the presence of ancient tombs or shrines. Often the river itself was enamelled with petals tossed into it after being discarded as offerings.

In places, the jungle foliage grew down to the water's edge and was broken only by natural glades. Emma saw deer grazing in one, their young gambolling about them. Monkeys were easy to spot . . . and if the shoreline occasionally became boring, there was the river itself to contemplate. Crocodiles and water snakes were common, but Emma watched in vain for the large man-eating *muggers*, and the smaller *gavials*. She glimpsed porpoises and too many birds to identify.

"Along the banks, you will see kingfishers, osprey, ibis, storks, and more, if you watch carefully," Mr. Kingston informed her. "Whole flocks of birds can be found at the various mouths of the Ganges, especially around the Sundarbans, an area of trees like mangroves which have knotted themselves into an impassable jungle."

"Oh, I should love to see that!"

"One day, you shall. If I can, I'll take you there."

The promise ignited a warm glow in Emma's heart. Perhaps he was just being nice . . . but maybe he really meant it. Oh, how she hoped he did!

As much as Emma loved the wild places along the river, she also enjoyed the civilized ones. They had entered the well-populated state of Uttar Pradesh, and the towns lining the river boasted impressive *ghats* or landing places, as well as a variety of architectural designs. Emma posed many questions about the history, religion, and inhabitants of the towns, and made mental notes of places she one day hoped to visit. It was fascinating to glide past an obviously bustling, busy metropolis, and then to suddenly be swallowed up in pristine wilderness again. The contrasts were startling, and she relished this chance to prepare for the immensity and variety of the country from a safe, sheltered distance.

That night, she fell asleep with her head full of images: a small steamship, hardly bigger than their own boat, pulling a separate cook-boat behind it; wood-covered cliffs shimmering in the sunlight; a Hindu temple half-hidden in the jungle; a cluster of native huts; a ruined native fort; a half-burned body being shoveled into the river at a funeral *ghat*; crocodiles basking in the sun; graceful Indian women carrying pots of river water on their heads as they filed homeward . . .

Emma had seen more in one day than most people saw in a lifetime, and when she awoke the next morning, ready and eager for more entertainment, she knew she had fallen in love with India . . . and perhaps with the man revealing it all to her.

It started out to be a good morning, but deteriorated rapidly when Mr. Kingston refused breakfast because of some problem with the boat's steering mechanism. Emma knew the problem was serious, because Sakharam and Mr. Kingston stood in the stern, arguing with the head boatman, while at least two men stayed up by the bow, and several scrambled in and out of the hatch.

Until now, she had paid no attention to the boatmen, but as they argued back and forth with Mr. Kingston, she grew alarmed. Mustering the nerve to interrupt, she made her way through the obstacle course on deck to see if there was any way she could help.

"No, Miss Whitefield, and I would appreciate it if you would leave us alone until we solve the problem."

"Why, yes, of course. I didn't mean to bother you. I was only concerned." Her feelings hurt, Emma retreated. But she kept a sharp lookout in case she could be of any assistance.

A short time later, she was horrified to see Mr. Kingston begin stripping off his clothing. Without a smidgen of modesty—or even a glance in her direction—he tore off his shirt, kicked off his boots, and had started on his breeches when she abruptly found her tongue.

"Mr. Kingston! What on earth are you doing?"

Ten

Mr. Kingston paused in the act of tugging his breeches down over his hips. He wore something white underneath; Emma was too flustered to direct her gaze below the level of his navel and ascertain exactly what. It was bad enough she could see that intriguing indentation—and all the bronze, muscular expanse above it. The dark skin. The whorls of darker hair spread across his chest and arrowing downward across his trim abdomen. His flat masculine nipples. Those broad shoulders and well-defined upper arms, bulging with muscles. He was so . . . sleek. So beautiful. So manly. . . . How dare he strip in front of her!

"What are you doing?" she repeated, as all eyes turned to her, including his.

"If you don't want to watch, go up to the bow and turn your back. I have to jump in the river to check something under the boat, and I can't do it fully clothed, so I'm taking off everything but what's necessary for decency. If that offends you, just do as I said. Look elsewhere."

"But . . . but you can't go in the river! There are crocodiles down there. And man-eating *muggers*. And water snakes. And charred bodies. And—"

"I'm not going for a leisurely swim. This will only take a moment, and I'll climb back into the boat."

"But you can't expect me to . . . to merely stand here watching the scenery while you risk your life. What can I do to help? Is there something wrong with the boat? Have we sprung a leak? Please tell me what's happening."

"Nothing's *happening*, Miss Whitefield. At least, not yet. There does seem to be a problem with the steering mechanism. I think I know how to fix it, though we've been having some disagreement over the matter. In India, a *sahib* is expected to solve all problems. Therefore, it is my duty to go down and find out exactly what's wrong."

"But . . . but aren't the boatmen going to shut off the engine first? What if you get hurt? Really, Mr. Kingston, I don't think . . ."

The engine suddenly shut down, and except for the murmur of the river and the creak of the gently rocking boat, there was absolute silence—until Mr. Kingston resumed speaking. "This is a very minor matter. Nothing to be concerned about. Indians jump in the river all the time—to bathe, wash laundry, fetch water . . ."

"Not way out here, Mr. Kingston! Perhaps near the *ghats* or in shallow water, they do, but not where it's deep, and no one knows what's down there."

"What's down there is water, Miss Whitefield, and a few harmless fish. By the time the *muggers* discover me, I'll be safely back on the boat."

Emma squared her shoulders and prepared to do battle. "Can you even swim, Mr. Kingston? If you can't, I absolutely forbid you to jump in that river."

"*Forbid*, Miss Whitefield?" His tone implied that it was ridiculous for her to think she could stop him—and Emma silently agreed. But she couldn't come up with anything better to say, and she had to say something.

"I shan't let you do it. It's too dangerous."

"I can swim," he icily informed her. "Even if I couldn't, I'd still try. Someone has to go down there, and I'm the logical choice."

She knew he was right, but the idea of him jumping in

the river still horrified her. "Then if I can't persuade you to do otherwise, I must certainly help. Tell me what to do."

Her mind made up, she marched over to him, head held high as she swept past Sakharam who had watched and listened to the entire exchange without saying a word. Whatever he was thinking, his face didn't reveal a thing. Stopping directly in front of Mr. Kingston, she demanded, "Can't Sakharam go in your place?"

"He doesn't swim as well as I do, and he knows very little about steering mechanisms." Mr. Kingston's blue eyes drilled holes in Emma's confidence. "If you insist on helping, you may hold a rope in case I need it. But don't try to pull me up by yourself. You aren't strong enough."

"If I had to, I could pull you up," Emma huffily protested. "Fortunately, you have plenty of worthless servants available to lend a hand. If you're going down, please do it immediately and don't dally once you get there."

Mr. Kingston snatched up a coiled rope lying on the deck at his feet and thrust it at her. "Has anyone ever told you what a termagant you are? You should have been born a man, Miss Whitefield. You'd have made an excellent officer in the British Army."

She slipped one arm through the coil of rope and met his unwavering scowl without flinching. "I've been told many times to mind my own business, Mr. Kingston, and I *always* make it a point to ignore that piece of unwanted advice."

"I don't doubt it. Well, if you're ready, so am I."

He finished removing his breeches, while Emma averted her gaze. But it was hard to keep from watching when he leapt up on the railing, poised there a moment silhouetted against the sun, then dove gracefully into the water. His body made a perfect arc, piercing the rippled surface without a single splash, and he surfaced almost immediately—laughing and shaking water from his eyes.

"Come join me, Miss Whitefield!" he called out tauntingly. "The water feels great."

He swam about in a wide circle, completely at ease in the greenish-brown water, while Emma waited for some hungry sea monster to grab his leg and pull him under. "Do get on with it, Mr. Kingston." Leaning over the railing, she cupped her hands around her mouth to shout at him as he swam farther away from the boat. "You're tempting fate! Anything could happen to you out there."

In answer, he laughed and dove out of sight. Clearly, he relished scaring her half to death. Emma clutched the coil of rope tightly to her bosom and prayed that nothing terrible would happen to him. At the same time, she almost wished it would, just to teach him a lesson.

Catching Sakharam's eye, she couldn't resist telling him exactly what she thought of him. "Some servant you are! Letting your master endanger his life while you stand here as if nothing at all is the matter."

Sakharam never so much as blinked. "The *sahib* knows what he is doing. The boatmen didn't realize that anything was wrong with the boat. The *sahib* was the first to notice. He knows everything."

"The *sahib* is a fool. He should have sent you or one of the others down there. He could have rescued you if you needed help. But who will rescue *him* if he needs it—the sweeper? Would you even dare touch the same rope he's touching?"

Sakharam turned away from her abuse, which only confirmed Emma's worst fears. Everyone on board probably considered her and Mr. Kingston untouchable—no, wait. Sakharam had seemed willing, if reluctant, to touch Mr. Kingston during the train wreck. It was *her* he wouldn't touch. Still, she couldn't depend on him. If anything happened, it was up to her to save Mr. Kingston.

Not seeing him resurface on the side of the boat where he had first disappeared underwater, Emma raced to the other side, but didn't spot him there, either. "Where *is* he? Why hasn't he come up yet?"

"He will surface soon, *Memsahib*. He had to go down deep to check under the vessel. Never fear. He swims like a fish."

"Oh, you don't know what you're talking about!" Emma rushed from one side of the boat to the other, anxiously searching the murky waters for Mr. Kingston's sleek wet head. "What if a *mugger's* got hold of him?"

She pictured a huge reptile opening its cavernous jaws and chomping down hard on Mr. Kingston's bare leg. Panic welled up in her, and new catastrophes danced in her head.

"If a *mugger* hasn't got him, he could have struck his head on the hull of the boat and even now be drowning—too stunned to make it to the surface. *Where is he, Sakharam*?"

"I . . . I don't know, *Memsahib*. He does seem to be staying underwater for an unusually long time."

As Sakharam and the other men began to peer into the depths of the river, Emma succumbed to hysteria. She was certain Mr. Kingston had either struck his head, become ensnared in seaweed, or been grabbed by a ravenous crocodile. Every moment they delayed meant disaster. She couldn't wait any longer; she had to do something. Had to find out what had happened and see if she could save him. Gathering up her skirts and still holding the rope slung over her shoulder, she climbed up on the railing as she had seen Mr. Kingston do.

"*Memsahib*! What are you doing? Wait! I think I see him."

But it was too late. Emma was already launching herself from the side of the boat. "Bugger you, Sakharam!"

It was the worst insult she could think of—something a lady would never say—and it gave her great pleasure to say it. One moment she was in the air, her skirts flying, and the next, she was in the river, gulping a huge mouthful of air just before she went under. Water closed over her head, enfolding her in its cool wet embrace.

The closest Emma had ever come to swimming was when, as a child, she had once removed her garments on a hot afternoon and paddled around naked in a pond on the White-field estate. She had just been getting the hang of it, when her father spotted her, dragged her out by the hair, and nearly screamed himself into a fit of apoplexy.

She had been sent to bed without supper, and all of her future attempts at swimming had been confined to furtive moments of wading barefoot; even for these, she had been punished. Ladies simply didn't go around with their skirts hauled up around their waists; their lower limbs bared for all the world to see.

Emma wished now that she had persevered in defying her father until she had actually learned to swim. She struggled valiantly to kick her way to the surface for another breath of air. At the same time, she opened her eyes wide and attempted to locate Mr. Kingston's trapped, mutilated, or mangled body. She couldn't see anything but mysterious shadows and shapes in the green gloom. Nothing looked like a man. And she couldn't breathe. Her lungs were ready to burst. The harder she kicked, the deeper she sank. Her skirt, petticoat, and other garments entangled themselves in her legs, and the string from the waterproof pouch into which she had sewn her jewels and her deed wrapped itself around her upper thighs, further impeding her movements. The weight of her clothing dragged her down . . . down . . . and down.

I can't drown! I've got to save Mr. Kingston.

Her own thoughts mocked her. How could she possibly save him when she couldn't save herself? The rope on her shoulder hampered her struggles, and in her mad flailing, she finally managed to dislodge it. But she couldn't free herself from her skirt and undergarments. She kept her mouth shut tight against the water, desperately resisting the urge to breathe through her nose—and inhaled a huge snootfull of water anyway. That was when she realized she really was going to drown.

Her own folly had been her undoing. She was dying and couldn't do a thing about it. Her head, nose, and lungs ached with an exploding sensation. A great pain racked her chest. Starbursts of light danced behind her eyes. Otherwise, it was dark . . . dark as midnight. Dark as the river bottom. Dark as a grave. Down . . . down . . . she spiralled downward, fighting the pain and the darkness.

Just as consciousness slipped away, she felt something—or someone—grab her about the waist. Maybe it was a *mugger.* Or Mr. Kingston! *Oh, God, if I survive this, I will never go near a river again. I will stop being so stubborn, opinionated, and rebellious . . . everything my father—no, not my father but my stepfather—had ever called me.*

Emma had one last thought before she slipped away: now, she would *never* find Wildwood. . . . Worse yet, she'd never be kissed again, not by Mr. Kingston or any other man. She never would discover if kissing was all she had hoped it could be.

"Wake up, Miss Whitefield. Damn it, wake up."

Alex knelt on the deck and leaned over the wet, bedraggled body of the woman he had hired to be nanny to his children. He slapped her pale cheeks and chafed her hands, but she remained bluish and cold, a step away from death if she wasn't drowned and dead already. Sakharam hovered nearby, but of course, he wouldn't touch Miss Whitefield—nor would anyone else on board except for the lowly sweeper, whom Alex deemed too filthy to put his hands on Miss Whitefield.

"Damn it, Sakharam, what happened? She was supposed to toss me the rope when I came up yelling that I had a cramp. I was going to pull her overboard and then save her. That was the plan. She wasn't supposed to jump in after me when I was still under the boat."

Alex spoke in English so the rest of the men couldn't understand, and Sakharam responded in English, well aware of the need for secrecy. "She was worried, Sikander. We were all getting worried. You stayed under too long. We thought something bad had really happened to you. I myself had grown fearful."

"Nonsense. I grew up teasing crocodiles in the Narmada. You know what chances I took. Yet I never got caught or even came close to drowning."

Alex rolled Miss Whitefield onto her side and proceeded to clap her on the back with gentle violence. It was hard to be gentle, but he didn't want to break another rib or hurt the one already broken, assuming Miss Whitefield was still alive and could feel what he was doing.

"The little fool! She can't swim, and she has on so many clothes she would have drowned even if she knew how. I just hope she was wearing that pouch or packet containing her deed. If she wasn't—isn't—we've killed her for no good reason."

"I do not count her life as any great loss," Sakharam sniffed. "Though she did show great courage when she jumped into the river to save you. Still, you wouldn't hesitate to shoot a thief intent on stealing what you most value; why would you mourn Miss Whitefield if she dies? Once she's gone, you need worry no longer. She cannot possibly harm you or the children by claiming part of Paradise View."

It was a good question, one Alex intended to ponder when he had the time. Mother India fostered ruthlessness in those who loved her, and he had learned her lessons well. The law of the jungle was kill or be killed. The law of man—the *unwritten* one, anyway—was the same. The Raj had imposed a veneer of justice and civility on the country, but men were as ruthless as they had ever been, albeit in a more bloodless manner, resorting to murder only when all else had failed.

Alex had hoped to avoid violence. All this stubborn woman had needed to do was toss him a rope, and his plan would have worked. Until she had taken it upon herself to actually jump in the river in an effort to save him, the plan

had been working. She had been as easy to deceive and ma-
nipulate as a witless child.

*Dear God, great Shiva, merciful Buddha, blessed Yahweh,
sweet Jesus, powerful Kali . . . don't let her die.*

Alex prayed to every deity he knew. As he sent his pleas
heavenward, guilt and shame consumed him. He had only
meant to pull Miss Whitefield into the river and get her
clothes wet; instead, he had murdered her. Who could have
guessed she would be so brave, so reckless, so heedless of
her own safety? Alex had risked his life to save others from
the burning train, but each time, he had calculated the risks
and decided that if he was careful he could survive.

Miss Whitefield hadn't given a moment's thought to her
own safety; apparently, she hadn't even thought of her deed.
Her courage was the purest, most selfless kind, and Alex felt
humbled by it. He himself had never put another's life and
welfare before his own. He would gladly do so for Victoria
and Michael, his own flesh and blood, but for a near stranger?
Someone he had met only a short time ago?

"Come on, Miss Whitefield." He thumped her harder between the shoulder blades. "I can't let you die. I *won't* let
you die. My life isn't worth the sacrifice of *your* life. If you
really knew me, you wouldn't have done this. You'd have
said 'he deserves to die young. Look at all the bad things
he's done. Look at who he is, for Christ's sake.' "

Miss Whitefield suddenly made a gurgling sound. A moment later, water gushed from her nose and mouth. Elated,
Alex pounded her harder, until she groaned in protest.
Coughing and gagging, she spewed water across the deck,
then rolled over on her back, opened her eyes, and heaved
a long, heavy sigh.

"Miss Whitefield, you're alive." Alex's throat swelled. His
eyes watered. "I can't believe it. You're still alive."

"What . . ." she began and stopped, her voice as deep as
a frog's. She coughed, cleared her throat, and tried again.
"What bad things have you done, Mr. Kingston?"

Alex couldn't help it; he burst out laughing. She was actually alive and once again posing outrageous questions. "That, Miss Whitefield, is none of your damn business. I thought you were dead, and here you are, eavesdropping. If you do it again, I'll take you across my knee and give you a mighty wallop or two, just as I do my children."

"You never strike your children," Sakharam objected, taking him seriously. "Nor would I permit you to do so."

"You have walloped me quite enough for one day." Miss Whitefield struggled to sit up. Her hand went to her throat, and she grimaced. "Dear me. Did I swallow half the river?"

"You barely left any for the *muggers*."

Alex waved away the boatmen, his bearers, the sweeper, and the other servants who had crowded about them, unable to understand what was being said, but fascinated by the drama, all the same. They were all chattering at once, expressing great joy at Miss Whitefield's survival. Not because they actually cared, but because her death aboard the boat would have brought bad luck. Boatmen were a superstitious lot; they might even have insisted upon burning the vessel to appease whatever gods or goddesses had been angered.

"Can you stand, Miss Whitefield?" Alex offered her his arm. "We must find you dry clothes and make certain you are really all right."

"I'm fine—now. But what about you?" Her great green eyes were unusually large in her still pale face. With her wet hair plastered to her neck and shoulders, she more closely resembled a drowned rat than a woman, but Alex had never seen anyone prettier.

"What happened to you?" she earnestly inquired, rising without his assistance. "I thought you were caught under the boat; you didn't come up for a terribly long time."

"I can hold my breath longer than most human beings. When I found a loose part that needed tightening, I stayed down to fix it."

"You don't have to go down again?" She gripped his arm so hard that his guilt was overwhelming.

"No, it's done. The boat should run well for the remainder of the river journey."

"I'm so glad. I was frantically worried about you. I was sure you had drowned."

Not a word about her own near-drowning. She wasn't even thinking of herself. Her concern was all for him. What a truly amazing, unselfish woman!

"You are the one who almost drowned. And if you had your deed to Wildwood with you, the river water has probably ruined it. If you do find the place, you'll never be able to prove that it once belonged to your mother." He didn't have to work to keep the triumph out of his voice; he didn't feel any triumph. All he felt was guilt for his own misdeeds and admiration for her courage and character.

Miss Whitefield paused near the partition. Water still streamed from her hair and sodden garments. Her face lit with a sudden brightness that completely dispelled the lingering bluish tint to her skin. "I'll check to make certain it isn't damaged, but I'm not worried. I knew we'd be traveling on the river, so I cut a piece out of my mackintosh and stitched up a waterproof packet for it. Wasn't that clever of me?"

Alex felt as if a mule had kicked him. "Yes . . . very. You think of everything, don't you, Miss Whitefield?"

"I try, Mr. Kingston. Oh, I do try! I admit I wasn't thinking soundly when I jumped into the river after you. I was acting on instinct, permitting panic to rule me. Now, I'm embarrassed that you should have witnessed such foolish behavior on my part."

"You must learn to curb your impulsiveness. This can't be the first time it's gotten you into trouble."

"Oh, it isn't!" She laughed a bit shrilly, as if she still hadn't recovered from her close brush with death, or was just now coming to terms with it. "I vow to curb it from now on; I swear I will. After all, you may not always be available to save my life, will you?"

He had saved her life, yes, but he had also been the one endangering it. Alex had never been more disgusted with himself. Relinquishing her arm, he rearranged the partition to give her more privacy. "I'll make certain no one disturbs you while you change, Miss Whitefield. Let me finish adjusting this, and then I'll have Sakharam make us some tea."

"Tea would be lovely. It will soothe my raw throat."

"We'll get underway again, too. I'll tell the head boatman that the problem has been fixed."

The problem that never really existed. Alex blessed his good fortune that Miss Whitefield wasn't mechanical. Otherwise, she'd have stuck her nose into that business also, and discovered his deceitfulness . . . and it had all been for naught. She still had the damn deed! Sewn into a waterproof packet, of all things. How was he going to destroy it now? What should he try next? And how could he keep her safe while he did it?

The first thing Emma did when she reached the privacy of the partition, which Mr. Kingston had rehung to form a small dressing chamber, was lift up her dripping skirts and check her oilskin packet. It appeared unharmed, but she took a small scissors and slit open the tiny stitches. The very top of the deed was dampened and curling. Even worse, a line of moisture had blurred a small portion of the ink, but the writing was, thank God, still legible.

The paragraph wasn't a very important one anyway, and the map sketched on the back was completely intact, as were the legal signatures and the description of the property. Emma resolved to cut still another piece from her mackintosh and make a double lining to protect the deed. Considering their misadventures so far—a train wreck and her own near-drowning—she couldn't be too careful.

Thinking of that near brush with death, Emma could scarcely make her fingers work properly. Reinserting the deed and gems into their original pouch and stuffing the pouch back into the packet, she set about peeling off her wet things and stripping down to the skin.

By the time she was dressed and had combed out her hair, she felt better—more in control. More like her old self. This was one more adventure she could tell her grandchildren, if she ever had any. Suddenly, she wanted children and grandchildren with a desperation she had never before experienced. Today, she had almost died, and if she *had* died, she would have left behind no legacy, no one to follow her or mourn her passing, no one who shared her blood and would affectionately celebrate her memory.

Rosie would miss her, but Rosie had her own life, complete with husband and maybe one day, a family. Her brother had made it clear that he was only too happy to sever their relationship forever. No one on the whole wide earth would mourn her in the special way she still mourned and remembered her own mother. Miss Emma Whitefield would simply cease to exist, and the sun would keep rising and setting just the same as it always did.

Lowering her comb, Emma sank down on a small stool and glumly studied the growing puddle where she had dropped her wet clothes. When all was said and done, what difference had she made in anyone's life? She had fought injustices, but injustice still existed; she had tried to help the poor, but poverty was everywhere. She had had adventures, but the great experiences of a woman's life still eluded her: marriage, childbirth, true love. . . . If she had just experienced true love, like her mother, death would not be so terrible. Her other failures wouldn't matter so much. But she had never loved any man—never even come close to it. Perhaps she was unlovable . . . but hadn't she loved today, for one single, glorious moment?

When she had thought Mr. Kingston was drowning, she

had done a stupid, incomprehensible, totally daft thing. She had jumped in the river to save him, when she couldn't even swim. If that wasn't love, what was? Would she have done the same for Percival Griffin? Or Sakharam? Or any of the nameless boatmen and servants aboard this boat? Probably not. Mr. Kingston would have saved them. Or she would have thought of some other method to assist them short of endangering herself. No, she had risked her life, *because it was Mr. Kingston.*

I love him. I must love him, or I wouldn't have done something so risky and foolish. Was that what love was—a willingness to jump into rivers to save the beloved? Her head ached from these unanswerable questions. . . . Oh, she was so confused!

"Miss Whitefield? Have you finished changing? Your tea is ready."

The warm masculine voice sent a tremor through Emma's limbs. She mustn't be in love with Mr. Kingston! She mustn't. For he could never love her. It just wasn't possible. A man with his looks, courage, money, and strength of character needed a young, beautiful, wealthy woman to help further his cause in society: to enchant stuffy British matrons, turn the heads of high officials, and give him confidence at the balls and entertainments where business deals were made on the side.

She knew exactly what he needed; she wasn't it.

"Miss Whitefield?"

She jumped up. "Yes, I'm coming. I'm coming, Mr. Kingston."

A tear trickled down her cheek, and she hastily dashed it aside. Smile, she told herself. Smile and look happy to be alive. But as she went out, she wasn't happy. She wasn't happy, at all.

Eleven

The remainder of the trip up the Ganges proved mercifully uneventful—except for Mr. Kingston's attentiveness to Emma. He explained the sights as usual, constantly inquired after her comfort, and when there was nothing else to do, engaged her in a game of whist. To compensate for the fact that there were only two players, instead of the usual four, they each played double hands. At times, they simply read together, sitting side by side on deck chairs, absorbed in books Emma had brought along despite Mr. Kingston's warning to pack lightly, carrying only necessities. Books *were* necessities, and she was overjoyed to discover that he thought so, too, and didn't mind that she had hidden a dozen in her belongings.

A week later, they reached the impressive stone *ghats* of Varanasi, which were a long series of stepped landings on the river front, linked with narrow crowded streets crammed with pilgrims and devotees of the Hindu religion. Here, Emma was treated to a brief tour of the city by palanquin, while Sakharam restocked the boat for the remainder of the journey to Allahabad.

Like Rome, Varanasi was an "eternal city," which had survived through the ages under the rule of Lord Shiva, the presiding deity of the town. According to common belief, all those who died here would be close to God in the other world, which explained why there were so many elderly worshippers in Varanasi, making it a city of old men. It boasted countless temples, of which the historic mosque of Aurangzeb, built in the eighteenth century, was the most conspicuous. The antiquity of Varanasi could be traced back to the middle of the first millennium B.C., but Emma was more impressed by the bazaar where colorful silks, shawls, brocades and embroideries, brass idols of Hindu deities, and children's toys could be purchased.

Over Mr. Kingston's protests, she bought two toys for his children: a small brass top for his son, and a tiny, exquisitely carved teak figurine, complete with silk *sari*, for his daughter. Mr. Kingston refused to bargain for her, so she wound up paying outrageous prices.

"You don't even know my children yet," he scoffed. "So why are you purchasing such expensive gifts for them?"

"Precisely because I *don't* know them, and they don't know me. These gifts will serve as an introduction—a way of telling them I was thinking of them even before I met them. Is Michael too sophisticated to enjoy a brass top? Perhaps I should have bought him something else instead."

"Michael has a dozen brass tops."

"You should have told me that. Why didn't you?"

"Would you have listened?"

She couldn't help smiling. "Probably not. A child can never have too many tops; this will simply add to his collection. I'll tell him it came from Varanasi and is therefore special."

"*You* are special, Miss Whitefield."

As he handed her into a palanquin after their shopping excursion, he held onto her fingers a moment longer than necessary. Her breath caught in her throat as she gazed into his brilliant blue eyes. People jostled them on every side, but it suddenly seemed as if they were completely alone.

"Why, thank you, Mr. Kingston. So are you," she lightly added as he released her hand and stepped back so the four bearers could carry her to the boat.

Their next, and last, stop before Allahabad was Mirzapur, famous for its plush woollen carpets. Emma would have liked to explore the bazaar and enjoy the beauty of the colors and designs in the rugs, but Mr. Kingston would not permit it. After a brief disappearance that left her wondering where he had gone, he rushed her through the marketplace and spirited her back to the boat less than an hour later.

She was somewhat miffed, until he presented her with a small but absolutely magnificent carpet of crimson, blue, and gold wool, woven in an intricate geometrical design. "Why did you buy this for me? I've done nothing to deserve so lavish a gift. Really, I am quite astounded."

He gave her a smug, self-satisfied grin. "If a boy can't have too many tops, a woman can't have too many carpets. You don't have any, do you? This carpet is a luxury you may shortly come to appreciate. As we trek through the wilderness, it will remind you that India can be a civilized place, as well as a wild one. Take care that dampness and insects do not destroy it. When you are not using it, give it to Sakharam; he will take care of it until we arrive at Paradise View."

"No, no—I can care for it myself. I will wrap it in what's left of my mackintosh—and I will treasure it always. Thank you, Mr. Kingston."

"Think nothing of it, Miss Whitefield. It's but a small token of my appreciation for your having jumped into the river to save me when you thought I was drowning."

She wished he hadn't explained the gift on the basis of gratitude, but she wasn't about to quibble over motives. It was the first gift she had ever received from a man, and nothing could have delighted her more. The carpet wasn't a useless item, nor a particularly feminine one. It would endure and last forever, bringing a warmth and vibrancy to whatever chamber, or tent, it graced.

As they drew nearer to Allahabad, the sun grew more fierce. Even Mr. Kingston took to donning his helmet, and Emma did nothing without her *topi*. She still managed to get sunburned from the reflected light off the river's surface. When, at last, they tied up at the stone *ghat* in Allahabad, she was both sad and happy to see the river portion of the journey end. After sending Sakharam ahead to announce their arrival, Mr. Kingston suggested they walk to the home of his friend. It wasn't that far, and the sooner they got there, the sooner they could get out of the hot sun.

Emma's ankle was now good as new and her rib nearly healed, so she eagerly agreed. They set out in the late afternoon through the quiet, half-slumbering city. When she remarked on the general peacefulness of the town, Mr. Kingston told her that it was one of the holiest places in the country. Consequently, life there moved at a slow pace.

"It does come alive every twelve years, when the *Kumbha Mela* is held. Allahabad then becomes the meeting ground for various Hindu sects and their ascetic orders, attracting hundreds of thousands of pilgrims."

Emma strove to match his long strides. "I should love to see that. I don't normally like crowds, but for something like the *Kumbha Mela*, I would make an exception."

"You wouldn't be permitted to witness the religious ceremonies, I'm afraid." He took her arm to steer her around a group of scruffy boys playing a crude game of cricket in the street. "Aside from the crowds blocking your view, you're a woman—and British. You'd not be welcome."

"I'd dress up in one of those tents with slits for the eyes. Then I could go where I pleased."

"You mean a *burqa*. Forget it, Miss Whitefield. Your height would give you away. . . . Ah, there's my friend's home, just a short distance away. I hope he's there."

Emma gaped at the Indian palace they were approaching. Mr. Kingston had described the Akbar Fort, a legacy of Mughal times, and a beautiful garden called *Khushrobagh*, which contained the tomb of the Mughal Prince Khushro and his family. Could this be the same place? The exquisite compound stood on a slight rise, dwarfing everything around it.

"You didn't tell me that your friend was living in a Mughal palace. If he lives here, he must be a prince."

"This—a palace?" Mr. Kingston laughed, somewhat bitterly, Emma thought. "I wouldn't call it a palace, nor would my friend, but yes, it was built during the period I told you about. And my friend *is* a prince—though not a ruler. When the Raj came to power, it deposed his family and installed another less inclined toward rebellion in his ancestral home. The place where he should be living is three or four times the size and beauty of this one."

"Goodness." Emma didn't understand how the British could have been so arrogant as to decide who should rule in this country and who should not, rebellion or no rebellion. Mr. Kingston's attitude surprised her; it was distinctly *un*-British, almost as if he faulted the Raj the same as she did. But if he did, he was the only *sahib* in all India to condemn the behavior of the sacrosanct East India Company.

"Miss Whitefield," Mr. Kingston stopped and turned to her. "There is something I must warn you about."

Emma took a deep breath. "Yes, Mr. Kingston?"

"Don't look as if I'm about to throw you to the *muggers*. 'Tis simply that you will probably have to spend tonight—and every other night we are here—in the *zenana*, or women's quarters. We will not be dining together this evening or sharing any of our meals. Food and drink will be generously provided, but you are expected to eat alone. Don't touch or handle any objects but those given to you for your exclusive use. I won't instruct you on what to say to the women in the *zenana*; it won't matter because they don't speak English."

Emma resented the implication that she might embarrass him with her lack of manners. "I shall try not to offend your friends. Are these precautions because I am untouchable?"

Mr. Kingston nodded. "Yes, and if you think the British

have too many proprieties to observe, you will soon discover that their rules of etiquette are nothing compared to the dictates of the upper-class Indian family. The culture may be different, but the snobbish attitude is as bad or worse. The very best families regard the British as barely civilized."

It was Emma's turn to laugh. "Oh, my! Do you know the first thing I was told when I arrived here in this country? An old British matron who stank of barley water informed me I must never shake hands with an Indian, because 'you never know where his hand has been, my dear.' How is that for snobbery?"

Mr. Kingston's eyes sparkled, either from amusement, anger, or a combination. "Not bad. Did she mention that an Indian might not want to shake hands with *you*, and for much the same reason? I'll bet she didn't know that Indians keep their right hands scrupulously clean for eating and use only their left ones for ablutions and the dirtier chores of life."

"I didn't know that." Emma was chagrined at her lack of knowledge; it echoed that of Rosie and her circle of friends, all of whom considered themselves a cut above Indians.

"My friend's *khansama* will conduct you to the *zenana*. After that, you are on your own."

"*Khansama*? Do you mean a head servant or chief of staff like Sakharam?"

"Yes, and you will be amazed at how alike the two men are in dress and manner. They are a breed unto their own."

He resumed walking toward the palace. High sandstone walls and elegant wrought-iron gates enclosed it. Emma hurried to catch up to him. "Wait a moment, please, Mr. Kingston. What about the women of the *zenana?* Is there anything more I should know about them?"

"Just that you should not be nervous, Miss Whitefield. They will be curious—as will you. Some are my friend's wives and concubines. Others are only servants. You'd need a month to sort them all out."

Emma had heard that Indians had plural marriages, but

she hadn't dreamed that wives and concubines co-existed together. "Isn't it awkward, a man's wives and lovers all living together under the same roof? What shall I say to them?"

"I've already told you. You won't need to say much of anything since you don't share the same language. Relax, Miss Whitefield. You won't find it awkward in the least. If the women aren't embarrassed, why should you be? My friend's mother rules the *zenana*; pay your respects to her. She will probably visit you and sit silently watching while you eat. It is her job to see to your comfort . . . and I promise you we won't be here long. In a few days, we'll be on our way again."

"A few days! Oh, I hope we can leave before that!" Emma was suddenly terrified, but intrigued, too. No one of her acquaintance had ever set foot inside a *zenana*.

"I'll need a few days to prepare for our trek across country. Then, too, friendship demands that I spend some time visiting with my friend. I haven't seen him for a long while, and he'll be most unhappy if I rush off too soon."

"How did you meet him, Mr. Kingston? When did you become friends?" As they entered the wrought-iron gates enclosing the large pink and white structure, Emma found her curiosity about this relationship growing. Mr. Kingston had probably met his friend in some business capacity—the usual way in which British and Indian men became acquainted. But few ever felt free to visit one another's homes; she recalled Rosie's explanation that it just wasn't done.

"You forget, Miss Whitefield, I was born here . . . and the man you are about to meet is Sayaji Singh. I might as well tell you now as later, before you hear it from someone else. Sayaji is not only my friend but a distant relative, one of the few with whom I am still on speaking terms."

Emma nearly tripped over her own feet. So it was true! Mr. Kingston *did* have Indian blood. Everything said about him in Calcutta, all the rumors about his pedigree, were instantly confirmed. He was not wholly British, but exactly what she had been warned against: a despised *kutcha butcha*.

Mr. Kingston's handsome face betrayed no emotion. "Watch your step, Miss Whitefield. The path may be unfamiliar, but that's no reason to stumble and fall flat on your face. Keep your eyes open, and you should have no problem."

He might as well have said "Keep your mind open, too."

"I . . . uh, yes, thank you."

While Emma was trying to recover from the shock of these unexpected revelations, servants engulfed them. Mr. Kingston apparently knew many of them and immediately lapsed into their language, leaving Emma an outsider, a foreigner, as he enjoyed a welcome such as might be given to a long-lost brother.

They were ushered into an inner courtyard where fountains tinkled and lush flowers bloomed. There, a slender dark man wearing white garments embroidered with gold thread and a turban adorned with a large ruby and an egret feather rushed out from between the pillars and unabashedly embraced Mr. Kingston. The servants presented garlands of flowers, though no one said a word to Emma until the slender man finally acknowledged her presence with a deep bow.

"Welcome to Allahabad, *Memsahib*," he said in perfect, precise English. "Sikander tells me you are the new governess and teacher of his children. My *khansama* will take you to my mother, the *Begum*, who will make certain you lack for nothing. We are pleased you have come to visit."

Sikander. Mr. Kingston's Indian name was Sikander; it sounded like the Indian version of Alexander. Emma recalled Sakharam calling him that after the train wreck. Sakharam was standing off to one side, almost lost in the shuffle of white-coated, smiling servants who differed from him only in the color of their cummerbunds; his was white, theirs yellow.

The term *begum* had also caught Emma's attention. Mr.

Kingston had told her that Wildwood had reverted to the Begum of Bhopal after the Mutiny. The conversation now seemed like eons ago. If their host's mother was a *begum*, then their host must truly be—or ought to have been—someone important, a *nawab* or *nawabzada*.

"Thank you, Mr. Singh." Emma almost called him Your Majesty, for it wasn't difficult to imagine Sayaji Singh in the role of a maharajah. He had enough servants to play the part. As if she herself were a mere servant, he ushered Mr. Kingston away, leaving her to the care of his major-domo, a man with the same air of authority as Sakharam.

The *khansama* said something to her and bowed, which Sakharam smugly translated. "He wishes for you to accompany him to the *zenana, Memsahib*."

Sakharam's thin lips curved in a knowing smirk; obviously he relished delivering the message.

"I know what he wishes, thank you, and I shall be delighted to accompany him." Emma picked up her skirts to follow the man through the maze of arches and corridors that fronted the pink and white building. She had gone from ruling class to caged bird in the blink of an eye, but she was determined not to show how disgruntled she was. How unfair that she had to be confined to the women's quarters, while Mr. Kingston went where he pleased! Was this how Indian women felt—restricted, ignored, and set aside, having no importance in the world of men?

She told herself it was just another social situation in which she must bite her tongue and do the expected, but it galled her that Mr. Kingston had gone off with his friend— no, *his relative*—without a backward glance. If she knew the language, it wouldn't be so bad, but he had neglected to tell her what language was spoken here. Was it Urdu, or as it was more often called, Hindustani? Or was it one of the hundreds of dialects she would never be able to understand, no matter how hard she tried?

Emma's pique lasted until she arrived at a pair of intricately carved wooden doors. The *khansama* stepped back and motioned her inside. As Emma entered, the doors softly closed behind her . . . trapping her in a mysterious, exotic, and fascinating world—a world such as she had never imagined existed anywhere on earth.

She stood in a large, cool chamber with immense thick walls of sandstone, decorated with beaded or embroidered wall-hangings, and lovely, airy screens of latticework, some of stone, others of bamboo. Some were filled with colored glass; others provided a view of various parts of the compound, interior gardens, and even the street outside. The chamber opened into other chambers or inner courtyards, and Emma suspected that all of them were beautifully furnished with carpets in jewel-like colors, exquisitely carved screens and wall-hangings, large tasseled pillows, and potted plants. Flat walls were painted or otherwise embellished with country scenes, geometric designs, or leaves, birds, and flowers.

The air smelled of exotic perfumes and spices, and a faint jingling sound could be heard. The jingling sound grew louder, someone laughed softly, and suddenly, veiled figures appeared from behind arches, screens, and doors. The jingling came from jewel-encrusted gold and silver bangles, earrings, and necklaces which created a delightful music with each step of bare feet across the plush carpets.

Emma stood transfixed as well over a dozen women descended upon her, murmuring, giggling, and shyly peeking out at her from behind the concealment of their *saris*, one corner of which they held across their faces. She caught glimpses of dark flashing eyes, slender hands adorned with rings, and was acutely conscious of the whirl of rich colors and scents as the women crowded around her.

They were all so beautiful—with their black eyes and hair, bronze skin, and feminine grace. It was hard to tell how old they were, but some of them looked barely out of childhood.

Emma was simultaneously enchanted and appalled. Did all of these gorgeous creatures *belong* to Sayaji Singh?

While Emma was busy examining them, they were busy exclaiming over her hair, clothing, *topi*, shoes. . . . She felt tall, ugly, and poorly dressed next to these bright, vivacious butterflies and was almost glad she couldn't understand them. When several reached out to finger her hair or clothing, Emma backed up a step and waved them away.

"Ladies, you mustn't. I'm not sure it's at all proper for you to touch me—nor I you. Oh, I wish there was someone here who spoke English!"

A loud clapping made all the ladies fall silent. In the sudden hush, Emma could hear the soft whisper of silk as a new figure glided into the chamber. Her pink and gold garments seemed to float on the air, and her sparkling jewels put the adornments of the other women to shame. She stopped in front of Emma and lowered one corner of her *sari* to reveal a serene, unlined face of great dignity and nobility.

Silver laced her coal-black hair, and her eyes radiated a warmth and composure. She smiled and nodded at Emma, who returned the smile and dropped a curtsy, as if she were greeting royalty. Emma didn't know why she did it, except it seemed the proper thing to do, and she hoped to make a good impression. Too late, she realized that as the daughter of a viceroy and woman of the Raj, *she* held the senior rank.

"Good afternoon, madam," she said. "I presume you are the Begum of whom I have heard. I am the Honorable Miss Emma Whitefield."

A titter of laughter erupted. The Begum frowned at the ladies responsible, then motioned for Emma to follow her. She did so gladly, for she was eager to see more of the beautiful, fantastic *zenana*. The Begum escorted her through several smaller chambers, each a perfect jewel of a room, and into a compartment with a high ceiling where a long, silk-covered divan occupied the very center and a second group of women huddled respectfully in a corner.

Four large copper vessels exuded fragrant steam, and three silver bowls, each filled with an oily substance, were laid out next to the divan. A chest of beaten gold held folded cloths, sponges, various vases and pots, and brass ewers.

Was this a bathing room?

No sooner had the thought formed in Emma's mind, when the Begum motioned for the women in the corner—women who wore no jewelry and were clad only in simple cotton *saris*—to come forward. The women immediately surrounded Emma and in a brisk, no-nonsense manner, began to divest her of her clothing.

"Stop! Wait a moment. What are you doing?" Clutching at her bodice, Emma backed up against the divan.

The Begum's delicate black eyebrows rose in surprise. She gestured toward the copper vessels of steaming water, the bowls of oil, and the folded cloths, and made washing motions, indicating that Emma must be bathed.

"I'll be happy to avail myself of . . . of your hospitality, but really, I can do this myself. And without an audience." Emma glanced around helplessly at all of the lovely women crowded into the room. There was barely space for so many; did none of them understand English?

They were all watching expectantly, ready to enjoy the spectacle of her "bath." The Begum picked up a small jar containing a thick, disgusting-looking green paste and handed it to one of the attendants. The woman took it, dipped her fingers in it, withdrew a large glob, and dabbed it on Emma's head. The cold, gooey mass promptly slid down Emma's forehead and plopped on the floor.

She suddenly realized that she could protest all she wished, but no one would understand, and she'd only make a fool of herself trying to avoid the inevitable. "All right, ladies. If this is what you want, so be it."

She sank down on the divan with a sigh. "Do your worst. As I am greatly outnumbered, I'll try to get through this with a semblance of good cheer. However, when I see him, I'll wring Mr. Kingston's miserable neck for subjecting me to this."

The Begum nodded and smiled, full of graciousness and concern as she watched the attendants ministering to Emma. Within moments, Emma was stripped down to bare skin and laid out on the divan like a victim on an altar. One woman worked on her face, another on her hair, and others tackled her limbs, torso, and even her feet. Consumed with embarrassment, Emma closed her eyes and prayed that her bath might soon be over.

Twelve

Alex had drunk too much. Sayaji had pressed whiskey, wine, and brandy upon him, and courtesy dictated that he join his host in indulging in all of them. Fortunately, his old friend wasn't given to smoking a *hookah* or taking opium; it was bad enough Alex had drunk more than he wished and eaten enough food to feed a small village.

He longed to go to bed. The hour had grown late, but again, courtesy kept him listening and nodding as he and Sayaji lounged on pillows around a small, low table, still set with silver goblets, while a *punkah*-fan kept them cool in his friend's lavish personal quarters. They had discussed family matters, politics, the state of the Raj, the futility of trying to regain the lost power of Sayaji's family, and finally progressed to personal problems.

With a long, drunken sigh, Sayaji morosely kicked a pillow onto the floor. "I wish I could leave Allahabad for a stint of *shikar*, but I dare not do so while my son is in such a delicate state of health."

Alex roused himself from his cups. "You are worried about your son?"

After a string of daughters, Sayaji had finally produced a son and heir, now four years old, and Alex knew how devastating it would be for his friend to lose him. Sayaji loved nothing better than "a stint of *shikar*," or hunting; he must be frantic if he was willing to forego it.

"My son is not well. One day he is full of energy, but the next, he is pale and quiet, barely able to enjoy his meals. I know not what ails him, nor can anyone tell me. I dare not leave him nor subject him to the rigors of hunting when his strength is so uncertain."

"Take him to Calcutta or someplace where a British doctor can tend him. Don't entrust his health to anyone in Alla-habad. Intrigue is everywhere; perhaps someone wants him dead, so your family line dies when you die."

"Why should anyone want that?" Sayaji airily waved a bejeweled hand. "Everything my family once owned has been confiscated; I have little left to lose."

"You still possess personal wealth, Sayaji. That makes you a target for the greedy and unscrupulous. I myself must always watch my back, because I never know when someone will attempt to stick a dagger in it."

"Hah! You speak of Hyder Khan—or one of your half-brothers. They are merely jealous that you have managed to achieve so much when you had so little to start with. You are the only man I know to have gained great wealth by dint of his own labor, rather than through birth. It must be due to that British education Santamani arranged for you to have in England. Or else it was the climate while you were there. For so small a country, England seems to breed more than its fair share of rulers and successful men."

" 'Tis true," Alex agreed. "Not about the climate or my education in England, but about Santamani. I owe all my success to the mother of my worst enemy. She would never permit me to waste time in self-pity. While her son was play-ing all sorts of nasty boyhood tricks—slitting the girth on my horse's saddle, hiding cobras in my bedchamber—San-tamani was encouraging me and plotting my future. She's a great lady; I wish there were more like her."

"She has spoiled you for all other women, hasn't she? You've not married again, I see. I have so many wives I can scarcely keep track of them, while you have naught but a single concubine in your entire household. You should marry, Sikander—not just one woman, but several. If you did, you'd be much happier."

"I don't need women for anything but sex, Sayaji. So why should I marry? I already have two children. As for companionship, well, I can find that elsewhere, too."

Alex thought of Miss Whitefield, whose companionship had been such a delight—or challenge—since the day he'd met her. He had Lahri for sex, and Miss Whitefield for intellectual stimulation; what more did a man need? The thought of love—and its accompanying complications— made him uneasy, even frightened. For love, he had Michael and Victoria; that was more than enough.

"If you say you don't need more women in your life, I will try to believe you, but I'm filled with doubts. . . . Ah, well, 'tis too bad you and I cannot enjoy *shikar* together. A man-eating tiger roams the region through which you will soon be traveling. Indeed, I had made preparations to go after him, but then decided I had better not do it—not until my son's health improves. That's why you will be able to leave so soon, by tomorrow, if you wish, because I have all in readiness for a trek into the wilderness."

"I'm sorry you cannot accompany us partway on our journey. If I find that tiger first, I will have to kill him, you know, not leave him for you. I can't refuse such a golden opportunity."

"If you get to him first, it was meant to be, Sikander. Don't deny yourself the pleasure of killing him on my account. He's been blamed for several deaths in the area. When the people discover your presence, they will demand your help. They have been sending messages almost daily—begging for my assistance."

"If the opportunity presents itself, I'll take it. But I won't go looking for it, either. Don't forget: I'm traveling with a *memsahib*. It's dangerous to hunt tiger while she is with me."

"Find an elephant. If she's safe in a *howdah* on the back of an elephant, you needn't worry she'll get in the way."

"A good idea, my friend." Alex concealed a yawn. He could barely keep his eyes open. To his relief, Sayaji also yawned, then sat up straighter.

"Forgive me, Sikander, but I grow weary. I must seek my bed. There's no need for you to do so. Would you care to adjourn to the Love Pavilion? I'll send you a girl from the *zenana* to keep you company. I know just the one to please you; she's an attendant to one of my wives, and I've been saving her in case you one day came to visit. She's well-born, of high enough caste to make an excellent concubine, or even a wife. She's also a beauty and has had some training. Why don't you try her and see if you like her?"

"I don't mind retiring to your Love Pavilion, Sayaji. The air should be cool there, and the sleeping good. But don't send me any maidens tonight. I want to leave early tomorrow. I need to conserve my strength for the journey."

"Ah, Sikander. . . . You do not enjoy yourself enough. You do not play; all you do is work, probably a legacy of your British education. I deeply admire you, but I also pity you. Let me send you the maid; if she doesn't appeal to you, you can send her back again. No harm will be done by looking."

Alex sighed. Sayaji would send her no matter what he said, so he merely nodded, intending to send her back again as soon as she arrived. He had no wish to make love to a stranger, beautiful or not. He'd made love to lots of beautiful strangers in the past, but tonight, the prospect did not entice him.

If he was going to sacrifice sleep for the sake of a woman's company, he'd rather spend an hour with Miss Whitefield, finding out what she thought of the *zenana*. He was sure she'd be bursting with opinions. This would be her first encounter with women who had spent their lives in the seclusion of *purdah*, never baring their faces to the sun or to any man not sanctioned by their fathers or husbands. Sayaji did not allow any of his wives, concubines, female children, or their attendants to be seen in public. *Purdah* was the ultimate protection and defense of womanhood, but Alex suspected that Miss Whitefield would not view it in the same way as Indian men—and most women—did.

He chuckled to himself as he tried to picture her reaction. His lethargy and stupor vanished as he conjured a mental image of Miss Emma Whitefield condemning *purdah* as "a suffocating institution invented by men to keep women under control," or some other such nonsense.

Yes, that's what she would call it; he could almost hear her saying it. He bade Sayaji goodnight and followed the *khansama* to the Love Pavilion, a small, delicate, three-sided structure overlooking the garden and fountain. What would Miss Whitefield think of having a special building just for the pursuit of seduction and sensual pleasure?

Sayaji's pavilion was about the same size as his own, and like his, was draped in sheer netting to keep out night creatures. It had similar sumptuous appointments and erotic wall frescoes, but lacked the view of the jungle and the gurgle of a stream spilling into a pond that Alex had built at Paradise View. The large silken divan looked comfortable; that was all he cared about at the moment.

Sayaji's *khansama* provided him with an embroidered robe to wear and a brass basin and pitcher of water for washing, turned down the single lamp, and then quietly departed, leaving Alex alone in the dimly lit Love Pavilion. Not bothering to remove his trousers, he changed from his shirt into the robe and sat down on the divan to await the arrival of the promised maiden. At least Sayaji was sending a female and not a young boy, as had once happened to him in the house of his degenerate cousin, Hyder Khan.

Hyder Khan had meant it as a deliberate insult. Either he thought Alex's appetites were abnormal, or else, he wanted to make the point that with his impure blood, Alex shouldn't take the chance of impregnating some poor female and producing inferior offspring. At Santamani's request, Alex had consented to visit Hyder Khan and forgive him his past sins—but he had awakened on his first night under his cousin's roof to find a youth of no more than eight or nine years old curled up beside him in bed.

"My master has sent me to entertain you, *Sahib*," the child had said. "I promise you I am clean; I bathed just before I came, and I have even been anointed with oils and rare perfumes. . . . I am my master's favorite, Sahib—and well tutored in the erotic arts."

Thoroughly incensed, Alex had banished the boy and left his cousin's house that same night—never to return. And he hadn't explained his reasons to Santamani. It just wasn't something one told a mother about her son—and Santamani had never forgiven him for refusing to make peace with Hyder Khan. Alex had tried to see her, but she had denied him access, sending only a note with the cryptic message: "Love me, love my son. The bad blood between you must end. If you cannot bear to sleep in Hyder Khan's house, you need not sleep in mine."

Hyder Khan must have told his mother many lies, and Santamani was blind to his true nature. Hyder Khan was cunning, deceitful, jealous, and evil to the core. Alex had spent most of his life keeping one step ahead of him. They played a constant, dangerous game, with Hyder Khan always crouching in the shadows like a stalking tiger, and Alex thwarting his unseen attacks. But why was he thinking of Hyder Khan now? Sayaji would never insult him; Sayaji was only guilty of matchmaking—trying to find him a new wife or concubine, hoping to brighten his life in some small way.

Alex lay down on the divan to await the maiden. He tried to keep his eyes open, but couldn't quite manage it.

"Too much drink," he muttered to himself. It was his last coherent thought.

* * *

Emma stood before the solid-gold framed mirror and stared at her reflection. She saw a tall, slender, and very beautiful stranger garbed in a floating, lime-colored *sari* that made her eyes look as green as the jungle and just as mysterious. Behind her, the circle of women giggled and chattered, murmuring what could only be comments of approval. They had *not* approved of the garments she'd been wearing when she arrived. During the three-hour bathing ritual, Emma's clothes had mysteriously disappeared. The only thing she had managed to keep in her possession had been her oilskin packet. She had staunchly refused to relinquish it, and once again, it was safely secured around her waist beneath the *sari*.

But oh what a difference the new clothes, free-flowing hairstyle, and rigorous, Indian-style beauty regimen had made! Emma could not believe it; she did not look at all like her usual self. She had been transformed into an exotic butterfly like the women surrounding her. With a slight shake of her head, her long, fragrant, shining hair swung around her shoulders like a silken cloud, and with every movement of her body, her *sari* whispered and shimmered, giving her a grace and elegance she had never possessed.

The artful application of cosmetics had made her eyes appear huge and luminous, her skin glow, and her lips resemble luscious roses. She was beautiful. For the first time in her life, she was truly beautiful. She felt so vain and silly standing there admiring herself, but it would have been an insult to the women of the *zenana* if she had *not* admired their handiwork. They were clearly delighted, even the dignified old Begum who had—only moments before—given her one last smile before departing, presumably to seek her bed after the hard work of overseeing Emma's transformation.

One of the remaining women suddenly came up to Emma, lifted her arm in front of Emma's nose, and gently shook it, making music with her bangles. She waited for Emma to do the same. Emma lifted her own arm where eight or ten circlets of gold and inlaid pearl encircled her wrist. She gave them an experimental shake, and the jingle of the bangles made everyone laugh joyously.

Emma couldn't help joining her new-found friends. They all seemed so innocent and childlike, but mischievous, too, especially when the old Begum turned her back. With her disappearance, the women had become noisier and more playful, and Emma greatly regretted her inability to understand their language. . . . But when did they all sleep? It had to be close to midnight—if not later—but the women showed no signs of wanting to seek their pillows and couches. Emma sensed that her presence in the *zenana* was such a novelty that the women couldn't bear to waste a moment of it. At this rate, she would be up all night.

A brass gong sounded in the distance, and the women hurriedly covered their faces with one corner of their *saris*. A moment later, the *khansama* strode into the chamber, uttered a short announcement, and crooked his finger at a young girl, beckoning her to follow him.

The girl could have been no more than twelve or thirteen years of age. She had been sitting on a small gilt stool, but now she leapt to her feet, her eyes huge and stricken. Dropping the corner of her *sari* in her agitation, she began protesting whatever the *khansama* had ordered.

The *khansama* looked shocked, then angry, and finally began to berate her in furious tones. The child burst into tears, loudly sobbing, while the other women gathered about her, making sympathetic noises, patting her shoulder, or otherwise showing their distress and support.

"What is it? What's going on?" Emma already knew no one would understand, but she couldn't help asking the questions. She boldly marched up to the *khansama* and reached out to tap his shoulder to get his attention. When he saw who she was, he shrank away with a horrified expression.

"Sakharam. Go fetch Sakharam. If you won't get him to translate and tell me what's happening, I . . . I swear I'll touch you." Emma reached for the man's immaculate white sleeve, and he all but leapt out of reach. "Sakharam," Emma demanded. "Find Sakharam—or the *Sahib*. I wish to speak to one or both of them and determine for myself exactly what is going on here."

Her tone of authority made all the women stare. They were clearly unaccustomed to giving orders and expecting instant obedience—at least, not where men were involved. But Emma had the blood of generations of aristocrats flowing in her veins, and she had had enough of being polite and accommodating. Had the Begum been there, she might have left the matter to her, but since she was not, Emma felt fully within her rights to demand an explanation of what was happening and why this poor young girl was so upset.

The *khansama* nervously retreated from the chamber and returned a few moments later with a sleepy-eyed Sakharam in tow. At his appearance, all the women turned their backs and did their best to hide not only their faces but every glimpse of skin, hair, hand, and ankle. They stepped into dark shadows and even extinguished several of the nearest lamps. Emma suspected she was violating some strict taboo, but she didn't care. Nothing on earth could have kept her from finding out what was wrong.

"Sakharam, please ask this girl why she is crying. What do they mean to do with her? Why has she been sent for in the middle of the night?"

Sakharam retreated to the corner of the chamber and hastily conferred with the *khansama*. The two men bent their turbaned heads together and whispered like old women sharing tidbits of gossip. At last, Sakharam turned to Emma.

"*Memsahib*, this is not your concern. No harm will come to the girl. Of that, I can assure you."

He regarded her gravely, showing no surprise whatever that she was dressed like the other women. Sakharam certainly had a gift for hiding his emotions.

"You have not answered my question. What is going to happen to her? Why is she so distressed?"

"*Memsahib*, she does not wish to obey an order she has been given."

"Is she a servant? Not a wife or a . . . not a wife?" Emma refused to call that mere child what she might possibly be.

"She is subject to her master's authority," Sakharam replied evasively. "And she does not wish to do what she has been told."

"What exactly has she been told to do?"

"I am not at liberty to say, *Memsahib*. Let me simply suggest that she is disappointed she has not risen as far as she had hoped to rise in this household. Her expectations far exceed her actual worth to her master. That does not mean she will be mistreated in any way. . . . As I said, this does not concern you, *Memsahib*. You must not interfere."

Emma had gone to battle too many times before for one of the world's unfortunates to be nervous about the prospect of *this* paltry conflict. It was familiar territory, and she had somehow always sensed that one day she'd be battling Sakharam. She narrowed her eyes at him. "Wherever the *khansama* is taking her, I will accompany them. Tell him that, if you please."

Sakharam showed no signs of being cowed. He was indeed a worthy opponent. "Of course, *Memsahib*."

Sakharam conferred with the other man whose dignity was far more ruffled than Sakharam's. He shot Emma a look of pure horror, babbled low and worriedly, then violently shook his head, which only increased her determination to protect the young girl from whatever it was she so dreaded.

His face mask-like, Sakharam stepped closer to Emma. "The *khansama* begs you to drop the matter, *Memsahib*. You cannot accompany this girl out of the *zenana*. You must remain here, while she performs her duty. Then she will be returned—unharmed in any way."

"I *will* accompany her. Short of laying hands on me and holding me back, you cannot stop me. And if you dare call a sweeper to restrain me, I shall inform Queen Victoria herself of the outrage—and that is *after* I've complained to Mr. King-ston, the British East India Company, the Viceroy, and the highest officials of the British Army. I will make no end of trouble, Sakharam, so I think you had best step aside—or else tell me where she's going, and why she finds the idea so dis-tasteful."

Sakharam seemed to pale slightly at the threats Emma was tossing about so confidently. "I cannot say why she doesn't want to go, *Memsahib*. I can only say she is foolish to be so fearful. If you *insist* on accompanying her . . ."

"I *do* insist."

"Then we shall all go together. I don't know what else to do. This matter is beyond me." Sakharam said something to the *khansama*, who in turn addressed the girl, who fell to her knees in front of Emma and began kissing the hem of her *sari* in tearful gratitude.

"Tell her to stop that. Such groveling is unnecessary. Let's go where we're going and be done with it. I *should* like to sleep sometime this night, if at all possible."

After the girl had risen and wiped her eyes, both Sakharam and the *khansama* salaamed to Emma, a much more obse-quious bow than the ones she had received thus far. It was annoying; a salaam was usually only performed to someone of great importance, and Emma didn't know if they were doing it to honor her or to mock her.

"After you, *Memsahib*." Sakharam indicated the door with a flourish.

"No, please—after *you*. I don't know where I'm going, remember? So it makes no sense for me to lead the way."

"You speak truly, *Memsahib*. You do *not* know where you're going."

A small sound—a gasp—awoke Alex. Opening one eye, he sought to focus on the source of the intrusion. Four figures stood before him. Blinking, he recognized Sayaji's *khansama* on one side of two *sari*-clad women, and Sakharam on the other. At sight of the women, he lost his temper.

"Damn it, Sakharam, get those females away from me! I told Sayaji I didn't want *one*; now, he sends me *two*. Take them back to the *zenana* at once. Tomorrow, I'll send them sweetmeats in apology, but I can't be bothered with them tonight. My head's throbbing like a bunch of *tabla* drums. If you want to do something, fetch me an herb, not a woman—and certainly not two of the useless creatures."

"But *Sahib*," Sakharam protested, and that was when Alex sensed something was wrong, unusual, or different.

Sakharam would not be addressing him as *Sahib* unless. . . . Alex squinted at the two women in *saris*. One was tiny, a mere child, about the age, height, and size that Indian men liked when they took a concubine—or for that matter, a wife. Sayaji would never consider a servant girl for his own wife, of course, because marriage among Indians of his stature involved ritual, ceremony, and delicate negotiations between two families. But Sayaji would think she was perfect for *him*—a mere *kutcha butcha*, who need not adhere to such stringent customs.

The other woman was tall. Abnormally tall for an Indian. Even in the dim light, he could see that she had brown hair, light skin, and green . . .

Alex bolted upright. "Miss Whitefield? What are you doing here—and . . . and dressed like that?"

Alex indicated her diaphanous green *sari* with a wave of his hand. With the lamp glowing behind her, he could see through her *sari,* and he was utterly dumbfounded. He almost hadn't recognized her—and no wonder. She didn't look like herself. Instead, she was . . . dazzling . . . breathtaking . . . sexy . . . a woman from a man's dreams. Her hair was just the way he had always imagined it—soft, shining, and loose, flowing like water down her back.

Her face was stunning, her figure perfect—delicate, slender, graceful, but lusciously curved in every place that counted. He couldn't take his eyes from her; he devoured her from head to foot . . . and discovered that her beautiful face did not look happy. She was aloof. Anger simmered beneath the aloofness. Actually, she looked furious.

"I am here to defend the virtue of this poor child." Emma nodded toward the young girl who stood beside her. "Did you or did you not send for her? And if you did, for what purpose? She wept when she received the summons, and now, I begin to understand why."

Alex glanced at Sakharam, but his cowardly servant seemed disinclined to come to his rescue. "She insisted upon accompanying the girl, *Sahib*. I regret the intrusion, but I could not persuade her to stay away. So we all came together."

I will beat you with my bare hands. When I get you alone, Sakharam, I will personally flog you.

"There . . . seems to be some misunderstanding here." Alex struggled to think through the fog in his head. "I . . . I was feeling unwell, and Sayaji, our host, wanted to send a woman to minister to me . . . to make me feel better."

"And just how was she supposed to *minister* to you and make you feel better, Mr. Kingston?"

Alex had never realized it was possible to pack so much scorn and suspicion into a single question. He felt desperate and cornered. "Why . . . she was supposed to sing to me. Singing is said to relieve the worst headaches."

"*Sing* to you? I've never heard of such a thing." Miss Whitefield's scorn didn't dissipate; it only increased.

"I told him I didn't want anyone; I preferred being left alone. But . . . the customs . . . the culture. . . . You understand, don't you? He feels responsible for me. I'm his honored guest. Courtesy demands that he try to ease my pain, so he sent someone anyway."

"And this place? What sort of place *is* this? Out here in the darkness, with flowers blooming all around it, set off by itself. . . . It's a perfect location for . . . well, what happens here would not be innocent. I'm quite sure of it."

Alex hoped she didn't choose to examine the paintings on the three walls around them. If she did, she'd be even more sure of it. She'd see more exposed *lingams* . . . and women pleasuring men, and men pleasuring women. It was a Love Pavilion, for God's sake. He prayed she wouldn't glance up at the ceiling, where a particularly lurid painting actually seemed to move when the light hit it just right. Fortunately, the single, dim lamp didn't illuminate too much. If he acted confident and a bit wounded by her suspicions . . . if he seized the offensive . . .

"This is a Sleeping Pavilion," he drawled. "What else did you imagine? Is it possible you have a perverted mind, Miss Whitefield? Did you honestly imagine I would welcome this . . . this *child* . . . into my bed? She's been sent here to sing, and I imagine she's terrified. She's probably never performed for a stranger before . . . Sakharam! Reassure her that I won't bite. Then ask her to sing to me and get it over with. That way, we can all go to bed, and perhaps I can sleep without interruption until morning."

"You expect me to believe that this child was only supposed to *sing* for you?" The snow in the Himalayas couldn't be frostier than her tone. "She could *not* have been that frightened, if all she had to do was sing."

"Did anyone tell her that was all she was *supposed* to do? Perhaps she thought differently, but that's all *I* expected from her. When I saw the two of you, I thought you were both coming to keep me awake with your caterwauling. That's why I was less than cordial in my welcome."

A direct hit! Emma's face told him he had finally made some headway; he *had* complained about the appearance of the women, thank God. While she came to grips with that fact, Sakharam spoke to the girl, her face brightened, and she ceased looking as if she expected Alex to pounce upon her and drag her protesting to his bed.

To the *khansama*, Alex said in Urdu, "What's the matter with her? Does she really fear me so much?"

"Who can divine the minds of females, *Sahib*? I know not if she fears you, but she was most disappointed that she was called to entertain you and not my master. She is only a servant to one of my master's wives, but I think she dreamed of becoming his concubine. If she first lay with you, she could not then go to him. Her chances would be ruined."

She would be contaminated if she lay with me first, and I would be obligated to take her home with me. Sayaji is a sly old fox, albeit he has my best interests at heart. Or what he supposes are my best interests.

"Is that true?" Alex asked the girl directly. She had regained enough composure to shyly peep at him from beneath her long black lashes. "Do you love your master so much?"

"Were I his wife, or even his concubine, I would commit *suttee* for him when he dies."

Alex was impressed. *Suttee* was the self-inflicted suicide of Hindu widows who—despite the act having been banned by the Raj some years ago—still chose to throw themselves on the funeral pyres of their husbands rather than live life without them. With all the tragic emotion of idealistic youth, the girl added in a whisper: "But I am too unworthy, *Sahib*. I see that now. I am naught but a servant girl. I have no value to him—not if he wished to give me to you."

"What are the two of you discussing?" Emma interrupted. "I *must* learn the various languages of this country if I am ever to truly understand what is happening under my nose."

Alex gave her a bland, innocent smile. "We were discussing my musical preferences. Unfortunately, the girl doesn't know any of the songs I would like to hear, so I can safely send her to bed without fear of offending her."

"*Her* bed, back in the *zenana*."

"Of course, *her* bed, Miss Whitefield. What a suspicious mind you have!"

"But what about your headache? What can we do to relieve it while we are here?"

Emma was beginning to look concerned, rather than outraged. Alex pressed his advantage. "Miss Whitefield, if you really want to help me, I'll tell you what you can do, but you won't like it."

"What? I'll do whatever I can. But whatever it is mustn't take too long. It's late, and this poor girl ought to be fast asleep by now. After all, she's only a child."

Only a child who's been trained to please a man in ways you can't begin to imagine, Miss Whitefield. Only a child who's willing to leap into the flames to satisfy her notions of romantic love. Ah, Miss Whitefield, you are the only naive innocent among us.

"Sakharam, Miss Whitefield is right. You and the *khansama* had better take the poor girl back to the *zenana*. Miss Whitefield will be along shortly."

"Wait a moment." Emma jerked her head up so fast that the fine veil skimming her shining brown hair drifted to the marble floor. "Perhaps they shouldn't go just yet. I shouldn't be here alone with you this late."

"Come back in an hour, Sakharam," Alex instructed. "By then, my headache should be gone."

"But . . ." Miss Whitefield raised a slender hand. "First, you'd better tell me what you want me to do."

Do? Miss Whitefield would be amazed at what he wanted her to do. But he could never tell her. Alex hadn't been to English schools for nothing; he had learned to be inventive when necessary. "I am going to lie down on this divan, while you, Miss Whitefield, sit on that three-legged stool which I will first bring over here for you. Then you will gently massage my temples. It's the only way I've ever been able to get my headaches to go away."

Sakharam's brows lifted at this lie; Alex very rarely *had* headaches, and when he did, he simply went to sleep. He didn't have anyone massage his temples.

"Can't Sakharam do that? Oh, I forgot. He can't. If it doesn't violate the caste system, it will wound his dignity. All right, I shall stay and massage your temples. But only for an hour. Is that agreed?"

"It will be so much better than singing to me, Miss Whitefield, and I'll be eternally grateful. While you massage my temples, you can also tell me how you came to be gowned in a *sari*. What happened to your own clothes?"

"I wish I knew, Mr. Kingston. While the women were bathing me, my clothing somehow disappeared. All I managed to retain was the packet with my deed in it."

I should have known you'd still be wearing that.

"You must tell me about it." Alex took Emma's hand to lead her over to the divan. Behind her back, he waved Sakharam, the *khansama*, and the girl away.

"*Two* hours, Sakharam," he called out softly in Urdu as the men retreated. "Make it at least two hours before you return to rescue Miss Whitefield."

Thirteen

Emma was so relieved that Mr. Kingston had allayed her initial suspicions regarding the young girl from the *zenana* that she ignored her misgivings about being alone with him in the Sleeping Pavilion so late at night. As he set the stool near the divan and lay down on the divan itself, she asked him what he had said to Sakharam as the servant was leaving.

"Oh, I just reminded him that he had better return no later than an hour, for I wouldn't want the ladies in the *zenana* to start wondering what happened to you."

"The girl—I don't know her name—will tell them where I am." She began limbering her fingers in anticipation of the massage she had promised.

"Don't worry about what they might think. I'm sure Sakharam will explain why you remained. . . . Put your hands here." He pressed her fingertips to his temples as she bent over him, then closed his eyes with a small sigh. "Mmmmm. You smell delightful, Miss Whitefield. Like a field of wildflowers. I can't seem to pick out just a single scent."

"I don't doubt it. I must have been anointed with hundreds of scents." Hoping she was doing it correctly, Emma slowly stroked his temples in a circular motion. Never having massaged anyone's temples before, she couldn't be certain of the proper procedure.

"Yes, the bath the women gave me was an amazing experience," she continued after a moment. "I never smelled so many fragrances as they used during it. If it wasn't hundreds, it must have been close to it."

"Ah, that feels good. . . . Tell me about your bath. I wish to hear all the fascinating little details."

This struck Emma as an odd—and personal—request. But Mr. Kingston was always surprising her. She never knew what he was going to do or say next. Needing something to take her mind off the intimate aspects of massaging his temples, she launched into a detailed description. "Well, first they lathered my hair using a disgusting green paste. . . . I've no idea what it was called or even what it was made of."

"*Thali*. I know of it; it's made from freshly plucked leaves."

"Thank you. Then they rinsed and washed my hair with some sort of oil and dried it with a thin, porous material."

"Coconut oil. And the thing with which they dried you is called *tortu*."

"Well, after that, they washed my . . . uh, the rest of me . . . and applied an odd sort of powder—"

"*Gram*. Made of chick peas. Did they then remove it with a circular sponge?"

Emma nodded. Mr. Kingston couldn't see it because his eyes were closed, but she had the sudden suspicion he was picturing all this in his mind—and *knew* that she had been lying naked on a divan while the women did these things. "Yes, it was a . . . a fibrous tool they scraped all over me."

"An *incha,* they call it. And after that, they washed you again, didn't they? With warm *Nalpamaravellam* waters, blood-red in color and made by boiling together the bark of forty different trees."

Emma paused in her massaging. "How do you know all this, Mr. Kingston? You are obviously well-acquainted with Indian bathing rituals; do go on and tell *me* what happened next."

"Next, Miss Whitefield?" He opened his eyes and gazed up at her, sending an arrow of sensation straight through her heart. The sensation—not unpleasant, but poignant and piercing—spread to her belly and lower in rippling waves, as if a stone had been dropped into the middle of a still pond, and its impact felt on the shore.

"Why, next, Miss Whitefield, they massaged and oiled your pink and white flesh from head to foot, even the soles of your feet. And it wasn't sensual, because it was only women doing it to you, but it *was* very, very relaxing, and it made you melt inside and wish that a man—some special man—was doing it to you instead."

"Mr. Kingston!" Emma removed her fingers from his temples, but he reached up and captured her hands in his and held tightly, so she could not pull away. He was grinning at her upside down, and she was annoyed with him, but also amazed, because he had described exactly the way she had felt while the women were fussing over her.

"They were careful not to get the oil on your hair, weren't they?" he continued matter-of-factly. "Because the oil most likely contained saffron, which is said to prevent hair growth. Finally, when they were done oiling and massaging even your most intimate places, they dried your hair over fragrant smoke from an iron pot called a *karandi*. It was filled with live coals and all sorts of herbs. Then they brushed your hair with long, slow strokes until it gleamed like the finest silk, and finally, they rubbed a powdered herb down the parting in the middle," he finished smugly. The smugness dissolved into a particularly engaging, little-boy grin.

Emma stared down at him, feeling as if he had entrapped her heart along with her wrists. His seductive voice and imposing presence had captured her mind, heart, and body. "Yes," she whispered. "But why did they rub the herb down the part in my hair? I could see no sense to that."

He rose on one elbow and turned on his side to face her, somehow managing to keep hold of her hands while he did so. "To prevent colds. I don't know if it works, but *they* think it does. What do you think, Miss Whitefield?"

She lowered her lashes to hide her tempestuous emotions. His nearness and the caressing quality of his voice made her tremble, quiver, and quake inside. "I don't know what to think. I never in my life had a bath like that—and I never wore garments like these. They feel so soft and wicked against my skin. Why, it's almost like wearing nothing at all."

She blushed when she realized what she had said—and to Mr. Kingston, of all people!

"Do you know how beautiful you are in a *sari*, Emma? Do you have any idea how seductive and sensual you become with your hair down and your feminine charms displayed to their fullest advantage?"

Emma. He called me Emma. And he is dishing up honeyed compliments that couldn't possibly be true—but oh, how I wish they were!

Her cheeks flamed, and she could scarcely breathe. "If silken garments and cosmetics do indeed make me beautiful, I assure you it is just an illusion, Mr. Kingston. The women of the *zenana* know how to make anyone beautiful."

"Why are you so self-critical? Your skin, hair, and eyes are all beautiful; they need no special enhancement, Emma. Even your face is beautiful—your features—and your hands . . ." He pressed her palms to his lips and kissed them. "The *sari* and the cosmetics simply call attention to what has been there all along. Just as the garments you normally wear conceal your natural beauty, these reveal it."

"You are flattering me, Mr. Kingston. Everything you're spouting is just empty flattery."

"Say my name," he commanded. "Say it, Emma. I want to hear it from your lips. I want to drink it from your mouth."

He reached up and drew her head down as if he meant to kiss her. "Say it, sweet Emma."

Emma felt bewitched; she had lost control. Anything at all might happen between them, and she might allow it. "Alex," she whispered, savoring the sound of his name. "Alexander. Alexander Kingston."

"No." He shook his head. "Sikander. Say my real name, the one my mother called me."

Was it from his mother he learned about the bathing rituals of the zenana? Or has he been bathed by laughing, chattering women in his manhood, perhaps even in his own zenana? How does he know the rituals so well?

When she hesitated a moment too long, he drew back to study her face, disappointment darkening his blue eyes. "Does my Indian name disgust you? Do *I* disgust you? Can you not say Sikander?"

The hurt in his tone tore at her heart. He had openly admitted he was part Indian; now, he was asking if she could accept it. He wanted some sign from her—some proof that she would not reject him because of his mixed blood. She thought of what Rosie's friends would say, what Rosie herself would say. . . . This man was forbidden fruit. He was an outcast from two different cultures. She ought not to trust him, to want him. Yet how could she refuse to say his name, when she *did* want him so very much?

"Sikander. . . . My dear Sikander. You could *never* disgust me."

He pulled her down and kissed her—a tender, burning kiss that flooded her heart with bittersweet yearning. She tasted brandy in his kiss, but the flavor only served to intoxicate her, as if she had drunk deeply from the bottle, not merely from his mouth. Her hair swirled around them, creating a cocoon of privacy as he rose from the divan, drew her from the stool, and took her into his arms.

Standing now, he molded his body to hers, his robe falling open so that she was pressed against his bare torso. Without the obstruction of traditional English undergarments, Emma felt naked against him; she fancied she could detect each contour of muscle and protrusion of bone. . . . But it was no bone that extended from his lower regions. She knew what *that* was—his *lingam*. The part of him that made him a man.

The thought of it—and the reality of his desire—made her

knees buckle. She leaned against him to steady herself. Lifting her off her feet, he held her firmly imprisoned against his blatant masculinity. "Emma. Sweet, sweet Emma . . ."

His kisses grew more ardent. His hands cupped her bottom, so that she felt the pressure of his *lingam* like a white-hot sword in the juncture of her thighs. She opened her legs slightly, and he rubbed himself between them, creating an intimate friction—and a dampness—that both shocked and excited her. When she opened her mouth to breathe between kisses, he teased her tongue with his tongue. Then he set her down and cupped her breast in his palm, while he nibbled along her neck. "Emma, Emma. . . . Let me make love to you. Let me show you how delicious it can be between a man and woman."

"I. . . . *Mr. Kingston!*" she gasped as he rolled her nipple between his fingers, producing a powerful sensation that reverberated throughout her untried, virginal body.

"Sikander," he gently corrected. "From now on, you must call me Sikander. Mr. Kingston belongs to that *other* woman—the one who wears her hair skimmed back into a tight little ball, and dresses in plain, dark colors, and hides her beauty under an ugly *topi*. When we are like this, when you are all fragrant hair and silken skin and shimmering eyes to match your *sari*, then you must call me Sikander and say it with a little soft moan of desire . . . telling me you want me, my sweet Emma, as I want you. I want to drive inside you, to touch the core of you . . . to plunge in and out of your body until you scream with the pleasure of it. . . . But first, I want to undress you and caress you all over, and taste you, teach you, tease you, love you. . . . Tell me you want it, too, Emma. Say 'I want you, Sikander . . . I need you. . . .' "

He lay her down upon the divan and stretched out on top of her—taking his weight with his elbows, gently fitting his body to hers. Emma's flesh prickled; she was simultaneously hot and cold. She inhaled great gulps of air and wanted nothing more than to arch against him and draw him downward . . . but some small part of her still resisted. It was all too new—too fantastic. She could not believe this was really happening, that she was behaving like this, dressed like this, pretending to be something or someone she was not.

She had never said "I want you" or "I *need* you," to any man, and she couldn't seem to formulate the words now. She *did* want him, she yearned for his touch, his kiss, and the hard, hot invasion of his *lingam* . . . but she couldn't say it. *I want you, Sikander.* It was just too difficult, too foreign. Years of repression, of submerging her femininity, of being alone, of hardening her heart to her innermost needs, of convincing herself that she *didn't* need any man, and that she *wasn't* vulnerable . . . all stood in her way like a solid stone wall. She needed time . . . more time.

Opening her eyes, she glanced up at the ceiling—and something died inside her. Right there above her, depicted in rich, sensuous colors, was a scene of such shocking intimacy that it reminded her of what she had witnessed in that pagan temple of *lingam* worship.

A naked man and woman lay sprawled together on their sides, arms and legs intertwined, his face pressed to her genitals, hers pressed to his. As she watched in total disbelief and a growing sense of betrayal, the figures appeared to *move.* . . . And what they were doing to each other passed all the bounds of decency as she knew it . . .

"Get off me!" Emma shrieked, pushing and shoving at Sikander's shoulders.

He drew back, startled. "What is it, Emma? What's wrong?"

"You said this was a . . . a Sleeping Pavilion! But you lied. *You lied to me!* That girl must have been sent to you for purposes other than singing. And this place—it's just what I thought it was! A place for disgusting, vile, depraved—"

"Emma, stop." Sikander held her down with the weight

of his body and grabbed her hands to keep them still. "What happens here is *not* disgusting, vile, and depraved. But you are right; I lied to you. I told you this was a Sleeping Pavilion, when in reality it's a Love Pavilion. It's where my friend, Sayaji, can be private with one of his wives or concubines. It's a place for pleasure and intimacy and exploring the delights of the flesh. But that's not why I came here. I came to sleep. I ordered Sakharam to take you and the girl away. Do you remember, Emma? . . . Emma, listen to me. Do you remember what I said when you first came into this chamber?"

He gave her a little shake, but her heart was pounding almost too loudly for her to hear him clearly. "Don't call me Emma! I am not Emma to you; I'm Miss Whitefield. And you are—and always will be—Mr. Kingston."

"You are not just Emma—nor Miss Whitefield—nor *Memsahib*. You're a flesh and blood woman, a sensuous, passionate being made to love and be loved by a man. What is so terrible about that? And what is so shocking about the tender intimacy depicted in the painting on the ceiling? Or by the paintings on the walls?"

"On the walls?" Emma struggled even harder. "Do you mean to say the walls, too, are filled with paintings of naked men and women doing all sorts of wicked things to each other?"

With grim determination, he held her down. *"Yes*. Yes, Emma, only they aren't doing wicked things. They are just behaving as men and women lost to passion are sometimes inspired to behave. You, too, could feel like that and be inspired to behave that way."

"No, no, I couldn't!" she sobbed, but she knew in her heart that she *could*. Mr. Kingston could entice her into doing those wicked, wonderful things; he could sweep away all her inhibitions . . . and that was what terrified her. *He could make me lose control. He could awaken feelings in me I have*

*never allowed myself to feel. And what then? What would
happen after that? What would become of me?*

If she gave her heart, mind, body, soul, and will into this
man's keeping, he would trample on them and destroy them.
She knew it with the same certainty that she knew the sun
would rise in the morning. He was from one world—she,
from another. They could have no future together. To suc-
cumb to passion was to invite great pain. . . . Pain was inevitable, and she didn't think she could endure it. How could
she go back to being the woman she had been before, once
she had become someone else with Mr. Kingston? Would
the new Emma Whitefield survive? Could she dare raise her
hopes and expectations so high?

No, it was better to deny herself at the beginning—to resist
her own weak nature. To cloak herself in the comfortable,
familiar attitudes and platitudes she had always known, and
fight the *un*known. Fight the person she might really be underneath, the woman she secretly *wanted* to be.

"Get off me, Mr. Kingston." No longer struggling, she lay
stiff as a board beneath him.

"Emma, you don't know what you are refusing. I would
never hurt you, I promise. I know how to make it good for
you—not just good, but exquisite. Earthshaking. Trust me,
Emma."

"Trust you, Mr. Kingston? Oh, I trust you could make me
behave like a wanton—make me want to give you my body
and . . . and act like the woman in that painting up there . . .
but no, I don't *trust* you, Mr. Kingston. Mere passion isn't
enough for me; I want more from a man than just his *lingam*.
I want so much more . . ."

She couldn't read his expression, but she thought she detected a flash of comprehension, compassion—and fear—in
his shadowed blue eyes. He knew what she was talking about,
and he *knew* he could never give it to her.

He levered himself off her, pulled the two halves of his
robe together, and tied it most efficiently. "Exactly what

more do you want, Miss Whitefield? Declarations of affection? Promises of eternal happiness? A guarantee that nothing will ever go wrong between us? Vows to bind us together until death do us part? . . . Why do women always make more of sex than a man ever intended? I am attracted to you; you are attracted to me. Why can't we simply enjoy that attraction without making promises we can never keep? . . . You were willing to flout convention by insisting on becoming a nanny to my children. Are you honestly prepared to become a permanent outcast from society by becoming my wife? By marrying a man who'd never be accepted into the homes of your dearest friends?"

Emma sat up, clutching her *sari* close around her. "Are you proposing, Mr. Kingston?"

He fixed her with a steely-eyed glare. "Would you say yes if I were?"

"I . . . I don't know. I would have to think about it."

"So would I. We . . . are very different, Miss Whitefield. Our differences go deeper than just the color of our skin. I, for example, find nothing offensive about the paintings on these walls and ceilings. They were done to put lovers in the proper frame of mind—the proper mood, if you will—to explore the delights of intimacy in all its charming variety. Nothing a man does with his wife or concubine can be considered ugly, at least not to the Indian mentality. Sayaji has chosen to celebrate that intimacy here in this chamber, and I find it stimulating, rather than offensive."

"Well, I find the very idea of concubines, Love Pavilions, plural wives, and sending young women to entertain men who are not their husbands offensive. If you had taken that young girl to your bed tonight—and gotten her with child— what would have become of her?"

"If I had done that, which I didn't, I would have provided for her until the end of her life. She would have lacked nothing. Society here in India is never so cruel as in England where a man—particularly a member of the gentry—can beget any number of by-blows on maids and serving wenches, without feeling the need to acknowledge them, much less care for their mothers indefinitely."

Was he telling her that he had his own *zenana*, his own concubines? Was that what *she* would be to him—a mere mistress? And if he did marry her, would she have to live with the knowledge—and the presence—of all the other women with whom he had ever been intimate? Would *their* children play with her children? She couldn't imagine living like that.

"I think we have discussed this enough for one night, Mr. Kingston. Please call Sakharam to accompany me back to the *zenana*."

Behind her, she heard a slight movement. "I am already here, *Memsahib*."

Dear God, how much had he heard? How much had he witnessed?

She lifted her chin. "Aside from the licentiousness, another thing I cannot abide about India is the complete lack of privacy. Servants hanging on your every word and spying upon you when you least expect it."

"If you dislike it so much, then leave. At the risk of repeating myself, I suggest you go back to Calcutta—and from there, return to England. In England, you can live the rest of your life trussed up in corsets and ridiculous social customs that violate the laws of man and nature. Those customs create females like you—women unable to enjoy their own sexuality, or to give and receive love . . ."

"I shan't ever go back!"

"Why not?"

"Because . . . because I just can't. All I have in this world is the inheritance my mother left me. . . . So I shall remain here with you—but only until I find Wildwood. And when I do . . . when I finally find Wildwood . . ."

"You will do what, Miss Whitefield?"

"I'll fight to regain control of it and make it profitable.

I'll fashion a new life for myself. Women can have ambitions, too, Mr. Kingston. We can be every bit as ruthless and determined as men. I'll do exactly as you have done—I'll *take* what I want from life, and damn anyone who stands in my way! Including you and your nosy, intrusive head servant!"

To her great surprise, Mr. Kingston didn't laugh. He didn't scoff. He didn't even point out how difficult, even impossible, it would be for a woman alone in India to achieve her dreams. He merely stood there watching her, thinking his own thoughts but not revealing them.

At last, he said, "What will you do if I refuse to take you farther? If I insist upon leaving you here in Allahabad?"

"I will go on by myself. I will hire a guide and continue the journey alone."

"To Paradise View? But you would be unwelcome there. We'd be severing our agreement here and now."

"To *Wildwood*. I would go first to the Indian officials in Bhopal; someone there will speak English, and someone will know the location of my land. I'll knock on every door, harass every official, I'll—"

"Enough, Miss Whitefield." Alex sighed deeply. " 'Tis very late, and you are overwrought. I sincerely regret what happened here tonight. It ought never to have happened. Let us pretend it didn't. We are two reasonable, sensible adults; let us put tonight behind us and continue exactly as we were. I still need a nanny for my children, and you still need a safe way to pursue *your* goals. Tomorrow, we'll set out cross-country for Paradise View. Sayaji will lend us everything we need. All I want from you is your assurance that you can ride as well as you claim. . . . Since it appears we cannot be lovers, can we not at least be friends? . . . Emma?"

It was on the tip of her tongue to insist that he call her Miss Whitefield. She would never again call him Sikander, or even Alex. Besides being too informal, Alex didn't fit him, not the way Sikander did. But Sikander implied an intimacy she was determined to avoid.

"If you wish . . . Mr. Kingston. And yes, I can ride as well as I claim. Tomorrow, I will prove it to you. No matter what pace you set, you will hear no complaints from me."

He smiled—a grim, humorless smile. "Then goodnight, Emma. I'll see you in the morning. . . . Oh, be sure to wear your usual attire. A *sari* isn't too practical on horseback."

"I will. Sleep well, Mr. Kingston—if you can avoid looking at the ceiling and allowing your imagination to run amok."

Emma knew she ought not to have added that last parting jab, but she couldn't resist. It *was* a form of debauchery to decorate one's walls with obscene art—and if Paradise View had something similar, she herself would take a pail of whitewash and paint it over. She'd do it for the sake of her two charges, Michael and Victoria, if nothing else.

She turned to follow Sakharam out of the pavilion when Alex suddenly called after her. "Emma? . . . Don't judge *all* Indian houses by what you have found here. We don't all have multiple wives and concubines, you know."

She was dying to ask him what he did have, but wasn't sure she wanted to find out. She couldn't deal with any more tonight. Couldn't bear the thought that she had almost given herself to a man who might have two, four, or even a couple dozen women in his *zenana* just waiting at his beck and call.

"In case you're wondering, *I* don't have multiple wives and concubines," he added softly.

Swept with an acute sense of relief, Emma almost spun around and ran back to hug him. *Keep walking, Emma. Don't look back. If you do, you're well and truly lost.*

Fourteen

They left Allahabad the following morning mounted on the finest horses Emma had yet seen in India. She was particularly pleased with her mare, a sleek, leggy animal with a shiny black coat that reminded her of the mare she had left behind in England. This one seemed to have a less explosive temperament, but she was Morgana's equal in conformation, if not in size.

Slightly smaller, the mare possessed an unusually long mane and a tail that swept the ground; she also had a white snip on her nose, instead of the star Morgana had sported on her forehead. Emma silently dubbed her Morgana II and eagerly rode ahead of Mr. Kingston, Sakharam, and the half-dozen *syces* and *pattah-wallahs*, whose job it was to see to their comfort and safety on the journey and to make certain the horses made the trip in good order.

Glancing back once or twice, Emma noted that all of the servants Mr. Kingston had selected to accompany them could ride quite well, though none looked as much at home on a horse as Mr. Kingston himself. She wished *she* could have ridden astride, instead of sidesaddle, but she supposed she was fortunate a sidesaddle had been located, or she might not have been permitted to ride at all.

Her heavy, cumbersome riding habit made her skin itch, and as usual, her *topi* felt as if it weighed as much as a blacksmith's andiron. But no matter how hot or uncomfortable she became, she was determined to enjoy this adventure. Just being on a good horse again was sheer joy, and she felt she *had* to canter on ahead instead of keeping to the sedate pace of the others. Morgana II seemed to feel the same way, for she pulled on Emma's hands, attempting to break into a gallop.

Emma let her out a bit as they crossed a level flat plain outside of Allahabad. Ahead of them and off to her left, steep blue-green hills crouched in the morning mist. Soon, they would be in the jungle where cantering—and galloping—would be unwise. Emma had gone but a short distance when she heard hoofbeats pounding behind her.

"Emma! . . . Miss Whitefield! Slow down, you little twit. Do you intend to lead the way for the entire journey? You already made a wrong turn back there at that track we passed."

Mr. Kingston came abreast of her on his handsome gray gelding, and Emma quickly brought her mare down to a walk. "I'm sorry. I didn't see a track back there. I thought we were going in this direction for a time."

"Well, we aren't. We must angle more to the south. Don't go off by yourself anymore. It's too dangerous."

His concern was comforting, but it rankled that he had called her a twit. "What can be dangerous about it? We're not in the jungle yet. All I see is high grass."

"That's what makes it dangerous. You can't tell what's lurking there." Lowering his voice, he assumed a less combative tone. "If your horse should startle, trust its instincts. Your mare will let you know if something's out there—providing she senses it in time. If you're galloping, that's hard for her to do."

Somewhat mollified, Emma patted her mare's glossy neck as they returned to the others and corrected their course. "She's a splendid animal. If you bred her, you should be very proud of the result, Mr. Kingston."

"I am. Don't you want to know her name? I'm surprised you haven't asked."

"I don't need to ask; I've given her one of my own. While I am riding her, she will be called Morgana."

"Morgana. I like it. It suits her better than her hard-to-pronounce Indian name. Perhaps I shall give my gelding a different name, too—an easy-to-say English one."

"Such as?" Emma stole a furtive, sideways glance at him. Today, surprisingly, he was the proper *Sahib* in buff-colored hunting attire all buttoned up neat and tidy, complete with *topi* and Hessian boots.

He smiled engagingly. "How about Jack?"

"Oh, he's much too elegant for so simple a name. And he's powerful-looking, too. Plain Jack isn't quite right."

"Then I shall call him Captain Jack. How does that sound?"

"It will do." Emma suddenly realized he was doing it *again*—charming her with only the slightest effort. Putting her at ease. Behaving as if nothing had happened between them last night . . . but it had. She was back to being a plain, prim, and proper sparrow in her drab, unattractive feathers, but she could never forget that for a few brief hours she had been a glorious swan . . . and Mr. Kingston had desired her and wanted to make love to her. That changed everything.

She could think of nothing more to say to him after that, and they rode along silently for the rest of the day . . . and that night, Sakharam erected three tents—one for her, one for Mr. Kingston, and one for the rest of the men. They dined on white linen, drank from crystal, and could scarcely find a word to say to each other. Yet all during the meal, Mr. Kingston watched her . . . simply watched her . . . as if searching her face and form for the woman he had nearly seduced the night before.

Bone-weary, saddle-sore, and achy all over, Emma lay awake a long time on her netting-draped pallet in her tiny tent, where Mr. Kingston's crimson carpet provided the only note of luxury and color. The journey was going to be twice as difficult if they could not find a way to resume the casual ease they had managed to adopt earlier in the trip. She resolved to get past this awkwardness and not allow it to spoil everything. He had probably only had too much to drink last night; she *had* tasted brandy on his lips. Now he was regretting—even as she was—everything they had said and done. Today it had been easier to recall that he *wasn't* responsible for the paintings on the walls and ceiling of Sayaji Singh's pavilion, and he *had* protested the appearance of two females in the chamber. Maybe the girl really had been meant to sing for him, regardless of *her* interpretations.

While Mr. Kingston's behavior had not been entirely blameless, Emma had held him accountable for more than was actually fair. He wasn't responsible for the sins of all India—but only for his own sins, of which there were more than enough. Once before, she had promised herself to reserve judgment and withhold criticism—and not to fall in love with the man!—until they reached Paradise View. She must stand by that decision, come what may in the meantime.

Emma finally managed to get some sleep, and the next several days passed without any confrontations or terribly embarrassing moments. The single exception was the time when she loosened her mare's girth during a rest period, and then remounted without remembering to tighten it. Morgana shied at some fowl rising up in a flap of wings, and the saddle slipped sideways, leaving Emma hanging on for dear life, clutching Morgana's mane, and screaming for help.

She would have suffered a nasty spill if Mr. Kingston hadn't once again rescued her. "Always check your girth before you mount, Emma," was all he said, but Emma stewed over the incident for most of the day. Checking her girth was something any competent rider ought to know without being told—and she *did* know it. She had just forgotten. Mr. Kingston had that effect on her; he made her forget all sorts of important things.

On the fourth day out of Allahabad, they came upon a village at the edge of a jungle. The natives poured out of their huts to watch them approach, and when they had set up camp for the night near a small stream cutting through the area, a delegation from the village came to visit. Emma could tell from the modest attire of the village officials that they were a simple people, living quiet lives, barely subsisting on what they were able to grow or harvest from the jungle. They treated Mr. Kingston as if he were a god and besieged him to resolve disputes among neighbors, find answers to village problems, and rid them of a certain local menace.

Emma found out about the menace only after the delegation had departed, following a lengthy visit that lasted until after dark and necessitated the villagers returning to the village by torchlight. Mr. Kingston had already told her that he could not leave the area until he had held court the following day, and now, he added, he must also solve one other minor "problem" before they could be on their way again.

"What must you do?" Emma asked, peeling a banana she intended to eat as part of her supper.

They were seated on stools beside a merrily blazing cookfire which provided illumination and deterred the pesky mosquitoes and other night insects. The tents were up, and Emma was eagerly anticipating the moment when she could retire, peel off her sticky clothing, and sponge away the day's grit and perspiration.

"Oh, nothing much actually. A tiger's been causing problems hereabout, and I have to kill him."

Emma dropped the half-peeled fruit in the dirt. "What tiger? What problems?"

"I told you we'd be engaging in a bit of *shikar* as we traveled. The tiger has mauled and killed several people in the area, and as the only *sahib* to appear here in months, I must dispatch the beast. It's my duty."

"But why you? Isn't there some local Indian official who could do it?"

"Not really. Only members of the Raj or Indians of royal blood can hunt tiger. Lesser men aren't worthy enough. They don't possess the proper weapons or aren't good enough shots. Hunting in India is much the same as in England. It's a sport for the rich and titled, not the common man."

"But we don't have tigers in England! Won't it be dangerous—going after a tiger?"

Mr. Kingston nodded. "Yes, but it must be done, especially when the tiger is a confirmed man-eater. Once he's tasted human flesh—and discovered what easy prey men are—he must be killed. The first *sahib* or high-born Indian who's available for the job is expected to assume it."

"But . . . but . . ." Emma desperately tried to think of reasons why Mr. Kingston should be exempted from this onerous responsibility. In Calcutta, she had heard nasty stories about the dangers of hunting tiger; it was a favorite topic at dinner parties. Women sometimes participated in the sport, in company with their husbands. Hunting was considered a perfectly respectable pastime for women, providing they had men along to protect them.

Emma had enjoyed the stories, but she had no wish to get within mauling distance of a tiger—and she didn't want Mr. Kingston to be endangered, either. Considering all that had happened on this journey, he must have exhausted his quota of good luck by now. Deliberately hunting a tiger was pushing things a bit far.

"You'll be perfectly safe, Emma. I told the villagers they must bring me elephants if I am to dispatch the tiger. Elephants and beaters. The beaters will flush the tiger from its hiding place, and I will then shoot it. You can watch the whole thing from the safety of a *howdah*, the carrier an elephant wears on its back."

"But . . . but what about Morgana and the other horses? Will they be safe while we are off riding elephants? And how does one ride an elephant? I know nothing about controlling one."

"You won't have to worry about controlling it; its handler or *mahout* will do that. We use elephants at Paradise View to harvest our timber. In most circumstances, they are quite docile and obedient; I think you'll find the hunt an interesting experience."

"Did you *know* about this before we got here?"

Emma wasn't surprised when he nodded. Just as she had thought, Mr. Kingston had given a great deal of thought to the matter and was actually looking forward to it. "Sayaji told me I might be asked to kill the tiger when we passed this way. He had intended to see to it himself, but fortunately, I got here first."

"Fortunately? I think it's *un*fortunate. I wish you would leave this particular task to someone else." But Emma knew Mr. Kingston would never do that; he accepted it as his *karma* that he personally face up to whatever challenges, disasters, or accidents he encountered.

"Women sometimes hunt tiger, too, you know," he continued in a blasé manner. "Even Indian women. I know of an old Maharanee who kept the strictest *purdah* at home, but when she accompanied her husband on the hunt, was as eager as he to bag a big cat."

"I know about *memsahibs* doing it, but Indian women? That is truly amazing. And I suppose you are telling me this only to whet my appetite for riding an elephant and watching you shoot some poor beast who may or may not be the one responsible for the deaths and maulings."

"No, actually I was hoping to persuade you to remain in camp while I hunt the tiger."

"Absolutely not. If you are going to endanger yourself, I will accompany you. And I should like my own rifle, in case you need my help."

Mr. Kingston expelled a huge mocking sigh. "Somehow I knew you would say that. You will have your rifle, Emma, but you must promise not to do anything stupid. If I should somehow miss the tiger, Sakharam will get it. He's an excellent shot—and anyway, I'm not the one who'll suffer if I should miss. It will be some poor beater, one of the villagers, most likely. If I only wound the tiger or miss him altogether, he'll try to break through the circle of beaters and escape. That's when men get hurt."

Emma's heart constricted with fear. This, too, she had heard about—a beater whose body had been slashed to ribbons by a few swipes of a tiger's wicked claws. "When are we going to do this? And how will we know how to find the tiger?"

"Bait. The villagers will set out bait for him. There are several ways to hunt a tiger: by following the drag of the bait during the daytime when the tiger is sleeping, then putting up a cot above the kill and waiting for the tiger to return to it in the late afternoon or early evening. Another is to study the ground, work out where the tiger will lay up during the day, and using beaters and elephants, drive him into a ravine or someplace where hunters on raised platforms are waiting to kill him. I myself once used a monkey tied to a string; I put him near the bait, and when he began to chatter and issue warning noises, I knew the tiger had come."

"Is that what you are going to do this time?"

"No." Mr. Kingston smiled, clearly relishing the thought of the careful plans he had already made. "No, this time we will let him take the bait the night before, but early the next morning, at dawn, we'll use beaters to surround him. We ourselves will be on elephants, slowly working in toward the bait, in hopes of catching the tiger still on or near it."

"That sounds so . . . risky."

"Trust me, Emma. It's the safest method. I killed my first tiger in just this fashion, from the back of an elephant, when I was only a boy. I wasn't supposed to take the shot—my cousin was, but I took it anyway . . ."

"Do you mean . . . Sayaji?"

"No, no, not Sayaji. Another, who never forgave me for it. I was younger than he by two years, only ten at the time . . ."

"Only ten!"

"Yes, and he was twelve. Having lost that opportunity, he had to wait another two years before he bagged his first tiger, and it wasn't as big as mine had been. Mine was a ten footer, while his was only eight." Mr. Kingston gazed off into space, remembering. "Perhaps that's why Hyder Khan has always . . ." He stopped, laughed sheepishly, and apologized. "Forgive me for boring you with tales from my childhood."

"I'm not bored! Do go on." *Please go on*, Emma silently begged. She wanted him to tell her everything about his childhood, to explain all the mysteries, to share his deepest, darkest secrets, to . . .

"No, that's enough. I've rambled on far too long as it is. Tomorrow night the villagers will set out the bait, and on the morning after, we'll shoot the tiger. It will be very simple, easy, and safe. You'll see."

"I hope so." Emma's skin prickled with cold foreboding, banishing the heat that lingered even after the sun had gone.

The next day proved to be long and boring; Mr. Kingston spent all his time hearing cases for the villagers. He did not even break for tiffin. If Emma could have understood what was being said, she might have enjoyed it, but as it was, by mid-afternoon, she had lost interest and decided to go exploring.

Saddling Morgana, she rode off by herself before anyone spotted her. Sakharam would have gone directly to Mr. Kingston to protest, and any of the other servants would have gone to Sakharam. Emma wasn't worried, because she didn't plan to go too far anyway—just to explore the village and ride along the perimeter of the jungle where no beast would be foolish enough to attack in broad daylight, even a maneating tiger. If a tiger did appear, Morgana would carry her to safety.

As Emma passed through a grove of coconut palms, Morgana's hooves clattered on stone. Looking down, Emma saw a pitted stone walkway, overgrown with weeds. It led off into the jungle, in the direction away from the village. Intrigued by this evidence of advanced civilization, Emma followed the path, all the while hoping and indeed expecting to find an old temple or mosque at the end of it.

At this time of day, the jungle was a lush, green, silent place—seemingly devoid of the teeming wildlife that inhabited the area around it. During the past four days, Emma had glimpsed the large deer called *sambur*, sloths hanging in the trees, partridge, quail, snipe, monkeys, cranes, and once, the spotted coat of what might have been a cheetah or leopard.

But today, this close to the village, there was no life whatsoever. It was absolutely silent and eerily green. Only the brilliant splash of an occasional flower or beam of sunlight alleviated the gloom. Emma grew uneasy when she had ridden for a few moments on the stone path and still had not discovered its destination. She was about to rein Morgana around and give up, when she suddenly spotted a patch of bright light; sunshine was pouring down through the trees a short distance ahead.

Urging Morgana into a trot, she soon arrived at a clearing which was fast losing the battle of survival to encroaching vegetation. Vines and creepers had wrapped themselves around the ruins of what did appear to be an ancient temple. The architecture was a fascinating blend of Hindu and Muslim styles, with stone archways, intricate carvings, and something that might have been a turret, except it had toppled. One whole side of the structure had collapsed, but the other side was intact, and Emma longed to peek inside.

Perched on her sidesaddle, she debated the wisdom of dismounting. She had no weapons with her—no pistol or rifle. Mr. Kingston had not yet given her one, and she was alone, except for Morgana. Any female with a lick of sense would have ridden back to camp and returned at a later time with an armed escort, Emma decided. But she wasn't the usual female.

"If I were some fluttering young miss afraid of dark shadows, I wouldn't be here in the first place, now would I, Morgana?" She swung her skirts to one side and dismounted. "We won't be here long enough to get into trouble, will we, my girl?" She rubbed the mare's velvety-soft nose, then led her to a twisted, gnarled tree with low-hanging branches. Lest the mare pull back and injure her mouth on the bit, Emma did not tie her securely, but merely looped the reins over a branch.

"You don't suppose there are any tigers about, do you?" She patted the mare's neck. Morgana wasn't wary or nervous. Her serenity fueled Emma's courage and eased her fears.

"If there were, you would have told me by now, wouldn't you, girl? Still, I suppose I'm a twit for taking such risks. . . . Then again, this close to the village, no self-respecting tiger would dare show his face. Stay here and munch a few leaves, Morgana, and I will be right back—as soon as I've peeked inside to make sure there aren't any idols with precious jewels embedded in their navels."

Emma laughed softly to herself; it wasn't unheard of for treasures to be found in old ruins, especially temples. At the very least, she hoped to find clues to the building's former inhabitants. Giving the mare one last pat of affection, she picked up her skirts, and keeping a close watch for snakes and other wildlife, headed for the ruins.

It was nearly evening by the time Alex realized how late it was getting. Two of the village officials dressed in *dhotis* and turbans had brought a young goat to be used as bait for the tiger. They called a halt to the proceedings so they might inquire as to where the bait should be staked out.

"Where has the tiger been spotted most recently?" Alex asked. The men responded that it had several times been seen near some old ruins in the jungle, approximately halfway between the *sahib*'s camp and the village.

"Then we'll take it there," he told the white-bearded old men. "Wait a moment until I get my rifle. We don't want to go into the jungle without it at this time of day—especially not with a tasty young goat in tow."

Alex summoned Sakharam and several servants to accompany him and carry extra weapons just in case they were needed. It was always wise to have more than one loaded rifle at hand; if he had to discharge a gun suddenly, he liked to have another ready and waiting—not that he expected to encounter the tiger. That would be too easy. Tigers did not normally make instant targets of themselves. It was far more likely that he might make the sudden acquaintance of a band of wild pigs or *pariah* dogs or even a python.

The little group set out at a brisk pace, but the village elders found it hard to keep up. The goat wasn't happy, either. It loudly protested, which was just what Alex wanted it to do when he left it tied at the ruins. Its pathetic bleating would call the tiger even from a far distance.

"Sakharam, take the goat. Gentlemen, can you give us directions from here? We'll get there faster if we leave you behind and continue on alone."

"Oh, 'tis not hard to find, *Sahib*," the senior official insisted. "Just follow the stone path. It will take you there quickly. Do you see? It begins here."

They were standing in the middle of a coconut grove, an unlikely place for a stone pathway, but Alex discovered there was one—and it led straight into the jungle. To his surprise, he also saw something else: the mark of a perfect hoofprint. He was reasonably certain there were no horses in the village, and neither he nor anyone else in his group had ever ridden through this grove.

"Sakharam . . ." He motioned for his friend to join him. Sakharam had hold of the rope around the noisy goat's neck, and he had to fight to bring him over to Alex.

"Sakharam, where is Miss Whitefield? Did you see her at camp before you left there to bring me my rifle?"

"I thought the *memsahib* was with you, Sikander. Listening to the cases you were deciding."

"She was with me earlier, but then she left. I assumed she had returned to camp."

"I did not see her there, unless she was inside her tent."

Alex wished he had more time to study the hoofprints, but if he delayed any longer, it would be dark by the time they reached the ruins. The men had brought along torches for the return trip to camp; nevertheless, he wanted to get there in time to scout the place and determine where the tiger would be most likely to hole up and sleep after it had eaten. It might sleep on the same premises, which would be ideal for his purposes. In the morning, he could return by elephant and quickly kill the beast, using the beaters to keep it from running past him into the jungle. He could possibly trap the animal against a wall or inside a portion of the structure.

Too bad he had no opium; he had always considered it unsporting to sprinkle the bait with opium—or force the drug down the throat of the bait—but it was an effective measure for slowing a tiger and inhibiting its escape. In this situation, where the tiger was particularly dangerous—and he had Miss Whitefield to worry about—he would have used the opium without a qualm.

He just hoped Emma hadn't been her usual independent-minded self and gone off alone on horseback. She could get lost or even thrown from the horse and herself become bait for a tiger. Well, he had warned her, and she couldn't be that foolish, could she? Yes, she could, his inner voice told him. After all, this was the same woman who had jumped into a river to save his life when she couldn't swim and was terrified of crocodiles.

"Sakharam, I'm going to take my rifle, run ahead, and scout the ruins while it's still light. You and the others come as soon as you can—or I should say as soon as you can persuade that little goat to embrace his destiny."

Sakharam was tugging one way, and the goat the other. "We shall have to throw him down, tie him, and carry him, *Sahib*. Otherwise, we will never get there."

"Fine, just do it." Hoisting his rifle over his shoulder, Alex set out at a lope, but he hadn't gotten very far into the jungle when he heard someone galloping toward him. Hoofbeats clattered on the stone, and he had just enough time to jump off the stone walkway when a black, riderless horse, mane and tail streaming, burst out of the vegetation and thundered past him. The horse was Morgana, and hanging off her side was the sidesaddle—but no Emma.

"Emma!" Alex shouted her name before he realized what he was doing, then he tore down the stone path in the direction from which Morgana had come.

Fifteen

Fool. Twit. Stupid, stupid female.

Emma exhausted herself thinking of names she ought to be called. This was the most ridiculous thing she had ever done, the most irresponsible, the most foolhardy. Why hadn't she had enough sense to remain on her horse and keep out of the jungle, or stay back at camp in the first place and sit twiddling her thumbs, if necessary, rather than plunge herself into this dangerous situation?

She wasn't bored now; she was in one fine mess. Something had spooked Morgana. The mare had pulled back on the tree limb, dislodged her reins, and taken off as if a tiger were at her heels. Now, it was getting dark, and Emma had a long, lonely walk back to camp. Her face and hands were already puffy from mosquito bites, and she didn't have even a parasol to jab at a tiger or panther if one should appear.

Stupid, stupid. Such recklessness might be more excusable—or explainable—if the ruins had contained something wonderful to justify the risks she had taken. If it ever had contained any treasures, they had long since been removed. Inside, there had been nothing but rubble and cracked walls. Some long ago upheaval of the earth must have pulled the building down, and the passage of time had done the rest.

Well, she wasn't going to dissolve into a puddle of helpless womanhood just because she had made a mistake. The first order of the day—or night—was to protect herself against the whining insects appearing in clouds with the setting of the sun. In the center courtyard of the ruin was a broken fountain, where she recalled seeing a trickle of water. Emma made her way there, formed a paste from the water and a bit of dry earth, and smeared it on her exposed skin. The mud had a cooling effect and afforded some relief. The next thing she did was locate a walking stick among the scattered limbs and brush littering the courtyard. With the stick, she intended to tap her way along the path in the darkness and alert snakes and other creatures to her presence before she got there.

Thus armed and prepared, knowing that darkness was only moments away and moonrise wouldn't be for another hour, she turned to begin her walk back to camp in the fading twilight . . . and that was when she saw him: an enormous tiger, a truly magnificent beast, standing motionless at the edge of the jungle—and watching her with glinting green eyes.

Alex had a stitch in his side from running. He was out of breath, and his lungs were burning. Soon, it would be completely dark, and he wouldn't be able to see the path. He had to keep going—had to find Emma. He had ceased being angry with her and now was merely terrified. Thinking of her lost or hurt, alone in the jungle at night and in the same vicinity as a man-eating tiger, made him frantic with worry.

He wanted to destroy her deed, but he didn't want her dead. No, he most definitely didn't want that. If anything happened to. . . . Damn! He blamed himself for this. He never should have ignored her for so many hours. Knowing how headstrong she was—and how naive—he should have realized what would happen. Trouble seemed to follow Miss Emma Whitefield. Indeed, she went looking for it.

Gasping for breath, he paused long enough to readjust the rifle slung on his shoulder—and heard the full-throated roar of a furious, frustrated tiger.

His flesh prickled. His hair stood on end. Was he too late? . . . But he couldn't be. The tiger wouldn't be roaring if he had already brought down his prey. Alex would be hearing different sounds—the rending, tearing, grunting, satisfied noises of a feline slaking its hunger.

Readying his rifle for a shot, Alex headed in the direction of that angry roar. Slipping from tree to tree, straining to see through the gathering darkness, he finally arrived at the ruins. What he saw made his blood churn, and his heart seem to stop beating.

The tiger had trapped Emma atop the wall. Somehow, she had managed to climb the crumbling barrier, and there she stood, poised on top, with the tiger pacing below, bellowing his displeasure that she was out of reach. Why he hadn't yet gotten her, Alex didn't know—for it was a simple leap to the top of the wall for a tiger of his size.

He was very nearly the biggest tiger Alex had ever seen, a superb specimen, measuring over ten feet from the tip of his nose to the tip of his tail. His thick striped coat glimmered in the darkness, reflecting all the available light. Knowing he had but a single shot to kill the beast, Alex took careful aim. But before he could shoot, the tiger leapt—a crippled, pitiful effort that revealed the source of his great frustration. Something was wrong with his left hind leg. It wouldn't support his great weight or give him the impetus to climb the wall. His claws scrabbled for purchase. Since he couldn't reach the top, he fell back down again, roaring in anguish.

In the breathless moment before he tried again, Alex recalled the best hunting advice he had ever received. It had come from his uncle, Hyder Khan's father. "Don't lose your nerve. Take a steady aim, wait for him to present a broadside, and then let fly at the heart."

Alex waited until he got a chance at a broadside, then slowly pulled the trigger. The discharge was deafening. The tiger leapt into the air and slammed against the wall. Emma, who had been silent all this time, screamed. In the distance, Alex could hear the bleating of the terrified goat.

It was all over in seconds. With a few protesting twitches of its tail, the tiger died. Holding one hand over her mouth, Emma made inarticulate sobbing sounds. She didn't see Alex; her wide-eyed gaze was fastened upon the tiger, and her face said she didn't believe he was dead.

"Emma . . ." Alex stepped out of the dark shadows and slowly approached the fallen tiger. "It's all right. He's dead. You can come down now."

She hiccupped and took her hand from her mouth. She looked down at him, and then at the wall, as if surprised to find herself standing on it. "How . . . how shall I get down?"

"How did you get up there?"

She shook her head. "I . . . I don't know. I honestly don't know."

"Sit," he said. "Sit on the edge, and then push yourself off. I'll catch you."

Like a frightened but trusting child, she obeyed. Dropping the rifle, he caught her as she fell. Immediately, she flung her arms around him and burst into tears. "Oh, Sikander! I was so frightened."

She didn't notice she had called him Sikander. But *he* noticed. Her agonized cry shafted his heart like a spear. He gathered her closer, feeling the rapid thump-thump of her heart to the depths of his being.

"It's all right. You're safe now. The tiger's dead, poor fellow. Some inept hunter must have wounded him and let him get away. He had to become a man-eater to stay alive."

As if she hadn't heard him, she suddenly wailed. "How could I have been so stupid? Why am I always doing things like this?"

"What do you mean—like this? Just how many times have you taunted crippled tigers from the top of a wall?"

"Sikander, why have I always been different? If someone says no, I must always say yes. If someone says up, I must insist upon down. Tell me not to do a thing, and I must run off and do it. I am a misfit. Yes, that's what I am—*a misfit!* I've been one all my life. Even when I know I shouldn't, I seem *driven* to confront, challenge, disobey, rebel . . ." Clinging to him, she sobbed against his neck.

"Emma, Emma . . ." He held her while she wept. He patted her back and tried to comfort her, but her words reverberated in his soul. They were two of a kind. All his life, he had done the exact same thing. He knew precisely what she was talking about. And he knew her hurt, her pain, her sense of being ostracized, alone, and cut off from everyone else. Neither of them belonged anywhere. They did not fit the mold; they didn't behave as the world said they should.

Emma rebelled by riding off alone into the jungle or jumping into rivers when common sense said she shouldn't. He rebelled in his own dark ways. Brave, beautiful, foolish Emma. She was his soul mate—the woman he had been seeking all his life. She was also his nemesis, the woman who could bring him down, the one who could destroy the world he had so carefully built for himself. In some ways, he was more afraid of her than he could ever be of a tiger.

"Sikander! *Sahib!*" Sakharam burst into the clearing brandishing a rifle. Several men followed, carrying the protesting goat who was trussed, tied, and hanging upside down from a tree limb. "We heard the shot. Are you all right? . . . Ah, but that is a huge tiger. Worthy of a viceroy or maharajah."

His arm still around Emma, Alex joined Sakharam in examining the beast he had just killed. "As usual, you are too late, my friend. You missed my big moment. I think you do it on purpose; as I recall, the last time I hunted tiger, you only appeared after the animal was dead."

"I came as quickly as I could. I am still out of breath from running. The *memsahib*—she escaped injury?"

Emma had her face hidden against Alex's chest. She showed no inclination to study the tiger up close. Alex could still feel her shaking. "Emma? Are you all right now?"

She lifted her head but would not look at the carcass. Her face was streaked with dirt and tears, her hair disheveled. She swiped at her nose self-consciously. "Quite all right, thank you. Except for my pride. Forgive my hysterics, will you? I ought to be horse-whipped, not comforted."

"First things first. A shoulder to cry on—and *then* we horse-whip you."

She gave him a watery smile that didn't last long enough to suit him. "What about Morgana? Did you see her?"

"I imagine she's safely back at camp by now, telling the other horses what a terrible experience she's suffered."

"One of the men caught her, *Sahib*," Sakharam gravely informed him. "She was unharmed."

"Thank goodness." Emma breathed a sigh of relief. "I can't believe I endangered a fine horse like that."

"Hush," Alex scolded. "Stop berating yourself. Leave that to me. I promise you I can do a better job of it any day of the week."

He succeeded in winning another reluctant smile from her. "What will you do with the dead tiger?" She eyed it warily.

"Make a carpet out of him to put in your chamber at Paradise View," Alex suggested.

Emma shuddered. "Please, no. Don't put him anywhere near me. I never want to see a tiger—dead or alive—at such close range again."

"Then I shall put him in *my* chamber—or my son's. He would be delighted. Come along now, Emma. It's time we got you back to camp."

She nodded. "I agree. I wish to check on Morgana and satisfy myself that she suffered no ill effects."

As the first torches were lit, Emma gave a cry of dismay. "But why is that poor goat tied up like that? He's bleating as if the end of his life were imminent."

"It almost was," Alex told her. "That goat is the bait. We had intended to stake him out at this very spot for the tiger to find."

"But . . . but . . ."

"Yes, he would have been killed, Emma. So you see, your foolishness saved his life. Good came out of a moment of silliness."

Emma stared at him, her eyes very bright in her mud-smeared face. "Then I'm *glad* I did it. It's a cruel thing to tie up an innocent goat, frightened and bleating, for the tiger to find. The goat has feelings, the same as we do. It would have suffered greatly; it's suffering now."

"Untie the goat and set it free," Alex ordered, glad that Emma had never witnessed the favorite sport of many a young Indian ruler, not only in the old days before the Raj, but now.

A goat would be hung by its hind legs from a scaffold, and the young horseman would unsheathe his sword, ride at a gallop, and attempt to slice the struggling creature in two with one stroke. Before Alex himself had learned how to do it properly, he had many times botched the job in his youth, trying to prove that he was as skilled as his cousins. Sometimes, it had taken an hour or more for the goat to die—which had always made Alex feel terrible.

When it was untied, the goat tottered about on unsteady legs before it ran maaa-ing into the jungle, where some other carnivore would likely get it. But at least Emma would not have to witness its demise. "Back to camp everyone," Alex shouted in Urdu. "But first, skin that tiger."

Taking Emma's arm, he began steering her down the stone path.

That night Emma dreamed. In her dream, she was pursued by a tiger—a ravenous beast who looked exactly like the one she had barely escaped. She managed to climb a crumbling wall, which the tiger repeatedly threw himself against. And each time, he came a little closer to scrambling on top. He stretched a little more, leapt a little higher, and roared a little louder.

She gazed into his great cavernous jaws and heard herself bleating like a doomed and frightened goat. She glimpsed death in his eyes and smelled it on his foul breath. She awoke drenched with perspiration, her nightdress soaked, her body trembling. Would she ever get a good night's sleep again? She was sure she would dream the same dream over and over, night after night, a fit punishment for succumbing to a foolish impulse.

The next day, with the tiger skin securely fastened on the back of a skittish packhorse, along with Emma's portmanteau, they resumed their journey. They entered the depths of the steamy jungle, whose wild, rampant beauty almost made Emma forget her fear. She thought she ought to hate the jungle, as a place where tigers and panthers roamed, but instead, in her usual perverse way, she loved it—so long as there were no more encounters with savage beasts.

The jungle made her feel small and insignificant, but at the same time, it heightened her appreciation for all life and growing things. It was as if nature had gone a little crazy in conceiving the jungle; everything was larger than normal. Trees and flowers were bigger, the heat and humidity worse, insects exaggerated in size. Logs often turned out to be huge pythons, butterflies came in the size of parrots, and parrots trailed enough feathers to be mistaken for peacocks. It was unnerving—but wonderful. And Mr. Kingston—Sikander, as she now thought of him—seemed to relish her discovery and enjoyment of it.

Wherever the jungle terrain allowed, they galloped madly along the trail which was often barely a trail at all. Leaning low over Morgana's neck, Emma joyously jumped the mare over obstacles that any sane rider would have avoided or at least dismounted to check first for safety. But she wasn't sane—and neither was Sikander. They seemed to have been bitten by the same bug, to be suffering from the same malady.

They were drunk on the beauty of the jungle and the exhilaration of being alive in it. If it weren't for the dampness and heat which sapped their energies long before noon, they would have spent every waking moment in the saddle.

As it was, they were only able to travel from first light until about midday, and then they had to rest and give the horses a chance to graze. Around tea-time, or what would have been tea-time if they were observing it, they would remount and continue farther, splashing through streams, trotting along the rims of steep gorges and hilly precipices, and going around villages and coconut, indigo, and mango plantations, traveling as far and as fast as they could before darkness fell.

Emma ceased asking what was in the cookpot. After she once found Sakharam skinning some sort of reptile and finely chopping it, she decided she no longer wanted to know. Sikander, Sakharam, and several of the other servants took turns shooting whatever game appeared. When none appeared, they made do without it. There was always something in the pot, and Sakharam and his assistant made it taste delicious, though some things he himself—and some of the bearers—refused to eat because they violated religious precepts.

A week after the tiger incident, they crossed a river—a dampening experience as the horses had to swim for it. Closing her eyes in sudden nervousness, Emma clung to Morgana's long mane and prayed that the crocodiles sunning themselves on the river bank had just eaten and weren't hungry for horse—or human—flesh.

It was late in the afternoon by the time they safely emerged from the water. Alex located a camping site in a grassy clearing a short distance from the river where a large, twisted old banyan tree spread its branches in welcome. Tents were hastily erected, fires lit, and everyone retired to change their soaked clothing.

Unfortunately, most of their belongings were also soaked.

They had spent a long time in the river; water had seeped into closed compartments and carefully wrapped bundles. Emma discovered that she hadn't a single dry item of apparel. Even her precious crimson carpet was waterlogged. She finally wrung out a few things as best she could and dressed in them, knowing that in the heat they would soon dry. It was no different than being caught in a rain shower, and she would have heartily welcomed a rain shower. There weren't any showers now, and the jungle was beginning to look dry and parched. A heavy dew still greeted them in the early mornings, but as it grew hotter, Emma expected that it, too, would disappear.

Wringing out her hair, Emma combed and brushed it, then turned her attention to the precious waterproof packet containing her deed. Slitting the seams, she pulled out the document. It was damp, but still legible. Smoothing it out, she spread it on a brass tray to dry, and then went out to join the others for the evening meal.

When Sakharam served it, he whispered something in Alex's ear, alerting Emma to the possibility that things weren't all they should be.

"What's wrong?" she demanded as soon as the servant had turned his back.

"Nothing much. Don't worry. There's naught to fear."

Emma didn't believe that for a minute; she could tell he was shielding her from some upsetting revelation. Several *pattah-wallahs* were studying the ground not far away. One was even on his hands and knees peering at the soil.

"Please tell me what's going on. If there's danger, I want to know it."

Alex set down his unfinished meal and regarded her silently for a moment. "All right. I'll tell you. There are tracks criss-crossing this area—tiger tracks. They look recent, and one of the men spotted fresh spoor under this very tree when he was setting up the tents."

"Do you mean we are camping on a . . . a . . ."

"A favorite haunt for tigers. Yes, I think we are. In my

eagerness to change out of my wet trousers, I didn't notice the pug marks. That was careless of me. They were made by more than one animal; some tracks are large and some small. It could be a female and her young, or a male and female, or . . . what have you."

Emma set down her own uneaten dinner. "But what shall we do? It will soon be dark."

"We'll keep several small fires burning through the night. The fires will help dry out our clothing and bedding. You see? Sakharam is already hanging up wet things on the branches."

As Emma watched, Sakharam flung her crimson carpet over a branch to dry. "The fires will keep the tigers away?"

"The tigers, leopards, or panthers—whichever they are. The pug marks are too unclear to be certain. I imagine they like this tree because the branches are low-hanging, easily climbed, and afford them nice, hidden perches from which to view other animals going down to the river to drink. They can lie here, twitching their tails and planning the dinner menu."

Emma shuddered. "I wish we could change our campsite. If the tigers like this tree so much, they can damn well have it."

Alex arched a brow. "Profanity, Emma? I didn't think a lady indulged in such."

"A lady doesn't. But there are certain occasions when nothing less will do."

Emma picked up her plate, but her appetite had fled. She toyed with her food, her attention on the bearer departing her tent with an armful of wet garments. When he began hanging up her underthings for all the world to see, she leapt to her feet. "Tell him to put those back in my tent at once!"

Alex burst out laughing. "Leave him be, Emma. He's just doing his job."

Emma rounded on him. "But . . . but those are my unmentionables! He shouldn't be handling them, much less spreading them on tree limbs like flags."

Alex motioned for her to be seated again. "Emma, will you never learn? This is India, not England. Your unmentionables have to be dried, or they'll rot. And you can't tell Sumair not to handle your things when he considers it his sacred duty to guard and protect them with his very life."

"Sumair? That's his name?"

Alex nodded. "He's extremely trustworthy. That's why Sakharam assigned him the task of looking after your belongings."

"He had better be trustworthy." Resuming her seat, Emma thought of her deed, spread out to dry in her tent, and her jewels which were still in the packet. "If anything of mine comes up missing, I'll know whom to blame."

"Yes, you will. But Sumair will never steal from you. He might beat your clothes to death, but he won't take them."

Emma winced as she watched the man do just that—take a few swipes at a fragile petticoat with a fallen tree limb, to beat the water out of it. "Do I really have to sit here and watch him do that?"

"You do unless you wish to bring him dishonor and disgrace. He's a proud man, with good reason. He was specially selected from hundreds of others to be one of my personal *pattah-wallahs.*"

"Then I suppose I must sacrifice my pride to spare his." Sighing, Emma averted her eyes from the display of every stitch of clothing she had brought along but wasn't currently wearing.

"Relax. Don't fret about silly things when there are more serious ones to worry about."

"Such as tigers," Emma mournfully agreed.

"Don't worry about them, either. I'll have Sakharam pitch my tent right alongside yours tonight, and I'll sleep with my rifle in easy reach. If you hear a tiger prowling the camp, I'll be there before he can get to you."

"Thank you," Emma murmured, relieved to know he would be so close.

They finished their meal and as soon as darkness fell, retired to their tents. Beside the tray where her deed lay drying, Emma found the usual thoughtful appointments: her ewer of water and a basin for washing. Since she had already had a thorough dunking that day, she decided to save it until morning. The night promised to be hot and sticky; come morning, she'd welcome the prospect of sponging herself clean.

The last thing she did before seeking her pallet beneath the wet mosquito netting was make certain her remaining gems were still in her packet. They were, and she lay down to sleep with less anxiety than she had been feeling earlier. Mr. Kingston—Sikander—was right next door. Nothing would happen to her during the night. She put out the lamp, and the fire outside made one wall of her tent glow a soft orange color. That, too, was comforting, and she climbed under the netting and stretched out on her pallet with a deep sigh of weariness.

The next thing she knew she was standing on the crumbling wall again, watching a huge tiger pace up and down below her. Occasionally, he stopped pacing and leapt at the wall, only to fall back with a roar of fury. That hair-raising roar finally woke her, and Emma opened her eyes to utter blackness. No warm orange glow lit the wall of her tent . . . and the roaring she had heard in her dream didn't stop. She heard it still—low and muffled, but a roar just the same. Somewhere nearby, a tiger was "talking," and in the distance, another was answering.

The sounds weren't the angry, frustrated complaints of the tiger who had tried to attack her, but they were still unnerving. The growls and whines made her flesh prickle. She began to tremble and perspire. What had happened to the fires that were supposed to keep the tigers away? Had everyone fallen asleep? What if the tigers came closer?

Emma sat up. She couldn't stay in her tent any longer and

listen to carnivores holding a conversation; maybe they were discussing how best to sneak into camp and eat all of the inhabitants. She had to awaken Sikander. Had to be near him. To hear his voice and his soft, mocking laugh. To see the humor in his eyes as he teased her about her fears.

Emma scrambled off her pallet, nearly entangling herself in the mosquito netting. Muttering under her breath, she broke free and hurried out of her tent. The fires had not completely died, but they had burned low and needed replenishing. No one stood guard. Apparently, everyone was sleeping. There was just enough light to make out the entrance to Sikander's tent.

Emma suddenly realized that she wasn't dressed; only a thin nightdress covered her nakedness, and she was barefoot besides. Her hair hung heavy, loose, and damp upon her neck. She wasn't properly attired for a late-night visit.

Hesitating in the tiny space between her tent and Sikander's, Emma debated her choices. Perhaps she should go back. Maybe she ought to heap more wood on the fires herself. Or get dressed first. Or start screaming and awaken everyone, then demand to know why someone wasn't standing guard and feeding the fires.

A low growl from the other side of one of the dying blazes galvanized her into action. She darted inside Mr. Kingston's tent. As if he, too, had heard something, he snapped upright on his pallet. "Who's there?" he hoarsely inquired. "Identify yourself, or the next thing you'll feel is a bullet in your gut. I don't like intruders coming uninvited into my tent at night."

"It's me—Emma." Emma strained to see him in the darkness.

"Emma?" The hostility faded from his voice. "What's wrong? Why are you here?"

"I . . . I had a nightmare," Emma confessed in a rush. "And the fires are out, and tigers are calling to each other."

"Come here." His tone was soft and cajoling. "Come on.

Don't be bashful. You're safe in here, but if you don't join me under this netting, the mosquitoes will carry you away."

"Oh, no! I couldn't do that. I just wanted to tell you about the fires and the tigers. That's all. I'm going back to my own tent now."

"Wait a minute. I'll light a lamp."

Emma paused. She wanted to stay; she honestly did. That was the problem. She wanted to stay too much. "Don't bother with the lamp. I'm going. Goodnight, Mr. Kingston."

"I like it much better when you call me Sikander." His voice was a throaty purr, as seductive as a kiss.

"Goodnight then . . . Sikander."

"Emma, wait, damn it. At least let me pull on my trousers, and I'll take you back to your tent."

"No, no . . . that's not necessary. Really."

He's not wearing trousers. But then what *was* he wearing?

Emma spun around and retreated from the tent. So eager was she to escape—to flee her own rash impulses and desires—that she forgot to listen for the tigers on her way out. Quickly, she scrambled inside her own tent, crawled under the netting, and lay down on her pallet, her heart pounding.

A moment later, an orange glow once again lit the wall, illuminating the interior. Another few moments, and a tall figure pushed through the partially closed flap. It was Sikander, naked from the waist up, tousle-haired, and so beautiful in his masculine fashion that she could barely breathe properly.

"I came to sit with you," he said softly. "Until you sleep. Perhaps my presence will banish your nightmares. I've heard you call out, Emma . . . when you dream about the tiger."

"I . . . I call out?" She was mortified that he should have witnessed such weakness on her part. She wanted to be strong—*had* always been strong, until fear began to chip away her confidence.

He knelt down beside her pallet. "Yes, you call out. You

say 'No! No, get back,' and sometimes, you whimper. Let me stay with you awhile, Emma, just until you sleep again."

"But . . . but I don't hear the tigers anymore. Does that mean they're gone?"

"Probably. In any case, the fires I just refueled will keep them away. That doesn't mean you won't dream." He lifted the netting and slid his large body onto the pallet alongside her.

Emma opened her mouth to protest, then closed it without uttering a word. She didn't know if she had gone speechless or was simply succumbing to needs too strong to deny. Sikander lay on his side and draped one arm across her bosom, where her heart was thundering.

Despite the heat and the trickle of perspiration between her breasts, Emma welcomed his nearness. The sultry night was full of unseen dangers, and she was afraid. She yearned to be comforted, held, soothed, and calmed. It felt so right that he should be here, and it felt wonderful when he began to nuzzle her cheek and move his arm ever so gently, lightly stroking her breasts through her thin nightgown.

Sixteen

Alex lay beside Emma and tried to restrain himself, but he couldn't resist her sweetness and innocence. She had come to him in the night, wearing her prim, little-girl sleeping gown, her hair all tumbled and curling in wisps around those lovely high cheekbones, her eyes wide and frightened. What was a man to do?

He was only human, after all, and she had teased, taunted, and tormented him long enough. He had to have her—to taste her sweetness, overcome her shyness, and awaken the passion he sometimes glimpsed in her eyes. It had gone on long enough: this unbearable tension between them, this simmering attraction, this obstruction and denial of what was obviously meant to be.

He turned her face to his, and she gazed up at him, her eyes luminous as emeralds in the soft orange light—her expression a study in conflicting emotions. She wanted this as much as he did, but she was wary and afraid. She didn't know what to expect. She trusted him, and yet . . . she didn't. She reminded him of a fawn beguiled by the sway of a cobra; she wanted to run away, but she couldn't. She was too curious and fascinated.

He bent his head and tasted the nectar of her lips. He kissed her gently at first, careful not to push her too far too fast, though he longed to drink greedily and hungrily of her sweetness. Fighting for control, he inhaled her faint, tantalizing, womanly smell, which only hinted of the mysterious fragrance he had first noticed during one of their earliest encounters.

Her hair was still damp, and so was the long white garment she wore. In his culture, white was the color of death and mourning; it was worn chiefly for funerals. In hers, it symbolized virginity and purity, and was worn by brides. Some might say those were stunning differences, but to him, they didn't conflict with each other. If a man did not awaken a woman's passion, did not teach her sensual delights and the joys of the flesh, would she be fully alive? He rather thought she would be a mere shadow of her potential self—not dead, but not totally alive, either.

He could not let Emma's precious, prickly femininity go to waste. But in order to persuade her to relinquish her white gown, he must lead her slowly down the path of sensuality and pleasure. . . . So he kissed her with gentleness and restraint, lingering on her lips before moving to the rest of her face. He feathered kisses along her temples and across her eyelids, stroked her silken hair, murmured endearments, and then returned to kissing her mouth until he knew she shared his intoxication.

Lifting her hands, she entwined her fingers in his hair and returned his kisses with ardent enthusiasm. Sliding his tongue into her mouth, he deepened the intimacy, and she did not resist. When he drew back for a moment to quickly kick off his boots and trousers and cover himself with a sheet, a soft whimper of protest escaped her. He had to remind himself that he mustn't fall upon her and frighten her with his growing impatience.

She lay still and trembling as he unfastened her bodice and reached inside to touch her breast. "Sikander . . ." she moaned, as he caressed and stroked her tender flesh.

Baring her breast, he took the swollen tip in his mouth. More than ready for the intimacy, she arched against him as he suckled her, her unabashed response causing an almost painful reaction in his own body.

Slowly. Slowly. Don't frighten her with your lust.

He fought an inward battle to keep from ripping her gown straight down the center and baring her entire body to his ravenous ministrations. Only his respect for Emma's inexperience enabled him to restrain himself when he wanted her as he had never wanted any woman. She held him in thrall as no other woman had ever done.

Always before, he had sought to pleasure his partner, but his own need for release had sometimes rushed him to culmination before his partner was entirely ready. Still, he prided himself on being a considerate lover and always tried to make up for his greediness later. But this time . . . this time, he wanted everything to be perfect, because the woman in his arms was Emma—and it was her first time.

His own satisfaction could wait. He wouldn't enjoy it half so much if *she* did not enjoy it, too—and he was well aware of the pain a first joining could cause a woman. So he lingered at her breasts a long time, until she was moaning and thrashing with need. Then—and only then—did he lift her gown and caress the core of her femininity.

She gasped when he touched her there, and he wanted nothing so much as to kiss those nether lips and stroke her with his tongue, not just his fingers. But she was still too green and untried for such wanton intimacies—as amply demonstrated by her shock at the painting on the ceiling of Sayaji's Love Pavilion. He dared not forget that.

As if to remind him, she clenched her legs together when his fingers probed too deeply, ascertaining her readiness for the act of lovemaking. Yet, her sudden shyness could not hide the fact that she was hot and wet, and he had to hold himself absolutely still for a moment, or he risked losing his seed in his excitement.

"Emma," he whispered against her hair. "Relax. Open for me. I promise I will not hurt you."

"But Sikander. . . . wait."

He kept his hand between her satin thighs and waited, praying she did not mean to refuse him now that things had progressed this far. Then he felt her hand searching for him— seeking him out—boldly exploring his body. When she found him, he stiffened, cried out, and nearly disgraced himself then and there. Gritting his teeth, he imagined himself diving into cold water, the chill of it quelling his arousal. "I . . . I'm sorry. Am I hurting you by holding you like this?"

How like Emma to ask questions at a time like this! But then, hadn't he always known she would? Would she now want to discuss the mating habits of all the species in creation?

"No, Emma. It doesn't hurt—not hurt, as it is generally defined. But if you continue doing that—no, don't stroke me!"

Sweat popped out on his brow. Alex grabbed her hand and held it away from him.

"But . . . don't you like it when I touch you?"

"I like it. *I like it too damn much!*"

"You do?" She giggled softly, a small, utterly charming manifestation of feminine glee and triumph. "Then I must touch you again. You cannot be the only one to be doing all the touching, Sikander."

She wrested her hand from his and reached for his right nipple. "What happens when I touch you here?"

He almost leapt off the pallet. "Emma, stop!" he hissed. "I am the leader in this. Not you. I thought you knew nothing about arousal and the joys of the flesh."

"I don't," she whispered, wide-eyed and not the least contrite. "That's why I'm trying to learn. If we are going to do this, I wish to do it right."

He could not believe it. It was more than he had dared hope to receive from a repressed, spinsterish female like Emma. At the same time, he was shocked. This woman not only aroused him, but also surprised him as no other woman ever had. She caught him unawares. Even women trained to be concubines usually had to be encouraged to employ their skills. They were afraid of offending—doing or saying the wrong thing. Not Emma. She seized the initiative and plunged boldly ahead, *demanding* to be told what pleased and excited him.

"Emma, whatever I do to you can safely be said to be pleasing to me. However, I am . . . I am particularly sensitive. Once you start touching me, you yourself had better be ready for our joining, because I can't guarantee I can hold back."

"Hold back? But why should you, if we both want . . . it . . . so badly?" She wound her arms around his neck and pulled him over on top of her. "I am ready, Sikander. In the morning, I will probably hate myself for this, but tonight I am ready. Will you please relieve me of my damn proper virginity?"

Her words brought a smile to his lips, but he hesitated to believe them. "Are you certain, my wild sweet Emma? Had I known you felt this way, I would have relieved you of your damn virginity long before this."

"If a tiger were to eat me later tonight, I would hate to die knowing that I . . . I never knew a man's possession, particularly *your* possession, Sikander. Tomorrow will be soon enough for regrets; tonight, I . . . I only want to be . . . to be one with you."

"No tigers are going to eat you, Emma. I won't allow it. But if you are truly going to regret this in the morning, we had better make it worth the suffering and self-recrimination, hadn't we?"

She nodded. "I'm so glad you are calling me Emma again," she murmured. "And you will be my Sikander. My beautiful, handsome, desirable Sikander, who has turned me into a woman I scarcely know."

"But *I* know this woman," he responded, placing his hand on her lower abdomen. "Oh, yes, I know her . . . and she's not at all what she's been pretending to be all her life up until this moment."

"What is she then? Tell me what I am, what you have made me become," she begged on a sigh. "Better yet, show me."

"Yes," he promised. "I'll show you, my little wanton."

Edging to one side, he slid his hand between her thighs again, and this time, she did not resist. She allowed him to do as he willed—and he made her ready. Made her wiggle and squirm and undulate her hips beneath his hand. Made her sigh, moan, whimper, and beg. Made her frantically reach for him and refuse to let go until he gave her what she wanted.

When he finally entered her, she gave a small gasp of surprise and pain. "Emma?" His own breath came in great heaving gasps. "Emma, are you all right?"

In answer, she placed the palms of her hands on his hips and wordlessly urged him to follow the dictates of his own wants and needs. He tried his best to be gentle, to give her body a chance to adjust to his invasion, but she arched eagerly against him.

"Don't . . . hold back," she begged. "Take me, Sikander. Make me yours. Make me a woman."

It was all the encouragement he needed. His release came quickly and explosively, surpassing anything he had yet experienced with a woman. He felt as if he were pouring not only his seed but all he was and ever would be into her; she was absorbing him totally. Wringing him dry. Taking all he had to give and then giving it all back to him.

The pleasure was rapturous—the satisfaction beyond his wildest fantasies. And it was still more than that; as they lay together afterwards—sleepy, sated, and bathed in well-being—he knew he had not had enough of her. He would never have enough . . . and that, too, was a feeling he had never felt before. She had truly become a part of him and he a part of her. He rejoiced in his masculine triumph—but beneath the triumph ran a vein of fear. What did it all mean?

He could not imagine letting her go after this. He wanted her with him always, in his bed every night or he in hers. He wanted to teach her every sexual delight a man and woman could share. He'd fight anything or anyone who sought to take her away. She belonged to him now, in the most primitive, elemental way that a man can possess a woman; he had just never realized that in possessing Emma, he would become possessed. . . . Would she stay with him? What would she think of Paradise View? Would she be satisfied to remain there forever and if so, in what capacity?

He thought of Lahri—his beautiful young mistress—and knew he must send her away, make some arrangement for her, and do it before Emma found out about her. The other women of his *zenana* could all be explained, but Emma would take one good look at Lahri and *know* what she had been to him. No, Emma must never find out about Lahri; he could possibly keep Emma away from the *zenana* for a time, but eventually she would discover the women's quarters. Before that happened, he must remove Lahri and locate a new protector for her.

Would Emma demand marriage? Nestled against his side, sleeping now, her face glowing and her hair all tangled, Emma looked as young as the mistress he was willing to set aside for her sake—but *marriage!* He couldn't imagine it, couldn't picture himself in the role of the proper British husband, or Emma as the proper British wife. *Because we wouldn't be proper.* It couldn't work. All the objections he had had before, he still had. He wasn't British, and the whole world knew it. Any sort of openly acknowledged, legalized relationship between them—or even a non-legal one—would cause a scandal in both British and Indian circles.

The only possible way they could be together without being ostracized all around, was to continue with their original plan—that she be nanny to his children and he be her employer. Even at that, he must get her a personal *ayah* as soon as they reached Paradise View and take care that visitors never discovered their secret—and that his servants didn't gossip with the servants of other houses.

If she did demand marriage, he must persuade her against it. He could not afford to sever all the fragile ties he had so carefully built over the years; they enabled him to conduct business among whites and Indians alike. He couldn't risk being shunned—and neither could Emma. She might claim it didn't matter, but how would she really feel being cut off completely from British society—and Indian, too? If she married him, she'd be cut off everywhere. A few—a very few—of his Indian friends, men like Sayaji, might remain his friend, but they would not be Emma's. Even if she was offered the friendship and hospitality of their wives and mistresses, Alex doubted she'd take it.

She wouldn't be willing to spend her entire life locked up in a *zenana*, living the narrow life of a proper Indian wife. She was much too British. Alex fell asleep pondering these problems and wondering what, if anything, could be done to resolve them. He awoke in the faint light before dawn and realized he must return to his own tent before the entire camp discovered where he had slept, which would surely be a great embarrassment to Emma. Quietly, he arose from the pallet.

Emma sighed and turned over, but did not reach for him. Her slow, even breathing informed him that she still slept. He wished he could stay beside her and awaken her with hot kisses and caresses, but discretion got the better of him and he began to collect his discarded clothing. As he bent to pick up a boot, he saw the deed. Emma's precious deed to Wildwood. . . . In the entire time he had been there, he hadn't once thought of it. But that could hardly be considered unusual; he hadn't been thinking of the future at all. Only of the present.

Yet here it was—Emma's deed, waiting for him to steal it. Or destroy it. She had obviously removed it from its waterproof casing to see if it was still intact after yesterday's river crossing, and she hadn't yet re-secured it.

He glanced back at Emma; she would know if he took it

with him. Could he destroy it without incriminating himself? He picked it up and held it closer so he could see it better in the dim gray light. In places, the ink was smudged, where the dampness had apparently damaged it despite all Emma's precautions. Too bad the dampness hadn't destroyed it altogether. Then there would be no need for him to betray her—and to feel guilty and ashamed.

How could he simply put it back and do nothing? He had been planning all along to gain possession of the deed and destroy it. He had almost left her behind in Allahabad—until she threatened to make her own way to Bhopal and confront the officials there, the last people on earth he wanted her talking to and persuading to undertake an investigation. The *Nawabzada* would be only too happy to use her claim as ammunition to force Alex into handing over a higher percentage of his profits.

Making love to Emma—and feeling about her the way he did—hadn't changed anything; the deed was still a threat to him. It was a threat to Michael and Victoria. From now on, he intended to take care of Emma anyway, so she didn't *need* her damn inheritance. Even if the deed were valid, which he knew it wasn't, Wildwood no longer existed. What little remained of the plantation itself lay in ruins; he would make certain she never found it. So why *not* destroy the deed? He would offer her Paradise View instead. If she would consent to be his mistress as well as nanny to his children, she'd have all the wealth and security she could ever want.

But she mustn't suspect he had destroyed the deed on purpose; the destruction must appear an accident. A quick glance around the tent suggested the perfect method—the ewer of water. It was sitting on the ground right next to the tray on which the deed had been spread out to dry. It *was* dry, but it wouldn't be for long.

He replaced the deed exactly as it had been, then knocked over the ewer, so it fell on top of the deed. It clattered, making a loud noise. Alex hastily snatched up his boot and clutched boots and clothing to his bare torso. He waited for Emma to stir, but she did not. He looked down at the deed; the water had formed a puddle right on top of the paper, and the ink was spreading. A moment more, and the script would be completely illegible.

Satisfaction and relief surged through him, followed by a tide of guilt. He'd make it up to Emma; he swore he would. The only thing she could have done with Wildwood was sell it—either to him or to his enemies. Paradise View in its entirety was far more than Wildwood could ever be, and she would have it all—through him. If she wanted it, she could have it, almost the same as if she owned it. And she would never have to worry about making it prosperous—harvesting the timber and transporting it to market, bargaining for the best prices, storing the wood until the most opportune time to sell, keeping good workers, maintaining the elephants necessary for harvesting the wood, ceaselessly fighting the jungle . . . driving off Hyder Khan and other competitors who were always looking for ways to destroy him. . . . Emma need not worry about any of that.

He had spared her both failure and endless heartache. No woman—not even his stalwart Emma—could successfully run a huge jungle plantation. And now, he need not worry she might try. The deed was destroyed. She could never prove the land did not belong to him. She couldn't even raise the suspicion.

By the time Alex left the tent, he was feeling good about having done it. He had managed to convince himself that he had done Emma a favor. With the deed to Wildwood gone forever, she would stop chasing a ridiculous dream and concentrate on realities. *He* was her reality now, the only one that counted.

Emma awoke with a leisurely stretch and a sensation of complete and total well-being. She lay still a moment, savoring the feeling and wondering about the cause of it—and then she remembered. Sitting up, she was relieved to discover she was alone. Mr. Kingston—her beloved Sikander—had had the good sense to leave—hopefully before anyone saw him. She didn't know if she could bear seeing a censorious expression on Sakharam's ascetic features.

It was an unnerving prospect to think of all the servants being aware of—and God forbid, *discussing!*—what had occurred in her tent during the night. She knew of *memsahibs* who thought so little of their Indian servants as to go naked in front of them, but Emma could *never* do that. She may not entirely approve of the Raj, but she still felt it was her sacred duty to uphold the dignity and high moral standards of the country she represented.

Still . . . it had been worth it. She would do it again in a minute. Hugging her naked bosom, she recalled her one glorious night of pleasure and wickedness. Oh, it had been so wonderful! She had never dreamed it could be so wonderful. Closing her eyes against the heat and glare of early morning sunlight already turning her tent into an oven, Emma savored the memory of each heated kiss and caress.

She blushed to think of all Sikander had done to her—and she to him—which had culminated in that dazzling moment when they came together, and she had learned what she had been missing all these lonely years. There had been a moment of pain, but after that, it had been marvelous. Awesome. Impossibly beautiful.

But now it was morning and time to resume their journey. Sikander was probably growing impatient for her to appear, but gentleman that he was—and knowing how she had spent the night—he had allowed her an extra hour of rest.

Rising, she reached for her nightdress, sighing as she did so. "What now, Emma? Where do you go from here?"

A soreness in a certain tender place reminded her of how much everything had changed since yesterday. But how much had actually changed? She and Sikander had made no promises, formulated no plans, volunteered no commitments. They had simply succumbed to a mutual impulse. She couldn't decide if she wanted more than that from him. If she did, there was so much else to consider—his children, for example. She hadn't yet met his children or seen his home.

"Emma Whitefield, you are surely old enough to refrain from leaping to conclusions or allowing your hopes to run amok." Languidly, she picked up a brush and dragged it through her tangled hair.

"Just because a man gets into bed with you, and you allow it, doesn't mean he's in any great rush to marry you. You are no dewy-eyed young miss who doesn't realize what she's gotten herself into. You went into this with your eyes wide open; you had no illusions. Rosie warned you about his reputation."

Yet even as Emma lectured herself, she couldn't help hoping that she wasn't just another conquest. Mr. Kingston felt something for her. How could he make love to her so tenderly, with such great passion and gentleness, if he didn't? It wasn't only desire that drew them together; it had to be more. But she knew instinctively that if she made the mistake of being too demanding, of *insisting* that there be more, he might be driven off by such aggressiveness.

She herself didn't know what more she wanted or expected. To actually become his wife? That depended on what sort of wife he expected her to be; she had no guidelines or clues. Better to remain discreet, simply enjoy the present, and let the future take care of itself. For now, it was enough that Alexander Kingston found her desirable. This was a miracle she had never expected, an experience she had never thought would come to her. Plain, proper Emma Whitefield had a lover—a handsome, virile, fascinating, sensitive lover. To ask for more seemed blasphemous.

"Take each day as it comes, Emma. And today is here, so you had better wash and get ready to travel."

Setting down brush and nightdress, Emma remembered the ewer of water she hadn't needed the night before. Turning to get it, she yelped in dismay. It lay on its side, all its contents dumped out. Her dismay became horror when she spotted her precious deed, all curled and ruined, the print on it dissolved into muddy puddles of ink and water.

Snatching it up, she sought to shake off the dripping liquid. It was useless. The print on both sides was no longer readable. Her deed, the legal description of her land, the map citing its location, the fine print as well as the large print, was completely destroyed.

How had it happened? Who could have done it? *She* hadn't tipped over the ewer of water; it must have been Sikander. She recalled how he had kicked off his boots and trousers last night as he lay beside her. It could have happened then, or even this morning when he gathered his things preparatory to leaving her. Or else some animal—a lizard or a snake—had tipped over the ewer. How could she have been so careless?

Her oilskin packet still lay where she had dropped it, and she knew without touching it that her gems were still safe, but the one thing she valued most in the world—her precious deed—was ruined. Ruined, ruined.

Suddenly, she had an overwhelming need to see Sikander and share the news of this terrible disaster. It made no difference that he hadn't placed any value on the paper anyway. She had to tell someone, had to unload her grief and horror. She had guarded the deed so carefully and taken such pains to protect it—oh, God! How could this have happened now, when she had managed to keep it safe for so long with the odds all against her?

Half-blinded by tears, Emma hurriedly cleaned herself, then struggled into the same clothing she had worn the day before. Hardly taking time to twist her hair into the knot that best accommodated her *topi*, she fled the tent in search of Sikander. He wasn't far away; he smiled when he saw her and held out a cup of steaming tea—until he got a good look at her face. Then he lowered the cup and led her a short distance away from the cookfire beneath the banyan tree, where Sakharam was preparing breakfast.

"Emma, what's wrong? You look as if you've lost your best friend." He paused and lowered his voice. "This doesn't have anything to do with last night, does it?"

She shook her head so violently that her hair came undone. "No, it's this." She held out the soft, soggy wad of paper that was all that remained of her deed.

"What is it?" He set down the cup of tea on a nearby wooden crate, took the gooey mass from her, and began to open and smooth out the paper. "Is this your deed to Wildwood? But what's happened to it? I thought you were keeping it safe in a waterproof packet. I assume its present condition is due to our river crossing yesterday."

"No, no. . . . Last night, it was fine, only a bit damp around the edges. I had spread it out to dry, but then . . . sometime during the night, an ewer got knocked over, water spilled out, and . . . and ruined it."

Her lips quivered from the effort she was making not to weep in front of him. She wished she could permit herself the luxury of bawling like a baby, but that wasn't her nature. She just wanted to tell him about it—and know he cared.

His expression revealed that he did. His blue eyes radiated concern, and a kind of realization dawned in them, as if he had just discovered something.

"Emma. . . . Emma, love, forgive me. *I* must have done it. I was fumbling about in the darkness trying to find my boots, and I knocked over the ewer. I know because I heard it clatter against a metal object. I never thought a thing about it. I wasn't worried—except that the noise might awaken you."

"Well, I never heard a thing. . . . Oh, I know it wasn't your fault, so there's nothing to forgive. You couldn't have known I'd left such an important paper lying about on the floor on a tray."

"But Emma . . ." He reached for her, as if to draw her into his arms, but mindful of Sakharam, she retreated a step and shook her head. "Emma. I know what store you set on that deed. I understand how you feel. Never mind that it's useless; your mother left the deed to you, so naturally, you're upset."

He understands. She was so happy he did. It made her feel so much better and enabled her to realize that all was not lost.

With a furtive glance at Sakharam, he did not again attempt to embrace her, but settled for merely taking her hand. "Emma, I'm so sorry."

She found the strength to smile through her tears. *I don't know why I'm crying over it. I've memorized every word on that paper. I can still search for Wildwood. And if I find it— when I find it—I can still plead my case with the proper officials. I'll simply explain what happened. I'll demand they search their records. If they ask if I have witnesses to my possession of the deed, I can tell them about you. You saw it. You read it."*

"Of course, I'll support you, Emma, in whatever claim you care to make. But nothing you or I say will do any good—not when Wildwood doesn't exist anymore. And now, neither does the original deed. You *must* give up this absurd idea that you can ever find the land and lay claim to it."

"But Wildwood is mine. It once belonged to my mother's lover, who left it to her, and she then left it to me. Yes, her lover. I can say that now. While she was married to my father—my stepfather, actually—she took a lover. Major Ian Castleton was his name."

"Major Castleton?" Recognition flickered in Sikander's eyes.

"Yes. Have you heard of him?" Emma grew excited. "You seem to know the name."

"No . . . no, I'm afraid not. But he must have been British—this Major Castleton."

"Yes, he was." On impulse, trusting him totally, Emma blurted, "He was also my father. My *real* father, though I grew up as the daughter of Sir Henry Whitefield. You see now why Wildwood is so important to me. It's the only legacy my parents left me—other than some jewelry. Sir Henry always suspected that I was not his true daughter, and he held it against me. When he died, he left me nothing—save a single shilling. The jewels would not have sustained me forever, so I had no choice but to come to India and claim my inheritance. I still have no choice. If I am to be independent and provide for myself, I must find Wildwood, or I shall one day starve."

"Emma, Emma . . ." Sikander lifted her hand and held it tightly in both of his hands. He gazed into her eyes, his expression intent and filled with emotion. "You don't need to find Wildwood," he said low and urgently, so that Sakharam could not hear. "And you most definitely won't starve. You have me now. You have a life awaiting you at Paradise View. For as long as you need it, for as long as you *want* it, Paradise View—and I, myself—will be there for you."

It wasn't precisely a proposal of marriage. But then, Emma hadn't expected that—not yet, at least. She had never thought to hear this much from him. It *was* a commitment, of sorts. And until she knew what she herself wanted, it was touching, reassuring, and more than enough reason to smile.

"Thank you. Thank you so much, though I am still not prepared to give up on finding—and claiming—Wildwood." She withdrew her hand with a little nervous laugh and a swift, piercing happiness. "We must be careful around Sakharam," she whispered. "And the others. I am not so brazen that I can hold up my head when my personal affairs become common knowledge and a topic for servants' gossip."

"I understand. For the rest of the journey, we will indeed be careful, but when we arrive at Paradise View, it will not be nearly as difficult as it is now for us to find time alone together. I will simply dismiss the servants from the house at an early hour and come to you whenever I wish."

Though the morning was typically steamy, Emma shivered at the prospect. "Then I hope the journey doesn't take too long," she murmured, expressing the urgency she already felt to be alone with him again.

Sikander laughed. "Oh, Emma, when you finally give yourself, you hold nothing back, do you? In a single night, you go from shy maiden constantly defending her virtue, to scheming seductress."

"I have no idea how to be a scheming seductress—but I would be happy to learn. Will you teach me, Sikander?"

His laughter rang out a second time, drawing a curious glance from Sakharam and several of the other servants. "Perhaps I should take you back to Allahabad and let you study the paintings on the walls and ceiling of Sayaji's Love Pavilion at your leisure. You may be ready for them now."

Emma blushed hotly. She still thought those paintings were obscene—but now she could actually imagine doing some of those things, but only with Sikander, of course. It *was* amazing what a difference a single night could make. "I'm not *that* corrupt yet. It's one thing to indulge yourself in the dark of night where no one can see you, but quite another to paint a picture of intimate activities on a wall where anyone can view them."

"Only Sayaji and his wives and concubines ever see them," Sikander countered.

"No, I saw them. You saw them. Sakharam saw them, and so did that innocent young girl."

"Emma, that girl has probably seen far worse. How do you think potential concubines receive their education?"

"From paintings on walls and ceilings?"

"No, from paintings in a particular kind of book, where various . . . ah . . . intimacies are amply illustrated."

"I don't believe you!"

"Well, you should. Such books are called Pillow Books, and they can be found in almost any Indian bazaar, as well as in many a *zenana*."

"That is outrageous."

"Nevertheless, it's true. . . . Come and eat your *chota hazri*, Emma. I can see that the old Emma is still alive and well inside the new Emma—and both probably need their nourishment."

His eyes lit with that mocking humor she found so infuriating and irresistible. She wished she dared fling her arms around him and kiss him, but even married couples didn't exchange intimacies in front of their servants. So she lifted her chin, assumed a haughty attitude, and followed him over to the cookfire . . . and as she ate her breakfast, she reviewed all she had said and done most recently.

Had she just agreed to become Sikander's mistress? She certainly hadn't objected when he mentioned how easy it would be to find time alone together when they reached Paradise View. And she had begged him to teach her to be a "scheming seductress."

Oh, Lord, he was right! In a single night, she had changed beyond all imagining—or perhaps she hadn't changed at all. Perhaps she was simply discovering her true colors, the woman she had been all along, only she hadn't known it.

Seventeen

"Come along, Emma. Don't look down. You should be fine. Give Morgana her head and trust her to watch her footing."

Sikander had twisted around on his horse to talk to Emma, but she devoutly wished he would forget about her and watch his own horse's footing. She couldn't believe they were really doing this—or that safety lay somewhere up ahead. To her right was a sheer drop of at least two hundred feet into a mist-shrouded gorge. To her left was a wall of rock broken only by a few tenacious jungle plants intent upon conquering the steep rocky promontory they were traversing.

The trail skirting the gorge had kept narrowing, until it was barely wide enough for Morgana; what if it disappeared altogether? There was no space to turn around and retreat back the way they had come. There wasn't even room enough for them to dismount. They had no choice but to go forward—and Emma was so nervous she couldn't feel the reins in her fingers. Her heart was pounding, her palms sweating, her breath coming in short little gasps. With the single exception of the tiger incident, she had never felt so terrified; even her near drowning hadn't inspired such dread.

"Don't worry," Sikander continued. "I bred these horses to be sure-footed, and they've all played enough polo to know exactly where to put their feet. Close your eyes if you must, but don't shorten your reins or snatch at Morgana's mouth. She needs complete freedom to keep her balance."

"I-I'm not holding her tightly. And I wouldn't dream of snatching at her mouth."

"You also have to remember to breathe. It will help if you breathe deeply. Stop clutching her mane. You don't want to give her the idea there's anything to worry about."

Emma willed herself to do as he said. She tried shutting her eyes and found it easier to relax if she couldn't see the yawning void right alongside her. In the past ten days, they had ridden over extremely rough and challenging terrain, but this was the worst yet. The jungle was so thick that she despaired of ever seeing civilization again. Lately, it was all up and downhill. Excellent hunting country. Marvelous for tiger and other big game. Incomparable for testing the limits of puny human beings.

Despite her fear, Emma continued to find it wildly beautiful. At times, she was filled with a poignant rapture that was part reverence for the land's beauty and part yearning for Sikander to join her in her tent at night. After that one glorious night of love-making, the same night her deed had been destroyed, he had kept a discreet distance and hardly spoken a personal word to her.

But then this sort of rugged wilderness inspired silence. Sakharam and the other servants had been quieter, too, all of them making a supreme effort to be efficient, but not saying much. At night, they slept like dead men, except for those assigned to keep watch. Watches were now posted every night, and Sikander took care to see that a fire burned all night long—which was only prudent considering that scarcely a night went by without the assorted sounds of animals hunting in the near vicinity. Emma was even learning to sleep through "tiger talks."

"You seem to be doing better, Emma," Mr. Kingston called back to her. "Does it help to keep your eyes closed?"

"Yes," she answered, realizing only then that she had been

so lost in thought she had almost forgotten to be afraid. Almost.

"Well, keep them closed, for we are coming to a particularly narrow stretch of this trail. Once we get past it, the trail widens enough to ride two abreast. If you find yourself brushing against rock on the wall side, just hang on and lean out over the precipice. I trust you fastened the girth on your saddle nice and tight at the last rest stop."

Emma's eyes flew open. "Of course, I did. I wouldn't make the same mistake twice."

"I was just asking," he responded mildly. "Don't take offense. Moments like these are why we have such rules for good horsemanship."

A wave of dizziness smote Emma as she chanced to gaze down into the chasm beside Morgana's shoulder. Her mare crowded the wall, catching the tip of Emma's boot and giving her foot a painful yank backwards. Emma futilely tried to flatten her skirts and make herself smaller. Since she was in a sidesaddle, her skirt and legs were all on the side nearest the wall, yet she feared leaning toward the precipice as Mr. Kingston had suggested. She wished to do nothing that might feel different or alarming to Morgana. Since he had never ridden sidesaddle, Sikander didn't understand the necessity of sitting perfectly straight and keeping one's right shoulder back, in order to balance both herself and the horse. Emma had done enough riding and jumping to realize that even the slightest shift of her weight was enough to cause problems.

The mare snorted, paused for a moment, and jerked up her head—causing Emma's stomach to lurch uncomfortably. She sat very still, giving Morgana a chance to regain confidence. Sikander kept going, widening the distance between them—a powerful incentive for the mare to scramble and catch up to his gelding.

"Easy, girl. Take it slowly now." Emma tried not to tense her muscles and add to the mare's wariness, yet she did grip harder with her right knee, clenching the high pommel of the saddle until her thigh ached.

"Mr. Kingston!" she called out as calmly as possible. "Can you please wait a moment for us to catch up?"

Sikander reined in his horse, and the *syce* in front of him did likewise. Behind her, Emma could hear the crunch of gravel that indicated that those behind her were stopping. Very carefully, Sikander turned around, and Emma could see the sheen of perspiration on his face beneath his *topi*.

"This isn't a good place to stop, Emma. Urge her along now; keep her moving quietly."

"But . . . she's afraid. She stopped of her own accord."

"No, *you* are afraid and communicating your fear to her. Once we start again, don't let her stop. Make her go forward, or she's likely to bound ahead when she finally decides to catch up—and there isn't room for that. Moreover, the horses behind you will think *they* have to go faster, too. A slow, steady pace is the only way to do this safely."

"I'm trying," Emma muttered.

"Well, try harder, Miss Whitefield. You can do it; I know you can." His tone had a hard edge to it, and the fact that he was calling her Miss Whitefield instead of Emma under-scored his annoyance.

Emma bit down on her lower lip until she tasted the salti-ness of her own blood. She waited for him to continue, and a moment later, he did. She urged Morgana to stay close behind Captain Jack, and the mare jigged along with a bouncy step that was half trot, half walk, as if she wanted to hurry and get to safety.

They went a little farther and again came to a standstill. The trail had grown so narrow that Emma was forced to hang off the side, leaning out over the void whose depths she couldn't see because of the mist covering the bottom.

"Emma? The ledge here has crumbled away, and we're going to have to jump a short distance to pick it up again." Sikander did not sound in the least alarmed. If anything, he seemed glad of a little excitement, as if the trip up until now had been boring.

"We'll go in order with no stopping in between. Try and remain calm and pick up a trot as soon as you land, so that the horse behind you has enough room to make the jump. Do you have any questions?"

"N–no." Emma hated the tremor she heard in her own voice. She drew a deep breath and suddenly didn't feel nervous anymore. It was out of her hands now. She had no choice but to trust Morgana; there was nothing else she could do. It was all up to the horses whether or not they survived this newest challenge.

"All right, the *syce* is going first. And I am following right on his heels."

Emma watched the powerful hind muscles of Sikander's gray gelding. The horse gathered himself, Sikander leaned forward, and together they sailed over the wide gap in the rocky trail. Emma urged Morgana to follow. She was careful not to look down—or indeed anywhere but straight ahead between her horse's ears. And Morgana did it!

Her hooves clattered briefly on the stones as she trotted eagerly after Captain Jack, hurrying at what seemed like break-neck speed along the narrow precipice. Emma could hear the other horses following Morgana, and then there came a terrible sound: a high-pitched neigh of terror. Someone behind her shouted. Hooves battered at rock.

It was too dangerous to turn around and look, and Emma dared not stop or the horses coming behind might run into her. A shrill equine scream told her that one of the horses hadn't cleared the gap in the ledge. There were a few sickening thumps, the sound of falling rock, a heavier thump somewhere far, far below, and then . . . silence.

"Don't stop! Keep going! Don't look down!" Sikander's commands were low and urgent. He lapsed into Urdu, and the men behind Emma answered him. They kept going, but Emma was by now trembling so hard that she didn't know how she remained seated on Morgana. She couldn't feel a thing except the heavy thundering in her chest which seemed to fill her whole body.

She managed to entwine her fingers through Morgana's long mane, and that was the only thing that kept her upright until—at long last—the trail widened and the ground became sturdy and solid. Sikander waited for her to catch up. As she reached him, he grabbed Morgana's reins.

"You did well, Emma." Admiration flashed in his blue eyes, then he was twisting and turning to see behind him.

"Who was it?" she demanded, half afraid to look. "Tell me who fell."

When he didn't immediately answer, she turned also and began counting heads. They were all there! The men had all made it. Only the last horse—the packhorse carrying the tiger skin as well as her belongings—was missing.

"I am sorry, *Sahib*," Sakharam apologized, coming toward them. "I should have led the horse myself instead of entrusting the task to another, less experienced man. We have lost not only a fine animal but the tiger skin, all of the *memsahib's* things, and some of your own."

"The elephant table?" Mr. Kingston asked, frowning.

Emma immediately remembered the tiny table on which they had taken tea and many meals. Could it have contained real jewels and ivory? Or did it simply have sentimental value?

"No, *Sahib*. Sumair has the table, but a small portion of our staples is also gone. Forgive me. This is all my fault. I should be punished severely. If you will not flog me, I will order another to do it."

"Stop it. I forbid you to be flogged or disciplined in any way. It was an accident; it couldn't be helped. The only thing I truly mourn is the loss of the horse. When we return the h̶ ̶s to Sayaji Singh, I will send another to replace it. It ̶ a better one than we lost."

"̶ ̶lease do not worry about my belongings," Emma

added, feeling a pang of loss over her beautiful rug. "They can all be replaced. For the remainder of the trip, I will have no trouble making do with what I have on my back."

"What I have done is unforgivable," Sakharam insisted.

The man never ceased to amaze Emma. She wondered if he would be so contrite had *she* fallen into the gorge.

"When we get to Paradise View, I was planning to have new things made for you anyway," Sikander reminded her, as Sakharam—his back straight as a lance—wheeled his horse around and rode back to rejoin the others. "We are not that far now. Another several days, if all goes well, and we'll be there."

"I'm growing anxious," Emma admitted. "Especially after today. Is there even the slightest chance that the poor horse who fell might still be alive?"

Sikander shook his head. "He could not have survived that fall. It's over three hundred feet, and the bottom of the gorge is littered with boulders."

"Three hundred feet! Then I'm glad I couldn't see the bottom, or I might have been more frightened than I was."

"You were actually frightened?" Sikander cocked his head, studying her with a gleam of amusement in his eye. "Why, I thought you were teasing—pretending to be nervous because that's what women are supposed to be in situations like this."

"Do you mean to say that *you* weren't afraid, Sikander? I admit you sounded completely confident. Indeed, there were moments when I suspected you relished the danger, though I can't imagine how anyone could."

"Danger is a part of life, Emma—the most interesting part. If there is no risk, there can be no triumph. Seeking safety and avoiding risk is a natural human response to being scared out of one's britches, but if a man—or woman—makes a habit of avoiding danger, he or she also makes a habit of avoiding the very things that make life worth living."

"So you are a philosopher, in addition to everything ꝯ'

"No, I'm just a man trying to make sense of life." Sikander smiled at her. "You do realize we could have all been killed back there."

She nodded. "Of course, I realize it."

They grinned at each other like two giddy children.

"But we didn't, did we?" he lightly inquired. "Which makes me think we must have been kept alive for some particular reason."

"Such as?"

He arched an eyebrow. "To take *more* risks perhaps?"

"Perhaps," she agreed, wondering where all this was leading and suspecting she already knew.

"You don't know how pleased I am to know you are a fellow risk-taker, Emma." He gave her a wink and a smile—and then cantered ahead to resume leading the way toward Paradise View.

They reached the plantation four days later. Emma first glimpsed it as they rounded a bend in the overgrown jungle trail. She suddenly spotted what appeared to be a mirage—that of a shimmering pink structure built on the order of the Taj Mahal. So strongly did the building resemble pictures she had seen of that magnificent monument that she came to a halt and stared in mingled wonder and confusion.

Sikander immediately reined his horse around and rode back to her. "Emma, what is it? What's wrong?"

"This? This is your home?" She gestured toward the airy, graceful, domed, two-story building whose octagonal shape and four tall minarets were an exact replica of what was perhaps the most famous monument in all India.

The building rose out of the jungle flora like some impossi￼ ￼am or imagined glory, an exquisite example of art- ￼beauty that brought a lump to Emma's throat. In ￼area in front of it, gazelles browsed, peacocks ￼brilliant plumage, blue-winged butterflies floated above lush flowers, and twin fountains tinkled merrily.

Emma had been mightily impressed by Sayaji Singh's home, but this one surpassed anything she might have imagined. The setting was so wild, the structure so incongruous, yet somehow it all went together, as if it were meant to be—and she felt a chord of recognition reverberate clear through her. Why did it all seem so dearly beloved and familiar . . . when she was seeing it for the first time?

Watching her closely, Sikander said, "Do you like it? Some people find it in bad taste—too ostentatious. But I have always loved the pure lines and simple majesty of the Taj Mahal, so I sought to reproduce it in my own humble way. I could not afford marble—except for occasional touches—so I used sandstone and wood. My version is also smaller. But then only I and my children—and now, you—actually live here. There are other buildings you cannot see from here which house my servants, my horses . . . and everyone else."

"Everyone else?" Emma wondered who else he could possibly mean.

"Guests. Visiting relatives, of whom there are very few. Passing government officials and the like."

She finally managed to tear her gaze away from the lovely main house. Perhaps I shouldn't live here, either. I mean, if your guests and relatives do not occupy the main house, neither should I."

"Nonsense. As the children's nanny, you must be nearby at all times. There are more than enough rooms to accommodate your presence—and besides, I *want* you there."

He wants me near him. So he can visit me in the night.

Joy leapt in Emma's heart. Just as she had not imagined the beauty of his home, she had never suspected she could be so happy to arrive here finally—and to be contemplating further intimacies with Mr. Kingston. She had begun to think he had changed his mind about pursuing a relationship with her, and she herself had begun to doubt the wisdom of allowing it. Not once had he so much as kissed her since their night of passion, which now seemed so long ago . . . and not once had he sought her out alone.

In some ways, she appreciated his discretion, but in others, she abhorred it. Despite the rigors of the journey or perhaps because of them, she yearned for his touch—and even more for the affirmation of his regard for her. Whenever her own doubts and hesitations arose, she struggled to squelch them. She could not recall feeling about any man the way she did about Sikander. If this was her one and only chance for love, nothing must destroy it. Like her mother before her, she was willing to risk everything.

"If you insist, I will consent to live in this beautiful dwelling," she told him. "Surely, the Taj Mahal cannot be any more elegant."

"It pleases me that you like it so much. Considering that I've chosen to fashion my home after someone's tomb, some people view it with horror. Sakharam himself refuses to sleep here—preferring a bed in the building behind this one, which is attached by a long covered walkway through a courtyard that lies between."

Sikander shot an accusatory glance in the direction of his bland-faced servant who gave him a slight nod. "I would do anything for you, *Sahib*. You know that. But I have my own tastes in living quarters."

"Hah! You'd rather bed down in the middle of a *mugger*-infested swamp than sleep in my house, old friend. Admit it. You are superstitious."

Sakharam maintained a polite silence, neither agreeing nor disagreeing.

"It doesn't look like a tomb to me," Emma exclaimed. "If anything, it reminds me of a place of worship—it's a mosque, isn't it?"

"A mosque, yes, but I doubt anyone would accuse me of an excess of religious fervor, dear Emma. However, no bodies

are buried here either. It is simply my home—built in a style
I admire. Therefore, I care little what others think of it. It
matters only what *I* think. Come. I am anxious to show it to
you."

He rode toward the gleaming rose-colored building, and
Emma happily followed, discovering new delights with each
step nearer. Despite the oppressive heat, which was almost
suffocating, an aura of coolness surrounded Sikander's home.
The fountains, lush flowers, and shady green tranquility of
the jungle setting conspired to create an air of refreshment.

Parrots, monkeys, gazelle, peacocks, and other jungle
creatures were able to come right up to the steps of the house
if they wished, but the top of the steps was secured by a tall
wrought-iron gate, and the house itself seemed to be set on
a high pedestal of pink sandstone. There was no need for a
wall, either for privacy or safety. The arched windows were
too high off the ground for any jungle creatures to enter, and
all around the top of the pedestal was a veranda enclosed by
more wrought iron. A person could sit or stand there and
watch tigers feed without fear of attack.

Looking up at the minarets, Emma spotted tiny wrought-
iron balconies where one could look down on the fountains,
flowers, and wild animals from the second floor. It all resembled a kind of natural zoo or Garden of Eden, where the
inhabitants of the house could live in harmony with the jungle—be a part of it, yet not too much a part—and Emma
loved it on sight.

She had imagined she would feel this way about Wildwood, but she wasn't creative enough to have thought of
conjuring the Taj Mahal in the middle of a jungle wilderness.
Sikander's home gave her tremendous insight into his character. Surely his cynicism and mocking smile hid a gentle,
romantic heart; what could be more romantic than living in
a replica of a monument to a beloved wife?

Sikander rode straight up to the steps of the house and

called out in a loud voice. "Michael! Victoria! Your Papa is home, and your new nanny has arrived."

Grinning at Emma, he shouted in Urdu. Emma caught a few familiar words and realized he was repeating his command in the native language. A moment later, two small figures appeared—one in a white turban, coat, and trousers identical to Sakharam's, and the other in a pink and gold *sari*.

Emma inhaled sharply; they were Indian children, right down to the caste marks on their foreheads. She had a sudden wild hope that they might belong to Sakharam or one of the servants—but then Sikander swung down from his horse and raced up the steps to greet them. A smiling *ayah* appeared behind the children, and servants hurried to open the wrought-iron gates.

Chattering in Urdu, the children embraced Sikander with a warmth and excitement Emma had rarely witnessed in British children. The little boy suddenly disengaged himself, stepped back, and executed an elaborate *salaam*, while the little girl clung to her father. Sikander picked her up, and she flung her arms around his neck and buried her small face in the crook of his neck and shoulder.

"Yes, yes, my little ones. I have missed you terribly, but now I am home to stay for a long, long while. . . . Michael, stop that bowing and come hug me again." He extended his free arm to the boy, but had to repeat his command in Urdu before the child obeyed.

They are all Indian, Emma thought in burgeoning dismay. *Appearance, dress, behavior, manners—they are all Indian. They don't even speak English.*

She tried to keep her shock from showing as Sikander turned to her, lifting his son in one arm and holding his daughter in the other. She saw it as clear as daylight. There was nothing British about any of them. Dark hair, dark skin, flashing white grins. Only Sikander had blue eyes. The eyes of his children were black as ebony. . . . No wonder he kept them hidden away in the jungle, and his British acquaintances had never visited here.

His home, his children, and everything about him proclaimed him Indian. Despite his dress and his blue eyes, he looked in that moment more Indian than Sayaji Singh or Sakharam. He lacked only a caste mark to proclaim his heritage.

Forcing her stiff lips into a smile, Emma calmly walked up the steps to join him. "So this is Michael and Victoria."

"Greet your new nanny, children." Mr. Kingston gave them a little squeeze, but the children only stared at Emma, their black eyes wary.

"I am Miss Whitefield, your new nanny," Emma said to cover the awkward moment. "Do you speak English? Can you say my name?"

The little boy shook his head solemnly, while the little girl lifted the corner of her *sari* and covered her face with it.

"They know a bit of English." Sikander sounded defensive. "They just haven't spoken it while I've been gone. I will insist they resume practicing at once."

"No English," Michael said sullenly, his small face rebellious. "Urdu. Hindustani."

Sikander gave him a mild shake. "Yes, you will speak English, Michael. We have discussed this, and you understand the necessity of it. Moreover, I am your father, and if you dare disobey me, you will regret it."

"Yes, Papa," Michael agreed, but his mouth had a mutinous slant, suggesting that he could be every bit as stubborn as his sire.

Oh, Lord! What shall I do with them? Emma wondered.

How would she ever manage to turn them into proper English children, when they bore the stamp of India so strongly and had no desire whatever to change?

Sikander caught her eye, his glance as determined as his son's. "I did it. So can they," he said, as if he could read her thoughts. "I am depending upon you to transform them completely."

Emma opened her mouth to protest, then snapped it closed again. This was hardly the time or place to object. "They are beautiful children," she said instead. "They look just like you."

"Not quite. They don't have my blue eyes, which is unfortunate, for if they did, things would go much better for them in the future."

Michael and Victoria glanced from Sikander's face to Emma's and back again during this exchange. Emma couldn't tell if they understood or not. She was afraid they didn't. Glancing past them, she found herself gazing into the unfriendly eyes of their *ayah,* who stood at a respectful distance but was keeping watch like a mother hen guarding her precious chicks.

The woman was tall for an Indian, slender and graceful in the Indian manner, and handsome, rather than beautiful. As soon as Sikander set the children down, she uttered a soft command, and they ran to her and clasped her hands, one on each side, presenting a picture of solidarity and innate suspicion toward outsiders.

Sikander appeared not to notice that all three of them—the *ayah,* Michael, and Victoria—were giving Emma a less than cordial examination. Dismissing the trio with a wave of his hand, he took Emma's arm. "Well, now that you've met my children, come along, and I'll show you the house."

Emma wanted to say, "Wait a minute. Introduce me to the *ayah,* too," but she didn't.

Sikander hadn't acknowledged the woman, which was surprising, considering that he was usually so considerate of his inferiors. Emma expected the children and the *ayah* to follow them as they inspected the house, but they immediately disappeared, and she was left to wonder where they had gone off to, while Sikander eagerly displayed the treasures of his jungle palace.

Eighteen

The house was much like Sayaji Singh's inside—furnished in a sumptuous Indian manner of rich carpets, decorative screens, low furniture and stools, string beds, and tasseled pillows which would have scandalized any British visitors. Emma saw no dining room nor any truly Western-style furniture; she realized she would have to confront Sikander about the lack of these, for she could never teach the children British manners without them.

The children probably took their meals seated on the little stools so beloved by Indians and thus had no idea how to conduct themselves during the traditional multi-course British banquet. In the entire house, there was but one small room—a kind of parlor—that would meet British approval. The furnishings there were the type found in a *dak* bungalow—a horsehair settee and a *punkah* fan, but the wall hangings and decorations were typically Indian. Sikander explained that this indeed was the room where he entertained the few government officials who visited Paradise View, but not many had ever made the trip, and he intended to keep it that way if possible.

"Fortunately, I am able to conduct nearly all my business with your countrymen while I am in Calcutta or Delhi. There's little need for them to come here."

"Fortunately," Emma dryly agreed. Sikander got the point

because he gave her a sardonic look which she chose to ignore.

His reference to "your" countrymen, rather than "our" had not escaped her. Here in his home, Sikander obviously eschewed all things British in favor of the Indian portion of his heritage. She wondered if he would ever trust her enough to tell her the complete story of his background and upbringing. Somehow, she doubted it.

On the second floor of the thick-walled building, he proudly showed her the separate compartments making up his suite of rooms, the children's, and the two remaining ones. Each had its own minaret and balcony overlooking part of the estate. The two front compartments belonging to him and the children overlooked the park-like entrance, while the suite he had assigned to her faced the back of the estate and provided her first view of the remaining buildings, the stable, and the distant polo field.

Standing on the balcony and looking down, Emma could see the roof of the covered walkway leading to the partially open courtyard that was itself connected to the next building.

"The kitchen and servants' quarters are there." With a cursory wave of his hand, he indicated the adjoining building. "Plus my office and a few other things. In time, you will learn the location of everything. Do you see the polo field way out back?"

Emma nodded. "I knew that's what it was the moment I spotted it. It could be nothing else."

He leaned on the balcony railing, and the sun struck blue glints in his black hair, reminding her yet again of what a handsome man he was. "That field is my pride and joy. It took months to clear away the jungle; keeping it clear and covered with sod requires more back-breaking, constant labor. I should erect a barrier to keep wild animals off it, but I haven't the heart to do so. Paradise View is a jungle plantation, and that is its charm and reason for being. The only place you'll find an actual wall is around the compound for the horses. I don't wish to keep them stalled all the time, especially when I am not here to help exercise them, so I've built several pens where they can be turned out for short periods. A high wall surrounds the pens so they can run free in safety."

Emma leaned out over the balcony railing. "I can see a portion of the wall from here. That, too, must have been quite an undertaking."

"It was." He smiled and straightened, turning to face her. "Paradise View—all you see here, including the large pond on the other side of the house—has been ten years in the making. And it still isn't finished. I am constantly thinking of new things to do, more improvements to make. Then there is the upkeep on all I've built. At last count, I had two hundred fifty servants."

"Two hundred fifty! Where do you keep them all?"

Sikander pointed to a spot that appeared to be solid jungle at one end of the polo field. "Back there is a small village where most of them have their own huts and gardens. Only the most important ones live close to the main house—Sakharam and the children's *ayah*, for example."

"The *ayah* lives in the children's compartment?"

"No, but she sleeps there occasionally and assigns another trusted servant to do so when she leaves. A servant always stays with them at night. As you have probably guessed by now, I live in the Indian manner, Emma. It far surpasses the British one when it comes to surviving in harmony with the jungle. . . . And after all, this is India," he added with a grin.

"I see." Emma wondered if now was the time to mention certain changes that would have to be made if she was to prepare his children to live in England and survive and prosper among the British.

"Do you like your new quarters?" Sikander gestured toward the high-walled compartment that reminded Emma of the *zenana* in the house of Sayaji Singh. . . . Where was the *zenana* in *this* house? And the Love Pavilion? If he was living in the Indian manner, he surely had both, but as yet, he hadn't mentioned them or pointed them out to her.

"It's quite beautiful," she assured him. "But far grander than I really need. Are you certain I should live this close to *your* compartment?"

Closing the small distance between them, he gently touched her arm. "Of course, I'm certain, Emma. For propriety's sake, I will assign you an *ayah*, but I won't permit her to share your quarters. These rooms are yours alone."

"All of them?" Emma couldn't quite believe it. The compartment was more appropriate for a wife than a nanny. It had its own bathing chamber, a large sitting chamber, a smaller one off the side especially for sleeping, yet another solely for dressing, and still one more whose purpose was a mystery. She already knew she would prefer sleeping in this one, hopefully with a cooling night breeze blowing through it from the open balcony.

He smiled at the question. "Yes, all of them. They belong to you alone, and no one may enter without your permission. Servants can come and go during the day, but at night, you may close that outer door, and no one will be permitted to set foot inside unless you allow it . . . and that includes me," he added in a husky whisper.

Emma stood there awkwardly, her cheeks burning, her heart pounding, afraid to say anything lest it be the wrong thing.

"Emma, Emma," he chided, reaching for her hand. He entwined his fingers through hers, his palm cool and wonderful against her fevered skin. "I know this is all a shock to you; I tried to prepare you at Sayaji's house, by admitting he was my relative. I wanted you to know what I am, and now you know how I live. As an Indian, Emma. Here, in the depths of the jungle, I can embrace my birthright and be who I really am. I need not pretend; I can be myself. That's why I invite no one here. Tales circulating through the British community would destroy my business contacts and ruin the empire I have worked so hard to build."

"But couldn't you have built that same empire as an Indian? Did you have to . . . have to . . ."

"Lie? What do *you* think, Emma? As a member of the ruling class, you should know better than anyone that I could never have achieved so much as a half-caste. A *kutcha butcha*. People speculate about my ancestry, but they don't know for certain who or what I am, so they let greed rule their actions. If I were honest, if I allowed them to get to know me, they would ostracize me. Even now, I don't enjoy social acceptance; I am merely tolerated."

"But what about the Indians? How do they feel about you—about all this?" She nodded helplessly at the scene around them.

"It's the same with them, Emma. I'm not good enough to marry their blue-blooded daughters, nor am I invited into all the best homes. Some show more tolerance than others, but my daughter can never marry among them, nor can my son. I must maintain a veneer of British respectability—for their sakes. For their futures. I want them to marry British, so that gradually our blood will lighten."

"You want them to *marry* British? But . . . but. . . ."

"You don't think that's possible? You think they are too dark?"

"But you've brought them up Indian!" she burst out, glad to pin the blame on that, rather than their coloring.

"Ah, but that is what *you* will remedy." He lifted her hand to kiss her fingers.

"You don't even have a proper dining room, yet you know the importance of good table manners to the British."

"Then we shall install one and eat there together every evening."

"They will need to wear British clothing!"

"I will send for a *durzi* this very day."

"They hardly speak English."

"From now on, they will speak nothing else."

"You expect me to turn their lives upside down? To change all that is familiar to them?"

"I expect you to do whatever it takes. That was our agreement, was it not?"

The enormity of the task stunned Emma. "I . . . I don't know if I can do it."

"You, my dear Emma, can do anything. Whatever doubts I had when first we discussed this have all disappeared. You've more than proven that you are equal to the task. You shall make my children more British, and in return, I shall make *you* more Indian."

"What do you mean—more Indian?"

He pulled her into his arms. "I shall teach you the Indian appreciation of sensual delights, my sweet Emma. If you will let me, I'll teach you all the delights of the Love Pavilion."

"So you *do* have one," she accused, but her words came out in a breathy murmur, as he held her close and rubbed his jaw along her temple. "Does it have paintings on the walls and ceilings? If so, I shall be forced to whitewash them to protect your children's morals."

"My children are forbidden to go there. But one day, I'll let them see it, for they were conceived in my Love Pavilion."

"I . . . I think I'd prefer to stay here then."

"Here will be perfect. Your door is right across from mine. No one will know when I visit you, Emma. No one suspects we were intimate that one single time in the tent. It has been difficult—very difficult—but I refrained from visiting you during the rest of our journey, because I wanted you to have time to consider this . . . and to be sure it is what you really want. Is it what you really want?"

"Oh, Sikander. I *think* it's what I want." Emma melted against him as he began to nuzzle her hair. "I wondered why you did not come to me again. I *wanted* you to come. And yet, sometimes I didn't. I wanted to see your house first, to meet your children, to feel as if I knew you better . . ."

He drew back, his brilliant blue eyes caressing her face. "And now that you have seen my house and met my children, what do you think, Emma? You still haven't said. In the clear light of day, can you bear to have me touch you and be your lover? Or am I . . . too foreign? Too unclean in the British way of looking at things."

Emma rushed to forestall the bitterness she heard in his tone; lightly, she clapped her hand over his mouth. "Sikander, don't. Cease maligning yourself. You don't believe it anyway. You are no less of a man for being a half-caste, and I am no more of a woman for being British. I see that clearly now; skin color is unimportant. What matters most is that you are tender, gentle, generous, loving, kind, courageous. . . . You can make me laugh and look at things as I have never seen them before. . . . You can make me feel things I've never felt before."

"Will that be enough for you, Emma?" He stood perfectly still, his blue eyes searching her face, probing her soul, and Emma suddenly knew the answer that had been eluding her all along.

"Yes," she whispered. "Before you, I had nothing but empty dreams. And now that I've found you, I'm unwilling to lose you. It will *have* to be enough, won't it?"

His hands moved to her shoulders, his grip on them tightening. "I'm not asking you to marry me, Emma. I would not do that to you."

Ask me. Ask me, and I will say yes.

"You . . . have no wish to marry again?" It came out flatly, revealing her disappointment.

"Emma, let's be clear about this. Let me speak frankly. If we marry, you will be ostracized, just as I have been. You will no longer be welcome in the homes of your British friends. Can you deny that?"

Miserably, Emma shook her head. It might be too much even for Rosie.

"And I would no longer be welcome in the homes of my Indian friends. Even Sayaji would probably reject me."

"I hadn't thought about that," she admitted. "I hadn't realized prejudice exists on both sides."

"Well, it does. It's a constant struggle to succeed in two such different worlds, Emma. You have not lived with it. You don't know how hard it is."

For you, I'd be willing to learn!

"I wouldn't want your friends to forsake you because of me," she murmured.

"For myself, I would risk it," he gallantly insisted. "But I must consider Michael and Victoria. Their futures come first. I could lose all you see here in an instant. My wealth lies in land and timber, which means I must keep harvesting the forests and investing the profits in other ventures—such as rice, indigo, and tea. I am still years away from true security, and always, I must be cautious, never letting anyone know how vulnerable I am, never allowing them to discover precisely what I'm going to do next. I've never discussed this with any other person on earth—except Sakharam. For I can truly trust no one. That's what it means to be *kutcha butcha*, Emma. So I cannot offer you marriage. . . . I'm sorry, but it would never work."

"I understand! Truly, I do. And I thank you for telling me all this. For being honest. I value your honesty more than anything, Sikander. Nothing in the world matters more to me. 'Tis another of your excellent qualities that makes me feel as I do about you." She forced a gay little laugh, but the sound emerged more like a sob.

"Emma . . ." He wrapped his arms around her. "Emma . . ." he repeated, as if he meant to say something more.

"What? You can tell me anything, Sikander."

He hesitated, then blurted: "May I come to you tonight?"

"Tonight?" It hadn't been at all what she was expecting.

She had thought he was going to reveal some deep, dark, troubling secret, but perhaps he had changed his mind.

"Tonight is too soon?" He looked crestfallen and disappointed. "You are too tired from the journey?"

"No! Oh, no. . . . 'Tis only that I'll want to bathe first and . . . and find something clean to wear. Perhaps one of your serving women can loan me a *sari."*

"I'll see you get all you need—and women to help you bathe."

"No women! I can bathe myself, thank you."

"Or *I* can assist you." He gave her a look that made her spine tingle. "I assure you it would be a bath to remember."

"I don't think I'm ready for that yet," Emma demurred, though she found the idea incredibly exciting.

"You'll be ready one day. Think how far you've come just by agreeing to let me visit you tonight."

"I've gone too far already."

"Ah, but there is so much more you have to learn . . . and Emma, while you are learning it, you need not worry about conceiving a child. That's another reason I waited to come to you until we arrived. Here, I can take precautions to ensure that my seed doesn't start a child growing inside you."

Emma's cheeks felt even hotter. "What sort of precautions? I don't understand."

"You've led a sheltered life, so I wouldn't expect you to understand. Leave it to me, Emma. Only do not worry. It isn't likely we conceived a child that one single time we lay together."

"I know we did not. I . . . I'm sure of it." Emma did not want to tell him that two days later, her monthly flow had begun. She was no expert on pregnancy and childbirth, but she did know that much; she had always been a good listener when other women whispered about these matters—particularly Rosie.

"I am relieved to hear of your certainty. From now on, we will take no more risks."

"How is that possible? I mean, if you come to me tonight . . ." She trailed off in embarrassment.

"Do you really want to know? . . . Never mind, I can see that you do, so I shall tell you. There is a device a man can wear on his *lingam* to prevent his seed from spilling inside a woman. I have such a device here at Paradise View, and I'll use it each and every time we are together. So don't worry anymore, Emma."

I wasn't worried! I want your seed in me. I want to bear your child one day!

"Thank you," she whispered. "I'm most fortunate that *you* worry about such things."

She tried hard—she really did—to keep the hurt from her tone, but it crept into it anyway. Worse yet, a single tear rolled down her cheek. To have a child, to bear the babe of a man she loved, must be a woman's greatest joy and triumph. How often had she heard Rosie express her longing for such a wondrous event! And in her own secret fantasies, she had dreamed of such a thing for herself, all the while knowing the dream was unobtainable. But Sikander was right. To bear a child without a husband was a woman's worst fear, her greatest disgrace, not an occasion to celebrate.

"Don't cry, my love." Again, he gathered her into his arms. "Don't be sad. Surely, you realize we *can't* allow ourselves to conceive a child. It will be hard enough building a life for the two children I already have, much less bringing another into the world—especially *your* child. Think what it would be like for you and me if we had a child together; think what our child would have to face."

"But it's so unfair! Why does the world have to be like this? Why does one race have to look down upon another— one culture reject all the good in a different culture? Why do adherents of one religion have to think it's the only *right* one, and all others are wrong?"

"If I knew the answer to those questions, Emma, I would possess all the wisdom of the universe. I could unite the world and create a loving, benevolent kingdom where no one is made to feel inferior. You and I alone can't do it. We are doomed to live by the rules others have made for us."

"Even here in Paradise View where outsiders so rarely come?"

"Even here, my love. The rules here are as strong as anywhere—perhaps stronger than most places. I have two hundred and fifty servants not because I actually need them, but because each person must do only those tasks allowed by the caste into which he was born. A Brahmin will never clean out the stable, and a sweeper will never touch food. And all those in between do only what is required of them. They call someone else if they perceive that a certain task is not appropriate. It is the Indian way."

"Then live in the British way! Or create a new way! You can choose what you want here!"

"But we are in India, Emma. Besides, I myself cannot accept all the foolish conventions of British society—and neither can you. You have already rejected more than half of them by coming here with me. . . . As for forging a new way, I'm not that brave, nor that eccentric. Will it truly help me to alienate both cultures any more than I already have?"

Emma sighed and shook her head. She could argue no further. He had obviously given a great deal of thought to the matter, while she was just coming to grips with it. "Forgive me for passing judgment on you, Sikander. At least between you and me, let there be understanding and tolerance. If we remain honest with each other—and respectful—we can at least be friends and lovers. More, I won't demand. Already, I am far more blessed than I ever dared dream I could be."

They embraced and shared a long passionate kiss that made Emma's head spin, for it hinted of what the night would bring. Then Sikander set her away from him. "Discretion, my love. We must continue to practice discretion—at least during the daytime. 'Tis time I leave you anyway, for I have been gone a long time from Paradise View, and there is much I must do now that I've returned. Rest and refresh yourself for the remainder of the day. Sleep, if you can; I intend that you shall not sleep much tonight."

Emma allowed herself the luxury of basking in his fiery regard. His eyes were smoldering. "May I visit with the children?"

He looked surprised—and pleased. "Of course. If you wish."

"Where shall I find them? I don't know their habits as yet."

"They will soon be in their chamber, for at this time of year, the afternoon's heat drives everyone to their couches. You may visit them any time and place you wish. I'll inform their *ayah* that you are taking charge of their schedule. In the mornings, they usually rise, eat, ride their horses—"

"Ride their horses? At such young ages?"

Humor lit his face. "When did *you* first learn to ride, Emma? I thought you told me you had been riding horses for years and years."

"Well, I have but . . ."

"But nothing. My children will be accomplished riders. When Sakharam is in residence, he himself oversees their lessons. You may attend if you wish. After that, their day will be yours to plan. Just remember all they need to learn: reading, writing, the rudiments of figuring, and all those elegant British manners. . . . Oh, yes. They must also take their castor oil once weekly. They take it now on Sundays. It makes their constitutions robust and keeps their bowels in good working order."

"You sound like an old British nanny yourself. Wherever did you learn about castor oil?"

"My mother's family once had a British governess whose purpose was to educate the young princes and princesses. We were all forced to sit on our little three-legged stools, called *chaurangs* and drink it out of a small bowl called a *katori*. Then we were allowed to suck on a lemon to remove the awful taste. Aside from the health benefits, I found it a character-building experience, and so will my children when they look back on it as I do now. After my cousins and I suffered the predictable effects, the nanny always carefully examined the contents of the royal thunder-boxes."

"And will *I* have to do that? Why, I hardly know what I'll be looking for. Do *you* know?"

His lips twitched with laughter. "No, but as you are the nanny, it will be your job, not mine. I only know that if the nanny didn't like what she saw, she doctored us with nutmeg, aniseed, or parsley seeds."

He executed a quick *salaam* and headed for the doorway, as if expecting Emma to throw something at him. She wished she had something to throw. Instead, she settled for laughter. "If I find something out of the ordinary, I will, of course, refer the matter to *you*," she called after him as he departed her compartment.

"Sorry, but I don't go near thunder-boxes unless I myself have a pressing personal need."

After he had gone, Emma wandered through her delightful rooms, briefly refreshed herself with some water and cloths she found in the bathing chamber, and then lay down for a short rest on the low, wide couch heaped with jade-colored pillows. She was much too excited to sleep—and it was far too hot in the stuffy little sleeping room. She returned to the main room and discovered that someone had closed the shutters to the balcony to keep out the heat. It was dim, quiet, and reasonably cool there. Still, she was restless. The evening seemed a long way away, and she didn't want to dwell on her conversation with Sikander. If she did, she feared she might yet change her mind about tonight and the path her life was now taking. She had consented to be his mistress—and she was eagerly anticipating their first night together in his house. . . . But had she made the right decision?

It was hard to be rational in his presence, when all she

could think about was what it felt like when he kissed her, held her, and made love to her. Given the recklessness of her emotions and the fact that she seemed powerless to control them, she would be utterly devastated if things did not work out between them. She didn't know how she would bear it, what she would do next, or where she would go. For that reason alone, she must persevere in her quest to find Wildwood. Just because the deed had been destroyed didn't mean she should give up. Nor should she abandon the search simply because she had been offered a home with a man for whom she deeply cared. Her mother, too, had thought she had found love in the wilds of India, and look what had happened to her!

A mistress had no real security. Sikander had promised to take care of her, but if their differences proved too great, or something else happened to separate them, she would need somewhere else to go. Returning in defeat to Calcutta and expecting Percival Griffin to accept "damaged goods" was unthinkable. It wasn't a viable option.

She mustn't delude herself. What she had with Sikander was so very fragile! She *wanted* to believe it could last forever, she hoped it would, but she dared not depend on it. Anything could happen to her, to him, or to both of them—including the possibility that once they had indulged their mutual passion, the attraction between them would wane, like a blazing bonfire that inevitably turns to ash.

Emma couldn't imagine that she would ever want Sikander less than she did now; he had awakened something in her that would *never* die. All these years, she had managed to submerge her femininity and deny her womanly needs, but once that box had been opened, it was useless to try and close it again. He had forced her to look inside, to discover the woman she really was, and now there was no turning back. . . . Now, she could only go forward and pursue her destiny—whatever it proved to be. Or so she managed to convince herself.

After a half-hour's pacing, Emma abruptly headed for the door and the children's quarters. It was time to confront them—and their *ayah*—with the reality of her new role in their lives. The sooner they got to be friends, the better. She just wished she hadn't lost the gifts she had brought for Michael and Victoria. The items would perhaps have warmed the children's hearts toward her.

Now she had nothing to offer but herself—and her knowledge. Because they were Sikander's children, she was sure she could grow to love them, and she intended to make them love her—or at least not hate her. But she wondered how she could win them over quickly and thus gain their cooperation and eagerness to learn.

Halfway to their quarters, it came to her: she *wouldn't* dose them with castor oil on Sundays, no matter what Sikander said. As a child, she herself had been subjected to the awful ritual; Monday had been castor oil day, until the rainy, gloomy Monday she had refused to open her mouth for the obligatory dose and declared that she was never going to take it again.

Her father—stepfather—had insisted it be poured down her throat, but she had retaliated by spewing it down the front of him. She had been locked in her room without food and water to repent of her sins and relent. She had held out longer than he had. Her mother had threatened to call the authorities, and even some of the servants—the butler, the cook, and two maids—had come close to resigning.

In the end, she had won. And what had infuriated Sir Henry all the more was that she had never suffered any ill effects from not taking it; indeed, she had been far healthier than her brother, who continued taking castor oil until well into adulthood.

Yes, she would take a stand on this issue. Her own experience had taught her that castor oil wasn't the boon to good health that most people thought. Rather, a healthful diet, plenty of exercise, and good fresh air were what counted most. Her father and brother would have been far better off had they put their faith in those things rather than castor oil. Tomorrow was Sunday, so it shouldn't take too long at all before she had Michael and Victoria Kingston wrapped around her little finger.

Nineteen

Emma spent over an hour in the children's quarters, but made little headway toward befriending either of them or their *ayah*. She did all the talking while they merely sat there, watching, as if they didn't understand a word she was saying. Perhaps the *ayah* didn't, but recognition and an occasional flare of interest lit the children's eyes as Emma promised to read them stories and poetry, as well as tell them about life in England. Victoria, especially, looked as if she wanted to ask questions, but couldn't make up her mind whether to do so or not, especially in front of her brother.

Only once did the *ayah* exert her influence over her young charges—when Michael rose from his stool without Emma's permission. The *ayah* frowned and shook her head, and it was obvious to Emma that this silent guardian intended to do her duty, whether she resented Emma's position or not. Michael walked around the room a time or two before returning to his stool, proving by the small rebellion that he had largely been permitted to do as he pleased, except maybe when his father was home.

When the children grew restless and fidgety, Emma rose to leave. Imposing her authority too quickly would only provoke more obstinacy when she was determined to gain their trust—hopefully by tomorrow. For now, it seemed wiser to retreat than to confront. Returning to her own chambers, she was delighted to discover a pile of brilliant-colored fabrics lying on her bed. Next to them was an assortment of pearl and gold bangles and a book bound in soft, crimson leather, trimmed with gold. Before examining the *saris* or bangles, Emma reached for the book to see what Sikander had thought she might like to read.

Opening it randomly, she knew immediately what he had sent. It was a Pillow Book wherein all sorts of sexual intimacies—and odd positions for the copulatory act—were painstakingly demonstrated. Heat rushed to her cheeks, and she snapped the book closed again, then timidly opened it at the beginning. The first few pages depicted simple kisses and caresses between two clothed figures. Emma breathed a sigh of relief as she realized that the book's vivid illustrations took into account the tender sensibilities of a woman for whom sex was still a new and shattering experience.

She sat down on a nearby stool to study the exquisitely rendered illustrations from the very first page, but was interrupted by the arrival of several cotton-clad women carrying tin pails of steaming water into her bathing chamber. When one of the women boldly approached her, Emma closed the book and tried to stuff it in the folds of her skirt, which weren't ample enough to provide concealment. Desperate to hide it, lest it be recognized for what it was, she quickly rose, set the book on the stool, and sat down on top of it, then smiled pleasantly at the servant.

Fortunately, the servant was far more intent on asking a question than discovering what Emma was hiding. If she found Emma's behavior odd, she didn't show it. Nervously twisting her hands together, she bowed and said, *"Memsahib . . . want . . . bathe?"*

"Oh, you speak English!" Emma exclaimed, delighted.

The woman doggedly shook her head in the negative. "No, no. . . . Want bathe?"

Having exhausted her entire repertoire, she lapsed into her own language and made hand gestures to indicate that Emma should retire to the bathing chamber where a tin tub full of hot water awaited her.

"Thank you," Emma responded, then experimented with the Hindu version of the word which brought a torrent of rapturous acclaim from the woman, very little of which Emma comprehended. "I'm sorry. You must speak more slowly. I might understand if you don't rush me too much."

But it was hopeless, and Emma soon gave up. Leaving the book on the stool, she ushered the servants out of the chamber. She wanted and needed a bath, but certainly not one such as she had experienced at Sayaji Singh's. She much preferred a British-style bath and intended to have it.

Moments later, she sat alone in the huge tub in water nearly up to her neck. The heat of the late afternoon, coupled with the warmth of the water, turned the entire bathing chamber into a steam bath. Emma's hair curled, and perspiration filmed her upper lip, but nothing could have induced her to depart the oily, patchouli-scented waters, not even a cobra suddenly rearing its head beside her.

She hadn't wanted anyone to enter and find the Pillow Book on the stool, so she had brought it with her into the chamber, and there it lay, next to the tub on a small stool, awaiting further perusal. Emma leisurely washed her hair, rinsed it, and wrapped it turban-style in a length of absorbent cloth, then leaned back in the tub and reached for the book again. . . . Surely, this was the height of decadence! To sit in a scented bath and study a book about seduction and sexual pleasure. She spent the next half-hour marveling at the variety and originality of the many ways human beings could make love to each other and give and receive pleasure.

Some of the illustrations made her laugh out loud, others made her blush, and some simply made her shake her head in amazement. To her great surprise, she discovered that none of the activities depicted in the book repulsed her. When she imagined herself as the female and Sikander as the male, such forbidden fantasies seemed perfectly natural. After a short time, her breasts began to feel heavy, her loins throbbed, and she was suffused with such languor and ennui that she doubted she was going to be able to leave the tub without assistance.

Sikander had done this on purpose! He *wanted* her to feel this way, as if every nerve ending and particle of skin was acutely sensitized and longing for his touch. She could hardly wait for the night to come.

"Emma Whitefield, you have truly become a wanton," she muttered, closing the book with a snap and replacing it on the stool.

Moments later, she climbed out of the tub, dried herself, and rubbed on some of the oil the women had left for her in a thin-necked blue flask. The simple act of working the oil into her flesh heightened her already full-blown arousal. She thought of Sikander stroking her body with oiled hands and wished she could go find him and make him come back with her to her quarters, so they could indulge her wicked fantasies. . . . But that was the price she must pay for consenting to be a mistress—a *secret* mistress—rather than a wife; she didn't have the right to do anything so outrageous.

Depressed by the thought, she wrapped herself in a length of colorfully woven Indian fabric and searched through her new clothing—still lying on top of her bed in the sleeping chamber. She hoped she could remember how to put on a *sari.* The women of Sayaji's *zenana* had taught her, amid much laughing and gesturing, but Emma didn't know if she could manage by herself.

By the time she had finished dressing, brushing and drying her hair, and arranging a lovely blue and silver *sari* to cover her head in the Indian fashion, it was early evening, and ardent feelings had given way to hunger. Still, she fussed with her appearance, using a huge brass tray hanging on the wall as a mirror. In it, she looked far more Indian than British. The *sari* floated about her like a cloud each time she moved, and she was enchanted anew with what the garment did for her—not just in the way she looked but in how she felt about herself.

Once again, she had become the swan—a beautiful, desirable, perfumed creature worthy of Sikander's passion. Like the woman in the illustrations of the Pillow Book, she was willing and eager to learn the secrets of lovemaking with the man she loved. . . . Yes, she loved Sikander. That could be the only explanation for her complete metamorphosis from prudish spinster to shameless fallen woman . . . and despite his professed inability to marry her, Sikander cared for her. She was sure of it. That was what made it possible for her to tell him she didn't need marriage; what they had was enough.

Certain she looked as beautiful as she possibly could, Emma stepped into the main room and discovered Sakharam setting a table for her. Nearby stood a servant with a tray of food. However, the table had only one place setting.

"Am I to eat my evening meal alone?" Acute disappointment enveloped her.

Sakharam didn't look up from his task. "If the *memsahib* wishes to dine with the children instead, I can take her meal to their quarters. But I think they have already eaten, and the *sahib* is presently occupied."

"Doing what? Did he send any messages for me?"

Sakharam calmly gestured for the servant to set the tray on the table. At last, he straightened and gave her his full attention. "He sent no messages, *Memsahib*. And I tell no one his whereabouts without his permission."

Both his manner and words were chilling. Somehow he had managed to remind Emma of her modest position in this house without saying a single word to that effect. She sensed his disapproval of her presence here in these rooms—and her manner of dress, too. His next comment proved it.

"Shall I have your regular clothing laundered and returned to you, *Memsahib?* No doubt you will want it in the morning.

I have already sent for a *durzi* to restore your entire wardrobe."

"Yes, I might want my usual gown in the morning." Emma barely managed to respond politely. "On the other hand, I may decide to wear *sari*s from now on, in which case the *durzi* will not be necessary. A *sari* is far more comfortable than my English garb, I find."

Sakharam pursed his mouth as if he'd just tasted a particularly sour lemon. "As you wish, *Memsahib.*"

As he turned to leave, Emma called out to him. "Sakharam!"

He paused on the threshold. "Yes, *Memsahib*?"

"Don't think I'm confined to these rooms. I'll go wherever I please whenever I please; do you understand?"

"I never expected anything different, *Memsahib*, especially from you. As the *children's nanny,* you are free to go wherever you wish."

So he was well aware of the nature of her true relationship with Sikander and wasn't happy about it. His emphasis on "children's nanny" reeked of sarcasm . . . and if Sakharam knew, others might also know or suspect, which gave her a peculiar feeling of vulnerability and shame. The one thing Emma had always merited from servants was their respect; to lose it was a severe blow to her pride. Yet she wasn't about to change anything because of it; for the first time in her life, she was going to obey her womanly instincts and be damned to anyone who thought less of her for it!

"Thank you for dinner, Sakharam." She allowed a distinct coldness to creep into her tone. He bowed and departed, leaving her to eat a lonely meal by herself.

Sikander came to her late that night, long after the household had settled down, and the moon had risen. Emma had dragged her bed into the main room and placed it near the balcony, and she lay beneath the mosquito netting and watched the moonlight gild the room's furnishings. It was hot and still; half-dozing, she did not hear him enter. But suddenly, he was there . . . gazing down at her, a tall dark figure clad in a loose silken garment fastened at the waist with a sash.

"What?" he drawled. "You are not reading? I had thought to find you immersed in that book I left for you."

Emma sat up, suddenly self-conscious in the thin, sheer garment she had surmised must be for sleeping—and seduction—because it was so light and airy one could see right through it. "I have already looked at the book you left. And I must say, it was . . . enlightening."

He raised the mosquito netting, took her hand, and drew her slowly to her feet. "Ah, was it? . . . What illustration enticed you the most?" His tone was light and teasing. "Do you wish to try some new position tonight—the Butterfly perhaps, or the Grasshopper . . ."

"I need no Pillow Book to stimulate my appetite for love-making, Sikander. That is like offering a tray of foreign delicacies to a woman who is starved for bread. What I need is . . . you. Here in my room, in my bed, in my arms."

Boldly, she embraced him, pressing herself against his hard length and discovering that he was naked beneath his silken robe.

"Emma . . ." he growled, rubbing against her so that she felt the thrust of his engorged manhood between her thighs. Spreading her legs slightly, she sought to hold him there, pressed against her femininity where the dew of desire was already making her slick and ready for their joining.

"I have been thinking of this all day," he murmured huskily. "And anxiously pacing my rooms waiting for it to be late enough to risk seeking you out."

"I missed you at dinner . . ." She slipped her hands into the slit at the front of his robe and touched her palms to his bare chest. "I wanted so much to be with you. I wanted you to see me in one of the lovely *saris* you sent. Thank you for sending them. They made me so happy, I'm not even going to ask where they came from or who wore them before me."

"I am here now, Emma. That's all that counts. If you did ask me, I wouldn't tell you. It doesn't matter. They are yours now. Let us not waste time regretting what we cannot change, thereby ruining the time we *do* have together."

"Would it be so improper for us to share our meals here in your house?"

"By ourselves, yes. But when we set up the dining room as you wish, why, then I see no harm in taking our meals in company with the children."

"Let's begin setting up the dining room as soon as possible." Emma burrowed into him. She didn't think she could bear it if the only time she could spend with him was late at night like this. She had grown accustomed to spending nearly every minute of every day with him.

He tilted up her face. "Tomorrow," he promised, and then he lowered his mouth to hers.

His kiss obliterated every thought except the need to be close to him and to assuage the aching heaviness she felt in her female parts. She wanted him to touch her intimately, and she desperately wanted to explore *his* body in return. The illustrations she had studied that day had shown her ways of loving she might never have thought of by herself— or if she did think of them, she would have been afraid they were too unusual and therefore, forbidden.

She now had the confidence she needed to be bold and experimental. When the long kiss ended, he simply held her to him as if savoring her nearness and fighting for control. But Emma began to kiss and nip at his neck while her hands explored his chest. She had already noticed that he had a generous portion of black curly hair on his chest while most Indian men seemed to have very little. And of course, she had discovered the sensitivity of his nipples during their first encounter. His chest was beautiful—wonderfully masculine and enticing. While her fingers roamed and caressed it, she bent her head to taste him and discover his textures. She found that she, too, could impart pleasure by suckling his nipples, but when she knelt in front of him and attempted to trail kisses down to his navel and lower, he seized her by the hair and gently pulled her back up again.

"One day, I shall let you do that, sweet Emma . . . but not tonight. At least, not until I have spent my passion the first time. Have you no idea what you are doing to me?"

She didn't really, other than what the Pillow Book and his responses suggested. "I assume you sent me that wicked book in order to give me ideas—but now that I have them, you won't allow me to put them into action."

"Come here, my eager little student. I will teach you a few things not found in books of any kind." He pulled her over to the bed, swept aside the mosquito netting, and started to press her down upon it. Then he stopped and removed her sheer gown and tossed it aside. "You won't be needing this anymore tonight."

She untied his sash with trembling fingers. "Nor will you be needing this."

His robe slid to the floor, and moonlight outlined his superbly sculpted body—including his enormous *lingam* which jutted toward her in all its masculine arrogance and power. Reaching out, she wrapped her fingers around it, marveling at the slick, velvety feel of him in her hand. Nothing so expressed his strength and masculinity as this part of him—and she suddenly understood how *lingam* worship had come about.

To worship him with her body—through her caresses and feminine possession—was so easy, so right. She wouldn't mind kissing him there at all; indeed, she yearned for it. But again, he rejected her first tentative overtures.

"Careful, my love. Let me do the loving first. Then you may have your chance." Pressing her back on the bed, he moved over her, settled himself gently beside her, and began to kiss and caress her in earnest.

Moaning softly, Emma succumbed to sensation. He worshipped her breasts, belly, hips, the insides of her thighs. . . .

His mouth fastened upon her feminine core, and she bucked and arched beneath him as he tongued and licked that most tender intimate place. When he began to suckle the small bud of pleasure he had ignored up until now, she gasped and tried to push him away. "Sikander, no! Stop, I beg you!"

Moving swiftly, he captured her hands and pinned them to the pillow above her head. "Let me do what I will, Emma. Don't be afraid. I would never hurt you. It did not hurt the first time I took you, did it?"

Emma recalled the sudden sharp pain she had experienced at their first joining—a pain which had quickly faded in the wonder of his possession. "It's not the pain I fear."

She didn't know how to put it into words. What exactly *did* she fear? She agonized over it for a moment, while he remained motionless, waiting for an explanation. She had none to give. She only knew that what he had been doing was an act so intimate, personal, and precious that it touched her deeply. It was an act a man should perform only with his wife.

"Forgive me," she murmured as tears gathered in her eyes, and her arousal began to ebb.

"There's nothing to forgive. You just aren't ready for that particular intimacy; one day, you will be."

She wanted to cry out, *I'll never be ready! Not if we never marry.*

But all she did was force a watery smile. "I promise to study the Pillow Book until I become ready."

"I thought you already studied it. Didn't it make you feel . . . amorous?"

"Oh, yes," she shakily agreed. "It did. And I am still feeling amorous. I'm just not ready to do everything depicted in its pages."

"We'll keep working on it, my love. Every night, we'll go a little further."

He resumed kissing and fondling her breasts. Despite her tears, she was soon ready for his full possession. He paused a moment, doing something in the dark to his *lingam*, and then mounted her, impaling her with a single long thrust. Holding still above her, he nuzzled her cheek. "Do you want me, Emma? Tell me you want me."

"I *do* want you. Oh, yes, Sikander, I want you very much."

With a low, inarticulate growl, he began to move within her. His *lingam* filled her completely, and she reveled in each thrust of his virile body. Meeting them with her own frantic gyrations, she became increasingly wild and lost control. She wanted him so much! The ache inside her grew unbearable, and the friction of his thrusting simultaneously soothed and provoked it, causing deep, fulfilling spasms that made her cry out and clutch him closer.

Again and again, he drove into her. She raked her nails down his back and sought to bring him closer still. Just when she thought she could bear no more, her body seemed to burst with pleasure. Great shudders rippled through her. At the same moment, he clasped her to him in one last desperate embrace. . . . It was like dying and being reborn. She lay still and spent as the last aftershocks of pleasure pulsed inside her and finally died away.

"I love you, Sikander," she whispered on a sigh, unable to restrain herself.

He lifted his head, and his expression was unreadable in the darkness, for the moon shone behind him. "Don't put a name to what you feel for me yet, Emma. Sex is still so new to you; you are just beginning to experience the wonder of it. I have given you pleasure, so you think you love me. You have given me pleasure, so I think I care for you in return."

"You care for me?" The admission thrilled her, though it wasn't precisely what she wanted to hear. "You honestly care for me?" she shamelessly prompted.

He nodded. "But I am far too cynical to admit to more, Emma. One should never place one's trust in declarations uttered in a bedchamber or Love Pavilion—or for that matter, anywhere else. Words are useless when all is said and done."

"You're right. You are too cynical. Your previous experiences with passionate declarations must all have been bad ones for you to be so suspicious and doubting."

He ran his finger along the curve of her cheek, his voice low and gently self-mocking. "Once, when I was a very small boy, my father told me he loved me. I believed him totally and thought that nothing could ever hurt me, because my father would not allow it. Not long thereafter, my father went away. He abandoned me and my mother because we were Indian—at least, my mother was. I was only a half-caste. But Anglo-Indian liaisons were no longer considered politic, so he ended the relationship by simply walking away from us."

"How awful! But where is your father now? Surely, he has regretted his actions and would willingly reclaim you as his son."

"He's dead, Emma. He died several years after he abandoned us. When I heard the news, I didn't weep or mourn; in my mind, he was already dead. Or perhaps I just wanted him to be dead. Whatever the case, I never again put any faith in declarations of affection. Members of my mother's family claimed to love me, too, but all of them rejected me at some point as I was growing up. My own mother abandoned me by marrying and bearing other children—pure-blooded Indians—and then by dying too young, before I was ready to relinquish her. So you see, I can't help but be cynical. I have good reason."

Emma pulled his head down to rest on her breast. "I will give you reasons to believe in love again, Sikander. We mustn't allow ourselves to become bitter because of the weaknesses and failings of others. We shouldn't close ourselves off from life—and from love—simply because we've been hurt in the past."

She was lecturing herself as much as him, for she, too, had suffered and wondered if love truly existed. Now, she was sure it did, for she had found Sikander.

"I would like to believe love is possible, Emma, but I'm consumed with doubt. I try to love my children; I will never abandon them as my father did me. But to say 'I love you'— it's much too hard. I can't do it. Because I know full well that love is too easily destroyed. Too quickly trampled and lost."

"You've never told your children you love them?" Lying still a moment, Emma absorbed that information. She remembered how she had *prayed* for Sir Henry to notice her and say a kind word—had dreamed of him professing his love for her on the front lawn of Whitefield Hall.

"They know I love them."

"Can you be so sure? You have to *tell* them, Sikander, or they will never believe it. You have to tell them many, many times, not just when they deserve it, but also when they don't."

He raised his head again "You want me to leave your chamber and go tell them now, this very instant?"

"Well, no, not now . . ."

"Good!" He laughed softly. "Because I won't do it. I've only just begun pleasuring you, Emma; I had hoped you had only just begun pleasuring me."

"But . . ."

"But nothing." He levered himself off her, breaking the contact of their bodies, and lay down beside her. Then he took her hand and placed it on his *lingam*.

"What . . . what do you have on?" she asked, distracted and excited at the same time.

" 'Tis the device I told you about—a kind of sheath made from a sheep's bladder."

"A sheep's bladder!"

"Yes, but don't worry," he drawled in his humor-laden tone. "The sheep was quite dead when its bladder was removed. Anyway, the device won't stop me from enjoying your touch. Touch me, Emma. I *want* you to touch me now."

Emma wanted to touch him—sheep's bladder or no. She

also wanted to urge him to show more affection to his children and tell them he loved them. But that was something to work on in the future. Slowly, she caressed him, restoring his full, rigid arousal.

"Is it really necessary for you to wear this . . . this device? I don't like having a barrier between us."

"It's necessary, Emma. You know it is."

"But I don't have to like it. I want to feel *your* skin, not the bladder of some poor dead sheep." Suddenly rebellious, she began to tug at the device which fit him like a second skin.

"Emma, stop!" He grabbed her hand and held it away from him, then rose up on one elbow. "I think you have had enough for one night."

"But I haven't." A nameless frustration and yearning filled her.

He rolled off the bed and stood. "Yes, you have, my sweet. I must leave you now anyway. But I'll come again tomorrow night . . . and I'll be wearing my protective device."

Quickly, he picked up his robe and donned it with an economy of motion. Emma slumped back on the pillows, watching him and feeling bereft.

"Good night, my love." He bent and brushed a light kiss across her temple.

It wasn't enough. Emma reached for him, but he was already leaving. As swiftly as he had come into her chamber, he was gone again. She struggled not to cry. If this was all she could ever have, she must learn to be satisfied with it. But she wasn't satisfied—not in the least. Her body was sated, but not her soul. She wanted all of him, not just his lovemaking, but the man himself—his seed in her body and more importantly, his love and commitment, his open acknowledgment of his feelings for her.

She thought of telling him it was over; it would never work out between them, and tears rolled down her cheeks. Turning her head, she let them spill onto the pillow that still bore his scent. She may not be happy with the way things were, but she couldn't leave Paradise View. She couldn't—not when she loved Alexander Kingston with her whole being.

"You love-sick little fool," she moaned, gazing up at the moon riding high in the night sky above the balcony railing. "Whatever are you going to do?"

Wildwood. Find Wildwood, a little voice insisted.

Wildwood would be something all her own. Now, she had only a borrowed lover, a borrowed house, borrowed clothing, and borrowed children. Even her job had been borrowed. It should have gone to Abigail Lundy. Tomorrow, after she refused to force castor oil down the throats of Sikander's children, she would begin her search.

Twenty

After leaving Emma and returning to his own rooms, Alex couldn't sleep. He tossed and turned restlessly for over an hour, thinking of Emma's dissatisfaction and regretting that he could do nothing to relieve it. She would have to accept things as they were; in time she would. . . . She had to, because he couldn't offer her anything else.

His body was tired and ready for sleep—or another bout of lovemaking with Emma—but he couldn't clear his mind enough to relax, so at last, he dressed, left his chamber, and headed for his office, located in one of the outbuildings near the stable. A huge pile of correspondence awaited his attention; he hadn't had time to sort through it since his return to Paradise View, and now seemed as good a time as any.

Mail intended for the plantation went to a small office he kept in Bhopal, and servants periodically picked it up. His absence had resulted in a stack of letters, packets, and old newspapers spilling off his big teak desk onto the red tile floor below. By the light of a coconut oil lamp, Alex began to divide the mess into small piles, according to order of importance.

Most of the mail appeared to be business related; there were progress reports on his various investments and inquiries from potential buyers concerning his rice and indigo harvests as well as his hardwoods. He pulled out several items of immediate interest: one was a letter from his aunt, Santamani, and the others were official-looking documents, two from the Government Land Office of Central India, one from the *Nawabzada* of Bhopal, and another—surprisingly!—from his cousin, Hyder Khan. He recognized the seals on all of them.

He tore open Santamani's letter first and scanned the brief message with a suddenly pounding heart. He didn't know what he had expected, since they hadn't spoken in years, but what he found made him grit his teeth in disgust and read the letter twice, to be sure he had caught every nuance.

"*My dear Sikander,*" it said in beautifully written English, in itself insulting since it emphasized the British half of his heritage. "*If you have ever cared for any of us, please give your most diligent consideration to a favor my son will soon be asking of you. Do not reject it out of hand merely because it comes from Hyder Khan. Despite what you may think, he is doing his best to protect and serve our people. This has become increasingly difficult due to the shameless manipulations of those now in power. Since you seem to have found ways to deal successfully with the Raj, I implore you to graciously grant his request. It is simple and completely harmless, though it may inconvenience you. If we had other options, we would never turn to you. I hope this finds you well and happy. Kindest felicitations, Santamani.*"

Hyder Khan was at it again—manipulating his mother to gain some advantage over him! Alex didn't want to open the cylindrical packet from his cousin, but his curiosity couldn't be contained. It wasn't thick enough to hold anything as dangerous as a *krait,* but Alex nonetheless handled it warily, for he didn't trust Hyder Khan one bit. It would be just like him to package a highly poisonous and aggressive reptile in some innocuous-looking container.

The letter inside was short and to the point; it, too, was written in English, as if Alex were too stupid to understand the language learned at his mother's breast.

"*Cousin,*" it said. "*Were it not for my mother's insistence,*

I would never write asking for your help. I had rather let our people starve to death. However, despite her advancing years, my mother still wields an amazing influence; therefore, I am writing. Due to the greed of our beloved Raj, who will one day bleed this country dry, I find myself unable to meet the needs of all those dependent upon me for their salt."

"Salt," as anyone who lived in India knew, was the Indian expression for the livelihood provided by a man's protector. In the feudal system of India, the peasants worked for their "salt," meaning they attached themselves to some great family or government entity, offered their total loyalty, and in return, received all they needed to survive. In the old days, the poor had flocked to the Maharajahs, hoping to attach themselves to their households or estates. Today, they were just as likely to flock to members of the Raj, offering themselves as servants working within the boundaries of the caste system.

With growing suspicion as to where all this might be leading, Alex read on. *"At my mother's suggestion, I am sending you some of my most skilled laborers whose services I no longer need and cannot afford. They have been instructed to give you the loyalty they once gave me and my family. I trust you will find some use for them and treat them kindly. If not, they will have to discover another means of survival, for I can no longer provide for them. The group will be arriving shortly, bringing with them their families, dependents, all their belongings, and in one case, an elephant. I would have kept the elephant, but his* mahout *refused to remain when all the rest of his family and closest friends were leaving."*

Alex uttered a loud curse, crumpled the letter, and threw it hard against the wall. He did not need to read further; there was only another line or two anyway, and he already knew all he needed to know. In a few days, an indeterminate number of impoverished Indians—most of them probably too old or too inept to work—would descend upon Paradise View.

Their sole value would be to spy on him and carry tales of his daily activities to Hyder Khan.

Oh, he had to congratulate his cousin on *this* latest coup! It was the perfect way to flood Paradise View with spies and informers. Under the guise of sincerity, benevolence, and concern for his people, Hyder Khan was sending him workers. No wonder Santamani had written in support! She no doubt applauded her son's generosity and nobility of spirit, never realizing his *true* motives.

Alex angrily recalled the time he had hired an extremely promising young clerk—only to discover that the man had once worked for Hyder Khan and considered it his duty to leak information about Alex's trade deals to his former master.

Well, his cousin's clever ploy wouldn't work this time, Alex swore; he'd send the whole lot back to Hyder Khan just as soon as they arrived. He'd have Sakharam post a guard at the furthest outposts of his land and turn them back there. As usual, Santamani would condemn him for his cruelty and hard-heartedness, but Alex didn't care. He couldn't support any more dependents, and he had to protect himself from what amounted to an invasion by his enemy—people who would remain loyal to the man they had always served no matter what he told them, *if* he actually *had* told them to switch their loyalties.

It was the Indian way to remain true to one's salt even unto death, if necessary. The worst sin a man could commit was to betray his salt. Hyder Khan had only to question these poor people at length, and they would tell him everything, because he had been their *ma-bap,* their mother and father, whom they and their families had been serving all their lives.

Muttering invectives, Alex grabbed a letter from the land office, opened it, and groaned in dismay from this new and punishing blow. The letter informed him that despite the claims he had refiled in the Calcutta office and the assurances he had been given that everything was all right, it would be absolutely necessary for a high-ranking official to tour his holdings to ascertain exactly where his stated boundaries lay.

The office had already received notice that counter-claims were going to be registered by certain as yet unnamed parties. Because of the size of Alex's holdings and the fact that the person or persons making the counter-claims was someone of lofty stature, the newly appointed British Land Administrator of Central India would have to make the visit himself. The letter didn't reveal the name of the man, but said Alex should expect him before the monsoon descended and made travel impossible.

The date on the letter proved it had been sent before Alex himself had departed Calcutta, which meant the land office had known all along that his claims were going to be disputed but had purposely neglected to tell him while he was there. It was one more demonstration of the Raj's prejudice toward a man who didn't meet their approval.

The second letter from the land office reiterated the information contained in the first letter, stating that the new administrator would most certainly be visiting Paradise View before the onset of the rainy season.

Fuming, expecting still more bad news, Alex picked up the letter from the *Nawabzada* of Bhopal. It turned out to be a flowery, not-so-subtle suggestion that Alex and the *Nawabzada* should meet to discuss the terms of their agreement regarding the harvesting of the trees on Alex's land. The letter alluded to the unfortunate loss of important documents in the Calcutta Land Office and suggested that since his right to harvest might now be under dispute, Alex needed all the support he could get from those in a position to help, such as the *Nawabzada* himself.

The young ruler must have had help from his greedy advisors and perhaps even from Hyder Khan in arriving at this conclusion, Alex decided. It was nothing less than a bold-faced attempt to bully him into increasing the *Nawabzada's* percentage of the profits on the venture.

Alex would have liked to ignore it—or better yet, tell the young man to stuff his *lingam* back in his trousers and stop trying to rape his own countrymen. But he didn't have the financial stability to fight such pressures; one day, he would. One day, he'd be big enough and diverse enough that he could refuse to cut down another tree, if he wished, which would leave the *Nawabzada* powerless to wring another rupee out of him.

What bothered Alex the most was that he could do nothing except begin planning for these unwelcome visits. Having Emma there would help create the impression that Paradise View was as much British as Indian. They must begin at once to make the changes she had requested. He had indulged his Indian tastes long enough; now, he would *have* to start living more like the typical Englishman.

Clearing a place to work, he sat down and began writing a list. His Indian furnishings would have to go; he'd send at once to Bhopal and Gwalior for the dark, heavy furniture so beloved by the British, and he'd put *punkah*-fans in every room, dress his children in British clothing, and serve typically British food at his table. Having known that one day he'd be overrun by officialdom, he ought to have been doing all this anyway.

Alex worked alone in his office through the remainder of the night and into the next day. He ate food a servant brought him and did not glance up from his work until Sakharam suddenly interrupted. "*Sahib*, you must come at once. The *memsahib* is looking for you everywhere. She is like a wild beast gone on a rampage."

"Over what? Has something happened?"

"I don't know when it all began, *Sahib*, but this morning, she stopped the children's *ayah* from giving them their weekly medicine—which pleased the children but not the *ayah*, because the order did not come from you. Then she began to move furnishings in the house, saying she was making changes, which she has no right to do."

Alex couldn't help grinning at the thought of Emma taking a stand over the castor oil. It was a deliberate refusal to do something he had expressly ordered, but he found it hard to be angry. If he himself had been rescued from the loathsome duty by his own *ayah* when he was a child, he would have worshipped the ground she walked upon. Emma knew exactly what she was doing—and apparently thought she had a good chance of having her rebellion overlooked.

"I have given Miss Whitefield the right to make whatever changes she desires," he told Sakharam.

"But *Sahib*, she was searching for you to tell you about them and found the *zenana*."

"So . . . the *zenana*. She's found it, has she?" Alex silently cursed his own forgetfulness. He should have taken Emma to the *zenana* before this and introduced all the women there, with the exception of Lahri. Had he explained the presence of each one, he would not be in this awkward, uncomfortable position. Now she could accuse him of misleading her.

"After she stumbled upon it by accident, *Sahib*, she *ordered* me to fetch you to her chambers at once."

"Well, I suppose I'll have to go and see what she wants, won't I?"

"Sikander. . . . Forgive me for asking, but does she know about Lahri?"

Alex shook his head. "No, and Lahri doesn't know about her, either. I've been meaning to have a little talk with Lahri, but I haven't yet found the time."

"You had best beware, Sikander. I have only seen the *memsahib* in such an agitated state one other time—at Sayaji Singh's, when he sent that girl to you. This time, I think she's *more* agitated. When I left her, she was pacing the floor and talking to herself."

Alex plowed a hand through his hair and sighed. "What was she saying?"

"She was saying, 'Six! There were *six* of them! . . . And he told me he didn't keep multiple wives or concubines.' "

Alex groaned. "I've badly mishandled this, Sakharam. Had I been forthcoming about the others, she might not have found out about Lahri at all. Now, her do-gooder British dander is up, and she won't rest until she rids my house of this supposedly wicked institution."

"I fear you are right, Sikander. It must have come as a great shock to Lahri also, to meet this foreign woman in your house."

"Why? She's the nanny I told everyone I was going to Calcutta to get."

"She's not just a nanny, Sikander. You needn't tell falsehoods to me. I *know* where you spent last night—and one other night on the journey home."

"Where I spend my nights and with whom is not your concern, Sakharam—nor anyone else's. And I'll run my pigsticker through the first person I hear gossiping about it."

"Yes, *Sahib*. If I hear any gossip, I will put a stop to it." His brows drawn together in deep disapproval, Sakharam made an elaborate *salaam*.

"You'd better. I value discretion more than anything in the men closest to me. You know that, and so do they."

"Forgive me for mentioning it, *Sahib*." Sakharam swiftly stepped aside as Alex rose and stalked around the desk on his way to join Emma.

As Emma paced her chamber, waiting for Sikander to appear, she resolved not to allow him to make some foolish excuse for the presence of all those attractive women shut away in their own spacious section of the house. The building in which the women were living was attached to the main house by a courtyard and covered walkway.

It *had* to be a *zenana*, and on the opposite side of the house from Emma's rooms was a small jewel of a three-sided structure overlooking the pond and fountain. It could only be Sikander's Love Pavilion, where he entertained his women. . . . Did he actually think she was stupid enough to mistake all those beautifully garbed females for servants?

One young woman in particular had been breathtakingly lovely. Emma had not been able to study her for very long, because within moments of Emma's appearance, the girl had quickly drawn up her *sari* to cover her face. If she *was* a mere servant, Emma would be only too happy to grovel at Sikander's feet and apologize for her suspicions—but if she was exactly what Emma thought she was, along with all the other women, then . . . then . . . Emma didn't know what she would do, but she'd certainly do something!

One look at Sikander's face was all she needed; one look and she'd know what those women were to him, and whether or not he had lied to her . . . deceived her . . . made her the *seventh* of his mistresses. . . . Oh, God! How could she bear it? The mere thought shattered her pride, devastated her soul, tore her heart into tiny fragments.

She hadn't expected that his entire past life had been lived in a celibate manner; but she wasn't prepared to share him with six other women! He should have told her about his harem—warned her—promised to send them all away. Instead, he had gone out of his way to assure her that he *didn't* keep a *zenana* at Paradise View.

Hadn't he anticipated she would go exploring? Hadn't he expected it? She had only been searching for him, after all. She was going to tell him exactly what she was doing today and why—rescuing the children from needless suffering and discomfort, and in the process, winning their approval. She was also starting to turn his Indian palace into a proper British castle.

She hadn't meant to poke her nose where it didn't belong; but why was she worrying about *her* behavior when *he* was the one at fault?

Pacing back and forth, growing more upset by the moment, Emma suddenly heard Sikander's voice outside her doorway. "Emma?"

Like a storm blowing into the room, he strode into the chamber with Sakharam at his heels. Emma said nothing. Slowly, she turned to face him, noticing that he looked tired, disheveled, and badly in need of a shave. His clothes—a simple Indian-style tunic over British breeches and boots— were worn and wrinkled. Despite all that, he was still the most beautiful man she had ever seen.

She thought of last night and the things they had done together, and she felt a surge of heat in the pit of her belly. As she remembered what had precipitated this meeting, an icy chill drove out the warmth.

"Emma, you have made a grave mistake. Those women you saw are *not* my concubines. If you doubt me, ask Sakharam."

"This has nothing to do with Sakharam. I prefer to hear the truth from *you*. You deny that you keep a *zenana*?"

He wore an expression of wounded innocence. Only then did Emma realize that even if he were guilty, he probably wouldn't *look* it; he'd had a great deal of practice at subterfuge.

"No, they are indeed living in my *zenana*. It doesn't necessarily follow that they must be my wives or concubines. One is a distant cousin. Her husband was so cruel she tried to run away and return home. Her family wouldn't take her back, so I offered her refuge here. Another used to be a concubine in the house of my cousin, Hyder Khan. He set her aside—threatened to turn her out to fend for herself. She's a gently reared, high-caste Brahmin, but she would have had to go begging in the streets of Gwalior. . . . And then there's Gayatri."

"Do tell me about Gayatri. No doubt there's a reasonable explanation—a heart-rending story—for each and every one."

"You refuse to listen?" Sikander's eyes were as dark as onyx. "You doubt what I'm telling you?"

"Let's go down to the *zenana* right now. You can make your explanations right there in front of them. I want to see and hear their reactions. Sakharam can translate . . . and don't think I won't understand what's being said. I can't speak it, but I know enough Urdu by now to follow a conversation."

It was a bit of a lie. Emma couldn't understand anything if the parties spoke too fast—but she was sure she'd be able to ascertain the truth by studying the faces of the women. They couldn't have Sikander's experience in masking their feelings.

"All right. If you insist. Sakharam, inform the women that we are coming to question them."

"No! He's to stay with us. That way he won't have the opportunity to persuade them to tell falsehoods."

Sakharam turned to Sikander. "*Sahib*?"

"Stay with us," he conceded. "Miss Whitefield doesn't trust either of us."

"You're right. I don't."

"Come along then. Let's go to the *zenana*." Sikander gave no hint of guilt or worry. He was smooth and confident, which only fired Emma's suspicions.

She preceded them out of her chamber and down the wide stairway. Soon, they arrived at the arched doorway of the *zenana*, where a beautifully carved door barred anyone from entering. A young man dressed like Sakharam stood at attention there. He was the same guard she had seen before, but just as he had not tried to prevent Emma from entering—probably because she was a woman—he made no protest when all three of them did so.

Why should he? Emma thought bitterly as he helpfully opened the door. Sikander was his lord and master; he could come and go as he pleased in the women's quarters.

They stepped into a luxurious, dimly lit chamber where a

single woman lounged against pillows on a thick rug in front of a screen. She was eating from a small brass bowl, but when she saw them, she immediately set down the bowl, rose, and covered her face with her *sari*.

Sakharam said something to her, and she hurried into the interior of the lush apartment. At Emma's look of inquiry, he explained. "I merely told her to fetch the others. I said the *Sahib* has brought the new English nanny to make their acquaintance."

Emma had caught the word for "visitors," so she made no further comment, but simply stood there, impatiently tapping a foot and wishing the women would hurry and arrive.

A few moments later, a small bunch of females filed into the room—their faces discreetly hidden behind the folds of their *sari*s, which had been drawn up to cover their heads. Sikander pointed to one, and she nervously stepped forward and gazed at the floor near Emma's feet. She was too shy to look at Emma directly.

Sikander cleared his throat. "This is Gayatri, the one I was trying to tell you about. She is my wife's elder sister who accompanied her to my home when we first married. Normally, she'd be married and living elsewhere, but since she is deaf, no man wants her. At my wife's pleading, I allowed her to remain. I thought she would be good company for my young wife—and so she was. She's still here, because her family doesn't wish to reclaim her."

The sad tale roused Emma's sympathies—until she remembered that everything Sikander was telling her could well be a lie. Lifting her hands, Emma clapped them together. The loud sound made the other women jump, but Gayatri never flinched, nor did she raise her eyes.

"She's ashamed of her affliction," Sikander added. "That's why she won't look at us. In all the time she's been here, she hasn't once looked me in the eye."

"I'd like to question the others myself," Emma said. "If you don't mind, Sakharam can translate."

"Of course. Satisfy your curiosity, Emma. You'll see I've been telling the truth. These women are here because they have nowhere else to go. They are all gently bred, but for one reason or another, can't live with their families—or their families no longer want them. Indian women are completely at the mercy of men; upper class women usually live in *purdah* all of their lives. They must have protectors, meaning that some man must be willing to provide for them. Even men like Sayaji have women in their *zenanas* who serve no real purpose, being neither wives nor concubines, but to toss them out would be—"

"I'd prefer to hear them speak for themselves. Mere nanny that I am, I haven't the right to make demands, but still I am asking, Mr. Kingston."

"Go right ahead, Miss Whitefield. That's why we're here; so you can ask all the questions you want."

Going to each of the remaining woman in turn, Emma asked her name and begged her to tell how she had come to be there. Sakharam translated, and it was exactly as Sikander had said. All of the women had perfectly plausible excuses for why they were there. Emma detected no hint of a lie or falsehood, and no shame or embarrassment regarding their positions in Sikander's household. To them, their dependency seemed quite normal.

When she inquired about their treatment and whether or not they were happy living there, the women insisted that the *Sahib* was a truly wonderful man whose generosity could never be repaid. Except for poor Gayatri, who looked puzzled and uncomfortable with the proceedings, the women began to relax and chatter happily among themselves. They seemed genuinely delighted to have a foreigner in their midst.

One by one, the women lowered their veils, and Emma could see that a couple of them were quite plain. One looked old. Emma was ready to concede that perhaps these females were *not* wives or concubines, after all, but then she suddenly noticed something. When she had first burst into the *zenana*, there had been six women in the large outer room. Now, there were only five. Where was the other one? . . . Or had Emma miscounted?

No, she decided, studying their faces. She had seen a lovely young girl with long black hair and beautiful black eyes. *That* one was missing—and suddenly, Emma knew *she* was the one to fear, the one Sikander didn't want her to know about.

"Are you satisfied?" Sikander gave her an arch look from beneath the slash of a dark brow.

"Not yet. One of the women isn't here. She was a lovely young lady—notable for being the fairest of the lot."

For once, Sakharam seemed to forget to guard his expression. He exchanged a quick worried glance with his master. Sikander's blue eyes revealed nothing more than mild curiosity and innocent puzzlement.

"Now, let me see." He seemed to be thinking. "Ah, yes. . . . You must be referring to Lahri, a mere child. Delightful, but extremely young. She's probably off playing a game somewhere."

His tone implied that Emma needn't worry about her, but Emma *was* worried. She knew instinctively that her only rival among these women was that beautiful young girl with the flashing black eyes.

"I should like to meet her, too." Emma congratulated herself on her calm, cool demeanor when she felt like a quivering compote.

"Certainly. Sakharam, ask one of the women to fetch her, will you? Miss Whitefield would like to meet Lahri. Then you may prepare us some tea. I'd like some tea after this, wouldn't you, Miss Whitefield?" He was being ridiculously formal, which made Emma all the more suspicious.

"Tea would be excellent."

Tea was always excellent, good for every occasion. In this, Sikander betrayed his British heritage. To the English, tea was the answer to everything, even a broken heart. In response to Sakharam's request, the women all scattered. Sakharam departed to make the tea, leaving Emma momentarily alone with Sikander.

"Emma . . ." He reached for her hand. "While we're alone, I want to tell you something."

"Oh? Is it about . . . Lahri?"

He nodded. "I'm afraid it is. Emma, she is . . . *was* . . . my mistress."

Emma withdrew her hand. "I *knew* it!"

"Emma, wait." His fingers clamped down on her wrist. "Listen to me before you jump to conclusions. Hear me out. It's true, she was my mistress before you came here. After my wife died, I was lonely, and Lahri was a pretty young woman in need of a protector. So naturally, she became my mistress."

"Naturally."

"I had planned to send her away—to find her a new protector. It will take time, and . . . and won't be easy. Lahri is devoted to me. Still, I hope to find someone pleasing to her. . . . I never intended to keep her once you and I—"

"Let go of me!" Emma pried his fingers from her shoulder. She couldn't bear for him to touch her; this was her worst nightmare come true. "Does she know about me? Have you told her you plan to send her away?"

"Emma, we only just got here. I haven't seen her since our return. Please try to be reasonable. I know you're hurt and angry, but . . ."

A piercing scream cut him off. A series of guttural noises, like a beast being torn limb from limb, followed.

"Dear God, what's *that?*" Emma gasped.

"I can't imagine, but I intend to find out. It's coming from the courtyard."

Sikander sprinted toward a screen, and when he got to it, darted around the obstacle. Close at his heels, Emma saw that it concealed an archway leading to a long stone corridor.

Sikander raced down the corridor, and picking up her skirts, Emma sought to keep up with him.

They made several turns and raced through a half-dozen rooms before reaching a covered archway fronting the enclosed courtyard which led to the main house. Sakharam emerged from the house at the exact same time as Emma and Sikander arrived there.

"What is it? What's happened?"

Emma heard herself asking the questions, but no one answered. People converged from every direction; the object of their interest was the kneeling figure of a woman—Gayatri. She was the source of the inhuman sounds. With piercing wails, she rocked back on her heels and raised her hands heavenward. Her screams made the back of Emma's neck prickle and burn.

Sakharam got to her first. In complete disregard for caste—unless he already knew she was acceptable for him to touch—Sakharam bent and helped Gayatri rise. And Emma saw the second body lying on the ground at their feet.

It, too, was a female—a young girl, twisting and writhing in great agony. Emma recognized Lahri, who was clutching something to her bosom. Pushing Sakharam and Gayatri aside, Sikander reached down and tried to take whatever she was holding away from her, but Lahri wouldn't let go. Emma pressed closer. Merciful Lord, the girl was clutching a snake!

The snake was small, dark, and rather harmless-looking, but Emma could tell from Sikander's behavior that it wasn't harmless—and she thought she knew what it was: a *krait*.

There were bite-marks on Lahri's throat and along her cheek. Her jaw was already swelling. But the girl wouldn't allow Sikander to take the reptile. Clasping it in two hands, she held it to her bosom and writhed in pain, as if the snake was still biting her.

"Give it to me, Lahri!" Sikander seemed not to notice he was shouting in English.

He finally managed to wrest the snake from Lahri, and

Emma gasped as he lifted it aloft and held it stretched out tight, one hand just behind its head with the tiny, wicked fangs, and the other holding the end of its twitching tail. He looked around helplessly, searching for something.

"The fountain, Sikander!" Sakharam cried.

Sikander plunged the snake into the water and held it there while it squirmed and struggled. Emma didn't witness its fate; she sank to her knees beside Lahri, Sakharam joining her on the other side. The girl tried to speak, but couldn't. Emma slid her arm beneath the fall of heavy black hair and lifted her up.

Her face and lips were turning blue and swelling horribly, but her mouth moved, and Sakharam bent his head to listen. Several agonizing moments slid past. Then Lahri stiffened and began to jerk uncontrollably.

Emma could do nothing but hold her as the women swarmed about, weeping and wailing, adding their bereavement to Gayatri's tortured sounds. The convulsions lasted only a minute or two, but to Emma, they seemed to go on forever. At last, Lahri went limp. A waxy cast spread over her delicate features, and the breath left her slender body in a long, broken sigh. She did not breathe again.

Shaken to the depths of her soul, Emma gently lowered the girl's body to the ground. "What did she say, Sakharam?"

The head servant still knelt beside her, his face grim, his eyes haunted. When he didn't answer, it suddenly became important to Emma to learn what the dying girl had said.

"Sakharam, what did she say? *Tell me.*"

Sakharam lifted his black eyes. "She said she took the *krait* from its basket and provoked it into biting her because she had heard that her master had brought home an English woman to replace her."

"She . . . she *provoked* the snake into biting her because of *me?*"

"Yes, *Memsahib.* Without Sikander's love, she no longer wished to live."

"What nonsense are you telling her?" Sikander—his hands empty now—sank to his knees beside them. He leaned over Lahri, peeled back one of her eyelids, shook his head, then pressed his ear to her breast.

" 'Tis hopeless, Sikander. She is dead," Sakharam said bitterly. "She killed herself out of grief that she had lost you."

Fury contorted Sikander's handsome face, turning it into the face of a satyr or a devil. "And how in hell did she *know* she had lost me? I hadn't yet told her. Was it *you* who betrayed me, Sakharam?"

"No, *Sahib*. As Allah is my witness, I swear to you I never said a word to her."

Sikander gathered the dead girl into his arms and lifted her. Cradling her body, he stood and glared at his head servant. "Someone told her. I demand to know who it was. Call everyone—all my servants—everyone in the whole damn household. Summon them to the front steps of the house. I will find out who did it. I will force them to look upon the consequences of their actions. A beautiful young woman lies dead because someone could not hold his tongue and allow me to handle my affairs in my own way. . . . Call them, Sakharam!"

Emma had risen when Sikander did. Frightened and appalled, she was also worried; she had never seen him so angry. In his present mood, he was capable of anything. "What do you mean to do?"

"Get out of my way, Emma. Whoever did this must be punished. Sakharam, call everyone!" He swept past Emma as if she meant nothing and his young dead mistress was all he cared about.

Sakharam disappeared into the maze of arches, and Emma was swept along in the crowd of women and servants who had gathered in response to the noise and excitement. From inside the house came the loud reverberations of a brass gong, and more people began to appear. Pushing past them, Emma hurried to catch up with Sikander.

He strode into the main house, traversed the lower level, and exited onto the veranda. At the top of the steps behind the huge wrought-iron gate stood a long bench of coral-colored sandstone. On this, he laid Lahri's body and then opened the gates.

The gong called Indians from every direction. They all gathered at the foot of the stairs. It was eerily silent; no one spoke. Quiet as sheep, they stood gazing up at Sikander and the still, small figure on the bench.

Filled with dread and not a little grief and guilt, Emma wondered what Sikander would do. Lahri was dead because of *her*—because she had taken the girl's place in Sikander's bed. It wasn't right to punish anyone else for something they had both done together. She hadn't known about Lahri, but Sikander had. They must share the blame for this terrible tragedy.

Emma wished it was a bad dream; the scene had dreamlike qualities. It didn't seem real—all the serious, scared faces of the Indians, Sikander's deep, murderous rage, the body of the girl lying so still on the sandstone bench . . . the knowledge that Lahri had taken her own life in a fit of jealousy and desperation.

Sikander began to speak, but Emma could understand only a little, for he was speaking in the local dialect. Then, apparently without realizing what he was doing, he lapsed into English. "I demand that you come forward. Whoever told Lahri about the *memsahib*, whoever dared to carry tales to wound this poor child, had better come forward and admit it. I won't rest until I know who you are and have decreed your punishment. Don't think I won't find out, for I will. I think I already know who did it. I'm giving you this chance to admit it. If you don't, my wrath will fall not only upon you, but upon your family, friends, and relatives. To spare them, you must come forward now."

Emma heard Sakharam somewhere below, among the Indians, repeating Sikander's threats in Urdu. Just when she thought no one was going to accept responsibility for the deed, a man dropped to his knees in the middle of the crowd and crawled forward, cringing and shaking as he approached the first step.

Everyone drew back as if he were a leper, and the man raised his arms and began to blubber. "*Sahib! Memsahib*. . . . Forgive. In the name of Allah . . . forgive."

Tears streamed down his anguished face. Emma recognized him as one of the *pattah-wallahs* who had accompanied them on their long journey to Paradise View. A good horseman, an excellent hunter, a man who knew the jungle well, he had proven himself an able servant. She didn't know his name, but had heard him speak halting English and many times seen him working near her tent.

Sometimes, he had helped Sumair pack her things. *He* had been the man holding the lead rope of the pack horse who had fallen into the gorge. Emma recalled how Sakharam had roundly scolded him for the loss. All the while she had been watching him, had he been watching her? Somehow, he had discovered that she and Sikander were lovers.

"Sakharam! Fetch me a bullwhip . . ." Sikander started down the stairs toward the man.

"Sikander, no! You can't whip this man for something *we* did wrong!" Emma cried. "All he did was gossip and carry tales. We were the real evil-doers. Had we not . . . had we not . . ."

Loath to say the words out loud, though most of the onlookers couldn't understand, Emma paused and gestured helplessly at Lahri. "She's dead because of us."

"No. She's dead because that cowardly, cringing jackal *told* Lahri about us. He violated my trust in him and breached the sanctity of my *zenana*. I should have suspected he would do something like this, and I should have taken steps to prevent him."

"How could you have known? Why *did* he do it?"

"Because before he was *my* servant, he was Lahri's. He came to me the same time she did—as a gift from the *Nawabzada* of Bhopal. He was part of her retinue of servants. I could have sent him to the forest to help harvest my trees—or to one of my rice plantations. But I didn't. I kept him near me. I grew to trust him. I . . ."

The crowd of Indians suddenly made a sound, a collective intake of breath. Sikander heard it too, and they turned at the exact same time. Sakharam stood over the kneeling man. The weapon he held high above his head wasn't a bullwhip. Rather, it was a long, slender spear—the kind used throughout India for pig-sticking. In breathless horror, Emma watched as Sakharam plunged it between the shoulder blades of the groveling servant.

Twenty-one

Emma had never fainted in her life, but she had the unnerving sensation that she was going to do it now. A buzzing sounded in her ears, the world seemed to be spinning, and her legs felt weak and shaky. Swaying on her feet, she reached for something to steady herself, but there was nothing nearby. Just as she crumpled in a heap on the hot sandstone, Sikander caught her. He held her upright, and she clung to him, desperately trying to maintain consciousness.

"Breathe deeply," he tersely instructed. "And you'll be all right."

Emma couldn't imagine ever being all right again. She was ripping apart at the seams. An inner earthquake was toppling the cornerstones of her existence. She couldn't speak or think. All she could see in her mind's eye was the image of a spear sticking straight up from the back of that poor man at the bottom of the steps . . . and blood. Blood had spurted from the hideous wound. If she looked down at him, she would see blood pooling around his body. She didn't have to ask if he was dead; she *knew* Sakharam had killed him.

Gradually, her breathing returned to normal. The world righted itself. She saw that Sakharam had come up the steps and was now standing beside her and Sikander. As usual, he looked calm and inscrutable.

"Murderer!" Emma pushed away from Sikander. "You

killed that man with no more thought than you'd give to swatting a pesky fly."

Steady as a stone, Sakharam gazed back at her. "It was my duty to discipline him, *Memsahib*."

"Discipline him! You took his life! . . . And for what? Because he told the truth?"

"He betrayed his salt, *Memsahib*. That is reason enough."

"What do you mean—he betrayed his salt?"

"His salt, *Memsahib*. He behaved without loyalty and honor. I punished him for it. Do you see anyone else protesting? No, because they know he deserved it."

Emma looked around at the Indians. They weren't protesting, weeping, or even looking at the body of the fallen man. Instead, they were slowly dispersing, as if justice had been done, they had witnessed it, and it was now time to go back to work.

"What's wrong with these people?" she shrieked, still grappling with the horror of the moment. "How can they witness a murder and walk away like that?"

"Emma, calm down." Sikander took her arm. "Come into the house with me. You're making a spectacle of yourself."

"If the *memsahib* would like some tea now, I shall see that it is brought at once," Sakharam said. "Do not worry; all will be taken care of here."

"Get your hands off me!" Emma slapped Sikander's hands.

He acted as if he didn't hear her. "Come along now, Emma. Soon, you'll feel much better. You can do nothing more here. Sakharam will see to everything."

"I'm going nowhere, except back to Calcutta and then to England at the first opportunity! You are both monstrous, this is a monstrous country, and I cannot *wait* to leave it and return to civilization. If you will not make the arrangements, I will leave here tomorrow morning by myself."

Sikander heaved a great sigh. "Emma, you are overwrought. You don't realize what you're saying."

"Yes, I do. I know precisely what I'm saying, and I mean every word of it. I'm leaving tomorrow morning. You can't stop me, Sik . . . Mr. Kingston, so you might as well resign yourself to the inevitable."

"Emma . . ." he began again, but Emma refused to listen. She had had enough—*more* than enough. She had had too much. India *was* a monstrous country. She never should have come here, totally unprepared for what she would find: the licentiousness, the sudden violence, the immoral social customs, the cruelty and poverty, the incomprehensible behavior of the people. . . . This day would live in her memory forever. No matter what anyone said, she was partly to blame for what had happened. And Sikander was to blame for the rest of it. Sakharam could possibly be forgiven his misguided sense of justice . . . but she could never forgive herself or Sikander. And she could never stay here and behave as if nothing whatever had happened.

"Emma, when you have had more time to think about all this . . . when you . . ."

She didn't wait to hear any more. Picking up her skirts, she fled into the house and sought the only refuge available—her rooms on the second floor.

It was very late that night by the time Alex summoned enough courage to visit Emma. Sakharam had handled the details involving the disposal of the two bodies; they had been placed in simple wood coffins and burnt on the same funeral pyre in a clearing deep in the jungle. Still, there had been much to do; for one thing, he had spent some time with the women in the *zenana*, comforting them and assuring them that he mourned Lahri's death and had meant to do right by her, despite having given his affections to the *memsahib*.

Gayatri, in particular, had been inconsolable. Alex wasn't sure how much she understood of what had happened and why, but it was clear that finding Lahri with the *krait* had greatly affected her. For hours afterward, she had made inarticulate noises of horror and sorrow. Yet Lahri had replaced Gayatri's own sister, so her grief seemed blown out of proportion. Alex didn't recall Gayatri grieving so terribly when his wife died; perhaps it was merely the fact that Lahri had deliberately taken her own life that so horrified poor Gayatri.

He had seen to one other important detail—the banning of dangerous snakes from being kept in baskets as pets. Cobras and *kraits* had lived for a long time in the *zenana*, but up until now, Alex hadn't thought much about it. To relieve the boredom of her life, especially when he was gone, Lahri had kept a small menagerie of jungle creatures, among them a cobra who had come up through the drain in the bath, and several *kraits* who had gotten into the house at one time or another.

Not wanting them to be killed, she had confined them in covered baskets and fed them rodents, which she paid for in sweetmeats and other delicacies when the children of the village brought them to her. It was a wonder she hadn't been bitten before this, but she had always been extremely careful, so Alex had indulged her in the weird fascination.

With Lahri gone, he had decreed that all the baskets must be removed and their inhabitants returned to the jungle; he had even freed Lahri's pet squirrel, a glorious creature with great golden eyes and a plumy golden bush for a tail. This had made the ladies of the *zenana* happy, for the squirrel had been given to sudden attacks and ruined many a fine *sari*.

Alex had been busy all evening, but his thoughts stayed with Emma. He couldn't allow her to leave—not now, when he finally realized what she meant to him and how desperately he would miss her once she was gone. Before Emma, he had somehow managed to endure a life he now saw as empty, greedy, grasping, and selfish. Yes, he loved his children, but in a rather distant fashion—for he often spent months without seeing them. Even when he was home, he left their upbringing largely to his servants.

There was no one like Emma; she challenged, exasperated, charmed, and coerced him into seeing things in a different light. . . . She saw him for what he really was, in all his bitterness and divided loyalties, and still accepted him. She filled a void he hadn't known existed—but he knew it now. If she left him, he would be alone again—truly alone, more alone than he had ever been in his life. . . . He *couldn't* let her go.

So he stood in the dark shadows outside her door and thought of what he might say or do to make her change her mind. How could he reach her? How did one apologize for being Indian, but at the same time British—and for making mistakes and behaving in the primitive manner he had been taught as a child? A cultural chasm separated them; it was also a rift in values and basic beliefs. For her sake, he was willing to change—to search for common ground between them. Emma was a slash of sunlight in the dark cavern of his soul. For years, he had brooded in the darkness, licking his wounds and plotting revenge. Emma revealed things he didn't want to examine too closely . . . but neither did he wish to hide in a black pit. Emma—Emma alone—could lead him to the light.

He had to make her stay. And suddenly, he realized how he might overcome what he hoped was only a temporary revulsion for him and all things Indian. His mind made up, he eased open the door and entered her room. Emma lay on the bed in a flood of moonlight that gilded the mosquito netting she had neglected to draw around her. Her eyes were closed, and a frown creased her forehead. Even in her sleep, she was still angry. Her glorious hair was spread in wild disarray across the pillows, and Alex felt a familiar tightening in his groin, a sudden surge of desire for this difficult, opinionated, impossible woman.

Standing over her, he shed his clothing with quick efficient motions, then, totally naked, eased himself into bed beside her. She did not stir, and he was able to settle himself and draw her into his arms so he could kiss, caress, and make love to her. This was his only chance to make Emma understand how much she needed *him*. She might think she didn't, but he knew better. Emma needed him every bit as much as he needed her.

Emma had fallen into a restless slumber, beset by nightmares and a lingering sensation of dread. Tossing and turning for hours, she had finally slid into oblivion, but shocking images repeatedly startled her awake. Over and over, she relived the horror of discovering Lahri clutching the *krait* to her bosom and writhing on the stones of the courtyard. Over and over, she saw Sakharam plunging the spear between the shoulder blades of the man who had "betrayed his salt."

The words echoed in her feverish brain. *He betrayed his salt.* Like a dog worrying a bone, she puzzled over the phrase. The concept was so very . . . Indian. How she longed to be free of this confusion and anxiety! How badly she needed consolation and comfort. Her dream abruptly shifted, and she found herself in Sikander's arms. *No! No, I mustn't let him touch me or make love to me ever again.* But her treacherous body refused to obey her mind. It felt so good to be held, stroked, touched, and kissed. And it was only a dream, after all; she wasn't responsible for her actions. She could overlook her weakness just this once.

Sikander feathered kisses over her face and hair. Reaching down the front of her gown, he fondled her breasts until they were full, heavy, and aching. He lifted her nightdress and stroked her thighs through her flannel drawers. He gently nudged her legs apart to gain access to her feminine core, slipped off her drawers, and rubbed, stroked, and rotated the little nubbin of flesh he had already taught her was the center of great delight.

Moaning softly, she lifted her hips in anticipation of his possession. He slipped his fingers inside her and diligently prepared her for penetration. . . . She awoke to find her dream turned into reality. Sikander was indeed lying almost on top of her, his fingers buried to the hilt in her female passage, his lips pressed to her temple. Her juices were flowing, her body throbbing with the first ripples of satisfaction, yet she forced herself to lie stiff and unyielding, to ignore what he was doing to her.

"Why are you here? I don't *want* this—not anymore. It's over between us."

"Yes, you do want it, Emma. I can feel that you do." He moved his fingers slowly in and out, stroked along her quivering flesh, then twisted them to press along her sensitized passage until she wanted to scream with the pleasure of it and the need he was building within her.

Her breath caught on a sob at her own shamelessness and weakness. She wanted to push his hand away and deny herself the release that was the ultimate result of his ministrations, but things had progressed too far. What made it worse was that he had *knowingly* brought her to the point where resistance was hopeless. She desired him far too much to reject him now . . . but she was unwilling to give *him* the pleasure he was giving her.

Let him suffer. Let him long for her to touch him and return the favor; let him yearn for the wondrous gift of physical release and satisfaction. She wouldn't give it to him. She hated him. Hated what he had done to her, how he had made her need him, how he had disappointed and betrayed her, how he had lied to her, and then expected her to instantly forgive him.

"Emma . . . Emma . . ." he murmured, stroking faster, longer, deeper. "Touch me, Emma. I want you. Need you. You can't deny what we feel for each other. Despite everything, we belong together. Surrender to me, Emma. Admit what you feel, damn it!"

Emma gritted her teeth to stop her body from obeying its ravenous instincts. She refrained from reaching for his *lingam* or turning her head to seek the contact of his mouth. She fought for separateness, cool detachment, disinterest . . . fought and lost.

With a small cry of surrender, she gave him what he wanted. Quickly, savagely, he mounted her. Ramming home, he rode her hard and fast, like a man gone wild, like a beast in the rut . . . and she gloried in it. She raked her nails down his back and sank her teeth in his shoulder. She grunted and groaned and rocked beneath him, wrapping her legs around his waist to take him as deeply as she could.

They reached cataclysm together—a release so shattering it more closely resembled destruction than pleasure. Emma was no longer the same person. She and Sikander blended together, their fragments so intermingled they could never again be separated. Almost without realizing what she was doing, Emma began to weep. Great, shuddering sobs racked her from head to foot. Taking his weight on his elbows, Sikander remained motionless above her. For several moments, he let her weep, never moving, never speaking. Then, finally, as her sobs subsided, he began to kiss her. Angry and ashamed, she sought to avoid his lips.

"Emma, don't. Don't turn away from me. I beg you to forgive me for not telling you about Lahri sooner . . . and for not realizing what might happen as a result of my bringing you here and flaunting you in her face. I blame myself, not you, not Sakharam, not the man who told Lahri about us. The blame is all mine. But what we share—what exists between us—is so strong, so powerful . . ."

"What we share is lust. That's all it is, *lust*. Don't try and make it more than it is."

"No, Emma, you're wrong. It's far, far more. And you know it; you don't need me to tell you."

She *did* know it, but it galled her to admit it. She refused to call it love; it was more like an obsession. A need so strong and terrifying that she didn't know how to escape it. When she was with him like this, locked in his arms, joined with his body, she couldn't think at all. She could only feel. Her emotions were a net entrapping her, robbing her of freedom. She could leave Paradise View, but she would never be free of Sikander. He would follow her, possess her, own her wherever she went. Body and soul, she belonged to him.

"Stay with me, Emma. Give me another chance. Give India a chance. Put this unpleasantness—this grief and sorrow—behind you. Behind *us*. Stay, Emma. Teach my children. Teach *me*. Let me learn how best to love you. Promise me you will stay."

She was somehow glad *he* was making no promises. She wouldn't believe him if he did make promises. There was no hope for the future, and even if there were, she herself lacked the courage to make plans or promises. . . . However, she also lacked the courage and strength to leave him. Leaving would compound her misery a hundredfold.

"All right," she murmured in defeat. "I'll stay. But only for a time. Until . . . until . . . we learn if it can work between us. . . . But you must help me find Wildwood! That's why I came. That's what I want: my own home, my land, my independence. It's the price I demand for remaining. If it doesn't work out between us, I must have a place of my own to go to."

"Emma, you know it's not possible for you to live alone in the jungle. Besides, you'll never find Wildwood. It's insanity to keep hoping—"

"I still have to try! And you have to promise to help me. If you don't, I won't stay. Do you hear me? Sikander, *I won't stay*."

After a long pause, he sighed. "You win, Emma. Soon, not tomorrow or the next day, but soon, we'll ride out and look for it. But I hope you won't hate me too much—and blame me—if we never find it, for I know in my heart we won't."

"All I ask is that you help me."

"I'll help you." Gently, he withdrew from her body, settled himself beside her, then stretched one arm and a leg across her in a fiercely possessive gesture. "Sleep now, Emma. Sleep."

Exhausted, Emma closed her eyes and slept.

In the morning, she awoke to the sound of giggles. Her eyes flew open. With one hand she felt the bed beside her. It was empty. The giggles came again, low and childish, brimming with mischief and glee. Clutching the bedclothes to her breasts, Emma sat up—only to discover that she was still wearing her nightgown. Last night, she had never removed it. That was fortunate for she now had visitors—two of them, hiding behind a beautifully painted screen in the corner.

A woman's voice sounded outside the door. The children's *ayah* opened the door and stuck her head inside. Bowing and murmuring apologies, she entered and looked around the room. Putting a finger to her lips in warning, Emma pointed to the screen. The *ayah* started toward it, but Emma shook her head and motioned for the woman to leave.

With a slight shrug of her shoulders, the *ayah* complied, and Emma then swung her legs over the side of the couch, stood, and tiptoed quietly to the screen. As the children peeped around one side, she peered around the other. Victoria shrieked with laughter, bounded from behind the screen, raced toward the bed, and jumped into the middle of it.

Her brother followed, and the two rolled about like playful puppies, until Victoria tumbled off and fell on the floor, banging her head on the tiles. Immediately, she screwed up her face and was about to release a howl when Emma clapped a hand over her mouth, forestalling the protest.

"Get up, Victoria. Don't cry over something you could have avoided but chose not to." *Good advice for you, too, Emma.*

Wide-eyed, the child gazed up at her, then scrambled to her feet. Emma sat down on the bed beside Michael and pulled Victoria into the circle of her arms. "Well, I'm glad you lively creatures decided to visit me today. I've been wondering when you would come to see me, and today is just the day I need you."

Michael cocked his head, studying her. "You aren't leaving, are you?" His English was perfectly clear. As Emma had already discovered, he could speak it well; Victoria was the one who saw no need to bother with the language. She seemed to understand it, but resisted saying much. When Emma told her she need not take her castor oil anymore, she hadn't even thanked her.

"Where did you get the idea I'd be leaving?"

Had the children witnessed yesterday's scene on the front steps of the house? Emma hadn't seen them or their *ayah* and had assumed they knew nothing about the incident.

"You told Papa you were going back to Calcutta." Michael sounded much older than five going on six. Both children were highly intelligent and perceptive, far more sophisticated and self-possessed than most youngsters of comparable age. Considering their father's identity, Emma wasn't surprised.

"You heard me say that?"

"We both did, didn't we, Victoria?"

The little girl nodded, very slowly and seriously, confirming Emma's suspicion that she understood everything, English or not.

"I didn't see you yesterday. Where were you standing?"

"On our balcony. Right above your head. We saw Papa put Lahri on the bench, and then all the servants came, and Sakharam drove Papa's pig-sticker through that bad man who betrayed his salt."

Emma closed her eyes and drew a deep breath. Had she actually thought she could leave these children to grow up alone in this cruel, barbaric world? Who would explain yesterday's doings to them? Who would suggest there might be a better method of dealing with problems other than what they had witnessed on that balcony? Not their father, certainly.

Suddenly, she saw how much she was needed here and what a contribution she could make—over and above Sikander's professed need for her, which was more physical than anything. Lifting Victoria onto her lap, she said, "About yesterday. . . . First of all, you needn't fear I will go away, for I have decided to stay."

"Good!" Michael announced, beaming. "If you went away, Papa or our *ayah* would insist we start taking our castor oil again. And we don't like it, do we, Victoria?"

"No," the little girl agreed with a shake of her long, silky black hair. "We don't like it."

"Well, I'm staying, so you won't ever have to take it again. Now, I do think we should discuss what happened yesterday, so if you have questions, I can try and answer them for you."

"Why did Lahri let the *krait* bite her?" Michael burst out. "Everyone knows that *kraits* are poisonous, and their bite can kill you."

"*Kraits* bad," Victoria echoed.

"Lahri was very sad—and jealous, Michael." Emma decided not to conceal the truth from this curious, bright child. He might overhear it anyway from the servants, or even his own *ayah*, and she would rather he heard it from her.

"The servant Sakharam killed had told her about me—how I had come home with your father and was going to be living here in the house with him as your new nanny. That made her very jealous and unhappy. She thought it meant that your father no longer liked her. So she provoked the *krait* into biting her."

Both children wrinkled their brows and thought about that for a few moments, and then Michael said, "Lahri was very foolish, wasn't she? She was all mixed-up inside her head."

The observation was amazingly astute, and Emma could think of nothing to add to it. So she merely nodded.

"Papa can have as many women as he wants, can't he?" the boy continued. "There's plenty of room for them. All he has to do is put more stools and couches in his *zenana*."

Emma sighed. Now was as good a time as any to start challenging the boy's assumptions. "That *is* the Indian way, Michael, but it isn't like that in the rest of the world. In England, where I come from . . ."

She launched into an explanation of British customs for courtship and marriage. When the children began to fidget, she stopped and again inquired, "Have you any more questions about what happened yesterday?"

"No," Michael assured her. "But I'm glad Sakharam killed that man for making poor Lahri feel sad."

Emma tried to think of how best to explain the British system of determining guilt, innocence, and the subsequent punishment of people found to have broken the law. No law had been broken in this instance, except by Sakharam, but she would need lots more time to teach the children these difficult distinctions.

"Let's go find your *ayah*," she wearily suggested. "I must bathe and dress now, and you probably need to . . . to do whatever it is you usually do at this hour. Later on, we will have a lesson in English grammar."

"What's grammar?" Michael frowned.

"Grammar! Grammar!" Victoria shouted. "I want learn grammar now!"

"You'll find out soon enough," Emma promised. "Come along, now. Your *ayah* must be growing anxious."

A week later, Emma warned Sikander that they had better start looking for Wildwood, or he was going to find her door barred against him. She said it teasingly but made sure he realized she was serious. Each night of that week he had come to her in the darkness, and they had shamelessly indulged their mutual desire for each other. No matter how many times they joined their bodies, they could not seem to sate their appetites. They were as eager to fly into each other's arms as they had been that first night at Paradise View.

However, the days were another matter; Emma rarely saw Sikander during the day. She spent the long, sweltering hours with the children—growing more and more attached to them. It was so hot that at night, she slept in the nude to spare herself the time it took to tear off her gown when Sikander appeared. Not only was it too hot to wear a garment, it was inconvenient. She knew she'd only end up naked anyway, so she figured she might as well save herself the bother of undressing and be ready for him when he came.

When another week of unrelenting heat had passed, and they still hadn't ridden out in search of Wildwood, Emma grew restless and increasingly annoyed. To be fair, Sikander had been busy preparing for a visit from some officials. He hadn't told her much about it, but she knew someone important was coming because he was working feverishly to prepare the house and furnish it in a British manner. A *durzi* had been found, and the man was sewing day and night to replace her lost wardrobe and produce British clothing for the children.

Despite all this, Emma was determined not to have her wishes ignored. At this rate, they would *never* find the time to search for Wildwood—not unless she made an issue of it. So she did, and Sikander finally agreed.

They rode out at first light the next morning and began scouring the countryside in the huge stretch of wilderness along the Narmada River. Sikander showed her the boundaries of his land, and they rode far beyond them, but didn't discover anything resembling an abandoned, crumbling plantation.

Emma was greatly disappointed. She had felt certain they would find *something*—some clue to identify the property her mother had left her. It was irrational and overly optimistic, but she fancied that her mother's spirit would somehow guide her straight to it.

"I'm sorry, Emma," Sikander apologized as they turned their horses toward Paradise View in the late afternoon. "I didn't think we'd be able to locate it, so I'm not surprised we haven't, but I know how disappointed you must be."

"Can we try again tomorrow? I had no idea how vast this area is and how long it would take to search it thoroughly. I see now that it might be weeks before we find a single clue."

"I can't spare any more time right now, Emma. Aside from preparing for my visitors, I must also harvest my timbers before the monsoon descends. Searching for something that doesn't exist is a luxury I can't afford."

Emma wanted to scream at him: Wildwood *does* exist. But she couldn't explain her faith to him or even to herself. It was simply a bone-deep certainty.

"I am exceedingly grateful for whatever time you can find to give me in the days and weeks ahead," she softly insisted.

"Emma . . ." He leaned over and grabbed Morgana's reins to make her stop and listen. "I'm not talking about ignoring *you;* for you, I will always have time. Have I neglected you lately? Have you been unhappy?"

Emma shook her head no. The past two weeks had been the happiest of her entire life. Her days were challenging, stimulating, rewarding. . . . She was making wonderful progress with the children, and even their *ayah* seemed to be warming to her. As for her nights . . . well, they far exceeded her dreams and expectations. She could wish for nothing more—unless it was to have Sikander openly acknowledge their relationship. Unless it was to become his wife, not just his mistress. She was trying not to pine for the impossible and was even managing not to dwell on the tragedy of Lahri's death and the brutality of the servant's murder.

"I have been very happy," she conceded. "But I can't help

wanting to find Wildwood. I . . . I just know it's out here somewhere—waiting for me."

"Well, it's not, Emma. You will have to be satisfied with Paradise View. I consider it *your* home, as much as mine, you know."

She didn't want to insult him by telling him it wasn't the same thing; *he* owned Paradise View, she did not. She was there on his sufferance. If he chose to take up with another woman, she'd be at his mercy—and the one thing she *didn't* want was to be at any man's mercy, not even Sikander's. Her experience with her stepfather and brother had been too painful and disillusioning. Sikander had given her far more than any other man, but it might not last forever. She had to prepare for what could still, possibly, be a precarious future.

"Thank you for your kindness, Sikander. I appreciate your assurances that I will always have a home with you—but . . . but you won't be angry if I ride out occasionally to continue the search on my own, will you?"

"Damn it, Emma! You had better *not* go riding out without me to search the wilderness. It's pure insanity. Surely, you've learned that by now—haven't you?"

"Yes, yes. . . . I *was* planning to take a *syce* or two with me. But if that doesn't satisfy you, then you *must* make time to take me yourself. Do you agree?"

"I will try," he said tightly, his mouth a grim slash. "Only I fail to see why you find it so necessary to keep searching. I *will* take care of you. Despite my failings, I do have a sense of honor. I will never abandon you or turn you out to fend for yourself. In this at least, trust me, Emma. Whether I deserve it or not, trust me."

Trust. Did she dare trust him? Considering all that had happened, how could she? Yet, in some ways, she did. Sikander had his own notions of honor and scrupulously adhered to them. That was the problem; *his* notions did not match hers. He tried—oh, yes, he did!—but he had enough trouble conquering his own demons, let alone taming hers.

She herself had to tame her demons and do it in her own way.

"Let's not fight, Sikander. Please don't spoil what we have by fighting over what we have not."

He sat on his horse stiffly, glaring at her, but then his expression softened, and he broke into a grin. "All right. Give me a kiss to hold me until tonight, when I mean to demonstrate how very much you mean to me, so that you no longer have any doubts."

She couldn't hold back a smile. "No, I will not kiss you. I had rather you come to me as eager as a stallion pent up in sight of a herd of forbidden mares."

Wheeling Morgana around, Emma took off at a gallop, laughing to herself when he bellowed, "Emma!" and thundered after her. They raced back to Paradise View and arrived just as twilight was swallowing the jungle in purple shadows. Heedless of any *syces* who might be waiting to tend their horses, Sikander slid off Captain Jack, strode over to her, and pulled her out of the saddle.

Wrapping his arms around her, he kissed her soundly in full view of anyone who might be watching. Emma was delighted. She kissed him back with all the love and longing that seethed inside her, threatening to explode if it did not soon find outward expression and recognition in the full light of day.

"I . . . can't . . . get . . . enough . . . of . . . you," he growled. "Look for me when the moon rises."

Emma nodded, and releasing her abruptly, he strode away.

Twenty-two

Several days passed, and Sikander still had not found the time to ride out with Emma again. From somewhere—she knew not where—a horde of filthy, exhausted, half-starved Indians arrived and overran the village with their children and animals. Sikander was unaccountably furious and wanted to turn them away, but even Sakharam defended them.

"Do not turn a blind eye on their suffering, *Sahib*, because you do not like their former master. I will tell them of the penalty for disloyalty. You must give them a chance to prove themselves. We can use the laborers to harvest the timbers—and the elephant is well trained and will be a good addition to our little herd that works in the jungle."

"Who was their former master?" Emma later asked the head servant.

"Hyder Khan," Sakharam informed her with a slight curling of his upper lip. "A man more dangerous and vicious than a *krait*. 'Tis difficult to believe he is Sikander's own cousin."

It wasn't the first time Emma had heard that name, but now she wondered if she would ever truly understand all the complexities of Sikander's background. There was still so much she didn't know and felt awkward about asking. Nothing had changed in that respect; Sikander still didn't easily share such confidences, and she had less opportunity now for private conversation than she had ever had. Here at Paradise View, they were too busy to see each other except late at night—and at the evening meal in the new British-style dining room, with the children in attendance. Emma sorely missed those long hours of togetherness and relative privacy they had enjoyed on their journey home.

She also missed riding, both for the physical exercise and the mental refreshment it provided. Sikander's stable was filled with beautiful horses—and Sikander rode almost every day, engaging in rough and tumble chukkers of polo, as the individual playing periods were called, with Sakharam and his *syces*. This, too, was denied Emma because of her gender and the danger of the game itself, especially the way Sikander played it. Chafing at her inactivity, she took to rising at a very early hour, before the children's day began and the day itself turned into an oven, and rode Morgana about the estate. Usually, she took a *syce* with her, but sometimes she rode alone, knowing that as long as she didn't stray too far from the main buildings, she wasn't in much danger.

On one particularly hot morning, she rode a bit farther away from the plantation than she had intended. Riding out alone, she had intended to look for the elephant compound, where the huge beasts who helped with the lumber work were kept and the new elephant had supposedly been taken.

Sakharam had told her the compound wasn't far from the polo field, but Emma explored the area all around the field without finding it. Discovering an overgrown track leading into the jungle, she rode down it, half-expecting to discover the compound at the end. Instead, she found a small, abandoned bungalow overgrown with weeds and bamboo trees.

At first glance, it appeared to be the original house where Sikander must have lived while he was building the beautiful sandstone version of the Taj Mahal. Rampant vegetation climbed over its walls and roof, but Emma could see enough of it to tell that the dwelling resembled the typical *dak* bungalow found throughout India. It even had a veranda running

along the front of it and surely had once been occupied by
an Englishman with a small retinue of Indian servants.

Emma urged Morgana closer so she could study the structure more carefully. This was exactly the sort of house that
must have been built to please an Englishman—*not* a man
who clung to his Indian heritage the way Sikander did. He
wouldn't have gone to the expense and bother of first erect-
ing such a nice bungalow; so what was it doing out here in
the middle of a jungle wilderness?

It *had* to be a former plantation house built by and for an
Englishman! Emma slid off Morgana, her heart thudding in
wild anticipation. Recalling what had happened the last time
she had explored some ruins in the jungle, she cast a wary
glance around the perimeter of the building. Closed shutters
secured all the window and door openings, and the house
looked completely intact; no tigers could be lurking inside.

As further evidence that all was safe and quiet, monkeys
chattered in the trees and a fat lizard sat on the edge of the
well and sunned himself in a stray sunbeam poking through
the thick green canopy overhead. Tying Morgana to a
wrought-iron ring on a hitching post in the front yard, Emma
saw evidence of what had once been a small courtyard and
perhaps a garden off to one side.

Someone had planted climbing yellow roses which had
run amok, entrenching themselves so firmly that they were
able to withstand both the heat and the dryness of the present
season. The purple, pink, and white blossoms of exotic jungle
plants crowded the veranda, creating an almost fairy-tale setting. This wild forgotten place had a beauty and charm that
years of neglect could not totally destroy.

Mounting the steps to the veranda, Emma wished this
could be Wildwood, for it was exactly as she had pictured
it—a lovely, private place buried in the jungle where very
few people would be likely to find it. This close to Paradise
View, Sikander *must* know about it and probably *had* stayed
here while his own home was being built. It was on his

land—almost in the very heart of his holdings. Why, she was barely a half-hour ride from his polo field!

He had never mentioned the place to her, but given his reticence to discuss personal matters, that wasn't unusual. However, it did seem odd he wasn't using the bungalow for some purpose, unless it was because it was too blatantly British. That must be it, she decided. Sikander had built an Indian kingdom, rejecting all that was British and thus rejecting this bungalow. It probably reminded him of all he was supposed to be and wasn't.

An exciting thought occurred to her: if Sikander didn't want this place, perhaps he'd be willing to sell it to her!

That way, if she never did find Wildwood, she would still have a place to call her own. She'd gladly sacrifice the remainder of her pearls—and the ruby, too—if it meant she could finally own a small piece of earth and her own house. She would have to convince him to part with a portion of his land as well, just enough for her to plant indigo or some other such crop. Since he himself wasn't doing anything with the nearby land, except harvesting the trees, maybe he wouldn't mind, after all. She would let him have all the trees he wanted, as part of the deal. And since he disapproved of the servants his cousin had sent him, he might allow her to put them to work.

Growing more and more excited, Emma set about prying away the board nailed across the front door to keep out intruders. Lacking the proper tools, she worked for a quarter of an hour before she managed to dislodge it. Praying that the door itself wasn't locked, she tried the brass door handle. It turned easily, and the door swung open.

Emma stuck her head inside. The interior was pitch black, lit only by the dim green light spilling through the open doorway. She could just make out the shapes of several pieces of furniture shrouded in dust cloths, and the *punkah* fan on the ceiling. Then she chanced to glance down at the floor.

It was alive and moving—snakes! Dozens of them. No,

hundreds, maybe thousands, all coiling, writhing, and slith-ering across each other. From their size and markings, Emma suspected they might be *kraits*. She closed the door with a thud and retreated several steps backward. No wonder the place was no longer in use! It was overrun with snakes. Well, they could have it; she was no longer interested.

Returning to Morgana, she was about to mount and head for Paradise View, when she decided it wouldn't hurt to ex-amine the immediate surroundings of the bungalow as long as she was already here. She discovered a large, sturdy lean-to, presumably for horses, and another structure which had probably housed servants. It, too, had a well out front and a hitching post. The roof was gone, and wild pigs had been rooting inside, for the door had been left ajar. A crumbling wall enclosed the roofless building, reminding Emma of the tiger she had so narrowly escaped, so she did not linger long.

On the ride back to Paradise View, her enthusiasm rekin-dled. If it was possible to get rid of the snakes, she would love to acquire the bungalow and enough adjacent land to support herself. Sikander might not like the idea, but she wanted independence too badly to reject the notion out of hand. He should be pleased by the bungalow's proximity to Paradise View—yet it was far enough away to satisfy Emma's yearning to have a place of her own.

She wouldn't necessarily have to live there; she just wanted to know it was hers—to do with it whatever she wanted. If she never found Wildwood, it could fill that aching void in her heart and give her a place to truly call home—a place that belonged to her alone, which no one could ever take from her. . . . She couldn't wait to ask Sikander if he knew of a way to drive out the snakes.

That night at the evening meal, she told him about the bungalow. Something flickered in his eyes as she eagerly described what she had found and confided her hope of ac-quiring and developing it. His reaction wasn't good.

Setting down his fork, he glared at her down the length

of the table, while the children watched intently from either side. "Emma, I cannot believe you went off by yourself again into the jungle. Close as the bungalow is to Paradise View, it is still much too far for you to have ridden there without an escort. What if you had been bitten by one of those snakes? If you persist in behaving so irresponsibly, I shall forbid you to ride Morgana. She must go back to Sayaji Singh anyway, so there's no sense forging a strong attachment to her."

Emma sat stunned and angry. He sounded exactly like her brother! Could this be the same man who had held her so tenderly last night and made love to her with such exquisite care for her feelings and responses? *This* was precisely why she wanted her own place—so no man could *forbid* her to do something ever again.

"So you do know about the bungalow." Setting down her own fork, she clenched her hands together on the crisp white table linen that had suddenly appeared, along with the furniture.

"Of course, I know about it. It's on my land, isn't it?"

"Not far from your polo field," she pointed out.

"I lived there while I was building Paradise View. But I never did like the place. It's . . . it's . . . haunted, or so they say."

"Haunted! Why, that's ridiculous. The only things haunting that bungalow are snakes."

"So *you* say, but my servants disagree. They claim they have seen and heard spirits there at night and even during the day. Once the house here was finished, I never saw a need to return to the bungalow, which also has a leaky roof. I was going to tear it down but never got around to it."

"Then you are absolutely certain it can't possibly be . . . Wildwood."

"Is that where all this is leading? You think that broken-down bungalow is your inheritance?"

"It *could* be! As you well know, my map wasn't specific,

but it did seem to place the location of Wildwood somewhere in this general vicinity."

"Give or take a couple hundred miles of virgin jungle," Sikander agreed with a sarcastic laugh.

"I should like to go through the house nonetheless. Only I can't while the snakes are in it. Do you know of any way to remove them?"

"Confound it, Emma. . . . Do you think I'm a snake charmer? Or that I have time to charm snakes when I am expecting important visitors at any moment?"

"No, but I did think you might know of some method, since you know so much about everything else."

"I know how to get rid of the snakes, Papa," Michael suddenly piped up. "Do you remember when they were inside the stable? The servants got them out with smudge pots."

"Smudge pots?" Emma was immediately interested. "I take it snakes don't like smoke."

"Michael, that was an entirely different matter and probably a different kind of snake. These snakes must have been there for years, multiplying and out of control. Take my word for it, Emma. That bungalow isn't Wildwood, and the structure is most likely unsafe by now. No one should be poking around inside it. Leave it be—at least until after my visitors have come and gone. Perhaps then I will see what can be done to get rid of the snakes."

He would *never* do it, Emma suddenly realized. Nor would he consent to her living out there alone if she decided she wanted to do so. She would have to solve the problem herself—behind his back, if necessary, but solve it she would!

"I shall try not to bother you anymore with my petty schemes while you have so much on your mind preparing for your guests. . . . Victoria, use a spoon to eat those figs; British ladies never eat with their fingers."

"Yes, Miss Whitefield," the child responded as Emma had taught her.

"Thank you for your forbearance," Sikander drawled. "I greatly appreciate it."

The meal continued in silence, while Emma busily made plans on where and how to obtain smudge pots and to convince Sakharam that she had Sikander's support for the project, so that he would assign servants to do whatever she asked.

Several days later, Sikander received word that the *Nawabzada* of Bhopal would shortly be arriving—within several days at most and accompanied by some other officials. Early the next morning, he promptly saddled Captain Jack, gathered a few *syces*, a tent, and food supplies, and prepared to ride off to greet him.

Up until now, Emma hadn't known precisely who was coming to visit. Sikander hadn't told her, and now, she understood why. He didn't want to fight over whether or not she should approach the *Nawabzada* about Wildwood. In saying his farewells on the front steps, Sikander told her he hoped she wouldn't cause any trouble by raising the issue with the young ruler.

"How would my asking him about Wildwood be causing trouble?" Emma was insulted. "Wildwood has nothing to do with whatever problems you are having with the *Nawabzada*."

"That's where you're wrong, Emma. I regret having to reveal this, but my entire future—and Michael's and Victoria's—depends on a good outcome from these visits by both Indian and government officials. Because of who and what I am, I am constantly under attack. Both sides, Indian and British, would like nothing better than to relieve me of all I have worked so hard to obtain all my life."

"I thought the *Nawabzada* was your friend."

"He is, but he is also under the influence of men who are *not* my friends. This visit was *their* idea, and my enemies will be quick to capitalize on it. For that reason alone, I prefer you do not give him another bone to chew while he is here. His attention mustn't be divided, for I'll have precious little time as it is to renew our friendship and nullify any lies my enemies might have told him about Paradise View."

Emma could not understand how anything she might say could hurt Sikander. This was the opportunity she had been awaiting—a chance to talk to the young official whose grandfather *must* have known about Wildwood. But she hated to increase Sikander's worries by refusing to honor his request. He had been so anxious and distracted lately that for three nights in a row, he hadn't come to her, nor offered any explanation for his absence.

Emma didn't want to make a scene about that, either, but faced with his imminent departure, she couldn't resist seeking reassurance. "All right, Sikander. I promise not to mention Wildwood at this meeting, but only if you promise not to shut me out of your life when you are worried and under siege. I have missed you these last three nights. I've lain awake wondering if you . . . if you still feel the same about me."

Mindful of his *syces* patiently sitting their horses on the lawn below, Sikander only whispered, "Of course, I do. And once this meeting is over, I'll prove it to you." His voice became husky. "Perhaps I'll lock you in your chamber for a full day and night and tell everyone you are ill with a contagious disease, and I'm the only who can care for you."

Emma wasn't able to suppress a smile. "You, naturally, will be immune to this terrible disease."

"Naturally. Then, when you are better, and all my own problems have been solved, perhaps I'll take you to visit the *Nawabzada* in Bhopal, where you can ask all the questions you want—bearing in mind that he won't be able to answer them with any degree of authority."

"Oh, Sikander! You would actually do that?"

"I said 'perhaps,' Emma." She sensed his withdrawal; he was only humoring her, and she ought not to take him too seriously. By then, he would probably have some other perfectly good reason why he couldn't take her.

"Well, I shall just have to hope, won't I?" she lightly teased, but she had already decided to smoke the snakes out of the bungalow while he was gone and couldn't stop her.

No sooner had he disappeared into the jungle when she approached Sakharam and told him a bold-faced lie. "Mr. Kingston has given me permission to clean up that old bungalow out past the polo field. He thought it would give me something to do with my time while he is busy entertaining his guests. Could you assign some servants to help? He suggested I employ some of the new ones his cousin sent. Oh, and I should like them to come armed with smudge pots, if you please, for I understand we have to rid the place of vermin. See to it, please, Sakharam. I wish to begin at once."

Sakharam regarded her suspiciously. "The *Sahib* said nothing to me about this project."

"He didn't need to, now did he? Not when he discussed it with me. I'll be waiting at the bungalow, Sakharam. I'm going there as soon as I speak to the children's *ayah* about their schedule today."

"Yes, *Memsahib*." Sakharam *salaamed*, and still frowning, hurried to do as she bid.

By mid-afternoon, there wasn't a snake left in the bungalow. At least, Emma hoped there wasn't. Looking doubtful and afraid, the servants hung about the doorway, but Emma bravely picked up her skirts and walked through the entire house. She encountered only one or two snakes which quickly slithered away at her approach. Elated, she began to search the sooty, smoke-filled rooms where the smudge pots still smoldered.

As the servants mustered their courage and began to follow, Emma motioned for them to open shutters and begin employing brooms, buckets, mops, and other cleaning tools. Once the place was thoroughly restored, Sikander would be forced to recognize its value and permit her to buy it. She intended to examine the entire premises before she was finished—and that included the leaky roof.

The day waned too soon, forcing Emma to return to the house where she shared a simple meal with the children, read to them before bedtime, and then fell exhausted into her own bed. Eager to begin anew tomorrow, she had no trouble falling asleep. Thus far, the bungalow had held few secrets, but in her dreams, it became a magical, enchanted place where she and Sikander could be alone together, far from the prying eyes of servants and whoever else happened to visit Paradise View. In the bungalow, they could be themselves and enjoy simple pleasures; no one but Sakharam would have to know where they were when they went there; it could be their refuge from the world.

Up early the next morning, Emma had it all figured out. She would take Sikander there and surprise him—*demonstrate* the purpose the bungalow could serve. It was all so wonderful and exciting, exactly the solution to the problem of never being alone with him during the day and having to sneak around to be with him at night. They could meet at the bungalow whenever they wished—tell the servants they were going riding or hunting, and then go there instead. They had to do something; Emma couldn't see herself living as she was now for much longer. She wanted more from Sikander than a few stolen hours in the darkness, and then only when it suited him. The bungalow was the answer to everything.

It was early afternoon by the time she got around to exploring the outbuildings. Poking into dark places with a stick first, she cautiously entered the crumbling servants' quarters. Debris lay everywhere, and she ordered several *pattah-wallahs* to start clearing it away. Picking through the rubble, they found broken pieces of pottery and remnants of simple furnishings. Emma watched for a while, but nothing of value appeared. She was about to return to the bungalow when a man walked past her carrying a square piece of wood resembling the top to a small table.

Emma had been wondering what she would do for furnishings if most of what she found proved unserviceable. Wanting to examine the piece of wood before the man hurled it onto a pile of rubble waiting to be burned, Emma stopped him. She indicated he should set it down on the ground face-up, then she bent to look at it more closely—and saw writing. Large, green-painted letters clearly spelled out a single word: WILDWOOD.

For the second time in her life, Emma thought she might faint. With great effort, she straightened and managed to pull herself together. She had found it. This was Wildwood, her inheritance, the very place where her mother had taken refuge with Major Ian Castleton, and she herself had been conceived.

Now she understood why she had experienced such a great sense of homecoming from the moment she had first seen it. Even the snakes had not been enough to discourage her. Her mother had probably planted those yellow roses, and earlier, while walking through the largest bedchamber, Emma had fancied she had caught a whiff of patchouli, her mother's favorite scent. She had thought she must be imagining things, for the odor of smoke had been overpowering, and no perfume from nearly thirty years ago could still be lingering there . . . and yet, Emma had smelled it. Somehow, she had known all along that she had finally come home to Wildwood; she had felt it in her soul.

Emma picked up the sign. It was so old and half-rotted it didn't weigh much. Taking it with her, she returned to Paradise View in the little dog cart she had driven to the bungalow that morning, hitched to a small horse Sakharam had assured her was well suited to the vehicle.

She found the house in an uproar with servants scurrying in every direction. As she entered the courtyard, carrying the sign, intending to take it with her to her quarters, Sakharam descended upon her.

"*Memsahib*! I am so glad you are here. The *sahib* and all his visitors have arrived. There are more than we expected—

an important representative of the Raj, as well as the *Nawabzada* of Bhopal. You must hurry and change into something more suitable. Forgive me, *Memsahib*, but your face and hands are filthy . . . and what is that dirty piece of wood you are carrying?"

Emma clutched the sign tightly to her bosom. She couldn't focus on what he was saying, but she wouldn't let him touch her precious sign—her proof that she had found Wildwood. "Do not concern yourself, Sakharam. It has nothing to do with you. Where is the *sahib?* I must see him at once."

"He is in the front room—what you call the parlor—with his guests. But you must change first, *Memsahib*, while I see to refreshments. The *sahib* has been asking for you. He was most distressed when I told him you had gone to clean out that old bungalow."

"Fetch your master's refreshments, Sakharam. Don't worry about me."

Walking past him, Emma headed for the front of the house and the parlor. She cared nothing for her appearance, nor was she worried about Sikander's guests. This was too important to be postponed until a more convenient moment. She had to know; had Sikander been aware all along that this was Wildwood land, the location of her inheritance? Had he not told her because he himself had *stolen* it—and feared she would take it away from him?

As if in a dream, she traversed the house, each step taking her nearer to the truth. Outside the parlor, she paused, uncertain whether or not she really wanted to discover the truth. With chilling clarity, she recalled Sikander describing the accidental destruction of her deed. Perhaps it had not been an accident. Perhaps he had been lying to her since their first meeting in Calcutta.

Setting emotion aside, she knew she must look at the facts. At every opportunity, he had discouraged her from searching for Wildwood. Over and over, he had insisted that Wildwood no longer existed. On the day they had ridden out to look for it, he had taken her *away* from the bungalow. And when she'd found it by herself, he'd tried to discourage her from exploring it.

The evidence was damning. She saw it all so clearly now. She finally understood how a handsome, rich, charming rake had been attracted to a tall, plain, aging spinster. . . . From the very first, he hadn't wanted *her;* he had wanted *her land*.

Sick at heart and trembling like a leaf battered by the wind, Emma paused in the hallway outside the open parlor door. As she fought for control, she heard voices within. One of them, Sikander's, emerged from the rest. He was speaking in English, his tone rife with anger.

"It is inconceivable that anyone can possibly challenge my property rights and boundary lines merely because a few original papers were destroyed in a fire. I have supplied copies of everything—all my agreements with the old Begum of Bhopal, the illustrious grandmother of our young *Nawabzada* here. What more could you want? What more do you expect? The issue of the percentage of profit I must pay to the Begum's heir is entirely separate from the main issue, which is that I do indeed own the land involved. No one can rightly dispute that. If you know of someone with a valid claim, you must produce this person immediately. Since I am currently in possession of the land, I should think *my* claim would be the stronger regardless—"

"Mr. Kingston, we have had inquiries," a second voice said. It was a very English voice and sounded faintly familiar, but Emma was too immersed in her own misery to speculate about the identity of the speaker.

"That's why I have come," the voice continued. "I went first to the *Nawabzada*, so as not to waste time conducting an investigation, if indeed, he supports your assertion. But he, too, raises some valid questions—and that's aside from the fact that other claimants have expressed a willingness to pay a higher percentage on the profits they receive from the land."

The familiarity of the voice nagged at Emma; she sought to pay closer attention to what was being said.

"Come now!" Sikander snapped. "Surely, you can see that this is robbery and coercion. My young friend has fallen prey to unconscionable jackals who seek to use him for their own personal gain. If you doubt me, why don't you ask him right now who is advising him to raise these questions?"

"Your Highness," the English voice said. "Since you understand and speak English, you know what Mr. Kingston has said. What say you? Is he correct in his assumptions? Have you raised these questions simply to bring pressure to bear on him in your own negotiations for higher profits? Did someone tell you to do this?"

" 'Tis a lie!" a young voice cried, cracking in that peculiar manner of a youth on the brink of manhood. "I make my own decisions and listen to no man. No one tells me what to say or do. Sikander isn't paying me all he should be, and he's taking trees from land that does not belong to him. I have witnesses who will testify to that. Not only is he cheating me, but he has trespassed on the lands of his own cousin, Hyder Khan. I have the same arrangement with him as I have with Sikander, except that Hyder Khan is willing to pay higher percentages. So I ask you: who is my friend in all this? Is it Sikander, who claims to be loyal but abuses my trust and thinks I will not know it because of my youth? Or is it Hyder Khan, who has opened my eyes to these injustices?"

Listening intently, Emma leaned forward, and the sign slid out of her chilled fingers. It clattered on the marble floor of the entrance hall, and just as she snatched it up again, Sikander appeared in the doorway, his blue eyes fierce. "What's going on out here? Emma? Is that you beneath all that soot? What are you doing skulking about in the hallway?"

Twenty-three

Emma needed a moment to collect herself, and then her fury erupted like a geyser. "I wish to speak with you, Sikander, and from the sound of things, it's about a matter that ought to interest your guests, as well as you."

Still clutching her sign, she marched past him into the room and saw a half-dozen males either seated on chairs or standing in corners awaiting orders. Two in particular caught her attention: one was a fantastically garbed youth wearing a crimson and gold-embroidered tunic, matching round hat, snow-white trousers, numerous gold chains, a jewel-encrusted sword, and gold slippers. He was only a boy, perhaps in his early teens, but he looked every inch a member of royalty. He also gave the impression of being outrageously spoiled.

The other was—of all people!—Percival Griffin, who jumped to his feet the moment he spotted her. "Miss White-field! Whatever are you doing here in the wilds of Central India? I thought you were in Darjeeling."

"Miss Whitefield is my children's nanny," Sikander swiftly interjected. "We . . . ah . . . met on a train, and I persuaded her to accept employment instilling manners in my unruly children."

How smoothly he can lie, Emma thought. How very, very smoothly.

"What a surprise to see you again, Mr. Griffin. I take it

you are here in the capacity of Land Administrator for Central India. I'm so happy you got the job." Emma managed a small smile, then turned to the *Nawabzada* and dropped a light curtsey. "And you, Your Highness. It's wonderful to make your acquaintance at long last. Please forgive my bedraggled appearance, but I have been rooting about in an old abandoned bungalow near here."

"And did you find anything?" A flare of interest lit Sikander's shadowed blue eyes.

Emma turned the sign around and pointed to the faded green letters. Somehow she found the strength to keep her voice from quivering. "I found Wildwood, Mr. Kingston."

His reaction confirmed her worst fears; his dark skin paled, and guilt flashed in his eyes. Quickly, he recovered and assumed an impassive expression. "You actually found Wildwood? Why, I can't believe it."

"Wildwood?" Mr. Griffin inquired. "Isn't that the name of the plantation your mother left you?"

"I'm amazed you remember, Mr. Griffin. Yes, it is. Despite everyone telling me how impossible it would be, I have found my inheritance, which consists of an old snake-infested bungalow and approximately eight hundred acres of prime virgin jungle."

She watched Sikander carefully, but he was such a master at concealing his thoughts that he merely smiled and briefly touched her arm. "I am glad for you, Emma. Truly glad—no matter where your land is located."

Emma didn't miss Mr. Griffin's reaction to Sikander's gesture of intimacy. His eyes widened, and he all but harrumphed in disapproval. Emma couldn't bring herself to care. Her personal interest in Mr. Griffin had died long ago. At the moment, her reputation barely concerned her. Indeed, it could be said it hadn't concerned her since the day she'd met Sikander.

"You are glad for me even if the land you've been calling yours all this time is actually mine? You don't mind that your polo field, stable, Love Pavilion, and house stand on it? You are honestly *glad*, Mr. Kingston?"

They might have been the only two people in the room; Emma knew she was being rude to the others, but she couldn't bring herself to care about that, either.

"Certainly, I mind, Miss Whitefield. But if you plan to dispossess me, I doubt you will succeed. Have you forgotten? Your deed was destroyed. It no longer exists."

He deliberately destroyed it. She no longer had any doubts on that score.

"The deed wouldn't be valid if it did still exist," he added. "You know this; we've discussed it in the past."

"Ah, but you've forgotten something, Mr. Kingston. Rather, you are unaware of it." Emma smiled sweetly, masking her utter devastation with an iron will. "Mr. Griffin knows all about my deed. I discussed the matter with him in Calcutta. Didn't I, Mr. Griffin?"

"Why, yes, Miss Whitefield, you did. On the night of that ball we attended together, where I first met you. I never saw the deed, but—"

Sikander never took his eyes from Emma's face. "You didn't see the deed?"

"No, I'm afraid I didn't, unfortunately."

"But any number of people in Calcutta *did*. When Mr. Griffin returns there, he can ask my friend, Rosie, and her husband, William. *They* saw it."

"Does he need to ask them, Emma? Are you staking a claim on my land?" Sikander's gaze pierced her soul, and Emma realized she had been avoiding that very question. Was she so shamelessly in love with him that she could forgive his lies, his subterfuge, his deliberate attempts to keep her from discovering the truth? Worst of all, he had pretended to care for her and desire her! That was what hurt the most.

"Yes," she said firmly. "I am staking a claim."

She turned away. "Mr. Griffin—Percival, I am definitely staking a claim on my inheritance. You can add it to whatever other claims you have already received regarding Mr. Kingston's holdings. I confess total ignorance on how such things are handled, but I authorize you to initiate an investigation on my behalf. While I am awaiting its outcome, I shall take up residence in the very same bungalow where I found the sign proving its identity."

"Emma, you can't . . ."

"I can!" Emma whirled to confront Sikander nose to nose. "You have no rights over me whatsoever! I hereby resign my position as your children's nanny. I want nothing more to do with you, for you knowingly attempted to deprive me of my rightful property. What you fail to grasp is that I only used *you* as a means of traveling to Central India to search for my inheritance. Now that I've found it—*right here where you live*—I don't wish to ever see you again, unless it is in a British court of law. . . . Mr. Griffin. What will happen if indeed it can be proven that *I* own this land?"

Mr. Griffin blinked rapidly several times and ran a finger around the edge of his stiff, white collar. He looked distinctly uncomfortable to find himself in the middle of this battle. "If it can be proven without doubt that you own the land, Mr. Kingston will either have to buy you out or vacate the premises and relocate somewhere else."

"That's what I thought. If I do own it, I won't sell it to Mr. Kingston. I myself will harvest the wood on it."

Out of the corner of her eye, Emma spotted a man dressed in white leaning down to whisper in the ear of the young *Nawabzada*. The youth then held up his hand, as if to interrupt. "Would the *memsahib* consider selling her land to me—assuming she owns it?"

The question caught Emma unprepared. "I . . . I don't know. I don't think so."

With no further prompting, the young man greedily insisted, "Whether you sell to me or not, you will still have to give me my rightful share of the profits. As the *Nawabzada* of Bhopal, I am entitled to that money."

"That is for Mr. Griffin to decide, not you," Emma corrected.

"Dear me. I have my work cut out for me, don't I?" Mr. Griffin said. "But surely, Emma, you don't wish to remain here in this wilderness. Why don't you go back to Calcutta? The *Nawabzada* and I plan to return very shortly to Bhopal, where I shall begin my investigations. I could send you to Calcutta from there, or even return with you myself, if I feel the need for more research in that vicinity."

"No," Emma replied. "I wouldn't think of leaving here before the matter is settled. I am moving to the bungalow to await the outcome of your investigation. You will have to report back to Mr. Kingston in any case, so you can report to me, too, when you return."

"This is all nonsense," Sikander protested. "No one can invalidate my holdings. I have been living here and conducting business for years and years. Yet you come like dogs sniffing around the kill of a tiger. . . . Emma! Is this what you really want—to join with the jackals? To fight their battles for them?"

Rage flared in Emma's breast. "I was never dishonest with you! You *knew* why I came here! But you have been dishonest with me. And now you will pay the price for it!"

Mr. Griffin pompously cleared his throat. "I may be new to my office, Mr. Kingston, but I can tell you I won't know if Miss Whitefield's claim is valid or not until I investigate. I promised her in Calcutta that if ever I became Land Administrator, I would look into the matter. Now, I shall be glad to do so. In the meantime, please do not berate the lady. It appears you have greatly wronged her, and if I could persuade her to come away with me, I would. Miss Whitefield and I have an understanding between us, of a personal nature . . . or at least, I thought—I hoped—we did. So I don't mind telling you I am not in the least happy to find her here at Paradise View and in such obvious distress."

Sikander almost sneered in Mr. Griffin's face. "Let me

assure you that whatever distress the lady is feeling is entirely of her own making."

"Stop discussing me as if I were not here!" Emma burst out. "Forgive me for being blunt, Mr. Griffin, but I have absolutely no understandings of a personal nature with anyone in this room—not anymore. Moreover, I've said all I have to say, so now I will excuse myself. Good day to all of you."

Dropping another quick curtsey to the *Nawabzada*, Emma fled the room.

Sikander came to her late that night—or tried to. Emma wouldn't let him into her chamber. She had shoved a large chest—the biggest piece of furniture in the room—in front of the door to block it, but Sikander still managed to push the door partially open. She stopped him by sitting down on the chest and adding her weight to its contents.

"Emma, let me in. I need to talk to you."

"We have nothing more to say to each other. Tomorrow, I will go to the bungalow, and if you dare show up there, I . . . I swear I will post guards all around and have them throw you off the property!"

"Emma, I realize I have greatly wronged you, and I wish to apologize. I truly care for you. Emma, I . . ." he drew a deep breath, then blurted, "Emma, I love you. Don't leave me, now. Don't let this separate us. Can't you understand why I had to protect myself? I still don't think your deed is valid. No matter how many people have seen it, no matter if Griffin is prejudiced on your behalf, you'll never be awarded Paradise View. Wildwood was only a small part of my total holdings; the investigation will show that, and it will also show I obtained the land in good faith. . . . Emma, listen to me. I've thought of the perfect way to settle the issue and make things right between us. We'll marry. Once, I would never have agreed to it, but at this point, we've nothing to lose. Your reputation is already destroyed. Now that Griffin knows about us, now that he's guessed—"

"I will not marry you! How dare you ask me now! Leave me alone. I never want to speak to you or see you again. I hate you! Do you hear me? *I hate you.* I can't possibly marry a man who's treated me so shabbily."

As Emma burst into tears, a new voice sounded in the hallway. "Mr. Kingston! What are you doing out here in the middle of the night? I demand to know what you are up to, sir."

"I might ask you the same question, Griffin. Have you forgotten that this is my house? . . . And why are you waving that pistol about? Do you plan to shoot somebody?"

"I was trying to sleep when I heard a commotion. If you have dishonored Miss Whitefield, if you have harmed her in any way, you will answer to me, sir. Stand back from her door. . . . Miss Whitefield, are you quite all right?"

"I . . . I'm fine, Mr. Griffin. I am not . . . not dishonored in the least. Please return to your room. Mr. Kingston only wished to speak with me, but he's finished now. We have nothing more to say to each other."

"Emma, I am *not* finished."

"Well, *I* am. Go away, Sikander. Go away all of you. I refuse to say another word to anyone."

"Miss Whitefield, wait!" Mr. Griffin sounded distraught. "I just want to say . . . to say that none of this changes my feelings for you. I am not withdrawing the proposal I made to you in Calcutta. Regardless of whatever has happened here, I would *still* be pleased and proud to make you my wife."

"Take his offer, Emma. If you won't take mine, take his. The man's besotted with you. Besides, he'd make you a perfect husband. He's lily-white, an exalted member of the noble Raj. And he's honorable. Respectable. Even virtuous. He'd never lie to you, never break your heart, never shame or embarrass you. He's exactly what you've always wanted. Marry him, Emma. Marry him and be damned to you both!"

"Get your pistol, sir! You've gone too far. We shall settle this matter once and for all."

Emma shoved the chest out of the way and opened the door. Hair sticking straight up on his head, hairy legs hanging out below, Mr. Griffin stood in the hallway in his night shirt, waving his pistol in one hand and holding a lamp in the other. Sikander wore only the embroidered robe in which he had come to her so often, ready to make love.

"Stop it, both of you. There will be no duel with pistols. Indeed, there will be nothing. *Nothing*, do you hear? I will not stand for it. Go back to bed, before you wake the children. In another moment, they will be out here, too. I implore you both to think of those innocents. The last thing they need is any more violence in their young lives. They've already witnessed more than they should."

"Are *you* thinking of the children, Emma?" Sikander gave her a look that prickled her flesh.

For the first time since she had found Wildwood, Emma did think of Michael and Victoria. Dear God, how could she leave them? . . . But how could she *not?* Oh, it was despicable of him to remind her of the children!

"They have you, Sikander. If you were the father you ought to be, they wouldn't need me. Stop abandoning them to others to raise. Give them more of your time, and they will grow up happily. But continue as you have been doing, and they will be miserable, always doubting themselves, always searching for a security and acceptance they can never find. You know the pain of a father's rejection," as she herself did, ". . . yet in your own way, you reject them simply by ignoring them."

"I *don't* ignore them! And I certainly don't reject them."

"Then why do they need a nanny?" she shot back. "You're perfectly capable of reading them bedtime stories and teaching them how to survive in this not so lovely world. Goodnight, gentlemen . . . and good-bye. These are my last words to either of you until the investigation is complete."

The next morning, Emma moved into the bungalow. Her parting from the children wrenched her heart, but she couldn't stay in the same house with their father. Clutching the hands of their *ayah*, Michael and Victoria stood on the front steps and silently watched her go. Emma's tears overflowed, but she was still adamant. Her relationship with Sikander was over. It had been the greatest joy and the greatest sorrow of her entire life. She would never love another; he had spoiled her for all other men—and in the end, he had spoiled her for himself. If only he had offered her affection, instead of betrayal . . . if only *he* had wanted to make their relationship work as much as *she* had. . . . *They could have made it work.*

She believed that now—but now, it was too late. He had destroyed something fragile and precious inside her, and she could never trust him or stay with him again.

Making the bungalow livable was the only thing that sustained her in those first few difficult weeks. Sakharam brought food, oil lamps, furnishings, servants, roofing materials, and everything else she needed. She paid for it all in pearls. When he showed up one day with Morgana, insisting that she needed a horse, she shook her head. "I cannot accept her. Besides, she belongs to Sayaji Singh."

"Not anymore. The *sahib* has bought her for you. She is a gift, along with the *syce* he has sent to care for her."

"I don't want any gifts from your master. Please take her away."

"You need her, *Memsahib*. If you are too proud to accept her as a gift, why don't you buy her? That pearl you gave me to pay for supplies was worth far more than what everything cost. Apply the excess to help pay for the mare."

Emma was sorely tempted, but knew that her heart mustn't rule her head. Not anymore. She would accept nothing from

Sikander. "I can't afford it. I will need everything I have to make Wildwood profitable."

Sakharam snorted—an inelegant sound from such an elegant man. "My master is right. You are too stubborn for your own good, *Memsahib*."

"I'm not interested in your master's opinions."

"You should be, *Memsahib*, for he cares for you greatly. He sincerely regrets the pain he has caused you. He does not sleep at night, does not eat, no longer plays polo—"

"Enough! Did he send you to plead his cause with me?"

"No, *Memsahib*, and I would never do so if it did not grieve me to see him so miserable. I never approved of your relationship with him, but I have come to see that my master needs a special woman. Of all the women he has ever known, you have come the closest to meeting his needs. If anyone could turn their backs on the world in which we live and create a *new* world, here at Paradise View, it would be the two of you. I no longer doubt this. I have been persuaded you belong together."

Emma didn't know whether to feel flattered or insulted, especially since Sakharam was only stating what she herself had once believed. However, she did know she wanted no favors from Sikander—not even the gift of Morgana. . . . Still, Morgana was too fine a horse to let slip through her fingers.

"Wait here a moment, Sakharam. I'll be back shortly."

She left him standing on the veranda, went into the house, and took yet another pearl from her fast dwindling supply. Not giving herself time to regret the decision, she returned to Sakharam and thrust it into his hand. "This is for Morgana and the *syce*. You may tell him to take the mare around to the lean-to in back."

The *syce* was still standing in front of the bungalow holding the horse's lead rope. His face brightened as he witnessed the transaction. No doubt he feared Sikander's reaction if he had to return to Paradise View.

Sakharam bowed from the waist. "A wise decision, *Memsahib*. But you have paid too much."

"I don't care! I won't be beholden to your master. Pay the *syce*'s wages out of that, if you must, but take it. Or else take the horse."

"As you wish, *Memsahib*. Consider the *syce* your faithful servant. I will tell him he owes you his salt. No one else—just you."

"Do that, Sakharam. Only bear in mind he is my servant—not my slave."

Emma watched as Morgana was led away to the lean-to, then she went back to work before it got so hot she had to retire to her room to rest. The bungalow was much hotter than Paradise View had been, with its extremely thick sandstone walls and cool marble floors. These days, the heat was almost unbearable. The roses and flowers around the bungalow had all withered and died, and the jungle itself was looking parched. Even the nights were sweltering and so long they seemed to last forever.

By day, Emma had to contend with carnivorous ants, snakes trying to return to their lair, and servants who pretended not to understand what she was saying and simply did as they pleased. But the nights were the worst—for that was when she lay awake remembering other nights and the joy of being in Sikander's arms. It was hard to convince herself that she actually hated him when she missed him so much . . . and she also missed the children. She had just been getting to know them; now, she might never see them again, much less become close to them.

She consoled herself with the wild beauty of her land. Even now, as the jungle withered in the relentless heat, it was still beautiful. Emma developed a fierce possessiveness, enabling her to better understand—if not to forgive—Sikander's behavior. She didn't really want to take his home away from him, but neither did she want to sell out to him . . . and marriage was unthinkable.

He had only proposed in order to protect his investment. He claimed he loved her, but she didn't believe it. She *couldn't* believe it. It had been an act of desperation. Fearing he might lose everything, he was apparently willing to take the smaller risk of marrying an English woman. Nothing else had been resolved or even discussed—how they would live, what customs they would keep, who would be their friends, if indeed they would *have* friends . . . if he would continue to keep a *zenana* or maintain mistresses as Indian men so often did.

Thinking of all the unresolved problems, Emma shuddered. No, marriage wasn't an option. She refused to build a permanent relationship on mere convenience or necessity. Her mother had tried to do that and hurt Emma in the process. Now that she had a chance at true independence, Emma would no longer consider marrying for anything less than total devotion, fidelity, passion, friendship, and affection.

Lust wasn't enough—and it didn't seem likely or possible she could obtain more from Sikander. He just wasn't capable of giving more. The only solution to the entire dilemma was for Sikander to purchase that portion of her holdings that constituted Paradise View—the land on which his buildings and polo field stood. She was willing to sell him that much, though he might refuse to buy it because her land would still surround him on all sides. Until she knew the results of the investigation, she couldn't be certain of her boundaries, but it was reasonable to believe that the bungalow stood in the center of her eight hundred acres.

There was no sense worrying about it until she knew if her claim would be honored. If the claim proved invalid, she would offer to buy the bungalow and a couple hundred acres—whatever her ruby would purchase. And if Sikander refused to sell, she had no choice but to return in disgrace to Calcutta. Whether or not she retained her good reputation depended entirely upon Mr. Griffin.

So the days passed, one upon the other, until the night a

fire mysteriously broke out in the servants' quarters. Emma was sleeping fitfully, when she heard shouts, screams, and a frantic banging on the front door.

Clawing aside the mosquito netting, she ran in her night-gown and bare feet to see what was wrong. Her house servants met her in the front hallway, and her major-domo—Sumair, who had recently been promoted to the position on Sak-haram's recommendation—flung open the door.

"Fire, *Memsahib!*" Sumair shouted, and then he joined the other servants in running to put out the blaze.

It took over an hour to get everything under control again. Dawn was streaking the sky by the time Emma determined that no one really knew how the fire had started; suddenly, the brightly colored ceiling cloths preventing insects and liz-ards from dropping on everyone had apparently burst into flame. Emma couldn't see how it could have happened unless someone had deliberately set the blaze—and she suspected she knew who that someone was.

Only one person in all India stood to gain if she gave up trying to hold onto Wildwood; only one person would be ruthless enough to try and scare her away.

Emma gave orders for Morgana to be saddled, then stormed back to the bungalow to wash and dress properly before she presented herself at Paradise View. She would confront Sikander directly, tell him what had happened, and warn him that she wasn't about to be intimidated by such bullying. Thankfully, no one had been hurt, and the damage could be fixed. She would have thought arson beneath him, but now that she knew it wasn't, she would be more careful, post a guard at night, and have her servants take precau-tions. . . . But first, she would tell Sikander exactly what she thought of him and then send word to Percival Griffin that if anything should happen to her, he would know where to place the blame.

* * *

Alex was in the children's rooms trying to teach them how to add three brass tops to four wooden ones to get seven altogether, when Sakharam informed him he had a visitor. Mindful of Emma's accusation that he wasn't spending enough time with Michael and Victoria, he had taken to instructing them for two hours each morning and evening, and had found he liked it so much that he resented being disturbed.

"Who is it?" he snapped, refusing to rise from his position on the floor with the children, where Michael's collection of tops was spread out before them.

"It is the *memsahib*, and she does not look happy, *Sahib*."

Alex jumped to his feet. "Is she all right? Is something wrong?."

"Yes, something is wrong," Emma said from the doorway, right behind Sakharam.

One look at her ruddy face and Alex knew that something was very wrong indeed. Even so, he couldn't stop the sudden tide of desire, gladness, and plain relief that swept over him—damn, but he had missed her! Even in her usual plain clothing and severe hairstyle, she looked good enough to eat, and he was starved for the sight, sound, and feel of her. He had lain awake nights picturing her, remembering their lovemaking, recalling every conversation they had ever had . . . and regretting all he had done to hurt and disappoint her.

He crossed the room in three strides. "Emma, what is it?"

She glanced nervously at the children. "Perhaps you should send them away first."

Victoria rose from the floor and ran to her, tripping over her gown, as she still wasn't accustomed to the new British-style clothing Alex had insisted the children wear. "Miss Whitefield! Papa is teaching us how to do sums—and now, he reads to us every night before we go to bed. But I still wish you were here. I miss you, Miss Whitefield!"

The child threw her arms around Emma's knees, and Alex was gratified to see the look of pain and longing that crossed her expressive face. Unlike him, Emma had never mastered the art of concealing her feelings, and she obviously returned Victoria's sentiments.

"Michael, take your sister downstairs to find Sakharam and tell him we would like some tea. Have him serve it in the dining room. We—Miss Whitefield and I—will be down shortly."

"Yes, Papa. Come along, Victoria." Michael scrambled to his feet and went to fetch his sister, but as he approached Emma, he lost his decorum and gave her a quick, fierce hug. "Miss Whitefield? Please tell Papa what you told us—that castor oil isn't necessary to make us grow up healthy. Ever since you left, *ayah*'s been giving it to us, and Papa won't tell her to stop."

"I . . . we . . . you must do as your Papa says, Michael. I am no longer in charge of you."

With a grimace of disappointment, Michael seized his sister's hand and all but dragged her from the room. As soon as they had gone, Emma fixed Alex with a baleful glare.

"Someone tried to burn down the servants' quarters at Wildwood, last night. It could not have been an accident. The women stay in the house with me, but the men stay out there, and they awoke to find the ceiling cloths ablaze. They were brand new, as was the roof, so someone must have set the fire deliberately."

"You're accusing *me?*" Alex couldn't believe it. Surely, she didn't actually think he would do something so despicable. But he saw from her face that she *did.* "By all that's holy, Emma, I would never try to hurt you or drive you away. I'm so damn glad to see you again that I—"

"Don't lie to me! Don't lie to me ever again. If you didn't do it, who did?"

Alex had a good idea who might be responsible, but he didn't want to tell Emma—didn't want to alarm her. It must have been Hyder Khan or even the *Nawabzada*. Such an action wasn't above either of them. He would know soon enough who had done it; Emma would receive another offer for Wildwood. Both men would give their right arms to possess eight hundred acres right in the middle of his holdings, especially when that acreage included everything he owned.

"Emma, whoever did this isn't after you. They're after me. You just happen to be in the way. It could be any one of a dozen people who've heard what's happened. Mr. Griffin and the *Nawabzada* must have begun spreading the word. All you have to do is wait and see who offers to buy you out."

"Then you completely deny any responsibility?"

"Of course, I deny it. Emma. . . ." He reached for her, but she jumped back from him like a frightened rabbit.

"Do you have a gun—a pistol or a rifle I can purchase? If not, I will have to send someone to Bhopal or even Gwalior."

"I will give you one."

"I will *buy* it from you."

"Emma, this is ridiculous. You must move back into the house where I can properly guard you. It isn't safe to stay out there now, all by yourself."

"I am not by myself. I have my servants. And the last thing I will do is move back here."

"Is it me you fear, Emma? Or is it yourself?" He moved closer, maneuvering her into a corner. "Are you afraid that if you *do* come back, you won't be able to resist sharing a bed again? You might have to admit you still care for me?"

She sought to push him away and escape, but he wouldn't let her go. Using his body and his arms, he imprisoned her against the wall. "Emma, listen to me. It doesn't have to be like this. All you have to do is find it in your heart to forgive me, and we can begin anew. We can start rebuilding. We can try and make it work, Emma. I've missed you so much! Haven't you missed me? Doesn't that tell you something?"

"You knew I would come," she accused. Tears gathered in her eyes. "If not to frighten me, you probably set that fire just to get me here, so you could do this. Well, it won't work, Sikander! I won't be swayed by anything you have to say to me, or by anything you do. I trusted you once, but never again. If your enemies—or your friends—set that fire, you can tell them I won't give up. I won't be scared into selling or leaving or running back to Paradise View. I'm staying at Wildwood, and that is that. . . . now, let me go. I've said what I wanted to say, and now I'm leaving."

He felt as if she'd driven a spear into his heart. "It doesn't matter to you that I love you—and that you're the first woman to whom I've ever said that?"

She gazed up at him with wounded, tear-bright eyes, so beautiful and so hurt that he felt the spear in his heart twisting and turning. "Once, it would have mattered. Oh, it would have mattered so much! But now, it doesn't. It's too little too late, Sikander. All I can see now is your ulterior motives. Don't bother denying you have them; if *you* can't recognize them, I can. So please, let me go now."

He finally realized that nothing he could say would make a difference. So he let her go. And once again, she fled.

Twenty-four

Over the next ten days, Emma received not one but four separate offers for Wildwood. The *Nawabzada* of Bhopal sent an emissary to negotiate with her—and so did Hyder Khan, as well as two others whose names she did not recognize. They all professed to have Sikander's best interests at heart, and hers, too, of course. She sent them away without giving them the opportunity to name a price.

It was amazing how fast word had spread, but then all four offers had come from people living either in Bhopal or Gwalior, the nearest towns. Any one of them could have been responsible for the fire meant to frighten her into selling. The mere fact that they were making offers fueled her hope that her claim might actually prove to be valid.

Emma wasn't ready to celebrate; for one thing, it was too unbearably hot. Too hot to eat. Too hot to sleep. Too hot to think. Each day was a struggle against the heat. Now at last she understood why her compatriots complained so much. It was too hot to move. Her servants coped better than she did, but they, too, took to their beds during the worst part of the day. They put up *khus-khus tattis,* or screens made of grass matting, over every door and window opening, and they kept them damp, so that if a breeze blew, it offered a small bit of refreshment. But it wasn't enough. Each afternoon, Emma stripped off her gown, collapsed on her bed, and suffered, wondering if she could last until the monsoon season arrived.

Whenever she asked Sumair or one of the other servants when it was due to arrive, she got only a smile and a vague reassurance. "Soon, *Memsahib*. One day soon."

One afternoon, Emma was lying on her bed half-dozing when she heard a loud cracking sound—almost like thunder. Hoping that was what it was, she snapped upright and listened intently. Several more cracking sounds reached her ears, followed by loud shouts and the distant murmur of men's voices. Spurred into action, she scrambled into her clothing, then ran downstairs and out of the house.

There, the sounds were louder, but she still couldn't see anything, and her servants had disappeared. Then she spotted Sumair, coming from the direction of the servants' quarters.

"Sumair! What is happening? What are those noises?"

He looked at her blankly. "Those noises!" She clapped her hands to illustrate. "What are those noises that sound like thunder?"

He broke into a white-toothed grin. "Not thunder, *Memsahib*. Trees come down. Bang! Boom! *Sahib* cutting trees."

"The *sahib* is cutting trees near here? But . . . he can't do that! Not until I know if they are *my* trees or his." Emma dashed back into the house to fetch her *topi* which she had forgotten in her great haste to discover the source of the noises. Once again, she wished for a rifle, but Sikander had neglected to send her one, and now she knew why. He was afraid she might use it on him.

Shaking with anger, she rushed back out of the house. "Sumair! Take me to the place where they are working."

"Yes, *Memsahib*. Right this way."

He led her deep into the surrounding jungle. Very soon, they came to a semi-cleared area where half-naked men and elephants were toiling in the heat—cutting down trees and hauling away the huge logs. Emma spotted Sikander almost immediately. He was standing atop an enormous tree stump and supervising the workers. He, too, was wearing a *topi* and immaculate, light-colored, British-style clothing.

When he saw Emma, he motioned for her to join him, which she had every intention of doing whether he invited her or not. "What is the meaning of this?" Head held high, she advanced upon him. "Just what do you think you're doing?"

"Harvesting my trees before the rains come," he informed her with a rakish smile. "I thought I'd work near the bungalow so I can keep an eye on things. Naturally, I've had guards posted ever since your fire, but it never hurts to take a personal interest, I've found."

He had posted guards to watch Wildwood? She hadn't seen any guards.

"You must tell your men to stop," she shouted over the din. "These trees are mine. You have no right to help yourself to them."

"I have every right. I've been harvesting them for years, and I intend to continue doing so until some recognizable authority tells me to stop."

"Mr. Kingston! Until we hear from Mr. Griffin, you must *not* attempt to make any further profit from *my* land."

"Until we hear from Mr. Griffin, there's nothing to prevent me from making a profit on *my* land, which this is."

"But . . . but what you're doing isn't right, and you know it!" She wished he would come down from that tree stump; she was getting a crick in her neck from looking up at him. Moreover, if she kept shouting, she was going to lose her voice altogether. "Will you please come down here so we can discuss this in a civil manner?"

Quite unexpectedly, he leapt down from the stump and landed not two feet in front of her. "Is this better?"

He was laughing at her, and she didn't know whether to join him or slap him silly. Next to the stump, she saw a large, heavy rifle, big enough to fell an elephant. He wouldn't be laughing if she turned that gun on him, now would he?

"I fail to see anything humorous in outright theft. These trees are as much mine as yours, and. . . . Goodness! Look at that elephant pick up that huge log as if it weighs no more than a piece of kindling!"

"Elephants are exceptionally strong; that's why we use them for this kind of work. They don't seem to mind the heat, either, as long as we let them have a cooling bath every now and then. They particularly enjoy rolling around in the mud."

"For such enormous creatures, they are certainly docile. Do they always behave this well for their handlers—their *mahouts*, as you call them?"

"Nearly always, unless they're mistreated or go mad for some reason. . . . But look, Emma. Perhaps you're right. I shouldn't be harvesting the wood if the land turns out to be yours, but neither can I afford to sit idle. What would you say to splitting the profits? I hate to let the season end without trying to get some of this wood to market. When the monsoon comes, it will be impossible. So how about it? I'm sure you could use the money, too."

"Well, I don't know. I'll have to consider the offer, especially in view of who's making it. *Split* the profits, did you say? I *might* be able to agree to that. . . . Oh, here comes that big elephant again, back for another log. Why didn't you tell me this was all so fascinating?"

"I never had a chance, Emma. But it *is* fascinating, isn't it? Almost makes you forget about the heat . . . almost."

Emma heard another sharp crack—this one sounding remarkably like a gunshot. Before she could identify the source of the sound, the very elephant she had been watching gave a great roar that shook the earth beneath her feet. Flapping his great gray ears, he rose up on his hind legs and pawed the air like a rearing horse. When he came down with a tremendous thud, he swung his trunk, lifted two men off the ground at the same time, and flung them into the brush.

His *mahout* gave a shout of alarm and attempted to regain

control, but without success. He soon stopped trying and dove for cover. Roaring and bellowing, the elephant began snatching up small trees, pulling them out by their roots, and flinging them about. All around Emma, men fled in every direction, but she couldn't move a muscle.

"Everybody watch out!" Sikander shouted. "Take cover! He's gone mad! I'll have to shoot him."

He leapt toward the rifle he had left standing against the tree stump, but Emma stood frozen in place, watching with a macabre interest as the elephant rampaged back and forth through the clearing. Other elephants answered the wild one's bellows, but didn't join in its destructive fury. The mad elephant was trying to destroy everything it could see . . . and its small intelligent eyes suddenly fastened upon Emma, the lone human being who hadn't had the good sense to flee or dive into the brush.

Emma wanted to run; she really did. But her legs refused to function. She had the exact same feeling of helplessness she had had when confronted by the tiger. In the grip of inertia, she could only stand there, staring, in awe of the huge mountain of quivering gray muscle and hide. Lifting its trunk, the elephant again reared, its huge feet churning the air. When it came down, it shook itself and charged Emma. She could feel the ground shaking underfoot, could smell the elephant's thick, musty odor, could see into its tiny eyes.

Muttering an oath, Sikander shoved her out of the way. Tripping over a tree root, Emma fell heavily on her hands and knees. As she rolled to one side, Sikander dropped to one knee, lifted the rifle, held it steady, and carefully squeezed the trigger. The report was deafening. The elephant stumbled in mid-stride. Forward momentum carried its huge bulk another few steps, where it abruptly collapsed to its knees.

A tiny blossom of red, like a crimson flower, unfurled in the middle of the elephant's forehead, between its eyes. Lifting its trunk in one last gesture of defiance, it swept the ground in front of it—and encountered Sikander. With a single sweep of its long, curling trunk, the dying elephant caught Sikander squarely in the chest, lifted him, and flung him hard against a tree trunk.

Sikander's head struck the obstacle with a sickening thud. The elephant groaned—an almost human sound—and rolled over on its side. After that, there was only silence, except for the excited screaming of the monkeys in the trees.

Somehow, Emma managed to get up and run toward Sikander. She reached him at the same time as Sakharam; until now, she hadn't noticed his presence. Trembling, she watched the head servant kneel and carefully examine his master.

"Is he . . . dead?" Emma could barely say the words, and Sakharam didn't appear to hear her.

Gently, with great tenderness, he lifted Sikander in his arms, cradled him like an infant, and stood.

"Sakharam, tell me! Is he dead?" Emma couldn't detect any signs of life. Sikander's skin was the color of an old clay pot, and he wasn't moving. His eyes were slitted, not open, not fully closed. There wasn't a mark on him, but Emma had heard that terrible thud. His head had hit the tree with enough force to kill him.

Sakharam shot her a scathing look. "He is not dead yet, but he soon will be. He has given his life in exchange for yours, *Memsahib*; but what have you given him?" His eyes sparked with fury, as if a dam had burst inside him. "You have given him nothing but trouble. He offered you his love, his home, and all that he is, but it wasn't enough for you. You demand the impossible and surrender nothing in return."

It was the most emotion she had ever seen in the man, and a corresponding emotion exploded in her. "What do you know about it? You know nothing! I do love him! I loved him long before he ever thought he loved me. *He* is the one at fault; he lied to me, manipulated me, used me . . ."

"You have a most remarkable way of showing your love,

Memsahib. Not once have you sought to understand him or ask yourself *why* he has done the things he has. . . . His life has not been an easy one; he has had to fight for everything. And he has done it all *alone*. Now—thanks to you—his fight is over. Step aside, please. I must get him home."

"I am coming with you. And I will help care for him. You can't stop me, Sakharam. I have as much right to be there as you do, and I *won't* let him die."

Sakharam did not respond; he simply kept going—finally reaching a cart in which he tenderly deposited Sikander's body for the short trip home.

Two days slid past with agonizing slowness, and Sikander did not regain consciousness. Emma and Sakharam kept day and night vigils, lavishing care—both British and Indian-style—upon him, but they were unable to rouse him. He was slipping slowly and silently away. Emma had to battle Sakharam nearly every time she wanted to try something new, for the head servant was deeply suspicious, refusing to allow anyone else to assist or even approach Sikander.

He has good reason, Emma conceded, for an examination of the dead elephant revealed the cause of its rampage: a gunshot wound in its hind leg. Someone had intended for the elephant to go mad—or else they had been aiming at something or someone else, and hit the elephant by mistake. Either way, it was clear that Sikander's enemies were closing in on him—and all because they knew he was vulnerable. *She* had made him vulnerable; by challenging his ownership of Wildwood, she had given his enemies a way to bring him down.

On the afternoon of the third day, as Emma was trying to pour water down Sikander's throat, Sakharam reached out and briefly placed his hand over hers to stop her. Emma was so startled by his behavior—his disregard for his precious caste—that for a moment, she could only stare at him. At last, she found her voice. "What do you want, Sakharam? Why are you touching me?"

"Let him go, *Memsahib*," the head servant softly entreated. "We are only prolonging the inevitable. Today, I will summon those few friends who might want to know about this and tell them that he is dying. By the time they arrive, he may be gone. But at least we can hold his funeral before the rains come."

The words pummeled Emma like a series of severe blows. They were the very antithesis of what she wanted to hear. "You're giving up? You—his dearest friend—are giving up on him?"

Her voice sounded overly loud and shrewish, but it wasn't bothering Sikander. He hadn't so much as moved a finger or blinked an eyelid since he'd been hurt. Clearly, he was dying, but she refused to accept it. He *couldn't* die—not with everything unresolved between them. Not without hearing once more that she loved him. Not without saying goodbye to his children, who had crept in and out like pale, teary-eyed, little ghosts for the past several days. *He can't die yet; I won't let him.*

"*Memsahib*, my master is gone. What lies here is only his shadow. Soon, it, too, will depart. We must think of the living now. The Maharajah of Gwalior must be summoned—and Sayaji Singh. So must Santamani, his aunt, who I think still loves him. I will send word to the *Nawabzada* of Bhopal as well, or he will be angry no one told him."

"Not him! He—or his advisors—may be the very ones responsible. Or else it was that Hyder Khan."

"I am certain you are correct, *Memsahib*. That is why I must summon Santamani, Hyder Khan's mother. 'Tis time she realized the treachery of which her son is capable. I can never forgive myself for urging Sikander to accept Hyder Khan's people—who are mostly now your servants. But I did not think any among them would do a thing like *this*. Yet someone did it. And when my master finally passes, I shall discover precisely who is responsible and punish him for it. I shall hunt down his murderer if it takes the rest of my life to do so."

"Stop talking as if Sikander were already dead! He's still breathing, his heart is still beating, and as long as we continue to supply him with nourishment . . ."

"No, *Memsahib*. 'Tis hopeless, and I will no longer be a part of it. Sikander would not appreciate our efforts to keep this . . . this husk alive. I beg you to stop. Sit and hold his hand if you must, but do not prolong his suffering by offering food and drink. I assure you; he would not want that, when his spirit is already gone."

"I can't give up yet." Emma raised Sikander's head and cradled it in the crook of her arm. "This is only the third day. It's still too soon. If you will not tend him anymore, that is fine with me. I will do it all myself."

"*Memsahib*, look at him! Look closely. The mark of death is already upon him. See how pale and still he is—how weak and wasted he has become in just three short days. His skin is drawn taut over his bones; his muscles are shrinking. If he does awaken, will he be the same man? Will he know who he is? Who we are? . . . I know my master, *Memsahib*. He would despise being an invalid—or worse, a madman or an idiot. End it now, *Memsahib*. I beg you—for his sake, end it now."

Perhaps Sakharam is right, Emma thought sadly. But she had no taste for playing God with the man she loved. If God wanted Sikander, God could take him without any help from her. Until the moment he breathed his last, she would fight God tooth and nail.

"Instead of giving up, it's time to do even more," she argued. "He must be fed the most nourishing broths. We must exercise and massage his muscles—three times daily and at least once during the night. If we keep his body strong, perhaps in time, his mind will heal."

"He has no mind left," Sakharam scoffed. "I wonder if

you yourself have not taken leave of your senses. The heat has affected your judgment."

Emma hadn't noticed the heat in the last few days; she had forgotten all about it. Now, she realized that if she hoped to keep Sikander alive, she must tend herself also. She had barely eaten and hadn't changed her clothes or brushed her hair since the accident had happened. Nor had she slept— except for a few brief hours slumped on the bed at his side. She had remained sitting on a stool the whole time.

"I am weary and heart-sick, but I am not crazy, Sakharam. Will you help me keep him alive?"

The muscles worked in Sakharam's jaw. He frowned deeply. "I cannot condone this, *Memsahib*. It is not what the *sahib* would want."

"You told me the *sahib* has always had to fight for everything; would he not want to fight for a chance at life, slim as it is? Give him another few days, at least, Sakharam. Then, if he is no better, I will seriously consider what you have suggested."

Sakharam sighed. "All right, *Memsahib*. I will help you— but only for a little while. We will keep him alive until his friends come, but then, if he remains as he is, I will insist you stand aside and let him go free."

"Is death the only freedom we can hope for, Sakharam? Is there no happiness or joy to be found in living?"

"You ask questions no one can answer, *Memsahib*. I only know that for Sikander, happiness was Paradise View. Here, he could be himself, raise his children, and live as he wished— until *you* came along. You changed all that, *Memsahib*." Amazingly, there was no bitterness in the accusation; it was a mere statement of fact. "For good or ill, you changed it."

Emma nodded. "Yes, I did, didn't I? So it's only right that I be the one to take extraordinary measures to keep him alive now. I don't really know if we can do it, Sakharam. But we must try. . . . Let's begin with exercising his muscles, so they do not waste away."

Sakharam joined her at Sikander's side. "Just tell me what to do, *Memsahib*."

They kept Sikander alive for another two and a half days, and still, there was no improvement—except in his color. Emma was sure he looked less like a corpse and more like a man who was merely sleeping. She took turns with Sakharam in resting on a pallet beside Sikander's bed. They fed him nourishing gruels, painstakingly spooning it into his mouth and encouraging him to swallow by stroking his throat. They enlisted the aid of two trusted *pattah-wallahs* and manually exercised each arm and leg for the periods of time Emma prescribed. They bathed him, massaged him, kept him clean, and prayed over him—reaching out, each in his or her own way, to connect with whatever deities might be listening.

Late in the afternoon of the third day, which was now almost a week after the accident, the Maharajah of Gwalior arrived. He was a thin, sallow, bearded young man—older than the *Nawabzada* of Bhopal, but still younger than Emma had expected. He strode into the chamber as if he owned it, went directly to Sikander's side, and stood gazing down at him in absolute silence.

As Emma watched, his thin shoulders began to shake, and tears rolled soundlessly down his sunken cheeks. Like the *Nawabzada*, he, too, was garbed in fantastically rich garments. They were too big for him, Emma noticed, when he suddenly removed his outer coat of purple cloth embroidered with silver and threw it on the floor. As he began to claw at the rest of his clothes, Emma jumped to her feet in alarm, knocking over the little stool on which she had been seated.

"Your Highness, stop! What are you doing?"

He gave her a look that suggested he had only just now noticed her—and then he answered in heavily accented English. "My friend is dying. Anyone can see that. Therefore, I shall don the garments of a beggar and smear ashes on my forehead to mourn him. I will also pluck my beard."

"None of that will help him, Your Highness. If you insist upon creating a scene, do it elsewhere. I am endeavoring to keep this sickroom a cheerful place." Emma didn't mention that she had had to fight all week to keep the wailing of Sikander's servants to a minimum and to prevent the women of the *zenana* from burning incense and otherwise fouling the air.

If the Maharajah insisted upon loudly indulging his grief, she'd soon have everyone on the plantation behaving without restraint—which *couldn't* be good for her patient.

"Who has done this terrible thing?" the Maharajah suddenly demanded. "Who is responsible?"

Emma exchanged a quick glance with Sakharam, who answered before she did. "We do not know, Your Highness. Someone shot an elephant. It went mad, and my master was hurt in the process of killing the poor beast. We have not yet found the man who originally shot the elephant."

"Say no more. I can guess who might be behind this wicked scheme. I myself will investigate. . . . But why have you prolonged my friend's suffering, when it is so obvious that he wishes to die?"

Oh, no! Emma thought. Not another proponent of Eastern fatalism. "*I* have kept him alive, Your Highness. And I intend to continue keeping him alive."

"But the accident happened a week ago, did it not? You cannot possibly save him—or if you do, he will be witless."

Emma's already frayed patience snapped. "I will not let him die! If he does turn out to be witless, I will spend the rest of my days caring for him."

"You—a mere female—have taken charge here?"

"Yes," Emma said. "And if you cannot display more optimism in Sikander's presence, then I urge you to depart, Your Highness."

The Maharajah looked dumbfounded. "*Memsahib*, are all

your countrywomen like you? You remind me of a tigress defending her cubs. Either that, or you are mad. Let me send to Gwalior for my personal physician and healer. He will tell you there is no longer any hope for Sikander."

"I myself have told her that, Your Highness," Sakharam interrupted. "But she will not listen. She keeps insisting he will eventually awaken."

Just then, there came a small sound—the barest suggestion of a moan. But Emma heard it; they all heard it. She bent over Sikander and anxiously searched his still face. "Sikander? Oh, my love, can you hear me? I'm here, Sikander. And Sakharam is here, too."

She picked up Sikander's limp hand and clasped it to her breast. "If you can hear me, my darling, give me a sign."

Another small sound escaped Sikander's pale lips—and then, miraculously, his eyes opened the tiniest bit. As they all watched breathlessly, his luxurious dark lashes lifted, he looked up at Emma . . . and smiled. She read consciousness and recognition on his face before he sighed deeply and closed his eyes again.

Emma bowed her head over his hand, kissed his fingers, and let her tears fall unheeded. He lived. He still lived! And he had known who she was. It was the happiest, most satisfying moment of her entire life.

"*Memsahib*," the Maharajah said quietly. "Forgive me for doubting you. It seems you knew what you were doing all along."

"He was dead, but she made him live," Sakharam echoed in a tone of reverence. "I witnessed it with my own eyes."

"He was never dead," Emma disputed. "Don't say that, Sakharam, for it isn't true."

"Then I will say he was caught between this world and the next, but you made him return, *Memsahib*. You brought him back. Were it up to me, he would have departed, never to return."

"It wasn't up to you. But it wasn't up to me, either. It was up to *him*. He was the one who decided to come back." *And I'm so glad you did, my love.*

That evening, Sikander's aunt, Santamani, arrived, along with the *Nawabzada* of Bhopal. Santamani was a handsome woman with silver-streaked hair, snapping black eyes, and such an air of authority that she intimidated both the Maharajah and the *Nawabzada* together. But she didn't intimidate Emma. Emma gave the woman her own quarters, but wouldn't allow any of the visitors to see Sikander that night. They all wanted to gather around his bedside, but Emma thought he needed rest and quiet more than ever now—so she stood her ground.

Begging Sakharam to care for the guests, Emma resumed her vigil at Sikander's bedside—and near midnight, she was rewarded with another miracle. This time, he opened his eyes, smiled at her, and *squeezed* her hand!

Her joy overflowed in fresh tears. As she wept silently, Sikander chided her in a whisper, "Stop that. No more. I can't bear sniveling females."

Astonished to hear his voice, Emma hastily dashed away her tears and leaned closer. She was too late; he had already drifted off again. Loath to leave him, even for a moment, she curled up next to him on the bed and promptly fell asleep. Twice during the night, she felt him stir against her and change position, but he was always asleep again before she could turn to look at him.

She had left the lamp burning, but it went out before morning, and in the gray light of early dawn, she awoke to find his arm around her waist and his leg over her legs, and that was when she knew—really knew for certain—that he was going to fully recover. He had regained the use of both sets of limbs and his voice; all her hard work had not gone in vain. Best of all, he definitely wasn't witless.

She slipped out of his grasp, intent upon seeing to her own personal needs, when she heard him whisper. "Emma . . . stay. Don't leave me."

He sounded weak and exhausted, as if the effort to call her back was almost too much for him. But Emma knew he would grow stronger; she would make sure of it. She climbed back into bed and wrapped her arms around him. "I am here, Sikander. I will stay with you. Go back to sleep."

His deep, even breathing told her he had done just that; apparently, he could fall asleep in the middle of a sentence. She suspected he would do that for a while. She stayed with him until Sakharam arrived with a breakfast tray. Sikander was still sleeping, so she finally left to make herself present-able to greet the day.

Over the next several days, Sikander's improvement was nothing short of incredible. He seemed to grow stronger by the hour. He started out eating broth and a little fruit, but quickly began demanding more substantial meals and asking to be served more frequently than custom dictated. He in-sisted upon getting out of bed, and when Emma argued with him, he impatiently agreed to sit in a chair in exchange for receiving his guests.

He spent well over an hour alone with Santamani, but only a short period of time with the Maharajah, and barely a few minutes with the *Nawabzada*. Between times, he wanted the children, but their boundless energy proved more than he could handle, and he thanked Emma when she sent for the *ayah* to come and take them away.

"I don't know why I'm still so tired," he groused. "All I've done for over a week is sleep."

"You weren't sleeping. You were unconscious. There's a big difference."

"I was sleeping," he insisted. "I know, because I was dreaming."

"What did you dream?" Emma was greatly interested.

"I relived my whole life. I remembered things I haven't thought about for years. . . . I also dreamed about you, Emma."

She waited for him to say more, but he didn't. She wasn't

sure what she *wanted* him to say. Or do. He had saved her from the elephant, and she had nursed him back to life. Except for his fatigue and a lingering headache, he was almost completely healed. They were even now. Yet nothing between them was settled; nothing had really changed—or had it?

There was still the matter of who shot the elephant; the culprit had yet to be found. And there was still the issue of who owned Wildwood. There was still . . . *everything*. Soon, Sikander would be his normal self again—and then what? Should she go back to the bungalow? . . . Ought she to stay? The question was presumptuous, for he hadn't asked her.

Emma was no longer angry with him; she supposed she had forgiven him. Still, nothing had been said, and there didn't seem to be a proper time to discuss the past. For now, it was enough that Sikander lived; what he or she would do with the rest of their lives—how they would handle this second chance they had been given—remained a mystery.

Twenty-five

"Thank you for telling me all that has happened between you and my son, Hyder Khan," Santamani said to Alex. "I am truly sorry it took a near tragedy to heal the wounds we have each nursed for so long."

"Thank you for coming here, Santamani." Alex stretched out his legs to ease a leg cramp. They were sitting on his balcony in the relative cool of the early evening, and Alex had just finished telling her, at long last, the secrets he had kept all these years—about all the hurts he had suffered at Hyder Khan's hands and the injuries he himself had inflicted. . . . He had told her everything he could remember, for he wanted her friendship again—and her love. She had come to see him when she thought he was dying, so the least he could do was be honest, even if it meant hurting her.

"How could I not come when someone I care for so much was reportedly dying?" She smiled sadly. "So often have I thought of you, Sikander. So often have I wished I had been wiser. I have wept many tears of regret over you."

"Why regret? You were always wonderful to me, Santamani, even when everyone else was terrible."

Santamani rearranged a fold of her pale blue *sari* and sighed. "My dear Sikander. You have told me nothing I do not already know tonight. For too many years I have watched Hyder Khan make one mistake after another. In my heart, I knew what he was doing to you—both when you were boys and later, when you became men. I saw his envy and his pettiness. I watched him scheme against you. Why do you think I offered to buy Wildwood from Miss Whitefield when I heard she might possibly have a valid claim?"

"You offered to buy Wildwood from her?"

Santamani nodded her silver-streaked head. "Through a party unknown to either of you, I did. However, she refused. I had hoped to keep Hyder Khan from getting his hands on it. I thought if I owned the claim, he would leave you alone. I understand he made his own offer, but Miss Whitefield would not accept it, either."

"That land means more than anything to Miss Whitefield."

"Not more than you, surely. I've seen the way she looks at you, Sikander. I've also seen the way you look at her. You would be dead were it not for her. So what is the problem? As long as you have her, you still have Wildwood. Neither Hyder Khan nor anyone else can take it from you. We must still find the man who shot that elephant, of course. Rather, we must find the man *behind* the man who shot the elephant. I swear to you, Sikander, even if it be my own son, I shall see justice done. This time, I will not protect him. He must pay for his folly. He has gone too far."

Alex was glad to hear she would not defend or protect Hyder Khan any longer. But she was wrong about him and Emma. They still hadn't solved their problems, and he could see no way to overcome her mistrust. Wildwood had initially brought them together, but now it was keeping them apart. Emma thought Wildwood was all he wanted—when in reality, he only wanted her.

"I hope, for your sake, that Hyder Khan wasn't responsible for shooting that elephant, Santamani. I wish your son and I *could* have been friends, instead of enemies."

" 'Twas impossible from the first, Sikander. He envied you far too much."

"He *envied* me? How could he—when he had everything,

and I had nothing? *I* was the outcast, the *kutcha butcha*, while he was the first-born son, the legitimate heir, the pure-blooded, high-caste, future ruler . . ."

"Are you really that naive, Sikander? Hyder Khan is short, fat, and not overly handsome. You are tall and have the face and form of a god. You killed your first tiger years before he did. You delighted your teachers with your intellect and thirst for learning. You were always running at life, eager to snatch it up, while Hyder Khan has ever been lazy—preferring to lounge on his bed and eat sweetmeats. . . . Oh, how he envied you! Precisely because you had nothing to start with and gained all you have through your own wits and hard work. Hyder Khan has never had to work for anything; it was all handed to him at birth. While your star was rising, his was waning. When the Raj came to power, he lost his birthright, but you learned to deal with the Raj and kept getting richer and more powerful. Nothing could hold you back."

"I am not loved by members of the Raj," Alex snorted. "They will always regard me with deep suspicion, if not hatred."

"Then why not marry your English woman? She will help smooth your path and the paths of your children. Embrace your British heritage, Sikander. You have spent enough years living as an Indian, and it has availed you nothing. 'Tis time now to go the other way. Once the British know you better, they will accept you. You have held yourself too much apart from them, and 'tis only natural they should fear what they do not know."

Her advice made sense. She had put into words what Alex himself had concluded—only he had been reluctant to give up his Indian ways. Now that he was ready, Emma wasn't.

"I wish it were that simple, Santamani—but my English woman doesn't believe me when I tell her I love her. She thinks I want only her land. In the beginning, that's all I *did* want. I lied to her, I hurt her feelings, I even destroyed the deed to her property, because of the problems her claim could cause. I never told her Wildwood was the most important part of my holdings; she discovered it on her own."

"Ah, I see. . . . You have driven a sword deep into her heart. What terrible things we do to one another! How much needless hurt we cause! . . . Do not do to her what you did to me, Sikander. Don't let years of silent anguish pass before you finally bare your soul to her and speak honestly. Tell her again how you feel. Beg her forgiveness . . ."

"It won't be enough, Santamani. That's not the way to reach her."

"Then think on the matter until you discover the right way, dear nephew. You know her far better than I; therefore I cannot advise you in this matter."

"I have been thinking. I *am* thinking—but still, nothing comes to me. All I do is make my head throb."

"Your head is throbbing because of your recent injury, and if you do not rest properly, you will never be well. I must leave you now, Sikander. I have already claimed more than my fair share of your time. Tomorrow, you should spend time with the Maharajah and the *Nawabzada*. Both of them need your friendship and advice; they would not have come here if they did not have some affection for you."

"They want Wildwood, too. I know the *Nawabzada* does; he has been making offers to Miss Whitefield also. If he can't get the land itself, he at least wants to make sure he gets his percentage of the profits from whomever does get the land."

"He is very young to be so greedy."

"His counselors are the greedy ones."

"Well, you will think of a way to deal with him, too, Sikander. I have the greatest confidence in you."

Santamani took her leave then, abandoning Alex to dismal thoughts. Exactly how *could* he convince Emma that he truly loved her and wanted to marry her for herself, not for her land? There must be some way to do it, but he'd be damned if he could think of it!

He couldn't lose her now, almost exactly as he had lost Santamani so many years ago—because of a lack of communication and honesty. Back then, he hadn't tried hard enough; he had just assumed there was no way to explain things to Santamani. But he had to reach Emma. She was the most important thing in the world to him—more important than Paradise View. More important even than his children. Michael and Victoria would one day leave him and go off to live their own lives. But he wanted Emma to share the rest of his days. She had become his reason for living; without her, it made no difference if he became the richest man in India. He would still be miserable and incomplete. . . . *How am I to reach her?*

It was early morning, and Emma was in the children's chamber, trying to reestablish a schedule for them with the *ayah*, when she heard a great commotion down in the front hallway. Ordering Michael and Victoria to stay where they were, she quickly departed and ran out to see what had happened. Santamani met her at the top of the stairway, and then Sikander appeared, along with the Maharajah, the *Nawabzada*, and lastly Sakharam and several other servants.

" 'Tis one of my men!" the Maharajah cried, racing down the stairs. "Nay, 'tis several come to report on the results of my investigation into the incident with the elephant."

A half-dozen men met him at the foot of the stairs, and there was a great deal of *salaaming*. One fellow groveled on his hands and knees at the Maharajah's feet. Emma watched a moment before she realized that the man was in great distress, and the others were angry with him. They kicked and shoved him when he tried to rise. Fearing another outbreak of violence, she was glad she had told the children to stay in their rooms.

The babble of voices carried up the stairwell, but Emma was too agitated to make sense of all that was being said. "Sakharam!" she hissed. "What's going on?"

"Wait a moment, *Memsahib*, and I will tell you . . . that man. The one on the floor. He is a *shikari*—a hunter—who often hunts with the *Nawabzada* of Bhopal. They are saying he is the one who shot the elephant. And he has admitted it."

"Then it was the *Nawabzada* behind all of it? That mere boy—that spoiled child—arranged to cause a terrible accident?"

Emma turned to look at the youth, and so did everyone else. However, the *Nawabzada* looked as stunned as anyone. "I didn't know about this! I didn't know, I tell you. Ask him. Ask my *shikari* if I knew."

"I'll ask him," Sikander volunteered. He lapsed into the native language, and he and the *shikari* engaged in a few moments of spirited conversation.

"Sakharam!" Emma pleaded.

Sakharam knew what she wanted. "He says he did it to curry favor with the *Nawabzada*, who has threatened to get a new *shikari* because this one cannot find tigers big enough for him to shoot and make his reputation as a great hunter. The *Nawabzada* didn't tell him to do it, but one of the *Nawabzada*'s advisors suggested this would be a good way for him to win his young master's approval."

Blue eyes flashing, Sikander turned to the young ruler. "Your Highness, what will you do with the man? How will you punish him?"

The *Nawabzada* looked ready to burst into tears. "I . . . I will have both him and my . . . my advisor—the one who told him to do this bad thing—executed by elephant. That would be a fitting punishment, since they plotted to have an elephant go mad and hurt you and your workers."

"Sakharam," Emma whispered. "Does he mean he will have an elephant step on their heads?"

"Yes, *Memsahib*. And that will be no more than they deserve."

"Sikander . . ." Emma began, but before she could say any more, Sikander held up his hand.

"I know, Emma. Give me a chance. Your Highness, I have a better solution. Turn the guilty parties over to the British Government to be punished. That way, you will show the Raj what an enlightened young man you are—and how mature, responsible, and worthy of their trust. You don't want to appear primitive and old-fashioned, do you? So you mustn't resort to old-style punishments."

Santamani suddenly spoke up. "Sikander is right. Turn them over to the British. Let British justice deal with them."

The *Nawabzada* seemed uncertain. "I . . . uh. . . . Perhaps I had better speak with one of my . . ."

"No!" Sikander snapped. "The one thing you must *not* do is speak with one of your damn advisors. It's time to make your own decisions, Your Highness."

"Listen to Sikander," the Maharajah urged. "More than any of us, he knows what he's talking about when it comes to the British. Let *him* be your advisor from now on. Better still, follow your own best instincts. You know the right thing to do."

"I'll turn them over to the British then," the young man announced, very pleased with himself. "And I'll keep to our original bargain, Sikander, when it comes to the trees you may harvest in the future. After all the trouble my men have caused, I owe you that much. And I won't listen to anyone who tells me differently."

Sikander grinned from ear to ear. "Your Highness, you are beginning to sound like a man I'd be proud to call friend. . . . Sakharam, lock up that poor devil until we can turn him over to the proper authorities—and send someone to fetch the *Nawabzada*'s advisor, the one who told the *shikar* to shoot my elephant."

Sakharam nodded and started down the stairs. Drawing

nearer to Emma, Santamani gave her a warm smile. "I am so happy it wasn't my son, Hyder Khan, who was behind all this."

"You were worried that it was?" The woman's candor surprised Emma, particularly since they didn't know each other very well and hadn't yet had time to establish a relationship.

Santamani laughed. "If you knew Hyder Khan, you would not need to ask that. Whatever you do about Wildwood, do not sell it to my son, Miss Whitefield. I intend to keep working to make a better man of Hyder Khan, but until I succeed, guard yourself and Sikander against him. Someday before I die, I hope to see him and my nephew become friends, but until then . . ."

"Don't hold your breath waiting, Santamani," Sikander interjected. "For I doubt it will ever happen. . . . Emma, now that the excitement is over for the day, I'd like to speak with you privately."

Emma's heart did a queer little flip flop. "Now—this very minute?"

"Sikander," Santamani scolded. "You really should wait for a more appropriate moment—at least until after we've gone. Now that the culprit is caught, there's no longer any reason for staying. I mean to convince the Maharajah and the *Nawabzada* to leave here this very day, before the rains come and trap us here at Paradise View. Hasn't anyone noticed the monsoon clouds beginning to gather?"

As if the sky itself had heard her, the brightness on the stairwell suddenly faded, leaving a feeling of closeness and expectancy. After days of relentless sunshine, it was now unnaturally dark. Then the sun reappeared, flooding the house with golden light and accompanying heat.

"Will it rain today?" she asked no one in particular.

"No, Emma. Be patient," Sikander gently chided. "The clouds will build for perhaps a week yet, before it actually starts to rain . . . and then you will find yourself wishing for sunshine, but the rain will be here to stay."

"I will never wish for more sunshine," Emma fervently promised.

Everyone laughed, as if they knew better, and in the ensuing conversation, Sikander did not repeat his request to meet with her. They had no time alone all that day, and after their guests departed, he still did not take her aside. Emma sensed that he was waiting for something; whatever it was, she couldn't rush him. He must come to her of his own accord—when he was good and ready.

Having lost so much time recuperating from his injury, he was suddenly in a fever to harvest more wood, and Emma saw less of him than she ever had. She used the time to supervise the remaining repairs on the bungalow and the roof of the servants' quarters and spent as many hours with the children as she could. But all the while she, too, was waiting . . . as tense and expectant as the parched earth beneath her feet.

As the monsoon drew closer, huge clouds piled high in the sky, forming a great dark mass. At times, the sunshine gave way to a strange hovering light, the color of pewter. There was no relief from the heat; it was hard to believe this was the month of June, for it was nothing like June in England. England seemed far, far away. Emma felt as if she had lived all her life in India—waiting for the rains and hoping Sikander would come to her soon.

One gray-green afternoon when the air hung as heavy as a shroud upon the earth, he finally came. "Emma," he announced, standing on the veranda of her bungalow. "Come back with me to the house, will you? I'm ready now to talk to you; I guess I didn't want to do it while I was still an invalid, and besides, I had something to do first."

He doesn't look like an invalid, Emma thought, as she grabbed her *topi*. No one would ever suspect that he had lain close to death for nearly a week in the recent past. He was so handsome he made her heart ache. These days, all she had to do was look at him, and a thousand butterflies took wing in her stomach. All he had to do was smile, and she wanted to throw herself into his arms.

With his usual distant politeness, he took her arm to help her down the steps. "Can you smell the rain?" He inhaled deeply, then sighed in appreciation.

Emma lifted her face to the pewter-colored sky. "I think you have all been fooling me; it's never going to rain. When it finally does, it will be too late. Everything's either dead or dying."

"That's where you're wrong, Emma. Wait until you see the resurgence of life when it finally rains. Why, there will be caterpillars the size of snakes, and moths as big as eagles . . ."

"You're exaggerating."

"Just wait; you'll see. The insects alone will overwhelm you, and suddenly your little bungalow will be swallowed entirely by the jungle."

"I can't wait. I'm so sick of this heat and dryness."

They were silent the rest of the way back to the big pink house. When they arrived, Sikander ushered her into the parlor where a British-style desk and chair had been set up, converting it into an office or study. In the center of the desk lay a sheaf of papers.

Sikander motioned for Emma to be seated, and then, very casually, he handed her the papers and leaned one hip on the edge of the desk. She scanned them quickly—stopped—and reread them more carefully. "This . . ." she picked up the top sheet. "Seems to be a deed for all of Paradise View, including Wildwood."

Sikander nodded. "It is. I had it specially drawn up to give to you."

"But . . . but it has *my* name on it, not yours. Your name is nowhere upon it."

"My name is there, on the bottom of the second sheet. If you read the papers closely, you will see that I've signed all my holdings over to you. All of Paradise View, that is, including Wildwood. I did retain ownership of several other properties which aren't located near here."

"But *why?* Why would you do such a thing? I don't want Paradise View; all I've ever wanted is what my mother intended for me to have—Wildwood."

"Emma . . ." Sikander's eyes were very blue and warm. "This is the only way I could think of to convince you of how much you mean to me. I am giving you Paradise View, the one place on earth that has always meant the most to me. Those papers are legal and binding. You now own three thousand acres, not a mere eight hundred. You also own this house, the polo field, the stable, the bungalow—everything on this land."

Emma was astounded. She didn't know what to say. She could only sit there and gape at him.

"Emma, close your mouth. You look like a fish." Moving away from the desk, he walked over to her, and dropped to one knee in front of her chair. "My dearest Emma, will you now believe me when I say I love you? Will you now accept that I have no ulterior motive, when I tell you I worship the ground you walk on? You own that ground now; I don't. I come to you with nothing to offer except myself. You can turn me away if you like; you can toss me off the land, and I'll go. God knows I deserve it. . . . But I do love you, Emma. And I want to marry you for your own sake, not to gain possession of your land. If we marry, it will stay in your name. . . . Why, this makes you one of the richest *memsahibs* in India! You don't need *me* anymore to make you happy— unless of course, you love me. If you don't. . . . I'll try hard to understand."

"Oh, Sikander!" Emma was dangerously close to tears. She lifted the papers. "This . . . this isn't necessary."

"It isn't? But it's all I could think of—the only way to convince you of my sincerity. Say you'll marry me, Emma. I swear I'll find new homes for all the women in my *zenana*. Before she left, Santamani invited them to come live with her. She said she would enjoy their company . . . and I'll throw away all my Indian clothing, institute reforms in my household . . ."

"Reforms? What sort of reforms?"

"I'll . . . I'll abolish the caste system. I'll make Sakharam treat the sweepers with more respect. I'll tell everyone they must treat one another as equals, I'll . . ."

Emma couldn't help it; she burst out laughing. "Sikander, don't make promises you can never keep! This is India, after all, and I've come to see that neither you nor I can make sweeping changes overnight. I imagine the caste system will endure for a long, long time yet."

"Will you marry me, Emma? Name your conditions; whatever they are, I'll meet them."

"You must be faithful to me," Emma blurted without hesitation. "As I mean to be faithful to you. And you must be honest. No more lies. No more subterfuge. That's all I really want, Sikander. . . . No, wait. There's one thing more. You must agree to disagree with me politely. When we do disagree, we must talk things out."

"That's all? It sounds so easy."

"No, it won't be easy. We'll continue to face many problems, Sikander. We may both become outcasts from our respective cultures. The Indians may never forgive you, and the British may never forgive me."

"Who gives a damn, Emma? I don't. Not anymore. When I lay flat on my back for a week, I came to realize that. My friends will remain my friends no matter what—just as my enemies will remain my enemies. I can't live my life in fear of what anyone else will think, except me."

"Sikander, you were unconscious. You could not have been thinking all these things during that week. First, you claimed you were dreaming, now you claim you were thinking . . ."

Sikander slid his hand around the back of her neck and pulled her closer, until her face was only inches from his. "All right, I admit it. I really only thought of all these things once I regained consciousness. But *something* happened to me during that time. That something was *you*, Emma. Because of you, I hung on. I felt a strong pull to go; there was a moment when I wanted to die, to escape everything. I wasn't afraid; somehow I knew it wasn't going to be nearly as bad as I always thought it would be. . . . Without you, Emma, I would have gone. You called me back. I realized I hadn't had enough time with you. I hadn't convinced you I really loved you. We have so much living yet to do, Emma . . . so much to share . . . so much to enjoy."

Emma crumpled the papers in her hands. Pulling back from him, she tore them in two—straight down the middle.

"What are you doing?" He looked horrified.

"The only papers I will accept are ones that show the land belonging to *both* of us, Sikander. And along with those papers, we must have one that clearly states we are leaving everything we own to the children—to Michael and Victoria—plus whatever other children we are fortunate enough to have."

"Yes," he whispered. "Yes, that's perfect. We must see to it at once. And I would also like to change the name of our joint holdings; instead of Paradise View, hereafter, our plantation will be known as Wildwood. That fits it better, don't you agree?"

Tears spilled down Emma's cheeks. "Oh, yes, Sikander! Wildwood it must be!"

Just then a voice intruded from the doorway. "Papa? Papa, why is Miss Whitefield crying?"

Emma looked up to see two dark heads and two pairs of black eyes watching her and Sikander. Victoria then darted around her brother and raced into the room. "Don't cry, Miss Whitefield! Please don't cry! It's only the thunder; there's nothing to fear."

She and Sikander exchanged glances. "The thunder?" Emma paused to listen. And then she heard it—a long, slow roll of thunder, moving like a train across the sky over the house. She rose to her feet, pulling Sikander up after her. "It *is* thunder! It's finally going to rain."

"Come and see." Victoria grabbed her hand, and Michael seized his father's. "Come and see!" both children chorused.

Smiling through her tears, Emma allowed herself to be dragged out onto the front steps. A curtain of rain was advancing toward them from the direction of the jungle. The thunder grew louder, reverberating from one end of the heavens to the other.

"You see?" Sikander shouted. "I told you the rains would come."

A cool, refreshing breeze, laden with the scent of rain, blew ahead of the wall of water. Breathing it, Emma felt giddy. She threw back her head and laughed; never had she felt so happy, so bursting with joy, so completely alive and intoxicated with the excitement of living and loving.

The children danced circles around them, and Sikander took her in his arms. "I love you, Emma," he mouthed to her, since the thunder was too loud for her to hear the words.

"I love *you*," she mouthed back at him.

Just as the rains hit, he pressed his mouth to hers in a kiss so searing that if it hadn't been raining, Emma would have gone up in flames. She melted against his hard hot body, and the rain was like a benediction pouring down upon them from above—cooling and refreshing, washing away all the hurt and pain they had ever known.

A single thought penetrated the rain-washed fog of passion and joy that enveloped Emma. What was there to do in the rainy season, except lie in bed and make love? That's all *she* wanted to do—and from the way Sikander was kissing her, that's all he wanted to do also.

Let it rain, then. Dear God, let it rain.

Epilogue

It was Emma's wedding day, and she had chosen to wear a red *sari*, red being the traditional color of Indian brides. However, the ceremony would be a British one presided over by Reverend Horace Barrington, who had traveled all the way from Calcutta, along with Rosie and her husband, William.

The rainy season had ended, and India was in the middle of its best, most beautiful season, so it had not been too difficult for the wedding guests to make the trip to Wildwood. Nearly all of the most important ones were now gathered in the front parlor: Rosie and William, Sayaji Singh, the Maharajah of Gwalior, the *Nawabzada* of Bhopal, Santamani and—surprise of all surprises!—Santamani's son, Hyder Khan, who had come at Sikander's invitation and a bit of arm-twisting by his mother.

No one had disappointed Emma by refusing to attend—with one exception. She had sent word to Percival Griffin, but hadn't heard from him. He hadn't responded or even forwarded the results of his investigation, though it must surely be completed by now. Nor could Rosie offer any explanation for the delay; she herself hadn't seen or heard from Mr. Griffin in months.

As Emma sought to arrange her *sari* in the most becoming manner, aided by the women of Sikander's *zenana* who were all aflutter over the wedding and their impending move to

Santamani's home, Rosie suddenly walked into Emma's chamber.

"Emma, dear, do you need any help?" She smoothed down her lace-trimmed, cream-colored gown. "Oh, my!" she exclaimed, catching sight of Emma. "My dear, you look truly lovely . . . alarmingly *Indian*, but truly lovely. That style does seem to favor you, though it would be a scandal if you wore it in Calcutta."

"I'm not planning on wearing a *sari* in Calcutta." Emma smiled at her friend. She was so glad Rosie had decided to come; it had not been an easy decision for her. Emma knew she still disapproved of relationships between Indians and whites. But both William and Rosie had managed to set aside their doubts in favor of friendship, and for that, Emma would always be grateful. She had prepared herself for rejection, but what a relief and joy to find acceptance!

"I decided to wear this because it will please Sikander— Alex, I mean. He loves to see me with my hair down and gowned in a *sari*. Indian garments are so very feminine and graceful."

"You're right. I don't know why I never noticed that before this." Rosie slanted a sideways glance at the lovely *sari*s Emma's attendants were wearing. "Alex does dress his servants richly, doesn't he?"

Emma did not tell Rosie that the women in the room weren't servants. One step at a time, she thought. Rosie had come a long way, but still had a long way to go. Emma could read her friend's reactions like a book, and Rosie was struggling with the notion that she and her husband were the only pure-blooded Europeans attending this wedding.

"Alex is very rich, Rosie, but he takes pride in sharing his wealth with those less fortunate," Emma diplomatically responded. "Do you know if Percival has arrived yet? I was hoping he would get here in time for the ceremony. I don't want there to be any feelings of ill will between us, but I'm afraid there might be, after all. When he was here the last time—or perhaps I should say, the first time—he again proposed to me. Of course, I refused and made it clear I'd never be interested."

"Then perhaps you shouldn't be upset he hasn't come. He's such a nice man, Emma. I still don't understand why you couldn't have been attracted to him."

"I tried, but we weren't suited to each other, Rosie—not the way Alex and I are suited. I've found everything I ever wanted and more here at Wildwood. It was here all along—just as I dreamed it would be."

"Then I'm happy for you, my dear. Truly happy." Rosie gave Emma a brief hug. "I wouldn't have missed your wedding for anything in the world. I hope you never doubted that."

"Oh, I didn't!" Emma fibbed. Catching herself, she grinned. "Well, yes, I did, actually. I worried you might disown me for marrying Alexander Kingston."

"If you are referring to his mixed pedigree as a reason for my disapproval, I suggest you don't mention it when you visit Calcutta. Pretend he's exactly what he has always portrayed himself to be—a dark-skinned Englishman—and you will be all right, Emma. Don't make a crusade of his heritage, and perhaps no one else will, either. If they do, they're boors. You know you can always count on me to stand by you; I'll defend you whatever you choose to say or do."

"I don't plan to say or do anything. Alex doesn't need an excuse for living, and I don't need to defend myself for marrying him. I love him, and that's all that counts."

"That's all that *should* count, Emma. When I see how happy you are—how content—I know you are doing the right thing. And somehow, you will make it all work. No doubt, you will even manage to convince the world that his adorable children are purebred English."

"His children are *my* children now, and I will fight to see they have every advantage. I'll also fight to make certain they don't forget who they really are. I want them to be proud of themselves, proud of their Indian heritage, proud of their father, proud of Wildwood . . ."

"Emma! Emma!" Laughing, Rosie held up her hand. "You will be a formidable mother; I can see that. Those children are extremely fortunate."

"No, *I* am fortunate. I'm not only gaining a husband, but a family. And speaking of family, I had better go make certain the children are ready to take part in the ceremony, for it's almost time to begin."

"I'll be waiting for you downstairs." Rosie gave Emma another quick hug. "Be happy, Emma dear. And plan to visit us next year, when I shall have my own little family to show off to you and Alex."

"Rosie! You mean you are finally going to have the baby you've always wanted? But why didn't you tell me at once?"

"I had to wait till we had privacy, for I haven't even told William yet. He wouldn't have let me come on this journey if he thought I was expecting a child. You are the first to know, Emma, but I will have to tell William soon or he might guess on his own."

"Oh, I hope he won't guess too soon, or he may insist on packing you off before we've had much chance to visit."

"A proper worry, indeed. Well, I'll leave you now. You don't want to keep Alex waiting."

No, Emma did not want to keep Alex—her dear Sikander—waiting. In deference to the arrival of their guests and the preparations for the wedding, Emma had not shared a bed with him for over a week. Thinking of the night to come, she indulged in a delightful shiver of anticipation and then hurried out of the room to check on the children.

The rest of the day passed in a haze of joy, excitement, laughter, and tears. The ceremony was lovely, the children perfectly behaved, and Sikander so handsome and attentive that Emma grew teary-eyed just looking at him. He had dressed like an Indian prince, but shortly after the ceremony, he changed into one of his half-Indian, half-British outfits that combined elements from the two cultures.

He had then gone to show Hyder Khan the stable and his finest polo pony, and Emma hadn't minded his brief absence, because she shared Santamani's obvious happiness that the two men finally seemed to be getting along. It would be wonderful if their years of mutual suspicion and enmity ended. When they returned from the stable, Sikander confided to Emma that Hyder Khan wished to breed two of his mares to Sikander's best stallion, and they had already made the arrangements.

The news delighted her, and Emma threw her arms around her new husband. "Now, if only Percival would appear, this day would be perfect!"

"I don't miss him," Sikander soberly replied. "If he's unhappy about this wedding, to hell with him. He's probably sulking. . . . However, I would like to know—for the sake of mere curiosity—what his investigation revealed."

"So would I." Emma had been hoping that Percival would tell her she did indeed own the land, and she could then make a wedding gift of it to Sikander. Considering that she hadn't much of her own to bring to this marriage, she had thought that presenting him with the deed to the original Wildwood would be the perfect wedding gift—particularly since he had tried to give Paradise View to *her*.

The wedding banquet was held outside, overlooking the clearing where jungle beasts occasionally gathered. They were in the midst of it, when Emma chanced to look up and see a small group of visitors arriving on horseback. With a cry of excitement, she recognized Percival Griffin—in company with an English woman!

She and Sikander hurried down the stairs to greet them. Both Percival and the tiny, delicate-boned lady looked tired and bedraggled from the long journey, but Percival's face glowed when he introduced the surprise visitor. "Miss Whitefield, may I proudly present my new wife, Lady Mary.

This is the Honorable Miss Emma Whitefield, Mary, and I hope the two of you will become good friends."

Emma managed to stifle her shock long enough to welcome the new arrivals. "I am so pleased to meet you, Mary. However, I am no longer Miss Whitefield, but Mrs. Kingston, now. Do call me Emma."

"Gracious! We've missed the ceremony, haven't we? And interrupted your celebration, as well. Oh, Percy, darling, I knew we should have hurried much faster to get here." Mary laid her small gloved hand on her husband's arm. "We tarried too long on our trip, Percy," she gently scolded.

Percy gazed down at the little woman with deep tenderness. "That's true, Mary, but I wouldn't have changed one moment of our journey in order to get here any sooner." Glancing self-consciously at Emma, he blushed to the tips of his prominent ears. "We married just before we left Calcutta. Our courtship was extremely—ah—rapid, and the journey was actually a kind of honeymoon."

"Please don't apologize, Mr. Griffin," Emma begged. "We are overjoyed you made it in time for the banquet. Come and refresh yourselves. Later, you can tell us all about it. I should love hearing how you met this charming lady."

His blush deepened. "Yes, well. . . . It was very sudden. Truth is, Mary swept me off my feet. But I still found time to complete my investigation into the matter of Wildwood. Of course, now that you and Mr. Kingston are married, it probably doesn't matter anymore whose claim proved to be valid."

"On the contrary. It still matters," Emma hastened to assure him. At the same moment, Sikander calmly refuted her. "Doesn't matter to me at all."

They exchanged glances, and Emma noted that Sikander looked surprised that she still cared so much. "We can discuss it all later," she said brightly, feigning a disinterest she didn't feel. Actually, she wanted to hear his report immediately, but in the interests of hospitality, knew she had to wait. She took

Mary's arm and steered her up the stairway to meet their guests.

Hours passed before Emma was able to reintroduce the topic. Night had fallen, the banquet was over, and despite the continued revelry of the servants, some of the guests had already retired for the night. For the past half-hour, Sikander had been signaling Emma to slip away with him, but Emma didn't want the day to end before she knew whether or not she could give Sikander his wedding gift that night. She certainly understood his eagerness to be alone at last, but she didn't think Mr. Griffin's explanation would take very long; surely they could restrain themselves for a few more moments.

"Sikander, Mr. Griffin's wife has gone to bed, but Mr. Griffin is waiting in the parlor for us. Please, can we hear what he has to say, before we, too, retire?"

"Mrs. Kingston, your lack of enthusiasm to be alone with me is most disappointing—especially on our wedding night. Can't it wait until tomorrow?"

"No, my love, it can't."

"Why?" he demanded.

"Because, it . . . well, it just can't."

Emma would have explained in more detail, but the din of music and merriment still coming from the courtyard, where the servants were celebrating, drowned her out.

"Please, Sikander? For my sake, be patient awhile longer, and come with me?"

"Well, I don't intend to sleep alone tonight, so I suppose I have no choice but to come. All I can say is he had better make his report short and to the point."

"He will, I'm certain. He wants to join his own wife. She is so sweet—so perfect for him!"

"As you are perfect for me," he growled, ". . . except in your little rebellions."

"Come along. This won't take long."

Mr. Griffin rose from his chair when they entered the parlor, and Sikander gave him a curt nod. "Out with it, Griffin. My wife is in a fever to know. What did your investigation reveal?"

Mr. Griffin nervously resumed his seat. "Goodness, I had no idea this would be so awkward. . . . Well, here it is. Emma does not, I am sorry to say, own Wildwood. It seems that a Major Ian Castleton *had* attempted to purchase the plantation at one time—before the Indian Mutiny—but he had only made a preliminary downpayment on the property. Before he had time to complete the transaction, he died. His initial payment then went to pay the taxes on the acreage. When no one immediately came forward to claim the land, it reverted to the status of government land controlled by the old Begum of Bhopal."

"But what about the deed?" Emma exclaimed. "My mother had a deed—or a copy of it."

"As nearly as I can figure out from studying old records in Bhopal, Gwalior, and Calcutta—what few records of those days still exist—a deed was drawn up, but never properly filed. Even if it had been, the land wasn't fully paid for, so the deed would have been invalid. Major Castleton apparently intended to pay for the land, but never had the opportunity before the Mutiny broke out—and he was killed in its aftermath. . . . Those were very unsettled times, you see, so it's no wonder things were left in such a muddle. In this case, however, the Begum of Bhopal clearly had the right to sell the land to Mr. Kingston, retaining only the stipulation that a certain percentage of all profits derived from the trees should go to the Begum and her heirs."

"I see." Emma sank down on a horsehair settee in front of the desk. "So I came all this way to India in search of a dream that didn't exist."

"Wildwood does still exist, Emma." Sikander sat down beside her and took her hand in his. "It's here; we've made it live again."

"Oh, Sikander, I know that, of course, but I still wanted

to have the pleasure of giving you something that belonged to me—that I actually owned. Wait a minute," Emma interrupted herself. "I still have something I can give you as a wedding gift—the ruby. I will give you my ruby, which I've been saving all this time. Aside from the few pearls I have left, it's the only thing of value I own." She jumped up. "Wait here. I'm going to get it."

"Emma, that isn't necessary. I don't *want* your ruby."

"Sikander, please! I want to give you something precious and dear to me on our wedding night. Something that symbolizes all you mean to me." She dashed out of the parlor and ran to get the ruby, returning breathless and excited a few moments later. "Here!" She uncurled her fingers and held the ruby out to him. "I will have it made into a ring or a pendant for you. Or if you prefer to sell it and use the money for something else . . ."

"I would never sell it! Not if it is a gift from you."

As Sikander reached to take the glowing red gem from her fingers, Mr. Griffin suddenly asked, "May I see that? I am something of an expert in fine jewels; it is my hobby. Perhaps I could suggest its value—not precisely, but I could come close."

"Oh, would you?" Emma handed the ruby to him instead of Sikander. "I've never had anyone knowledgeable look at it, and I'd be delighted to discover what it's worth."

"Well, as I said, I cannot be exact—not without my jeweler's glass, but I can tell a great deal by examining it closely." Mr. Griffin took the ruby, peered at it, turned it over several times in his palm, then held it up to the light from the nearest lamp. His expression turned grim.

"What is it?" Emma burst out. "What do you see?"

"Er . . . perhaps you should have someone else look at it, Mrs. Kingston. I . . . ah . . . the light isn't good in here, and without my glass . . ."

"Tell me. Whatever it is you think you see or don't see, I want to know."

"I can't be certain, of course, but . . . but my guess is that your ruby is made of . . . of glass. I'm so sorry, Miss . . . Mrs. Kingston. Really, you should have someone in Calcutta assess its value."

The news devastated Emma. First, her land did not belong to her, and now, her ruby wasn't even real. "Mr. Griffin, will you have a look at my pearls, too?"

"Emma, what difference does it make . . . ?" Sikander began, but Emma cut him off by starting for the door.

"Wait right there, Mr. Griffin—I'll get my pearls."

She was back even faster than before. "Here. Tell me what you think of these." Handing him the pearls, she refused to look at Sikander who was glowering at her from the settee.

Mr. Griffin held the half-empty string of pearls to the light. After a moment of intense study, he broke into a broad smile. "Why, Mrs. Kingston, these are truly magnificent. I've never seen finer. Were I you, I should never sell a one of them. If you have sold some, I hope you demanded a fortune for them, because that's what they are worth."

"A . . . a fortune?" She thought of the sums for which she had sold or traded them and realized that they could scarcely be called fortunes. "What do you mean by a fortune?"

He named a sum so high it made her heart plummet into her toes. According to his assessment, she had practically given away her pearls! Seeing her face, Mr. Griffin immediately backtracked. "I . . . I could be wrong, you know. Perhaps I am. But before you sell another one, do consult someone who knows more about gemology and the market for fine gems."

"No. I'm sure you're right," Emma said, reclaiming the pearls. "I've done everything all wrong. Sold my pearls for less than half their true value, guarded a worthless ruby as if my life depended upon it, and traveled halfway around the world to claim land I never owned. I've been rather deplorably stupid and impetuous, haven't I?"

"Understandable mistakes—all of them," Mr. Griffin said,

rising. "I just wish I didn't have to be the one to have given you such bad news—and on your wedding day, too. Please excuse me; I'm most dreadfully sorry, but Mary is probably waiting for me to come to bed. . . . She likes to have me near her at night, especially when she's sleeping in a strange place. Good evening to you both. Sleep well . . ."

Growing redder and redder, Mr. Griffin backed out of the parlor. Not looking at Sikander, Emma struggled to suppress her tears. She was mortified to think of how badly she had mishandled everything—how unwise she had been to leave England without having someone examine her pearls and ruby, how reckless and improvident to go haring off to India in the hopes her deed was truly authentic, how badly she had treated Sikander in her quest to gain her supposed inheritance. . . . She had subjected him to hellish inconvenience, at the very least, and for what? Only to discover that he had been telling her the truth all along; he owned the land, and she had no claim to it.

She couldn't resist a loud sniff. Catching her hand, Sikander pulled her to him. "Emma. . . . Why are you weeping?"

"Because I'm such a . . . such a . . ."

"A wonderful, dear, sweet woman—*my* woman. My beloved wife. How dare you weep over such inconsequential matters? Are you homeless? No. Are you unloved? Most definitely not. Are you unhappy? I would hope not. Why then are you weeping?"

"Because . . . because I put such store in those things my mother left me, and I'm disappointed they came to naught. I have so little of worth to give you, Sikander. Only a few pearls . . ."

"I'm not partial to pearls anyway. They would look charming on you, however, mounted in earbobs, perhaps, or—"

"This is not a joking matter, Sikander! I had meant to give you the deed to Wildwood as a wedding present. Now, I find I'm only a step or two above being a pauper. Yes, I still have some pearls, but even those I mostly squandered. Don't you see? Nothing has turned out as I planned."

"No, it has turned out better. Would you rather have me as your husband, or the undisputed ownership of Wildwood? What say you, Emma?"

"I want *both*," Emma stubbornly insisted.

"Forgive me for pointing out the obvious, but you *have* both. The only thing you don't have is a ruby, and if you really want one, I shall move heaven and earth to obtain one. A ruby the size of a hen's egg. Will that make you happy?"

"Oh, I don't care a fig for rubies, and you know it! It's just that . . . that . . . I wanted to give you a present that expressed my feelings for you, I suppose."

"Emma Kingston," he said, giving her a little shake. "Have we learned nothing from all this?"

"What do you mean?"

"Will you never believe I can love you for yourself alone? I cannot make love to some damn ruby—nor will a tree ever make me laugh or long for its company. As for the bungalow, I already live in a palace. Emma, the only thing that matters is our love; without it, we are truly poor and have nothing. *You* were the one who taught me that; must I now teach you?"

"Yes," she said, and smiled a little, her mood brightening. "I find myself desperately in need of a lesson on the importance of loving."

He pulled her closer. "Well, then, Emma. The first thing you must learn is that nothing can substitute for love, but love can substitute for all else, and do it quite nicely. Have you got that?"

"Not quite. I believe I need further convincing."

"Oh, you are a stubborn minx, aren't you?" He tilted her face up to his and kissed her—slowly and deliberately. "Now, do you understand?" he growled in a low, husky tone.

"I might be getting the idea. But . . . I still need more tutoring."

He shook his head in exasperation. "I can see this might take all night."

"That's precisely what I intend." Emma rubbed her body seductively against him. "Indeed, I'm certain it will take all night."

"You are incorrigible." He slid one arm around her lower back and another beneath her thighs and lifted her off her feet, cradling her snugly against him. She wound her arms around his neck and settled herself as close to him as she could get.

"*You* are wonderful," she purred. "You honestly don't mind that I have nothing to give you, do you?"

"You have everything to give me, Emma. You have a whole lifetime of living and loving here at Wildwood to give me . . . and that is really all I have to give you."

"Then let us begin," she sighed, entwining her fingers in his silky, black hair.

He kissed her again—soundly and passionately—and suddenly she knew he was right. Love was all anyone had to give, material things—land, jewels, money—might come and go. They could not be guaranteed to last forever. Only one thing could possibly withstand the ravages of time, and that was love. She would love Sikander forever. She had made her choice, her decision, her life-long commitment . . . and he had made his. Together, they would face whatever problems, joys, or sorrows came their way.

"I love you," she whispered, as he carried her up the staircase toward the bed they would share from this night onward.

"More than Wildwood?" he teased, his breath hot on her ear.

"You, my love, *are* Wildwood." She knew as soon as she said it that it was true. He was the culmination of her dreams, all they had ever meant to her—and all they would ever be. Wildwood. Beauty, mystery, danger, love, happiness . . . home.

Home, most of all.